Reaper
By
A P Bateman

Text © Anthony Paul Bateman
2018
All rights reserved
No part of this book may be reproduced, or stored in a retrieval system, or transmitted in any form or by any means, electronic, mechanical, photocopying, printing or otherwise, without written permission of the author.

This book is a work of fiction and any character resemblance to persons living or dead is purely coincidental. Some locations may have been changed, others are fictitious.

Facebook: @authorapbateman
Website (including contact and mailing list sign-up): www.apbateman.com

The Alex King Series
The Contract Man
Lies and Retribution
Shadows of Good Friday
The Five

The Rob Stone Series
The Ares Virus
The Town
The Island

Standalone Novel
Hell's Mouth

For my family

1

Georgia, Black Sea Coast

Fight fire with fire.

King had always undertaken a measured response to violence according to the severity of the attack. A lifetime of judgement. He knew there was no way a war - especially a dirty, secret war - could be won without the stark reality of ruthlessness. He had fought and won many of these wars. Some played out on the desolate terrain of Northern Iraq, in the mountains of Afghanistan or among the ruined streets of Syria. And some of these wars had been fought and won on the streets of Britain. In the back alleys, the shadows. Always ruthless, yet mindful to avoid the slippery slope of becoming nastier, more ruthless than his enemy. King had always been guided by his conscience, his ability to care enough about himself and the people around him over simply getting the task done.

He had never been afraid to question the chain of command. A trait that had made enemies for him within his own organisation, created a rocky road for him to travel, but allowed his horizon some clarity within the shadowy world he occupied.

But, until now, there had never been the personal involvement for him. King had witnessed vendetta and revenge. He had stood back and witnessed what revenge could do. He had seen mothers avenge their sons, husbands avenge their wives. When ISIS had reigned and ruled terror in Syria and Iraq, King had witnessed the tables turn. He had seen the bloodlust of normal people who had lost everything, the horrors of bloodthirsty vengeance satiated only by the hacking and burning of the bodies of the once powerful, suddenly defeated and beaten. For those people, the fight had been personal. And now, for the first time in a life spent plotting and killing in the shadows, King knew how difficult it could be to control that bloodlust. For the first time in his life, he *wanted* to kill. He wanted it more than he could ever have imagined.

King pulled the car over to the side of the road. The Black Sea shimmered beyond the pine trees on the rocky slopes. It was hot, late June. The sky clear and blue. The morning had been enveloped in a thick fog along the shoreline until well after dawn. The sun had now baked it off and the day didn't look like it would be anything but perfect. But not for some people. For some people, their day would only be getting worse.

King switched off the engine and got out, his desert boots crunching on the gravel. There was an air of calm, of unnatural silence. He hadn't seen a single vehicle on the drive across the plateau, traversing from one mountain to another. He stood stock-still, listened. A bird called a shrill tune, fluttered through the pines and disappeared. The slope of the mountain was still once more.

He walked around to the rear of the vehicle. Opened the boot and stepped back. The woman looked younger than her twenty-five years. But her features were familiar, there was no mistaking her. She blinked against the sunlight, strained against the thin rope fastening her wrists. She looked terrified.

King felt the adrenalin subsiding. He was aware of a stinging sensation, followed the woman's stare to his left arm. Blood ran down his forearm, trickling steadily from a graze above his left elbow. The blood had reached his watch, covered the face and permeated the stainless-steel links of the bracelet in a crimson glaze. He turned his elbow over, looked at the wound, was relieved there was no more damage. He had been lucky. Many men had not.

The girl looked at the pistol tucked into his waistband. She had been around weapons her entire life, but she seemed scared at the sight of it. King took out a handkerchief from his pocket and folded it before pressing it against the wound. He took it away, noted there was more blood soaked into it than he thought there would have been. He pressed it against the open wound again. The woman was watching him intently. King followed her stare, saw the patch of crimson spreading across his stomach. He placed the folded handkerchief against it, then took it away to see how much blood there would be. It wasn't good. He felt a wave of nausea wash over him, but it was soon replaced by anger.

He couldn't go down yet.

There was too much left to do.

He couldn't afford to be taken out of the fight.

The woman tried to talk but her lips were stuck together. Her nose was bloodied and there was swelling to one of her eye sockets. She swallowed like it was an effort to talk and licked her lips with her dry tongue. It must have helped her a little, because she asked, "Are you going to kill me?"

The words hung in the air, seemed to resonate around King, like an extra-sensory experience. King didn't simply hear her question, more felt a third party to it. It wasn't until the young woman asked him, that he realised the ramifications of taking her. What scared him most of all, was now she had asked the inevitable question, he simply didn't know. What he *did* know, was that she was now his bargaining chip in a game that had long become out of hand.

2

**One month earlier
Sodertalje, Sweden**

May was a spring month in southern Sweden, yet today was cold. The sky was grey, and darkness threatened to dominate the morning. King stepped out of the hire car, closed the door, yet left it unlocked, and crossed over the street. He adjusted the collar of his coat, smoothed down the front, casually checking the 9mm Browning pistol was securely in place.

They would have the jump on him. They had known when he would have been coming. They had known before he had even read the letter, so attempting to get there before them would have been a fruitless exercise. He would have to accept that he was on the back foot. Even so, he had managed to skirt the town and monitor movement. He had done this in the darkness on foot, then later at dawn circling the area in a wide loop. Finally, he had driven around, eased the car to a halt and watched. There had been nobody. Nobody out of the ordinary for a small town. Just people starting their days – commutes into Stockholm, school runs – everyday things. No vehicles parked up, the occupants waiting, scouting the streets for him. Which told King that the buildings across from the post office would be the only place from which they would mount surveillance. They would have eyes on for sure. A riflescope maybe, but only as a countermeasure. No, the game was about to commence, and King knew he was not yet walking into an ambush. The answer lay inside the post office, inside the safety deposit box numbered 4478. Soon enough he would know how much he would be played. And whether getting the woman he loved back safely was even a remote possibility.

3

The post office looked like it would have been more fitting in a remote Swedish village. King had noted an old fashioned sweet shop across the road. Perhaps both establishments belonged to a time when Sodertalje was smaller, a quaint township rather than a satellite of Stockholm's city limits. A place where commuters could afford more than they would in the city. Now that Sodertalje hosted a major industrial complex and commercial town along with housing developments of exponential growth, this part of town would surely change before long.

King stepped inside, closed the door and looked back across the street. He noticed a net curtain move. Encouraging. Only a rank amateur would do that. He waited a moment to see if there was another movement, but really, he knew there wouldn't be. He would be visible to them, but he would have shown them that he knew he was being watched, and that he had seen them. He stared intently, hoping he would be clear in the lens of a camera or even the sight of a rifle. He hoped they would see his eyes, cold, grey and cruel. They rarely sparkled anymore. They had simply seen too much; the worst that humankind could deliver. He continued to stare, wanted to show he was unafraid.

And he was.

He had crossed the line between self-preservation and recklessness. He would die one day, so it might as well be doing something worthwhile, something personal to him. He had laid on his bed last night, thought of the missions he had played a part in over the years, the risks he had taken. It had all paled into insignificance.

"Kan jag hjälpa dig?"

King broke away, looked at the young woman behind the counter. She was blonde, tall and beautiful. Scandinavian through and through. She wore her hair in plaits with a tight beanie covering the top of her head. "Sorry…" he said.

"Can I help you?" she repeated in English.

King was relieved. He had only visited Sweden once before, briefly. "I have a safety deposit box," he paused. "Number four-twenty-seven."

She smiled. "This way," she said, and she walked out from behind the counter and opened a door to her left. She held it open for him and nodded for him to go through. "There's a privacy curtain if you wish, but as you can see, it's quiet today."

King nodded and walked through. He quickly scanned the room, noted the smoke detector in the centre of the ceiling, two PIR sensors at each end. There would be a camera in one of them for sure. Why else did a room which would be locked when the building was closed need passive infrared sensors?

The woman closed the door behind him and King walked to the end and looked at the numbers. Box 427 was near the far end and King could see that there were no more than fifty boxes in total. He studied the numbering and realised that the first number dictated the row. Row four, box twenty-seven.

King turned his back to the PIR units and the smoke detector the best he could. He studied the door to the box, noted the dial and series of numbers. He knew the combination by heart. Had done since he had read the letter two days earlier.

4478.

He twisted the dial all the way round to 44, back to 78. There was no other way to do it because a single digit four could not be dialled in twice without a reset. The door to the box clicked open and King tentatively opened the door. He looked for signs of a trap – wires, tripping devices leading to an IED – but decided it would be fruitless. If they wanted him dead, they would have had many opportunities by now. They called the shots, held all the cards.

There were two envelopes. King removed them and walked over to the curtained cubicle. He could already tell there was a mobile phone in one of the envelopes – a slimline smartphone. Undoubtedly a burner – a non-contract, prepaid phone with an untraceable number. He glanced upwards and saw another smoke alarm directly above his head. Undoubtedly a hidden camera. He couldn't reach it to knock it down, so he angled himself the best he could to keep the contents of the envelopes shielded from view. He figured it was good enough and flipped the envelopes over. He discarded the first when he saw the single word scrawled on the front of the second envelope. His heart raced and he took a deep breath to calm himself, quell the adrenalin which now coursed through his veins. One name. Eight letters.

Caroline.

He tore open the envelope and turned over the single photograph. He couldn't remember having ever felt so nervous. Unsure whether to recoil in disgust and horror or take the photograph as a blessed relief.

Caroline had been beaten. Her blonde hair was matted to her face and her left eye was swollen and blackened. Her lips were swollen too. It was a terrible sight to behold, but the clincher, the relief was in the form of the proof of life. A copy of Le Monde - the leading French newspaper - with the date and front-page story of radicalised asylum seekers. The photo had been taken a week ago.

That meant she was alive, or at least, had been for a whole three weeks after she had been taken.

4

**One week later
Biarritz, France**

The second envelope had contained photographs of somebody else. He was a forty-year-old Russian named Pyotr Sergeyev. He was a wealthy man, yet nobody knew his net worth. His business interests ranged from construction, road haulage and nightclubs, through to people trafficking, drug dealing and murder. Sergeyev owned brothels all over Europe, where many young Muslim asylum seekers had ended up working off their passage. They would work there until they were too old for the punters, too worn and abused to appeal with their looks. And then they would simply disappear.

Pyotr Sergeyev had started out as a strong-arm for the early founder of one of the arms of the Russian mafia. His boss had been ex-KGB and when the wall had fallen, the satellite countries broken free and the Soviet Empire collapsed; KGB agents knew where the accounts were, the weapons, the disenfranchised young men with little future ahead of them. The money, contracts and opportunities were there for the taking and many men were catapulted into billionaire status, their sons free to stroll around Mayfair and buy football clubs on a whim.

When the fragile balance of power teetered, Sergeyev had been in the right place at the right time, with a gun in his hand. He had killed his boss, the man's wife, their two young sons and the man's closest aides. He had killed the man's elderly father, his brother, the man's wife and their daughter. He had thrown down a challenge to the men around him, and they had fallen in behind him. Each of them undoubtedly terrified by Sergeyev's ruthlessness. Because when someone crossed the young Russian, their family paid the price as well.

That had been ten years ago, and Sergeyev's power and influence had still not been successfully challenged. There had been attempts, but all had failed. The Russian mafia boss had either killed or put these would-be assassin's families into prostitution. He spared nobody, spoke loudly of what fate these people had suffered. He had kept two of his challengers alive long enough to see the extent of his retribution.

King looked at the photograph one last time, then put it back in the envelope, along with the dossier on Sergeyev and placed the envelope in the glovebox. He checked himself in the rear-view mirror. He had scrubbed up well enough. A close shave, a brush through his damp hair with his fingers. It was good enough. He had chosen a crisp white shirt to go with the dark blue suit that he had bought in one of the town's boutique shops, though went with the shirt left open and without a tie. It was a smart look, enough for the casino, and as smart as he had been in years.

King watched the silver Mercedes S65 saloon stop outside the casino. Sergeyev's security had already arrived in a garishly spec'd Range Rover Sport. Both bodyguards were brick outhouses. Twenty-stone a piece and well over six foot. They saw a lot of gym time. Both struggled to look comfortable in their suits and King could see unsightly mounds above their right hips. Both men carried large handguns in holsters and were obviously right-handed.

King wasn't armed. He thought it prudent not to test the casino's security. Sergeyev would have already bribed the house security to allow his own security such blatant disregard of France's firearms laws. He envisioned a great deal of money spent, both on the tables and on the bar tab, and imagined that the casino's security would be of no consequence if the Russian decided to merely do as he pleased under their roof. He noted that any action within the casino would not be his best approach.

The security was indeed laughable, because King was both swept with an electric metal detector wand and given a quick pat-down as he entered the foyer. Sergeyev and his two bodyguards had breezed straight through and were now in the bar. One of the guards was fetching chips, the other was clicking his fingers at a waitress while Sergeyev looked bored and impatient. King noted that the waitress left a table in the middle of placing an order to take the Russian's bar order.

The table, which was made up of two couples, looked outraged. One of the men got up and strode over, interrupting the order. He was irate and focused as much on the bodyguard as the waitress as he vented. King admired the man's tenacity, for the bodyguard was twice the man's width, but he stayed back and watched to see how it would play out. Inevitably, the bodyguard gave the man a shove, which was something akin to watching someone get it very wrong at the Running of the Bulls in Pamplona. The man travelled a good distance before hitting the mosaic floor with a slap that made King wince from his vantage point. He knew enough about fights to know that the man wasn't going dancing tonight, or perhaps for the rest of his holiday.

As the man lay still on the floor, his companions getting out of their seats to assist him, there were two things that could happen now, and King watched to see which would follow. Either the maître d'hôtel would be bringing out chilled champagne and a few hundred euros in complimentary chips for the table, or the house security would be taking the two couples outside before they had time to complain and cause a scene.

It was the latter. King watched as both the women and two men were roughly handled out through the bar and foyer by six well-built men with stubble on their faces and tattoos on their hands. They had all put time in at the gym and the four guests didn't stand a chance. Normally, King wouldn't have stood by and watched something so unjust, but he had to remind himself of the odds, and what he had on the line.

The Russian had this place sewn-up. His money was everything here. There was no touching him.

King ordered a beer when the waitress hovered over his table. She returned a few minutes later with a frosted glass, but a little too much foam on top. He didn't complain, but nor did he tip. He drank down half the meagre glass, stood up and walked out onto the casino floor.

The casino was running at about half capacity, with croupiers on every table, but plenty of seats at the *Chemin de fer* table and the bank of blackjack tables. There were poker games on raised plinths, three or four people at each table, and a whole host of slot machines with thousand euro pay outs. King changed up two-hundred euros and headed to the roulette tables. He played randomly numbered odd reds for twenty spins and walked away forty euros up. He had finished his drink and went to the bar for another. It was only when he had drunk half the glass and completed his fifth spin on even blacks and lost fifty euros, that he looked up and watched Sergeyev walk from the opposite roulette table to the nearest of the six blackjack tables. There was nobody else at the table.

One of his minders carried his chips, while Sergeyev managed to carry what looked like a large scotch all by himself. He sauntered over, ignored the croupier's greeting and tapped his finger on the table. The minder dutifully placed the considerable pile of chips beside his boss and stood back a pace. King wandered over as Sergeyev reached twenty-one and beat the house. He couldn't help wondering whether it was luck, or if he had been dealt a softener, something to ease his mood and bolster his ego.

King pulled out a chair, put down his glass and put his meagre pile of chips next to it. The croupier glanced at the Russian, then dealt King a card when the Russian did not look up. King flicked over the card, a seven. Sergeyev got a nine. The house got a six. King's next card was a six. The Russian got a four and the house dealt down a five. King took another seven and naturally held. Sergeyev got another nine and lost a whole lot of chips. The house got a three, then a ten. King won fifty euros. He watched the Russian's pile go to the house. He wouldn't have earned that much in a month, but Sergeyev already pushed another pile across, bigger than before.

"Something I can help you with?" Sergeyev said, without looking up.

King picked up his glass, drained the beer in one. "You can get me another drink," he said. "Or one of your monkeys could get one, if they're not too busy looking tough."

The Russian looked at him this time, his eyes hard. But King saw the flicker. Nobody had ever stared into his own eyes and come off better. King's were grey-blue and glacier cold.

"What?"

"Buy the winner a drink."

"You call that winning?"

"Sure," King said. "Hell, with what you've got in the bank, you didn't exactly lose just then. You've probably made more since."

"What do you know about me?" The Russian asked incredulously. As if to back up the man's disbelief, his minder stepped over behind King.

King smiled. "Now, I wouldn't recommend that," he said. "I won't go down like that poor fella in the bar." King turned around in his chair, looked at the minder. He was built like a side of beef. Looked as intelligent too. "Go and fill up your boss's Scotch. I'll have another house lager. But get them to work on the foam-beer ratio. They're making enough money tonight." He turned towards Sergeyev. "So, are you playing or what?"

The Russian smiled, but there was no humour behind it. "You know something of me, and you think you can talk like this?"

King shrugged. "Shitty world. Don't always assume you've done more, or worse than the guy sitting next to you," he paused. "Get your monkey to fetch our drinks, you might want to talk with me in private." He looked up at the croupier. "Deal another hand, will you?"

Sergeyev nodded to the croupier and she dealt out two cards. A ten for King and a seven for the Russian. The house got a nine. King was hit with another ten and held. Sergeyev got a seven. The house took a ten. Then the Russian was dealt with a nine. The house got a four. King won another fifty euros and the Russian handed over close to four-thousand.

"Well, it's one way of cleaning your money, I suppose," King said. "You own this place, don't you? You take money from drugs and arms and prostitution, and you lose it here. To yourself. Back in the system, cleaned and ready to go. Nice." He tapped his chips beside him. "Thanks for my win, by the way."

"Don't thank me. You won fair and square. Shame you won't spend it though," he paused. "Two things can happen when my bodyguard returns," said the Russian. "You pitch your angle and I like it, well, then you leave tonight, but with a beating. And without your winnings. Or, you say what it is you want to say, and I don't like it… well, you will get beaten like you wouldn't imagine possible, taken by car to the forest, dragged out pleading for mercy, and take a bullet in the head." He smiled. "So, I hope it was worth it."

"I'll be leaving around fifty euros up, so it's all good," King said. He watched the minder walk over with two glasses, but also accompanied by the other bodyguard. "And you're buying my drinks, so it's not all bad."

Sergeyev glanced behind him, then smiled back at King. "So, which of the two scenarios will it be, I wonder?"

"Well, you're going to need more guys. And I'll get to you first. Don't doubt that for a second. But I think I'll take the third one," King said coldly. "That's the one where I've already boarded your yacht in the harbour, neutralised your remaining three guards and taken your wife and child to a secure location. That's another scenario into the mix, and I think you had better shut up and hear me out."

5

She had become accustomed to the chloroform. She fought like hell, her heart and soul in the fight, but the inevitable had become more acceptable. She feared that the noxious chlorine would get into her system and damage her internal organs, give her cancer. She knew of the side effects, possibly why when her fight was over, she relaxed more in a bid to take in less of the chemical, expose her lungs to less danger.

Her hands were taped behind her back – she had already escaped once, gnawing at her bonds and making it out of the first compound they had held her in – and now her captors were taking no further chances. She knew she was inside a goods vehicle, as it rumbled along the roads, and she knew that as they had travelled across Europe with impunity – and the EU *Schengen Agreement* would give them that – with no borders or security checks, there was little chance of her discovery.

They had held her in France initially. She was certain of that. She had drunk the tap water, eaten bread they had brought her. It was unmistakable. The bread in France tasted like no other. There was a crust to it, a softness in the dough that differed to other countries, and certainly British outlets that marketed their produce as such. She could concede that they had taken her to Belgium, but it seemed unlikely. Other food had been distinctly French. A simple stew of beef and potatoes, but strong on garlic, yet with no pieces in it. The French always crushed their garlic with salt, like the Italians only ever sliced. The Spanish chopped it, and their bread always seemed a day-old. In truth, she realised she had perhaps had too much time and solitude to contemplate such matters. But, she had heard French spoken in passing, and there were smells which had taken her back to childhood camping trips throughout France. Spain had always been a little mainstream for her parents, and France, along with trips to Tuscany and the Italian lakes had been her holiday destinations. Or at least the ones she remembered the most.

She had lost track of time. Not just the hours, or the days, but she could not recall to the nearest week how long she had been held. Her training was slipping. She had done the forty-eight-hour escape and evasion courses, been held and interrogated, sleep deprived, then given a pat on the back, a Mars Bar and a cup of tea when it was all over. It seemed so trite now, so utterly fruitless. Such a tough course at the time, but one that had paled into insignificance when compared to her situation. Surely this could not go on much longer? She thought of Terry Waite, the envoy to the Church of England, and hostage negotiator, held captive for 1,763 days, the first four years of which, were in solitary confinement. What must he have felt? The thought made her draw on her resolve. It wasn't over yet. And she suspected, it wouldn't be for quite some time. She would have to be ready for an opportunity when it arose. A toilet break, a meal, a wash. When the time came, she would do what had to be done.

She did not remember the night she had been taken. Not much of it, at least. An attempt on her life. She had been struck on the head and later drugged in the boot of a car. She remembered coming round, for what seemed an age – groggy, sick and nauseous. The effects of her head injury, the excessive use of chloroform and the exhaust fumes from the boot of the car. She had been locked in a dark room, not given food or water until she had been as desperate as she could have ever imagined. She knew she had lost weight. Her filthy clothes had been loose, and her insides had rumbled constantly.

A shop-bought sandwich had been thrown to her, along with a bottle of water, and she had feasted like a wild dog. She had missed the opportunity of escaping, the door left open too long, in favour of eating. It had been a low moment. One of degradation and disgust, and one of knowing she had missed her chance.

The next time opportunity presented itself, she had struck her captor, sending him to the ground where she had stamped on his groin and fled out through the open door. She had bolted, clueless to either the time of night, or her surroundings. She had been a few hundred metres later, lights from what looked like a village nearby, so close she could taste her freedom. She had been beaten then, bound sadistically tight, and kept under guard. The guard had touched her at night, when the rest of the building had been dark and quiet. She had resisted, fought him night after night, sustaining bruises and cuts as he had kicked her like a dog. The beast had been persistent, and her energy had all but gone to keep fighting. It had been her lowest ebb.

But the one thing Caroline Darby promised herself, that kept her going - perhaps more so than even the slim chance she would ever be free, to see the man she loved, her family or her friends again - was that before this ended, in whatever way fate dictated, she would make the man hurt a hundred times more.

6

Biarritz, France

"We have a saying in the Urals, where I grew up," Sergeyev paused and sunk his Scotch in one mouthful. He did not grimace at its bite, but thoughtfully studied the remnants, the droplets of amber liquid running inside the glass. "You cannot negotiate with a wolf, while your balls are still in his mouth… but you can still kill him, if you care not for your own fate."

"There's a saying on the estate where I grew up," King said. "It's about shit and being full of it. Right now, your wife and daughter are being held. You are a tough and resourceful man, I get it. You took control of the brotherhood. And you did it by being a ruthless son of a bitch. Here's the reality check. There is always someone more ruthless, tougher and more resourceful. He's sitting here, drinking a beer and giving you one chance, and one chance only."

"You are brave," Sergeyev said. His hair was jet black and greasy. But it was product. He was sweating profusely, and the beads of sweat were trapped in the product. When they eventually ran, they formed thick rivulets. King noted that the man's colour had paled. The man was not riding this out with as much bravado as he made out. Sergeyev wiped his forehead with the back of his sleeve. "I could kill you. Right now."

"And never see your wife and child again," King said coldly. "Let me tell you, tough guy… that would look good to your monkeys here. That would make you look tougher than just about anyone. But you will burn and freeze and ache inside forever more. And besides, like I said, don't assume you'd win. And don't assume your two monkeys will beat me either."

"You are not armed," the Russian said. "You're very arrogant."

King sipped some of his beer and shrugged. "I've been asked to kill you."

"You're an assassin?"

"I suppose. I'm not here for financial gain, and I'm not serving my country. Somebody is holding the woman I love prisoner. They have me in a corner. They want you dead, and I don't think one death will cut it for them. So why the hell should I further their agenda? I want my fiancé back, but when this is all done, I don't want to have helped the person calling the shots. I don't want them to gain from this."

Sergeyev thought on this for a moment, then clicked his fingers. One of the man mountains stepped forward. Sergeyev snapped at the man in Russian and he seemed to protest. Sergeyev pulled him closer and spoke slowly and hoarsely into his ear, and he seemed to think better of it, turned around and walked to the bar. "More drinks," the Russian said.

"I've ordered you another glass of that piss you are drinking…"

"Thanks," King said, somewhat impassively. "You drink Scotch," he commented. "I thought you'd drink vodka."

"Peasant's drink," he replied. "We used to put garlic in the stuff we drank at home. It held the impurities which could otherwise make you go blind…"

King nodded. "Excuse me for a moment," he said. "I need the lavatory." He stood up and casually buttoned his jacket.

"Dimitri will accompany you," Sergeyev said emotionlessly. "Just to make sure you don't go anywhere before we've finished our little… chat."

King nodded. "Of course." He pushed past the hulking minder and watched him fall in behind him using the mirrors behind the bar. King walked casually, unhurried. He pushed the first door inwards, then when he reached the gents he opened the door, glanced at the Russian. "Are you coming in? I can't take a piss with someone watching."

"Tough shit."

"Well, after you then." He pushed the door wide and the Russian stepped inside.

King took a shuffle step and kicked the big man between his legs from behind. To be fair, the man had quite a package and King's size twelve leather brogue had no trouble finding the target. The man gasped, but as he dropped, King was already on him with a right, left, right combination of punches to his kidneys. He was felled and dropped hard on the tiled floor. King had watched the lavatory door as he played blackjack and talked to Sergeyev. He knew nobody would be in here, but he could not account for who would follow and when, so he stamped on the back of the man's head and drove his face hard into the tiles. King was already heaving his unconscious body into the furthest cubicle, the one that would give him more privacy. He bundled the man onto the toilet seat, pushed the door closed, then took a deep breath. He was lightheaded for a moment. The twenty-plus stone of muscle was dense and unpliable. King reached inside the man's jacket and retrieved a nickel-plated Colt .45 pistol with mother of pearl grips. Neither classy, nor a practical combat piece. Nickel reflected light big time and mother of pearl had all the grip capabilities in combat - where palms can be sweaty, and fingers seem numb - of a wet bar of soap.

The weapon was a solid design though, and King had used the big Colt many times before. He was always happy with the slow travelling, hard impacting .45 round. Usually a one shot, one drop weapon. He checked it over, saw that it was chambered but not cocked. A big mistake for the single action pistol. Safe to carry, but the hammer would have to be cocked back before firing, unlike most semi-auto pistols made from the seventies onwards, where they could be carried with extra safety on a dropped hammer but would require twice the trigger pull on the first shot. After the weapon had fired, cycled and a new round chambered, then the hammer remained back, and an easier trigger pull was given for every following shot. And this weapon, although mimicked and even made under license by other companies, was well over one-hundred years old in design. And completely unchanged from its first patent and subsequent use in the First World War. Testament to its capabilities yet flawed in many ways by today's standards. King got it though. The hefty weight and size, the appearance, the shine and bling. It was a drug dealer's weapon, a mafia's tool of the trade. It was noticeable and had most likely been waved in many faces as a warning. A taste of what was to come if deadlines were not met, if sales were not made and percentages not paid.

King checked the man's pulse, tucking two fingers with a lot of force into the side of the man's throat, pinching the carotid artery. He frowned, adjusted his position, then felt a weak thud. It was enough. The guy would either make it or he wouldn't. He couldn't worry about the little things. Sergeyev's instructions to the other monkey had been clear enough. He would be outside, calling in the troops. The Russian had not assumed, somewhat arrogantly so, that King could speak Russian. King had spent a lot of time either in Russia or fighting their agents in secret wars. He wouldn't pass for a local by any means, but he could understand and speak the language beyond conversational levels.

Sergeyev was a fearsome man. King could see that now. There was a reason he was still at the top, still the man running one of the most notorious of the Russian brotherhoods. A man willing to chance sacrificing his wife and child to remain top dog. He was hedging his bets on making King talk. Making him give up his wife and child, and if he did not, then that was the price he had been willing to pay.

King checked over the man's pockets. He went through his wallet. There were a few cards and five-hundred euros. It would come in handy, so he took it, along with a spare magazine for the Colt. That still only gave him fourteen rounds in total. Not enough for a proper shootout, especially with Sergeyev's men on route. King knew that the Russian had business interests in Biarritz, not least the casino. He would have to get out fast. But how? Casinos were like banks. Only with more security. He tucked the pistol into his waistband and adjusted his jacket, before pulling the door inwards and closing it carefully behind him. Once outside in the corridor he saw that the only other door was that of the female lavatories. Not even worth a look. The windows would be barred, as they had been in the gent's. No, his only chance was to slip behind the bar as he re-entered the casino lounge and try to get down to the works of the building – the pot-wash, kitchen and beer-cellar or wine-cellar.

King eased the door outwards, looked directly at Sergeyev, who was standing in front of him. There were four burly security personnel on either side of him. All had a variety of handguns pointing at him. King was fast, and he was *good*. But nobody is that good. He glanced to his right, where the house security stood. Unarmed, but they were loving the turn of events. He figured they would get a bit of him sooner rather than later.

"Give me Dimitri's gun," Sergeyev said quietly. "Slowly."

King reached slowly, as he was told, but even now, he was unsure which end to give the Russian. The muzzle first and a .45 bullet right between the eyes, or butt first and surrender? King had never surrendered before. He had been shot and captured, held and tortured, but he had never had to hold up his hands and accept capitulation. He eased the weapon out of his waistband. He could do it, was convinced he'd take down several of them, but it was a suicidal move. But he couldn't abandon Caroline. Right now, he was her only hope of survival. Play the game he had been pulled into and look for the right opportunity. King held the pistol pinched between his thumb and forefinger, held it out carefully.

"Easy," one of the armed men said. He stepped forward and caught hold of the barrel with confidence and familiarity. He twisted the weapon away from King and gained possession, before stepping back.

The unarmed men lunged forwards as one. A flurry of fists and elbows, but King was too akin to a life of survival to take a beating without a fight and reacted hard and fast, the men dropping around him clutching chopped throats, gouged eyes, broken noses and loosened teeth. King dodged and weaved and punched and kicked and with five men down, was starting to look like he could go all night and take on all-comers. And then he felt an impact between his legs and an indescribable pain through his testicles and his stomach. He dropped to his knees and took the slam to the back of his head. He fell forwards, rolled onto his side and saw the bulk of Dimitri in the doorway. The big Russian was holding his own groin and heaving for breath. He was pale and clearly pained, but he looked like he was pleased with his efforts. He'd certainly repaid King for the kick in the balls.

King gasped through the pain, struggled to get a breath inside him, as he watched the big Russian walk forwards and raise a size fourteen shoe above his face, hovering ominously.

Perhaps it was time for plan B? Plan A had gone to shit, he just hoped things would get better. There was no avoiding the stamping foot, nor the darkness of the unconsciousness which followed.

7

The pine forest smelled dry and fresh. The scent was strong, heady – like a pine air freshener. The forest was dry and hot too. A savagely-hot start to the summer, with long hot days and uncomfortably close nights, had dried the forest floor, the needles and the scattered pine cones.

King could smell this, and more besides. His own body odour in the confines of the vehicle's boot was not the freshest thing he'd smelled in a while. And the exhaust fumes that filled the boot had worked its way into his nose, his throat and his eyes.

He had regained consciousness on the drive into the forest. The car had been driven erratically along the twisting country roads. Many were straight, interspersed by cross-roads, but the road surface was of poor-quality. Seldom maintained, deeply rutted, which tested the vehicle's suspension.

The vehicle had slowed and pulled off the road, and King could tell that they had travelled on softer ground. Just as rutted, but foliage scraped underneath and occasionally, the vehicle would bottom out and the wheels would spin as the driver tried to maintain progress.

When the car eventually stopped, King realised he could hear another vehicle. There was the sound of doors opening and closing, and low voices. He could smell cigarette smoke, and he imagined the men gathering together to devise their plan or receive orders.

There had been a few times over his time with the intelligence services, that King had been convinced he was about to die. Fate, luck or happenstance had turned it around, but right now, bound and imprisoned inside the boot of the vehicle, this was one of those times. Possibly the definitive moment. Plan A hadn't worked out, and plan B was a work-in-progress. Whether he got out of this would depend on one thing. But now, after spending much of his time in confinement, he just hoped it had been enough.

The boot lid opened and even though it was close to sunset, the light stung his eyes. He blinked against it, then felt rough hands on him, some grabbing his collar, others grabbing him around the ankles. King was solid, a shade under six-foot and around fourteen-stone. But he was whipped out of the boot and thrown through the air as if he were a child. He looked up to see it had been three men who had got him out. The monkey named Dimitri, all twenty-stone of him, and two other men, similarly sized. Dimitri clearly had a grievance, and King couldn't blame him, but could have done without another kick to his ribs. He gasped, grit his teeth, and hoped he had not shown how much it had hurt. He couldn't get up with his hands bound behind him, but he got onto his side, more to take in his surroundings than in any hope of getting to his feet.

Sergeyev smoked a cigarette and watched with amusement. He was flanked by two more guards. He nodded to one of them, and the man dutifully walked around to the open tailgate of the Range Rover. He retrieved a shovel and a chainsaw and walked towards King, throwing the shovel at him. It hit the ground and bounced into his face. King recoiled, fell onto his back.

"I think getting a man to dig his own grave gets that man into the right headspace for what is about to happen," Sergeyev paused as he inhaled some of the cigarette smoke and blew out a thick pungent-smelling plume. "You *will* die, but before you do, you will tell me where my family are, and you *will* beg for a swift end. I guarantee it." He nodded to one of the men behind King and he bent forward, slashing the rope bindings with a knife.

King knelt slowly, rubbing some feeling back into his wrists. He looked around him. There was a glimpse of the ocean, the beach some fifty metres beyond the trees. He closed his eyes, a distant memory coming to him. Southwest France, the beach, the pine forest, the pungent cigarette smoke. King would bet anything it was a Turkish blend. The memory of a night of killing, the start of his career all those years ago. He shook his head to dismiss it. He needed to stay in the game.

King stood up, heard the safety catches release or hammers cock on the various pistols around him. For a moment he was reminded of the scene in the film *Blazing Saddles* and the gunmen lining up on the *Wako Kid*, hammers cocking. Comedic interlude in a dire situation. Gallows humour. He smiled to himself. He didn't have a gun, almost certainly wouldn't be as fast as Gene Wilder's character. The shovel was at his feet and he figured he could slice at least one man's head open before he went down. He figured that was the best he could hope for.

Plan B, still a work-in-progress...

"Dig," Sergeyev said.

King shook his head. "You risk never finding your wife and child."

"I'll pay the price for showing strength," Sergeyev smirked. "But it will not come to that. You will give me what I want to know."

"Don't count on it," King said.

"Who are you?"

King smiled. "Is that it? You think you're getting shit out of me? I told you – I have been told to kill you to free my fiancé. I gave you the chance to keep your family safe and for you to lay low while I sort this out. And you do this?" King gestured at the forest clearing. "There's no deal anymore."

"What did you want to deal?" Sergeyev frowned. "You captured my wife and daughter."

"Well, I misread you," King paused. "So now, I'll just have to kill you."

"Kill me!" Sergeyev screamed at him. He paced over and stood two paces in front of King.

"Look around you, dickhead! I am calling the shots! It is *I* who will kill you!"

"And you will never see your wife and child again. They are quite safe. For now. But they will die of thirst and starvation before you find them, or before anybody else does," King paused, held up his hand. "You control their fate. Don't be an idiot. I'll give you one chance, and one chance only. We'll put this down to ego, to theatrics. Emotion, even. Now, get your boys to put down their weapons and leave us alone to talk."

"Niet!" Sergeyev screamed. He pulled a gold-plated Makarov pistol out of his waistband and aimed it at King.

Sergeyev went down hard. The bullet striking him in the chest and throwing a mist of crimson in the air. Some of it went on King's face, but he was already moving and had the shovel in his hands as he rolled back up onto his feet. He saw the bewildered expression on Dimitri's face, right before he split the big Russian's head open through to the middle of his face.

Gunshots echoed out, but these were not the shots that were finding their targets. Instead, two of Sergeyev's bodyguards went down almost simultaneously. King dug the shovel out of Dimitri's face, went to swing at the nearest monkey, but the man went down, his head dissolving into a pink mist. King dropped to the ground, scrambled over to Sergeyev and picked up his pistol. He sighted on the last remaining guard, who looked at King in bewilderment, more than anger, and watched him fall into the rear door of the Range Rover, slip to the ground and lie still.

King was breathing hard. He had no cover, no target to acquire in the pistol's tiny sights. He stood up slowly, the pistol lowered down by his side.

The figure rose from a pile of broken branches, twenty-five feet from him and stood still, the rifle held with the muzzle pointed at the ground. He walked over, stepping over one of the dead Russians. He was dressed in an army surplus olive jacket and a pair of tan cargoes. His hair was as black as jet and his dark coffee complexion remained invisible in the dim light, right up until he stood next to King.

"You cut that fine," King said.

"Better late than never," there was a distinct brummie lilt to his accent.

"Better never late."

The man shrugged, cradled the suppressed M4 rifle. "You didn't give me much notice. Seems to be a habit. And you still owe me a pint from last time."

"I'll buy you a couple later."

"Do you know how hard it is to smuggle one of these out of Hereford? And through the border force lot at Dover?" he raised the rifle, then glanced at Sergeyev on the ground. "You've got a live one."

King turned around to see the Russian mafia boss trying to push himself backwards across the earth. The fallen pine needles were thick, and they were mounding up around his shoulders. He raised the pistol and Sergeyev stopped moving. He was bleeding heavily from the wound in his chest. The blood was almost black. The bullet had caught his liver.

"Bastard…" he said, his Russian accent thick and hateful.

"I gave you a chance. You were too much of a tough guy to take it," King paused, looked at his companion. "Rashid, find the keys to the Range Rover and let's get out of here." He looked back at Sergeyev. "Your wife and child are quite safe. I'll release them tonight. No harm will, or would ever have come to them. But I'm in a tight spot. Someone who wants you dead is holding my fiancé."

"So?" he rasped.

"Her name is Helena. She is from the Ukraine and she married an English billionaire…"

"Helena Milankovitch…"

"You know her then," he said flatly. "What's her issue with you?"

The Russian sneered. He touched his chest, then looked at his blood-soaked hand. He'd seen enough in his violent and unforgiving life to know his fate. He seemed to relax, as if knowing had knocked the fight out of him. "Fuck you," he grimaced. "Fuck you, and fuck her too…"

"We've got wheels!" Rashid shouted. "Stick a bullet in him and let's get the hell out of Dodge!"

King looked down at Sergeyev. He didn't see the tough and resourceful, unrelenting, unforgiving mafia boss who had risked the life of his wife and child in a show of strength to his men. He saw a dying man, whose violent past had finally caught up with him. Whatever it was, the mention of Helena Milankovitch had taken the wind out of his sails.

"Your liver has had it," King said. "You are going to die here, in this clearing. You're not going to talk about Helena, are you?"

"Niet!" Sergeyev glowered. His face was ashen, his torso now completely soaked. He forced a smile, perhaps a last-ditch show of bravado. "But mark my words," he said, his breathing laboured. "If she has your woman, she is as good as dead. You won't bargain with Helena." He smiled. "Your bitch is as good as dead…"

King looked at the Russian, then glanced around the clearing at the bodies strewn on the ground. He shook his head, angered with himself that he had let it get this far, taken this turn of events. He had tried to give a man a chance. Not that the man deserved it. A ruthless individual who would have caused untold pain and suffering to others in his world of organised crime. His quest to become more powerful, ever wealthier, had caused misery for so many. He wasn't a man who deserved a chance, yet King had attempted to take the moral high ground. To spare a woman the loss of her husband, a child the loss of her father. And when it had come to it, the man had been willing to risk their life for nothing more than his own ego.

King stared down at Sergeyev, ashamed at deviating from his instructions, from chancing Caroline's safety, to try and do the right thing. The right thing for a woman and a child he did not know. The right thing was whatever it took to get back the woman he loved. He shot Sergeyev through the forehead, dropped the gold-plated pistol onto the dead man's chest and walked through the clearing to where Rashid had the Range Rover idling.

Rashid was searching the radio station for something that wasn't French folk music. He found a rock channel playing *Steppenwolf* and *Born to be Wild*. King got into the passenger side as Rashid put the vehicle into drive and floored the accelerator. The wheels tore up the sandy earth, the pine needles scattering behind them.

Rashid turned the volume button up on the steering wheel and started to sing, "Get your motor runnin', head out on the highway! Lookin' for adventure, and whatever comes our way…"

8

It was completely dark when they reached Rashid's car. The SAS soldier was not pleased at leaving the leather throne of the Range Rover, but King had insisted any link to Sergeyev needed to be severed as soon as possible. The Russian mafia boss had many interests in southwest France, and one of his vehicles could easily be identified, especially by the police, which King would assume were privy to what the Russian did, or were in fact on the payroll themselves.

Rashid had pulled alongside King's BMW and King had swiftly got in, moved off and taken the lead for him to follow. He led the way out of Biarritz and through Bayonne to the gentle hills a dozen miles from the coast - the foothills of the Pyrenees. There were villages - some as old as the first settlers to the region - others purpose built, full of faux chalets and cottages for the summer tourist season, complete with micro-markets and pharmacies, medical centres and gift shops. Farmhouses dotted the rolling grass hills, visible only by lights shining within.

King used his phone's GPS to find the farmhouse. The darkness made it impossible to use the various landmarks he had noted during the day, but as he reached a crossroads with recycling bins packed tightly on the other side of the road, he recognised the farmhouse's entrance. He turned sharply to the left, crossing over the road and slowed over the potholed track. The farmhouse was the only property on the track. King had earlier scouted out the track, but it merely led to pastures and a large storage shed stacked with the last of the previous year's haybales.

King turned into the driveway, the lights of his car illuminating the chalet and its front garden. He switched off the engine, for a moment enjoying the darkness and silence it afforded him. Taking lives was not something that went without reflection. Or at least, not the older one became. It had been so long now, King couldn't remember if it had always been this way, or merely in recent years. He liked to hope, that on some level, it had always rested heavily with him. In truth, he suspected it had not. He looked up as Rashid's headlights swept over the chalet, dazzling him in the mirror. He doubted the young SAS officer was feeling the same way. He imagined him blasting out karaoke renditions to the rock station all the way up here. Hyped up on the adrenalin, trying to maintain its levels with whoops and calls, screams and shouts, playing back the shots in his mind and seeing the men drop as he moved the rifle's sights to the next unfortunate soul.

Rashid was a gifted marksman. He was also the first solider of Pakistani extraction to lead an SAS unit in Afghanistan, and had successfully infiltrated ISIS, which he had done by taking up arms against US-led Iraqi troops. A dark time in Hereford's history, and one that would forever be denied. Rashid had also helped King in both the fight against Muslim extremists and a Russian-sanctioned terrorist plot against Britain. In a world where he had few friends and had left little personal or emotional impression behind, King would call Rashid his closest and most dependable friend. Only now, for the third time in just over a year, he was further in the man's debt.

King got out of the car. The air-conditioning had cooled him, and the night air was warm and pleasant. He watched Rashid get out of his car – a ten-year-old Audi A4, that had seen better days – the M4 assault rifle held loosely in his right hand. He was chewing gum and still bobbing to the music, long after the stereo had been switched off. The man was wired and pumped and ready for a war. King wanted him to mellow. In fact, he wanted him out of the way entirely. There was no point in the soldier being a part of what was to happen next.

"Do a sweep of the area," King said. "Take up position fifty-metres over there," he said flicking his head down the road. "Enough to keep eyes on the house, and the road down here."

"What will you be doing?" he asked.

"What needs to be done," King said.

9

Anna Sergeyev looked up at King as he entered. She was scared and as all mothers would have done, she turned to look at her nine-year-old daughter. King felt a pang of anguish, of regret. He saw that the girl had fallen asleep, her hands still bound to the chair he had put her in. He had not involved himself with any contact with children in almost twenty years of service in the intelligence services. He had never considered them to be collateral damage, had gone out of his way and risked the outcome of entire operations to keep children coming to harm. Now, with the woman he loved taken as leverage, he had barely considered taking the girl hostage, of terrifying her, of using her as a pawn.

King walked across the room and eased at the edge of the duct tape covering Anna Sergeyev's mouth. He pulled at it gently, her lips stuck, but she did not have enough facial hair to make the process too uncomfortable. He said nothing, decided to leave Dina Sergeyev sleeping as he walked through to the open-plan kitchen and fetched a glass of water for the woman.

She watched him as he returned. He held the glass to her lips and she sucked some of the water off the top.

"I'm sorry," he said.

She pulled away from the glass having slaked her thirst. "You are going to kill us…" she said quietly.

"Your husband didn't go for it," he said. "I gave him the chance, but he barely considered it."

"You expected him to?"

"Of course."

"Then you know nothing of the Russian mafia. The brotherhood."

"So, it would seem," he said.

"Stupid man," she said, her accent a mix of thick Russian, guttural, with a hint of American. A woman who had grown used to watching and listening to popular culture, but couldn't quite shake off the motherland.

"Who? Him or me?"

"Both."

"Fair enough."

"Bastard."

"Me?"

"Him," she snapped. "How much did he ask about us?"

King shrugged. "Nothing."

"He sacrificed us?"

"In fairness, he was set on torturing me to death to find you."

"How far did he get?"

"He made a start," King said. "Drove me out to the forest, told me to dig my own grave."

She closed her eyes, took a deep breath, when she opened them again, her eyes were moist. "How did he die?" she paused. "How did you kill my husband? My daughter's father?"

"It was quick and painless," King lied, thinking of the man's exploded liver and that dark, unmistakable blood. He wasn't feeling unhappy about it. He hadn't been a good man. He felt something for the woman in front of him, the child asleep in the easy chair. "He was a big boy and he was playing big boys' games. He died by big boys' rules."

"How will you do it," she asked. "How will you kill us both? My daughter is sleeping…" she said, her voice catching in her throat. Tears had formed in her eyes. "You could do it now… while she's asleep," she paused. Her brow was perspiring suddenly, her face pale and her breathing more rapid. "Oh, God, no…" she said urgently, as if changing her mind in an event she had no choice over. "I don't want to die…"

King looked at her, took out his knife and opened the blade. "You fucking Russians are hardcore," he said. "My car is a hire car. I took it under an alias, so knock yourself out." He bent down and sliced through the bindings. She pulled her hands away and rubbed her wrists. "I have no way of knowing what will happen with your husband out of the chain, but a powerplay will put both you and your daughter at risk. Can you get to any money?"

"Enough," she said. "Enough to disappear and live well."

"That sounds good enough," said King. "This place is taken for two weeks. You can stay here, make your plans and be invisible. There are shops in the village for food and clothes, nobody will disturb you here. You'll be just another tourist."

She wiped a tear from her cheek. "Thank you," she said quietly. "But why?"

"Why, what?"

"Well, why let us go?" she rubbed her face, then took the glass of water off the table and drank most of it in a few large mouthfuls.

"You were leverage, nothing more. I'm sorry I scared you," he paused. "And your daughter too. I was desperate."

"Why?" she asked, seemingly interested, though she was sad. King suspected not so much by the death of her husband, but his willingness to sacrifice them to save face.

"Someone is holding my girlfriend, my fiancé. They want me to perform certain tasks. Killing your husband was one of them."

She stared at him. "Well, you stand to get her back then," she paused. "You win, my husband loses."

"And so do you. I'm sorry."

"I'll survive. Possibly longer now that he's dead. There have been many attempts recently, many betrayals. He has driven to those woods many times. He was scared. So, if not you, then somebody else.

Somebody even more ruthless. Perhaps you have saved me, my daughter too."

"I hope so. It wasn't my plan, but perhaps some good can come from it." He folded the knife, slipped it back into his pocket and tossed her the keys to the hired BMW. "Your husband seemed to know the woman behind his death, the woman holding my fiancé."

"Her name?" Anna peeled the remainder of the duct tape from her wrists, slipped the keys into her pocket.

"Helena…"

"Milankovitch…" she interrupted.

"Yes."

She shook her head. "I'm sorry," she said. "But your fiancé is as good as dead."

10

"I thought you were going to slot them both."

King looked at Rashid as he drove. "Really?"

"Well, you're pretty hardcore."

"Says the man who just took down the Bratva Mafia."

"Needs must," he paused. "I didn't hear you complaining."

King shrugged. "That sort of thing isn't my style."

"Complaining?"

"No, you tit. Collateral damage."

"Not yet, at least."

"Meaning?"

Rashid negotiated the slip road and accelerated to join the D817. "I just don't think you'll stop at anything to get Caroline back."

King didn't answer. Deep down, he knew the man was right. But it had only just started. He knew he was going to be put through the wringer. He just hoped he stood a chance of freeing Caroline. He thought back to what Pyotr Sergeyev had said before he died. King had merely thought it a taunt. The man knew he was dying; his injuries were too severe to hope to recover. But King hadn't been ready for Anna's comment. And no amount of asking would make the woman elaborate. She had history with Helena Milankovitch, knew her from old. He had seen from Anna's file that she was Ukrainian. He knew too that she had met Sergeyev in the club scene. It wouldn't be a stretch to assume she was from a similar background to Helena – a dancer, an escort or more.

Rashid carefully overtook a series of slow-moving trucks, keeping the Audi at a speed of around seventy-miles-per-hour. He was making timely progress but didn't want to push it. Not with a firearm on board. Especially when that firearm was a Ministry of Defence registered 5.56mm Colt M4, part of a requisition from 22 Special Air Service Regiment.

"Don't get me wrong," said Rashid. "I've done some stuff I'd rather not talk about, but I can't see this going well. Not unless you get some help."

"You helped," King answered tersely.

"Always glad to. Especially now I'm shining a chair with my arse."

"Really?"

Rashid smiled. "Wound up the wrong Rupert."

"*You're* a bloody Rupert," King corrected him. In the SAS, and now in many other units as well, Rupert was slang for an officer.

"Well, someone a lot higher up the chain than myself."

"What did you do?"

Rashid shrugged. "Well, he's in his fifties, a lieutenant-colonel. He has a daughter…"

"A sullied one now, I take it?"

"Oh, I imagine she was sullied a long time before she met me…"

King smiled. Rashid was a captain, and only recently promoted. He didn't say anything, but he had a feeling it wasn't just rank that irked the toy colonel. Rashid didn't seem remotely bothered, so he didn't mention it. The army was inherently racist, despite the recruitment films, and there would be those who would think Rashid had simply been promoted to fill a minority quota. King knew it was more likely because he was one of the best soldiers he had ever met.

"Well, getting caught AWOL with a weapon would do more than find you a desk," he said. "I appreciate it."

"Well, you still owe me a beer from the last time," he smiled. "Seriously though, you need someone helping you. What about 'Box?"

King shook his head. "Not yet. They wanted to, but I didn't want it. Not yet."

"Why? Just think of the resources, the manpower. Even a discreet investigation would give you a few pairs of hands."

"But they won't play it like it needs to be played," King paused.

"This woman, Helen Snell…"

"Milankovitch."

"Right," Rashid nodded. "So, let me get this straight. You investigate Anarchy to Recreate Society, a terrorist group founded to kill the richest five people on the planet and continue to do so until the rich offload enough money to get off the rich list. But it's not all it seems. Helena Snell, AKA Milankovitch, is the wife to one of the richest men on the list and she is sleeping with some guy and has been all along throughout her marriage."

"Correct," said King. "Viktor Bukov."

"The sniper killing all those lovely billionaires."

"Yes."

"And the same sniper I killed on the roof before he made his final hit."

"Yes."

"Now, this Helena, she has organised this whole terrorism angle to cover the real target, her husband?"

"That's right."

"And she's pissed at you for cracking it wide open. She blames you for not getting the money she thinks she deserved, and for the death of her lover."

"Who you killed," King said dryly. "Perhaps I should send her your number."

Rashid ignored the quip. He'd helped his friend, was glad to have gone up against a notable sniper. "And during your heroics, shutting down the rest of the group, she kidnapped Caroline."

"And now she wants her fun. But there's a completely different agenda. She has a past, and so far, two people knew what she was capable of. Sergeyev, before he died, said Caroline would be as good as dead. Not two hours ago, his widow told me the same thing. She has plans, and she's going to use me to see them through."

"And Caroline is the carrot dangling in front of your nose."

"That's about the size of it, yes."

"So how are you contacted?"

"A prepaid mobile phone. One number punched in. It diverts to other numbers like an old-school dial-up internet. Must be a dozen numbers diverting before I speak. Even then, I can only leave a message. I get a text in return."

"And you text back?"

"Yes. I've given up trying to call."

"So, what now?"

King hesitated, the phone in question vibrating in his pocket. He took it out, unlocked it and looked at the screen. "That's her."

"Shit, what are the chances? What has she got to say?"

He ignored him, studied the picture of Caroline now enlarged on the screen from the message. She looked to have had a wash and a change of clothes since the photographs he had collected at the post office in Sweden. She was expressionless. However, King recognised it as simmering anger. There was a fire in her eyes that he seldom saw, had only witnessed in a rare argument. He could see the headline of a newspaper, *L'Express,* a French language Swiss paper. He spread the screen with his thumb and forefinger to enlarge it further and saw that it was today's date. "I think she's being held in Switzerland," King said quietly.

"Are you sure?"

"Could be a ruse. There's a picture of her with today's newspaper. She could be anywhere in Europe."

"You need MI5. They can work with the European intelligence services, Interpol even."

"Not yet," said King emphatically. He read the text, frowned, then read through again. "I have to go to Italy first."

"Italy?"

"Tuscany."

11

**Four days later
Tuscany, Italy**

The town of Monteverdi Marittimo was sat on top of a mountain, approximately seven miles inland from the Mediterranean. It afforded excellent views of the sea, mountainsides thick with pine trees and well-tended meadows. On the west side of the mountain, grapes grew in organised rows in vineyards that remained unchanged since the height of the Roman Empire. Olive trees lined the quiet streets, with thick trunks and large canopies, the roots pushing up the paving and causing the road to peak and crack. At harvest time, even these decorative trees were harvested with the use of nets held by the women, and the trees given a shaking by the men, tourists invited to partake amid music and much *grappa* – the heady and intoxicating fortified liquor made from the waste in winemaking.

    King hadn't bothered trying to order a cup of tea. This was espresso country. He settled for a beer, which came well-chilled and in a frosted glass. The waiter had placed a saucer of nuts beside his glass. King picked at the nuts, sipped the cold beer and watched Luca Fortez order another espresso. King wore dark aviator glasses and scrolled on his mobile phone. Not the phone he had been left in the safety deposit box, along with his orders, in Sweden. He kept that one switched off, the sim card removed, until he needed it. He had removed what he could of the device and inspected it but found nothing unusual. The phone could not be traced unless it was switched on and the sim card was active. King used his own iPhone. Always two models old, but with upgraded software, keeping it as non-descript looking as he could. Between drinking his beer, picking at the nuts and checking his non-existent emails, he studied the folded tourist map, but watched the Italian Mafia boss discreetly in his periphery.

Luca Fortez had been born with a different name. He had then worked his way through another, as hitman and enforcer to the Mafia running everything north of Rome and south of Modena. He had settled on Fortez when he had reached the higher echelons and become a made-man. The killing and violence was not behind him, he ordered such things now, but he had made his way to the top of the pile with the blood of his own friends and family on his hands. His reputation was well-earned, and he commanded respect not so much through fear and intimidation, but by history. People who knew of him, who found themselves in the realms of the mafia's touch, feared the legend. And that was precisely what the man had become. A legend. Like the Bogey Man.

King had studied the man enough to know he was dangerous. Six-two, well-muscled. His biceps were large enough to indicate he was still extremely physical, despite being in his mid-forties – an age where many Italian men have learned to embrace pasta, wine and middle-age. But it was the man's eyes that told King he was dangerous. They were the eyes of a killer. The eyes King saw in the mirror every day. Unlike King's glacier-blue eyes, the Italian killer's eyes were dark, but they stared hard at everything he looked at. They did not blink either. Like a cobra's. He wore his sunglasses pushed fashionably high on his forehead, the lenses as dark as his lifeless eyes beneath.

There were two bodyguards. Both big and burly and clearly armed with sizable handguns and spare magazines under their linen suit jackets. They wore dark wraparound sunglasses, open shirts under their white suits and seemed bored. This was a quiet town, a village really, with a few tourists and locals milling through the street. A bakery, a convenience store and several bars and tobacconists. A church and tower were the key points of interest, along with a small piazza and regular open market. King had perused the market, bought some bread, deli meats and cheese, and placed them into a paper bag he had earlier prepared. He had placed the bag on the table, adjusted the lens of the camera to fit the hole he had made in the bag, and was now filming the Italian mafia boss and his two bodyguards, as he sipped his iced beer and picked at the saucer of nuts. King knew enough about surveillance to understand the importance of appearing natural. He looked at the mafia boss like he simply didn't care, mindful not to allow his stare to linger. He simply took in his surroundings, enjoyed the sunshine and the coolness of the narrow street, which funnelled the air through. A lone traveller, taking his time to soak up the architecture, the simplicity of Italian life in the Tuscan hills.

When the Russian arrived, it was with two security personnel ahead of him, three behind and one bodyguard a pace behind and to his right. All wore the same wraparound sunglasses, black T-shirts and black suits. All five men also wore heavy gold chains around their necks. The lead bodyguard wore more gold than a jeweller's window. It was by no means subtle. The exact opposite, in fact, a declaration of wealth. At odds with blending into the surroundings and lowering the threat. It was a show of force – the muscle, the wealth, the poor-fitting suits unable to conceal the bulging holstered pistols underneath. And it was as much a show to the Italian security as the rest of the world around them. Many of the people walking through the thoroughfare must have thought a rap video was being filmed. Some even stopped and watched. A few knowing locals walked on. Some would know Luca Fortez, and that would be enough to keep walking.

King watched, waiting to see what would happen next. He had noticed two men loitering at the piazza, and they sauntered over and joined the Italian ranks. Two more walked up the street from behind the Russian and his entourage. The Italians outnumbered the Russians now. The street was full and people walking in and out of a nearby bakery had to side-step the display of muscle. King sipped his beer, ate more nuts and adjusted his seat to put his face in the sun and his back to the show. He could not take in much from his occasional glances, but he would see everything he needed to when he played it back at his convenience. Hear everything too, as the camera was equipped with an amplified directional microphone, what the surveillance world called parabolic.

King was amused. The text had told him the premise. The Russian competitors to Sergeyev's brotherhood, a splinter group from the hostile takeover Sergeyev had made, was linking with one of three mafia's who held almost half of Italy. An uneasy balance, soon to be struck a deadly blow with the help of Russian resources. King could not see the end being a sweet and rosy one. With one brotherhood controlling the territory, surely the partnership would be in the sole hands of whoever did not blink first? When he studied the text message, along with internet links and a data download from iCloud, it was only obvious that Luca Fortez would find himself involved in another powerplay. Perhaps the Italian mafia boss would have that covered. But he would bet his life that the Russians would too.

The Russian was a forty-three-year-old named Nikolai. King had no more details, but he could see that the man was cast from the same mould as other men in his game. He couldn't see the man's eyes under his sunglasses, and the photo he had been supplied with had not been in high quality detail, but he could see the outline of the man, the shape of his face. All King knew of the man was that Helena had vengeance in mind. The man was his primary target.

King had hit the ground running in Sweden, flown straight in from Scotland, where he had received news of his fiancé. Until then, he had suffered the purgatory of her being a missing person. The half-life, if only for three weeks, of not knowing the fate of the woman he loved. That letter had been delivered by his immediate boss, Simon Mereweather, now director of operations for MI5. King did not dislike the man, but he was sure that in going to Sweden alone, without being part of the Security Service's operation to get their agent back, he would find few friends within MI5. But the letter had been clear, and King knew it had been intended all along for him to work off Caroline's freedom, and not negotiate her release. He had tried to search Helena Milankovitch's past, but had come up with a blank. There had been some online articles about Helena Snell, the Russian wife of Sir Ian Snell, the British billionaire assassinated by the terrorist group, Anarchy to Recreate Society. Her background as a model – glossing over her time lap dancing and pole dancing in the Black Sea resorts – with the focus on her charitable work and her failing fashion label. There had been hastily-written articles of her disappearance after her husband's death, but she was clearly old news. What King found difficult was finding details of her past prior to her marriage. She had clearly crossed paths with Pyotr Sergeyev and his wife Anna. And now, ordering King to kill the head of the *Bratva* - or Brotherhood's - competition meant that her Russian mafia connection went further than with Sergeyev.

King risked a glance, smiled to himself when he saw the attention the two high-profile entourages had made on the people of Monteverde Marittimo. He decided to make a move before they did. He dropped a ten-Euro note on the table and used the empty saucer to secure it in place. He gathered up his bag of groceries, tore a piece off the end of the bread and ate it casually as he checked his phone and ambled past the group of Italian heavies. He looked at the two men, engrossed in conversation and nursing two glasses of *grappa*, tripped and fell towards Nikolai. He didn't get very far. One of the men flanking him caught hold of King, ripping his shirt and stopping him in his tracks. Another had his hand on the grip of a hefty pistol, not quite drawing it from its holster.

"Sorry," King said meekly. "Thanks. I almost went there." He patted the largest of the two men on the shoulder. "Too many beers," he said.

"You took your time over that one," the man replied.

"I'm taking in the sights, stopping at each bar," King countered quickly. He was back upright now, easing himself away. "Are these guys famous?" he asked.

He was being moved past the two men. They had barely noticed, Nikolai barely pausing for breath. King noticed the man helping him on his way had been replaced by another equally large guard.

"Just businessmen," the man said, his voice almost devoid of any accent. He backed away without another word, re-joined the ranks.

King walked down the steep cobbles, negotiated the steps and crossed over the road to where his basic Skoda hatchback was parked. He had hired the car at Pisa airport. A generic hire car, devoid of character, and therefore invisible. Which was far from what he could see further down the road and on the other side of the road behind him. He guessed the Italians had the black Maserati Quattroporte and the two red Alfa Romeo Giulia saloons. The Russians, by contrast looked to drive three black Mercedes S Class saloons with blacked-out windows. A driver sat behind the wheel of all three vehicles. The Italian vehicles, by contrast, were watched by a single male, smoking a cigarette. He bought his clothes in the same emporium as his colleagues, and looked to be armed, judging by the poor-fitting shoulder holster. The man stood with one foot on the rear bumper of one of the Alfas and rested his elbow on his knee. King watched him stare at a Carabinieri patrol car as it drove slowly past. He neither changed his demeanour, and nor did the police car stop. Which told King there were few friendlies out here. He doubted the local police would be any different.

He took out the camera, attached an ear piece and scrolled back through the footage. His ruse of faking a fall had taught him a great deal. The Russians were on it. Not only had the lead bodyguard noticed King, seen how much he had drank, but King had been stopped well before he would have been a threat to their VIP. They were routinely armed, and as King had patted the man in thanks, he had noticed how physical he had been. Nothing but muscle under that suit. And a lot of it. The drivers were pros too. They had remained with the vehicles, wheels turned out from the kerb. Their drills put the Italians to shame. King had got as close to Luca as he had to Nicolai, yet the Italian muscle hadn't moved. Barely twitched. Which told King that the Russian would not be an easy target.

Which gave King an idea.

12

Somewhere in Eastern Europe

She had been travelling for three days. Hot and uncomfortable, tediously monotonous as the vehicle ate up the miles over motorway, potted back roads and tracks. She had no idea where she was, no clue to the direction she had travelled. Her confines were that of a wooden crate that she estimated to be one metre by two and just over one and a half metres high. Enough for her to stand if she ducked her head, to lay straight and to sit. She was no longer bound or gagged, but there was no way she could escape. She had pounded and kicked the wooden slats, and although they gave, emitting tiny shafts of light, she could not get them to break or lift out the screws that held them firmly in place.

One side of the crate opened to allow her access and was bolted with what sounded like an array of sliding bolts padlocked into place. The inside of the truck was not much larger than the crate and was lit by a single bulb above the rear doors. It was humid and airless, but they stopped every few hours, where she was taken at gunpoint by her two captors into forest or scrubland for a convenience break, given water twice a day, something to eat. No opportunity presented itself for escape – she was weak now, unable to get far if she managed to run. Her shoes had been taken after her last attempt, and one of the men carried a pump-action shotgun with a sawn barrel. She knew she would get no more than a few steps. She had the measure of the two men. They were well-muscled but had worked mainly on their comically over-sized arms, which were tattooed and on constant display. Both men looked tough, smoked incessantly and washed infrequently. Not that she could take the moral high-ground there. She yearned for a bath, a toothbrush and some clean clothes. She felt dehumanised, an animal. She was just thankful the beast with the wandering hands was not here to add to her humiliation.

      She knew she had reached a border crossing from Europe, or at least the European Union, to the east when the truck had pulled over and she had been roughly bound, trussed like a chicken and gagged. The ordeal had lasted over an hour at her best guess, and she heard voices, traffic slowing and moving off again, vehicle doors slamming shut. The truck had travelled a good twenty-minutes before she was untrussed, released to the relative freedom of her box once more. That had been what felt like hours ago, and the quality of the road surface had deteriorated considerably, but there had been a change recently, a stretch of road that had sounded both smooth and fast. It had come as a blessed relief. She had taken the opportunity to lay out flat and attempt to sleep. She knew that if she could rest her mind, allow her body to relax, then she would be in better shape to face whatever awaited her at the other end of her journey.

13

Tuscany, Italy

King had already familiarised himself with Luca Fortez's property. A vineyard and vast stone-built mansion on the south-side of a mountain near the town of Canneto, approximately seven miles north-east of Monteverdi Marittimo, but because of the switchback mountain roads and lack of overtaking opportunities, approximately thirty-minutes' drive. Or an hour, if there were groups of cyclists testing themselves on the gradients. King had studied the property using Google Earth for an overview and had parked further down the road and walked in to get a feel for the layout and scale.

Security was tight, but nothing compared to military compounds he had broken into in the past. There were motion sensors along the fence, but there were also birds resting on top of the fence in places, so the sensors would be set reasonably high to avoid false alarms. As well as the fence and motion sensors, the entrance was gated with CCTV cameras and an intercom. He could also see alarm boxes on the gable end. He had skirted the property and appraised the rear. A swimming pool and patio with open glass doors to the house. The pool was a feature for both relaxing and entertaining. The doors would remain open, adding to the spacious lounge and the capacious feel. An extension to the luxury within, and the breeze from the shaded forest side of the property would cool the house inside. So, here was his entrance point. A doorway to the house that would remain open right up until the inhabitants went to bed.

The villa that Nikolai had rented was entirely different. But not altogether less secure. A temporary rental, that King had checked with the agents, booked for a duration of six-weeks. A ten-bedroomed, split-level villa with two swimming pools, set amongst twelve acres of private forest and meadows on top of a mountain overlooking the Mediterranean some ten-miles distant. It was hemmed in by a ring of wire fencing that took in a full four acres of grounds. The fencing was to keep out wild boars, which were numerous in the mountains and a local delicacy when cured into hams by specialist butchers in the region. The fence was merely head-high, constructed from concreted metal posts and high-tensile wire, capable of withstanding persistent, three-hundred-pound wild boar intent on getting through to the well-tended gardens beyond.

There was basic security, a CCTV camera on the entrance and a further two mounted on each end of the property. King had taken details of the property from the letting agents - under the premise he was searching for a client interested in making property purchases in the area and all the way up to Siena, and who needed a base for these activities - and had familiarised himself with the layout. He was most interested in ideal surveillance locations and points of entrance and exit.

King was vastly outnumbered. He would be using the strengths and weaknesses of these people to help him with his plan. He had got the idea from the surveillance at Monteverdi Marittimo. The show of force and dominance had entertained King. For two organised crime bosses to meet in a low-key location could have been so easy. The security could have remained discreet. Instead, the meeting had created so much attention and been nothing more than a powerplay. King had finally formulated his plan when he had played back the audio in the car. He knew what the two men were planning, yet neither trusted the other enough to meet on anything other than mutually neutral ground. The Russian had compromised the most, meeting on the Italian mafia boss's home turf, so King guessed that was why he had turned up with such overt security. Luca had at first been more discreet, but his men had eventually outnumbered the Russians, even if they were not so professional in their approach to their vehicles.

Luca Fortez was going big. He was planning to take out the two competing mafia families and take over half of Italy for himself. To do this, he would need resources. These came in the form of Russian ex-soldiers, now working for Nikolai. The Russian could muster two-hundred and fifty men, and he could bring in the arms and equipment for their coup. They would mount synchronised operations using paramilitary and special forces techniques, and a whole host of heavy armaments from AK47 rifles and Makarov pistols, to explosives and rocket launchers. There would be no link to Luca Fortez, who would be free to cry crocodile tears, but assume the control of the entire region. He would strike while the opposition was down, rounding up the stragglers and either killing them or force them to swear new allegiance. It was a positively medieval plan, but it looked set to work. The coup would be organised and planned for next month, whereby Luca would pay three-million euros down-payment and a significant thirty-percent royalty per year of all money accounted by his new organisation. It was an outsourced operation, with no direct evidence pointing at Luca Fortez and his seemingly untouchable enterprise.

King locked the camera in the glovebox and stepped out of the car. He had parked in a shopper's carpark in the town of Castagneto Carduci, just five miles from the mountains and the town of Monteverdi Marittimo. The town was made up of many blocks of apartments, supermarkets, business centres and restaurants. It reminded King of towns in America with strip malls and clusters of businesses, each linked by roads running parallel to the main road which ran from Rome in the south to Pisa in the north.

King found a clothes and fashion accessories outlet in a small shopping centre. He made his purchases in cash. It was a twenty-minute walk to a shop he had seen on his way in by road, but before he reached it, he stopped at a tobacconist and stepped inside. The air-conditioning was a relief, it was thirty-degrees centigrade and the sun was strong and high, the sky cloudless and an azure blue from the sea all the way to the mountains, where it appeared washed out with white. The sky above the mountains always seemed to look that way, only to be as blue as the coast once you reached them.

The man behind the counter looked up, nodded, then returned to his magazine. The shop smelled heady with tobacco and leather goods, which ran along the walls. King looked around for a moment, then spotted what he wanted in a glass revolving cabinet towards the other end of the shop.

King always wondered how Britain had such terrible knife crime figures, when there were literally no places like this in the UK, yet throughout Europe, there was a place on every street that sold all manner of knives, and even swords, with as much ease and acceptance as shoes or wallets. King rotated the cabinet and coughed politely. The man looked up, put down his magazine and walked over. King did not want to engage in conversation, anything that would make him memorable. He pointed to a large military bowie-style knife, or what was increasingly called a tactical knife, and the man unlocked the glass door, picked up the knife and sheath and passed them to him.

King tested the blade for sharpness with his thumb, just enough for the blade to feel sticky. He turned the knife over, saw that the blade went all the way through the handle, what is called a full tang, and was happy with the three brass rivets securing it in place. It looked to be a sturdy design and well balanced with a fifty-fifty weight distribution between blade and hilt. The back of the blade was serrated, with an additional feature near the hilt, a W shape cut into the metal. He slipped it into the leather sheath and nodded. King noticed an array of flick knives, each sticking into a solid piece of cork. He reached in, pulled one out and checked it over. He closed the blade, then pressed the button and the blade flicked out and locked tight. He folded it, nodded to the man and handed it to him.

There hadn't been much change from one-hundred-euros, but the man had wrapped them in tissue and placed them in a thick paper bag without seeming to take any notice. King walked on and after ten minutes he found the sporting goods store. There was an outdoor pursuit section with climbing equipment, canoeing and paddle-boarding gear and mountain bikes. King bypassed all of this and looked at the guns behind the counter. Tuscany was hunting country, with walked-up game birds and wild boar, as well as deer and small ground game. This all required a variety of firearms including various gauges of shotguns, and .22 rifles through to heavy calibre hunting rifles in 7mm and .30-06. There were also a few handguns under the glass counter. King suspected Italian gun laws would be like most of Europe and would require licences, home security and hunting permits. He didn't even waste his time asking, but he did see the selection of crossbows hanging from the ceiling and he pointed to a rifle-style one that had 150lb written on one of the bow-limbs. The pedantic part of him wondered why it wasn't in kilos, but he knew the poundage was a universal measurement of power. He had used a fifty-pound recurve bow for a while, thought it would be a good hobby when he found the time, and figured the crossbow would be three-times more powerful. The young man unhooked it and passed it to him. King shouldered it, sighted through the open vee and pin sights and eased on the trigger. He took it away from his shoulder and studied it more closely. There was a safety catch and he could see the locking system, along with a foot loop for loading. He'd find a tree and have a practice when he got back to his villa. He asked for some bolts, knowing they were not called arrows, and the young man nodded and came back with a pack of twelve. Just to be sure, King asked for another pack and paid in cash. Another crossbow had been supplied, packed in a sealed box, which came with a multi-tool for assembly and some paper targets. King paid in cash again, little change from two-hundred euros and carried it in the bag the store supplied, along with his other purchases, back to the car.

The drive back up the mountain took longer than King expected, there was no overtaking room and if it wasn't clapped-out mopeds or motorcycle-pickup wagons with little in the way of horsepower and turning ability, then it was groups of Lycra-clad cyclists testing themselves on the twisty passes. It took an hour to get to his villa, just fifteen miles from Castagneto Carduci. It was a modest villa of two-bedrooms and a swimming pool set in well-tended grounds. King had taken it over the place he had been told to check into. He hadn't even considered the pre-paid villa that his paymaster had booked. He needed to perform what was asked of him to save Caroline. So, he would do it on his own terms. He imagined a property bugged and tapped, wired and rigged to cameras. He was damned if he would give Helena that much control. She texted the target, the photo and left documents in the cloud. That was what he needed to get the job done. He wasn't going to be her puppet. He was doing what he was good at, right up until he stood a chance to save Caroline, or he hoped, give her enough time to get control of her situation and get away. He had never met anybody more rounded, more capable. She was a force to be reckoned with, and she had proven that with her last assignment.

If only King could say the same about himself. He knew that Caroline was held prisoner because of him. Because of his sense of justice, his need to exact revenge. He had rescued Caroline, gone after the person who had attempted to kill her, but he should have done it differently. He shouldn't have sought justice for her victims. He should have simply detained her or killed her. But he had wanted her to know, to feel what was happening, that what she had done had caught up with her. It had taken him away from Caroline, and it had left her vulnerable. Helena had exploited this in ways King would not have imagined. And now Caroline was paying the price.

14

King laid his purchases out on the bed. He did so meticulously, counting out what he had bought and making a note of anything else he would need. It was too late for rethinking things. Outside forces had aligned locations, people and opportunity. There was no better time than now, not for one man with relatively few resources. He had resigned himself to thinking the plan was fluid at best, unrealistic and doomed to failure at worst. No, at worst it would be the death of him. But he didn't fear death. He didn't want to die, but he was not scared of dying. He had finally compartmentalised the emotion. What he feared was not fulfilling his objective. And now, as he started to get into the mindset of the task, it was no different. Ultimately, Caroline's freedom, her life, would be on the line. But he couldn't be blinkered by this, he needed to set himself objectives, process steps for the task. A to B to C. Nothing more. Nothing less.

He looked at his watch, figured he had time for a swim. The water and exercise would help him calm and finalise his plan. He stepped through the open glass doors and out onto the patio. The pool glistened in the late afternoon sunshine, the garden taking on shadows as the sun moved past the top of the mountain and warmed the western slopes of olives and grapes and tended meadows. King looked to the east, miles of pine forest mountain slopes, interspersed with the odd church spire or farmhouse.

The water was cool on his skin and he enjoyed the sensation as he swam the first two lengths underwater. He rose to the surface and settled into a crawl and got his rhythm, tumble-turning as he reached the side every ten strokes. He stopped after twenty lengths, pushed backwards and floated on his back, regretting it almost instantly as a persistent horsefly shadowed him, buzzed in front of his eyes and bit his cheek. He got to his feet and fended off other attacks. There were four or five of the insects in all, and they were going to town on him. The bites hurt as much as wasp stings, but the pain thankfully dispersed within seconds. It was both painful and annoying, to say the least. King dived under the water, flipped onto his back and blew through his nose to avoid taking water into his sinuses. He could see the insects buzzing above him, flitting on the surface. He spun, swam and pushed himself up when he reached the side. The flies were coming in again, and he flicked his towel at them as he made his way back up the lawns to the patio. He wondered if other villas in the mountains suffered the same infestations. The mountains were heavily forested, and villas had been constructed amid the wild land, without other habitation or amenities. He knew about the wild boars, had seen some crossing the lane on his way down to the villa. He had seen some sort of mountain goat on an impossibly steep, practically vertical mountainside on his drive down into town. He wondered what other wild animals lurked on the edge of his fenced-off and well-tended gardens.

King showered the chlorine from the swimming pool off his body with cold water, but did not use soap or shampoo, and when he towelled himself dry, he did not apply deodorant either. He would be infiltrating a hostile environment and knew the importance of keeping a neutral odour. Likewise, when he ate a small meal of bread, tomatoes, cheese and prosciutto, he chose not to eat the garlic and chilli olives he had bought earlier. He took his meal on the patio, drinking plenty of iced water and picking at the food as he looked out across the beautiful countryside.

It was the sort of place he would have loved to come to with Caroline. The hills, the mountains and forests, the idyllic mountain towns with its bars and restaurants, the ice cream and gelato parlours. The kind of delis and bakeries and butcher shops where Caroline would shop and prepare delicious meals for them both as they talked and read and watched the sun go down over the Mediterranean. He couldn't help longing for her, wishing he had not left her to hunt down a cold and callous killer, or that he had not wasted time exacting revenge for a family caught up in someone's agenda. If only he had stayed with her…

King pushed his plate aside. He was feeling wild and aggressive. He knew the task that lay ahead of him, and he breathed deeply to calm himself. He wanted to hurt the person behind this, but he did not want to lose control and fail. His target tonight was a clinical process, part of an equation which would ultimately lead to getting nearer to Caroline. That was the objective. Not getting even, and certainly not exacting revenge. That had been his downfall. He would learn. He would learn too, from his mistake in France. He had underestimated the ego and vindictiveness of the Russian mafia boss. Again, Rashid, who he had put in place for backup, had fluidly worked with events and saved his backside.

The target tonight was a cold and ruthless killer. A man surrounded by his own security. Those men would be armed, and King doubted the local law enforcement would turn anything but a blind eye. He had seen evidence of this at the town of Monteverdi Marittimo.

King would learn not only from his mistake in France, but from his enemy. Collateral damage was a phrase used by people behind the decisions to use lethal force. King found the phrase abhorrent. It had always been something he fought stridently against and tried to avoid. He had even hung onto his job when the new MI5 director was appointed by vehemently arguing the pros of a man on the ground against the cons of missile strikes by drones. He felt a hypocrite now, because tonight there would be people forming collateral damage in his plan. All he could hope for was that they remained unpunished from previous crimes. He would do his best not to kill, but he also knew the dangers wounded and scared men presented. They often felt they had nothing to lose, or they became charged-up with endorphins and adrenalin, often taking on superhuman strength and a will not easily broken. But King was wounded too. He felt a numbness inside, an emptiness that he knew would not go away until he held the woman he loved in his arms again. And yet, he was driven within by a force he had never experienced before. He would never give up on this. He would get Caroline back. Or he would die trying.

15

There were many tracks leading off the mountain roads. Some led to villas or farmhouses, others led to meadow pastures hemmed in by forest. Others simply seemed to lead nowhere. Enough room to turn a car, or to park a couple of vehicles. King assumed these were the starting points for hunters, climbers or hikers.

King had driven down several of these tracks until he was confident he had found the most suitable. He looked at his watch again, decided he could spare an hour, although he was confident it would take only half that time.

King opened the boot of the car and took out the crossbow. He had assembled it back at the villa but kept hold of the multitool and spare bowstring to be safe. He had rolled up a thick woollen blanket he had found with the extra bedding in the wardrobe. He had fastened it tightly with a length of washing line that he had cut down from two trees in the garden. He walked out across the opening and placed it against a tree trunk and paced out ten metres. He pointed the crossbow to the ground and slipped his foot into the loop and pulled back the string until it locked firmly in place. The bolt needed to slide back as far as the mechanism would allow and was held in place by a spring clip. King was aware that it felt less safe, less substantial than a gun. He made sure his finger was nowhere near the trigger as he shouldered the weapon and took careful aim at the roll of blanket. He flicked off the safety and squeezed the trigger. The string lurched off its hook and the bolt was shot forward at tremendous speed, but not much accuracy, missing the roll and disappearing out into the forest. King was pleased he'd bought two packs. He reloaded, but this time he was ready for the crude trigger release and the second bolt fared better but hit low of where he was aiming. He kept his aim-point and the next arrow tucked neatly alongside the other. He fired another and was relieved to see it near the other two. This was called grouping, and now King had to adjust the sights, confident that he was firing the weapon skilfully enough. He looked at the two adjusters and twisted the one on the side of the sight four clicks counter-clockwise to adjust elevation. The next bolt struck dead centre and three inches above the other three bolts. King fired two more bolts, and again, he had a grouping. He wound the elevation adjustment twice as much, and after another three bolts, he was bang-on target. He walked forwards and collected the bolts, surprised at the degree of penetration. The blanket was thick and had been folded in three before it was rolled, and King counted off seven layers. At twenty-one single layers, he likened the penetration of the bolts up there with a 9mm pistol. Or at least in the same ballpark.

Next, King walked to a firing point of around fifty-metres. He fired the first shot at the top of the blanket and was surprised to see it hit just a few inches lower. He followed up with three more, getting a good feel for loading and handling the weapon. It was cumbersome to handle, yet light and easy to fire. King was stunned at how quiet it was to fire. A slight twang as the bowstring relaxed. King was confident nobody would hear a thing if they were twenty-feet or so away from him. Hopefully, they would be a lot further away than that.

16

Georgia

She would never have believed how good a bath could be. To her disgust, the water had turned dark and after she had soaped and rinsed and washed her hair twice, she had drained the water and run a second bath, where she washed again, rewashed and conditioned her tangled hair, and languished in the warmth of the water, with the aroma of citrus shampoo and coconut soap attacking her senses.

She had checked the windows of the tiny bathroom, only to find they were barred. She had checked these too, heaving them, but feeling no give. She could see she was in a rural location, and thanks to the time she had been given alone, and the travel of the sun, she had ascertained which way was east, and from that, she had all four points of the compass in her mind, with the large hillock in the distance acting as a marker. She figured that by sunset, she would know the time to within an hour.

She had been given curt instructions when the man had handed her the clear, plastic bag of toiletries, which had included a single-blade disposable safety razor. All the bottles, even the toothbrush and hand soap were to be returned. The towel provided had been little bigger than a hand-towel, and that too, was to be returned.

When she had towelled herself dry, she opened the door into the bedroom and looked for something to wear. Her dirty clothes had been taken away. The towel was barely large enough to cover herself, let alone wrap around her, and she felt vulnerable once more. She heard a knock at the solid oak door, looked around and then pulled the sheet from the bed over herself. The door unlocked, then opened. The door had no lock or handle from inside, and the sound had been like that of a bolt and padlock.

The man looked at her impassively. She had not seen him before. He seemed a little embarrassed. He dropped a pile of clothes on the bed, held out his hand.

"Your toiletries," he said.

"I might want another wash," she replied.

"You smell clean now," he said, but he seemed embarrassed and hastily added, "The soap is strong."

Caroline looked at the man. She figured he was in his early twenties. He did not look the same as the brute who had touched her, or the two East-Europeans who had driven her here. "I am Caroline," she said softly. "Thanks for the clothes."

The man nodded. "I know who you are," he said. "I am to take your toiletries away," he repeated.

Caroline reached out to the table, struggling to keep herself covered with the sheet. She picked up the bag and handed it to him. "Here," she said. She looked him in the eye. She could see there was something there, something less cruel than the rest of her captors. She had been trained to make the most of every situation. She smiled again, "What is your name?"

The man hesitated, then said, "Michael." He had no real accent, not that Caroline could make out, at least. "Are you hungry?" he asked.

"Famished!" she exclaimed. "Oh, please, could you get me something to eat and drink?"

He nodded but said nothing more as he backed out of the doorway and closed the door behind him. The bolt slid home with a heavy thud. Ominous, final.

Caroline looked at the clothes. Nothing much, and a little calculated. Plain white cotton underwear more on the skimpy side than Bridget Jones, and a white linen dress. She put them on, pleased that the dress covered her knees and that all were a good fit. She looked out of the window, saw from the position of the sun that she was looking northwest. There was a distant mountain range ahead of her. The terrain looked like farmed pastures, with many knolls and clumps of trees, but otherwise open ground all the way to the mountains. She would guess the mountains were twenty miles away. Any escape on foot in that direction would be a fruitless task. Too much ground to cover, nowhere to hide and besides, what would she do if she reached the mountains? Cold, high and deadly. Not the best terrain for a summer dress and bare feet.

The bedroom windows were barred also. Again, she opened the window and pulled at the bars. They were solid. She left the window open, the cool early summer breeze felt good on her flushed skin after the hot bath.

There was a sharp knock on the door, then the sound of the bolt opening. Michael stood in the open doorway with a tray. Caroline went to walk forward, but he said sharply, "No. Stay there. I will put it on the desk."

Caroline shrugged, like it was no bother, but she knew that he had been briefed to take no chances with her. She knew that if she were to escape, then it was better attempted in the first few hours of a new location. But she also knew that her stomach was almost touching her spine and she had never felt so hungry, nor had lost weight so quickly. She looked at the tray of food and knew she would never chance escaping until she had eaten. The thought annoyed her, like she was becoming submissive, reliant on her captors, but she was a realist. She hadn't given up, she just needed to bide her time.

Michael stepped back, and Caroline hustled forwards. She picked up a chunk of bread and bit down. There was a satisfying crunch as she bit through the crust and she chewed quickly, then dipped the bread into a large mug of soup. She took another mouthful, but this time her mouth felt the explosion of flavour from the onion, garlic and beetroot. She knew it was *borscht* and that narrowed down her location a little. The flavour was overwhelming, and she knew it was only because she had not eaten in so long. There were slices of cold sausage on a tin plate next to the soup and she ate these quickly. She looked at Michael as he made to leave. "Thank you, Michael. It's much appreciated," she paused. "Please, stay," she said, taking a sip of the tepid soup. "I haven't talked to anybody in such a long time…"

"I am not allowed," he said. "I have to get more food…"

"Just a minute," she said. "I've been so scared. You look like a kind person, Michael. I can tell that. You look a bit like my brother," she said. "I miss him terribly. He'll be so worried about me…"

The young man looked at his watch. It was a cheap, plastic digital model. He wore gold rings on his fingers and was fiddling with one subconsciously. "I can't," he said.

"Where am I?" she asked. "I was travelling for hours, days even."

Michael shrugged. "I can't tell you," he said. "Now, I must go and get food for the others…"

"Others?"

"I can't tell you!" he snapped. The change in his expression shocked her, and he could see this, and his face softened. "Now, I must go," he said.

Caroline looked sadly at him. "Okay," she said. "But promise me you'll come and see me when you're done. You could bring more food," she smiled.

The young man nodded, and Caroline caught him staring at her legs as she tore off a piece of bread and dipped it into the soup. She was annoyed, there hadn't been a spoon or anything else that would be useful in her escape.

17

Dover, England

"It doesn't get any better than this. A Paki smuggling an assault rifle? Now, let's start again. Where did you get it?"

Nothing.

"For the tape, the suspect refuses to answer."

"For the tape, the officer just called a British citizen a Paki."

"Smart-arse, are we?"

"One of us is smart. I think the other is just an arse."

"What were you planning to do with it?" the second anti-terrorism officer asked. "An ISIS attack on UK soil? What, another random act of slaughter? "

Nothing.

"Again, for the tape, no answer. Look, we've got you for nine more days, sunshine. You've had four, you'll break sooner or later," the lead officer paused. "And it will be sooner, mark my words."

"Cakewalk."

"What?" the lead officer asked.

Rashid smiled. "Fairground game. Like musical chairs. It means this is a piece of piss."

The junior officer slammed his hand down on the table. "This is an interrogation!"

"Interview, shit head. And an easy one at that."

The lead officer turned over Border Force arrest notes in front of him. He looked at Rashid, shook his head. "What is it? ISIS? Al Qaeda?"

Nothing. Rashid stared impassively ahead.

"You were caught smuggling an assault rifle through the port of Dover."

"Nah, not me, mate. Someone must have planted it. Strapped it to my car's exhaust and were going to follow me, pick it up when they had the opportunity."

"So, you say," the junior officer commented.

"Are my prints on it? I don't think so." Rashid smiled. He had stripped the weapon, smeared it with a sheen of bleach and left it for an hour before oiling it and wiping it clean. The bleach would destroy any of his DNA. He had used gloves, wrapped it in bin sacks, strapped it underneath using duct-tape. He had dumped the twenty spare rounds for the weapon – no point carrying anything further incriminating. The ammo had come from Hereford but could not be traced to his absence. One or two rounds at a time over the years, pocketed after operations or drills and kept in his personal stash, along with a pistol and some ammo he had relieved a dead Taliban fighter of in Afghanistan – a man in Rashid's line of work could never be too careful and he knew he may need the weapon one day.

"You're a smug one."

"What? For a Paki?"

"I didn't mean that," said the lead officer.

"Charge me or let me go. You have nothing more than my unwitting possession of a firearm."

"You're AWOL. You're a serving soldier in the Parachute Regiment."

Rashid knew where their information would lead and where it would end. His military service history would terminate at the unit he served in before his time in the SAS. He was never under any obligation to correct them. "I was on holiday," he replied.

"That explains the gun," said the junior officer sarcastically.

"Does it?" Rashid shrugged. "I was travelling *to* Britain, not *away* from it."

"Maybe you're a traitor then? Maybe you're in the army and all the time, you're an extremist planning an attack?"

"So, I'd be bringing in a gun, why?"

"To harm British citizens!" The officer interjected. "Unless it has something to do with Russia's state visit in a couple of months. Is that it? You're not happy with their support of the Assad regime in Syria, want to help fellow Muslims?"

Rashid laughed. "Fellow Muslims would also be Assad and his soldiers. You have a great imagination there, you're obviously wasted as a policeman."

The officer slammed his fist down on the table, making his colleague flinch, but merely making Rashid smile. "Tell us about the gun!"

"What sort of gun was it?" Rashid asked.

"An assault rifle."

"Doesn't narrow the field much."

The lead officer looked at the notes, took out a photograph. "An M4."

"Nice," Rashid said. "Never used one. The Paras use the SA80. And if I were a terrorist, with access to an entire warehouse full of SA80 rifles, then I wouldn't have to travel to France to buy one. I'd smuggle one out of barracks."

"So, you're a hard para, are you?" the junior officer asked. "You think you'll breeze through this?"

"What, exactly?"

"This process of questioning."

Rashid looked at his watch. He had not been charged yet, but under the prevention of terrorism act, they had fourteen days before they had to charge or release him. But they also had to allow him six hours uninterrupted sleep and provide him with three meals, four drinks and as many toilet breaks as he required. A cakewalk to an SAS officer who had successfully infiltrated ISIS in Syria and lived amongst them as a spy for months.

There was a knock at the door and a detective walked in.

The lead officer looked around, then turned to the recorder and said, "Interview suspended at sixteen-forty-two, DI Blakemore has just entered the room…"

The detective whispered into the lead officer's ear. The lead officer was a DCI and he looked to be ten-years older than the DI. The DCI stood up, glanced at Rashid and ushered the DI to the corner of the room, where they talked animatedly in low voices. Both men left the room and a uniformed officer stepped inside to keep the two to one ratio.

The junior officer smirked. "Sounds like they've got something significant. Say a little prayer to Allah, you're fucked, mate."

Rashid tapped the top of the recorder. "You aren't allowed to talk to me without the tape running," he said. "That's a shame, because it won't pick me up saying how much I enjoyed giving it to your old lady."

The detective laughed. "I'm not married, dickhead."

Rashid leaned forward and smiled. "I know. I was talking about your mother."

18

Tuscany, Italy

King looked at himself in the rear-view mirror and smiled. He had learned the importance in maintaining a sense of humour in life. It had got him through tough and desperate times. The fact that Caroline was being held captive was always on his mind, but as he looked at the fifty-euro set of fake gold chain around his neck, worthy of Mr T, he couldn't help wondering what Caroline would say. It was off-set wonderfully by the black T-shirt and black suit. King had used butter to grease his hair and smear it backwards. His head now stank of rancid dairy product, but he didn't care. He looked every inch the Russian bodyguard. Every inch one of Nikolai's men.

King had parked his vehicle on a narrow mountain road approximately half a mile downhill from Luca Fortez's property. It was a tactical and practical decision. Exfiltration, and this one would be hot, was better made downhill. Less exertion, more speed – which in turn meant he would present himself as a more difficult target – and an uphill escape would mean that he would have to drive back past the entrance to the property.

King would have to skirt the property, hiking the steep hill for at least a mile and a half, before observing the property from above. He would then make his way down to the vineyard and enter the grounds to the property through the fence.

King found the walk uncomfortable. The late afternoon sun was hot on his back, the temperature a dry and draining thirty-degrees. The ground was arid, with the earth baked hard, and much of the terrain was sharp rock and loose shale, which made every footstep difficult, as he dropped backwards a few inches with every tread. The pine trees were scented and seemed to give off their own heat. He was using dead-reckoning, cursing leaving his button compass back in Scotland, simply using the sun and the mountainside as his directional prompts, although he was aware he could be veering drastically off course and away, or worse - head-on towards the vineyard. He had no friendlies out here, so as usual, he had left his mobile phone behind. There was no point in carrying it, and with the use of scanners, the phone's signal could be traced simply by a pulse receiver. The phone emitted a signal wherever it went, and this could be exploited. The people using the equipment may not know whose phone it was, but they would know that one was in the area and could easily home in on it.

He had slung the crossbow over his shoulder using a belt and tucked the bolts into his pockets. It wasn't an ideal way to carry them, but he had the sheath knife fastened tightly to his trouser belt and the flick knife in his jacket's inside pocket and was not dressed in tactical clothing. The suit had started to tear, and he was both hot and uncomfortable, the excess butter he'd greased his hair with had started to run into his eyes. The macabre sense of humour in him just hoped he didn't die out here and was left looking like this for someone to discover. A greasy-haired extra from a rap video with four-pounds in weight of gold-painted brass around his neck and a crossbow strapped to his back. The police would be scratching their heads for months.

When King had estimated the distance, he tracked across the mountainside and crouched low, listening to his surroundings. He took a 500ml bottle of water out of his pocket and downed the contents in a few mouthfuls. He wedged the empty bottle between some tree roots, and wiped his face with his sleeve, before taking out a crossbow bolt and standing up to cock the weapon. He tucked the bolt under the spring clip and kept the cumbersome weapon held in front of him. The going was much easier downhill, and he moved at twice the speed as his climb, taking care to watch the ground for loose rocks, tree roots and snakes. He had seen some big spiders, which looked like tarantulas to him, waiting patiently in the centre of giant webs, spanning five or six feet between the trees. He was sure they weren't too harmful, certainly not lethal, but he didn't want to put his face in one while he was watching the ground. He had to remind himself that he needed to keep aware not only of his footsteps and his immediate vicinity for natural threats, but to be ready for the human factor too. As he closed in on Luca Fortez's property, he realised that he was approaching one of the most dangerous and untouchable men in Italy. His men would be armed.

And that was what King was counting on.

19

Dover, England

"Have they treated you well?"

Rashid shrugged. He looked at the man in front of him. The recorder had been switched off and all police officers had left the room. There were two cups of steaming coffee on the table in between them, and a plain manila file.

"There will be no charges brought against you. I've seen to that."

"Cheers," Rashid said, his Birmingham accent making it sound somewhat noncommittal, as he reached for the cardboard cup.

"That's it?"

"What do you want? A dance?"

"Some gratitude would be nice."

"I've got some bitchin' blisters, you wouldn't want a hand job…"

The man stared at him, then shook his head. "I can see why you and King are friends. You love authority too…"

"I don't know anybody called King," Rashid paused. "Is that what you are? Authority? Sorry, I thought you were just some prick in a suit."

"I think we'd better start again."

"You can start by telling me your name and business," Rashid said coldly. "You're a spook, that much is clear."

"My name is Simon Mereweather, and I'm director of operations in MI5."

"Head shed."

Mereweather smiled and nodded. "I suppose," he said, picking up his coffee. "I'm joint deputy director. MI5, or the Security Service to use its proper title, has a director and two deputies. One deputy oversees administration, while the other oversees operations. That is what I do. And that is why I want to talk to you about Alex King."

"Like I said, I don't know anybody called King."

Mereweather shrugged. "When I said, no charges will be brought against you, I meant that is if I had your cooperation. Without that, then Special Branch can have you, and the rifle you were bringing in, and Christ knows what else they can get to stick to you."

"You going to charge me for the coffee too?"

"Please, take this seriously, Rashid," Mereweather said plaintively. "I need to find King. I need to help him get our agent back. You are aware that Caroline Darby, an agent with MI5 and also King's fiancé, was abducted by a suspect in an operation the two of them were investigating?" He looked at him, studied his eyes carefully as he let the silence envelope them. "Of course, you are. I can see you're in a quandary. Well, Captain. I can smooth over the heavy mob at Hereford, give you a cover story, black-ops stuff. They'll welcome you back, get you off that desk you're riding, put you back in the field. If you don't go shagging the nineteen-year-old daughters of commanding officers, that is."

Rashid smiled. "I still don't know this King bloke."

"Yes, yes. All very admirable." He opened the file in front of him. "Good shot, are we? Must be to be in the SAS." He took out a series of photographs. They were of a body and a crime scene. "Your handiwork?" He pushed the photographs towards Rashid.

Rashid looked at the photographs. He recognised the body, had seen it through the scope of his sniper rifle about a month ago. He looked up and shrugged. "No."

"I don't want a confession, Rashid. Just hear me out. Okay?"

"Not going anywhere, by the looks of it."

"You're friends with King. You met on separate operations that merged. You kept in contact, or whatever. Perhaps you bonded in the brief time your paths crossed. I don't know. But I *do* know that your bond was strong enough for you to take out a sniper for King during his last operation. There's enough CCTV in London. Don't play me for a fool. As it is, nobody is looking for the killer of a killer. The case is never going to be solved, because nobody is looking into it. It's been black-bagged. End of. The only thing that will open up that particular can of worms is if pictures of a serving SAS officer linking him to the killing of a man on a London rooftop find their way into the public domain."

Rashid looked at Mereweather. "And you think threatening me will get you my cooperation?"

"I don't have time for appealing to your better nature," Mereweather said, his tone clipped and harsh. "Or rather, my agent, my friend even, doesn't have time. Caroline Darby has been abducted. To get her back requires more than playing into her captor's hands. King has gone on a self-destructive mission to get her back. He is singing to their tune. He is doing what they require of him, and hoping he finds an in. A way to get close to them. It only takes one mistake, one run of bad luck, and King is dead and Caroline is gone forever. I'm not prepared to take that risk. Not for her."

"You're sweet on her?" Rashid smiled. "Well, I wouldn't let our mutual friend know about that."

"I like her. She's a long-time colleague, and now comes under my command…"

"Whatever," Rashid shrugged. "Not my business."

"I can get you out of here, Rashid. I can get you out of here, paint a picture of your shenanigans in France as a black-ops mission for MI5 to the regiment, even keep a lid on what you did in London. But I need your help in return."

"I'm not selling out King," he paused. "Firstly, because he's my friend. Secondly... well, he isn't the sort of man you sell out. You may want to remember that."

"It's nothing to do with selling him out. It's a contingency. And it's a second prong attack. King is haring around trying to buy some time while he gets a handle on this, and it's quite possible the man will slip up. I want to search for Caroline, use what we've found so far to get to Helena."

"Helena?"

"Christ, you don't know a thing, do you," Mereweather paused and sipped some coffee. "Look, agree to help me. Agree to help find Caroline, and in turn, help King. Let's agree that King is not infallible. Let's agree that he needs help with this."

Rashid nodded. "I can see where you're coming from," he said. "But right now, I'm still under arrest and AWOL from base. You can really make all of that go away?"

"Like it never happened."

"Well, let's talk some more," Rashid said. "But I want to see you pull a few strings first. When I've seen that, I'll listen to what you've got to say."

20

Tuscany, Italy

The vineyard was expansive. It surrounded three sides of the mansion's gardens and took up an area of what King estimated to be four football pitches. The rear of the mansion was laid to lawns and gardens, dominated by an elaborately constructed swimming pool that was all swirls and nooks and fountains, with barely an area for proper swimming. A place where drinks could be taken, and conversations whispered, and groups of people could disperse into couples.

There were two children playing in the pool. Even from this distance, King could tell it was a boy and a girl from their swimming attire. The boy was dive-bombing the girl and she was splashing him in the face as he returned to the surface. A woman and a man walked out from the patio doors, the woman looking in King's direction. King froze, worried that his costume jewellery would give him away, but he was aware of his surroundings, knew the sun was on his back. The woman pointed at a sun-lounger to the man and he obliged, dragging it to where she was now pointing. She had wanted the chair aligned with the sun, her feet acting as a pointer. She sat down, then reclined, her hands by her side, her face taking the full glare. The man walked away and sat at a chair and table in the shade. King could see that the man was one of Luca's men. The clothes, the body language. He was what every bodyguard eventually became to the rich and indifferent – an assistant. The man was an armed butler. He would not be switched on and alert. He had melded into his role. And a target.

King backed into the treeline twenty-feet or so. Enough to keep the property in view below him, but also enough to keep his profile interrupted by the trees. The ground was steep, steeper than he had found on the hike up. His pace was rapid, occasionally he would slip and needed to correct himself or he would be on his backside. After he had dropped down five-hundred feet in elevation, and around two-thousand feet in distance, he stopped and tentatively made his way back out to the treeline. He was beside the fence. At eight-feet high and topped with razor wire, he wasn't looking to get over it anytime soon. He looked around, found what he wanted at the base of a large pine. A clump of dried grass. He picked a blade of the grass, wet his fingers with spit, and rubbed the grass between his fingers. He then walked to the fence, rested the blade of grass against the wire. There was no noise, no tingle. He tried again, further up, then rested the grass on the stanchions fixing the wire to the posts. Nothing. A practical defence against rampaging wild boar, and a deterrent for someone to climb, but not an impenetrable barrier. Not in keeping with one of the wealthiest men in Italy, soon to be one of the most powerful crime bosses in Europe.

King studied the layout of the mansion. There was an array of cars parked in the lee of the building, and King could now see a series of outbuildings which had been redesigned or renovated into tiny villas. He thought they could be accommodation for both security and the vineyard workers. Or maybe they were offices and day quarters for the criminal operation. The cars ranged from hatchbacks through to the three Italian saloons King had seen at Monteverdi Marittimo. The hatchbacks would suggest domestic staff, gardeners or vineyard workers. The security personnel would be on higher salaries, would express themselves with more expensive vehicles. The collection of cars looked large and shiny, and King supposed they belonged to Luca's bodyguards. It was a large operation, and the fence seemed at odds with what lay behind it. It didn't seem a big enough deterrent.

King took another few steps, then froze. He waited, chanced it, pulled back into the treeline and hurriedly made the crossbow ready. If he hadn't thought the mafia boss had enough security on the perimeter, he had changed his mind now.

21

Caroline worked on the wingnut, hard to move at first, but now turning slowly and stubbornly on the bolt which had been carelessly painted during its haphazard restoration. The dressing table had been given a new lease of life by someone, a coat or two of eggshell white, fashionable in a New England beach house way. It was one of the rear legs, and if she could remove the leg, complete with the three-inch bolt embedded deep within the wood, then it would be a formidable weapon at close quarters. Finally, the wingnut cleared, and with a little force, breaking the seal of two coats of paint, she got the leg out. She examined it closely, then replaced it, carefully pushing the dressing table to the wall to keep the leg in place. She held the wingnut in her palm, turned it over, then wedged it between her fingers. One end of the wingnut pressed firmly into her palm as she made a fist, and the other end protruded almost an inch. It would make a decent knuckleduster. Something to give her an edge.

    She hadn't seen Michael since. She had drunk some water from the bathroom tap but was feeling hungry still. The sun was going down now, edging its way west. She felt the chill already and had kept the bedsheet near, planning to use it as a shawl. To go to bed, tuck herself under the covers and chance a sleep felt too submissive somehow. Like she had given into her fate. She couldn't take that step. Not while she still had fight left in her.

Caroline had a sinking feeling, knew that taking these steps was a morale boost. She had thought back on Michael, he seemed different to her captors so far. Certainly, a different man to The Beast. What was his role? A house keeper, perhaps. But he had said he had to get food for the others. Those words had played on her mind. Were the others her captors? Were there other captives here? And who were they? Women like her? She hoped not. Not only for their fate, but for her own. Because if there were others, then Caroline knew that she was close to her destination. And more worryingly, the *reason* she was here.

22

The man carried an Uzi machine-pistol in one hand and a two-way radio, or walkie-talkie, in the other. It was an old fashioned-looking handset with a long, rubber antennae. King supposed the mountains made receiving a clear reception difficult and he knew that smaller units with discreet, or built-in aerials often struggled in remote areas, so there was purpose to the choice of equipment. Either that, or Luca Fortez had not reinvested his money into security. He supposed men with Uzis should be enough. But it put King in a quandary. He had not wanted to kill the mafia guards. They were bystanders to his plan, for the most part, and his primary target was Nicolai. But, intentionally wounding a man with an Uzi was as dangerous as pulling on the tail of a tiger. King couldn't breach the fence while the man was there, and he was running out of daylight. For his plan to work, he needed to move now. He hadn't wanted collateral damage, but he hadn't wanted Caroline kidnapped either. He didn't know this man, knew that his career choice didn't make him a choir boy. This man would have done terrible things, and he would have earned good money from it. If you wanted to dance, eventually you've got to pay the band.

King had a clear shot of the man, hoped the bolt would pass through the mesh fence without clipping a link of wire. He had a good sight bead on the man's neck and figured it would go a long way towards silencing him as well as stopping him in his tracks. The guard tucked his radio into his pocket and fiddled with a packet of cigarettes. King waited. Eventually the man would take his hand off the grip of the weapon and his finger away from the trigger. Lighting a cigarette was one of those tasks. The man pulled the cigarette out with his lips, pocketed the packet and reached for his lighter, proving King wrong. He lit the cigarette, savoured the flavour and aroma, the hit to his senses. King steadied his aim and squeezed the trigger. The bolt shot through the fence and whipped through the air missing the man by less than an inch. The man straightened, dropped his cigarette and turned. King had the bowstring pulled back but was struggling with loading the bolt. Time, as it always did in close quarter battle, slowed. The man pointed the Uzi out like a handgun and fired. King blinked, hearing the dry-fire of the safety. The man looked stunned, brought the weapon back and held the fore-end with his left hand as he flicked the safety over with his right thumb. He had the machine-pistol back out, but this time aiming more carefully with both hands, the sight lining up with his right eye.

King had already moved to his right, putting the post of the fence between them and had got the bolt under the spring clip and was aiming carefully, but this time he centred the sights on the larger target – the centre of the man's chest. He fired, and the man shuddered. He glanced down at the bolt, which was lodged under his diaphragm. His white shirt was growing red, the blood looking like a rose, but some foot or so across. It had hit the aorta, and King assumed from the man's build and the length of the bolt protruding, that the wicked-looking hunting tip would have exited near the man's spine.

King reloaded the crossbow. The Uzi was still in the man's hand, and although he didn't look as if he was going to get it back up to aim, he couldn't risk the man firing the weapon and warning the security in the property below. King aimed, was about to fire, when the man fell backwards, and the weapon clattered out of his hands and across the rocky ground.

There was no time to waste, and he had started the ball rolling. He dropped the crossbow by the fence, took out his tactical sheath knife and slipped it between the links of the fence. The W shape in the haft of the blade, near the hilt, was a military grade wire cutter. He slipped the wire into one of the vees, then twisted and pulled the knife downwards. The wire was severed, and King worked quickly until he had enough room to pull the wire back and slip through. He replaced the wire, leaving it tidy enough to pass a walk-by inspection.

The man was dead. King rolled him onto his side, saw that the head of the bolt had been broken in the fall. No point pulling the bolt out, and it would have been a grisly task that King was happy to avoid. He took the spare magazine out of the man's pocket and picked up the Uzi. It wasn't a precise and accurate weapon, but it could make a good noise and strafe targets at fifty-metres with little skill. King could comfortably take this to volleys of aimed shots out to one-hundred metres with great effectiveness. He checked the action and magazine, each one held thirty rounds of 9mm, but sixty rounds in an Uzi wasn't going to last long. He slung it over his shoulder on the worn leather strap and picked up the crossbow. The radio came with him too. His Italian was poor, but he could cause some problems for them with the radio when the opportunity presented itself.

King skirted the fence, moving quickly down the steep gradient. He could see a group of guards milling around where the driveway met the gardens. He could still see the pool as well, the two children playing and the woman sunbathing. The light was getting low, so she would not be there much longer. King imagined her changing into something long and sheer and flowing and sipping cocktails beside the pool later. The bodyguard was still at the table, apparently uninterested in a roaming patrol or even a change of position. He was stale, and King hoped he could exploit this soon.

The next guard seemed more alert. He was cradling an assault rifle in both arms, and the way he paced, turned and watched reminded King of somebody with infantry experience. King kept right up against the fence, he was coming from the east with the sun above him. It was borderline for a stealthy approach, but it was still in his favour. The guard was sixty-metres away, and King knew it was now or never to take a shot. The man was more alert than his dead colleague had been and King imagined he would track a look towards him at any moment. But King wasn't worried, because the man had the right hardware and things were going to get noisy now.

23

The top floor of Thames House had recently undergone a complete refit. The glass was quadruple-glazed ballistic composite, impenetrable by 20mm anti-aircraft rounds. The thickness also made the windows soundproof and would deflect parabolic microphones. To keep up with the added security measures, lead and titanium sleeves now lined the walls between the grade II listed stone walls and the plasterboard within.

It had been a deniable act of terrorism by Russian extremists that had necessitated the refit and reconstruction of MI5 headquarters. The strike at the heart of the British intelligence establishment had called for more changes, and now each floor was guarded by heavily armed security officers from MI5's security group, the only non-police or military guards armed in the UK.

Rashid glanced at the guard, who was protected by a flack-jacket and body armour and armed with a Sig P226 pistol and a 7.62mm SAR rifle. He noted the heavy calibre. MI5 were not taking any chances. At the end of the corridor, another similarly attired and armed guard stood outside the director's office.

"A bit heavy," he said. "The PM hasn't got a show of force like this."

Mereweather nodded. "It's exactly that; a show of force. Foreign intelligence officers and dignitaries have been doing the rounds. We wanted them to go home with tales of the service's strength. The guards would normally be suited and booted, conceal-carry. The paramilitary boys are usually outside or on the exits and entrances."

"Where do they train?"

"With the metropolitan police."

"SCO19?"

"Yes."

Rashid said nothing.

"Anything wrong in that?" Mereweather asked.

Rashid shrugged. "A bit gung-ho."

"Care to elaborate?"

"We trained a few groups in Hereford, that's all."

"And?"

"They like Ray-Bans. Like, when it's dark," he paused. "And afterwards, in the bar, they keep their pistols on. Pose for photos, that sort of shit."

"Anything else?"

"When they find out you went to war, they always ask you if you've killed someone," Rashid said quietly.

Mereweather nodded. Rashid had a feeling the MI5 man would take it under consideration. He opened the door, ignoring the guard and ushered Rashid inside. There was an outer office and the secretary barely acknowledged them, as she tapped on her keyboard, and studied her handwritten notes. Mercwcather opened the second oak door and the two men stepped into the inner sanctum of MI5.

Director Amherst was seated behind his large mahogany desk. As usual, the chairs for his guests had been arranged in a semi-circle in front of his desk, with two low glass tables between. There were three chairs. One was occupied, the other two were empty. The man in the chair stood up, nodded at the men as they walked in. Amherst remained seated.

"Neil Ramsay," the man said, holding out his hand.

Rashid shook it but said nothing. Things were moving fast. He looked at the seated man, then back at Mereweather. He shrugged. "All looks official," he said.

"Do sit," Amherst said. He had been in the role for less than a year, but he was confident. He had paired some of MI5's more dubious expenses and increased the closeness of their working relationship with both GCHQ and MI6.

"Long and the short of it is; you are in the shit, so we'll get you off any charges if you work with us to locate our missing agent, Caroline Darby, and along the way, get Alex King back on the reservation," Amherst steepled his fingers, his elbows on the desk. "Can you help us?"

"Why me?" Rashid asked incredulously. "You have agents for this sort of thing."

Mereweather nodded. "But you know King. And he trusts you…"

"I'll not set him up."

"We're not asking you to," Ramsay said. "But the time will come when King will need to be approached, and we think he'll trust you, more than us."

Rashid looked at all three men in turn. "Have you given him a reason not to trust you?"

"Certainly not," Amherst replied, seemingly for all three of them. "King is not thinking straight. He's blinded by love, and I fear, revenge. He has jumped and danced to Helena Snell's, or should I say, Milankovitch's tune. We know he took out a Russian mafia brotherhood down in France, and we can assume he is planning another hit for Helena as we speak."

Rashid shifted uncomfortably in his seat. Technically he had taken out the Russians, or at least most of them. He'd even dealt Sergeyev a wound that would have killed him, had King not delivered a *coup de grâce*. "You can't blame the man," he replied. "He's buying time. He's not blindly haring across Europe killing people. He's finding out as much about the bitch as he can."

"And what has he found out?"

Rashid shrugged. "I want anything against me dropped. And I want something in writing. I want the terrorist sniper on the rooftop covered in that paperwork too. Queen and country, that sort of shit."

"So that *was* you," Amherst stated flatly.

"You know it was. I want a secondment to MI5, open-ended. And I want that agreed at Hereford."

"Anything else?" Mereweather asked sardonically.

"I imagine senior field agents earn more than SAS captains, so I want my paygrade to go northwards. Pension contributions too," Rashid smiled.

"You ask for a lot," Amherst commented flatly.

"I'm not asking for an Aston Martin or a jet pack," Rashid smiled.

"And a good job too," Mereweather said. "Our budget tops out at Fords and budget airlines. Now, in all seriousness, what did King tell you down in France?"

Rashid held up a hand. "Look, I haven't eaten all day. There's a McDonalds across the bridge from here. I'll be in there with a burger and a brew. You can meet me over there with the paperwork and my get out of jail free card. I'll need some expenses and a place to stay tonight. I'm not classy, a Premier Inn will do me fine. We can meet there at breakfast if you like, discuss transportation, flights and that sort of thing. Unless you want to get going tonight." He stood up and looked down at Mereweather. "You can show me out, Simon."

"Deputy Director Mereweather, if you please," Amherst said sharply. "You want the paygrade and entitlement, you can take the chain of command."

Rashid shrugged. "Fair enough, boss." He walked to the door and waited.

"I'll be out in a moment," Mereweather said. He waited for Rashid to close the door behind him, then looked back at Ramsay and Amherst. "Well?"

Amherst shook his head. "Well, I think we just added a bloody great hammer to our toolkit, when we needed a pair of precision snips," he said. "Seriously, what the hell is it with these sort of men and etiquette? Where did he say he'll be?"

"McDonalds," Ramsay said.

"Dear God…" Amherst shook his head. "Okay, Simon. See him out and come back up here. Neil, get what the man wants. You can take over now. Liaise with our new friend. I want you to accompany him, work with him to bring King back in. Simon, you keep an eye on this and report back to me, but I want you on top of this Russian state visit. We need to know where any Syrian radicals are, anyone with Syrian sympathy, ISIS connections, that sort of thing. There's a three-pronged war and resistance going on down there, and we don't want anything happening to the new Russian president on British soil. Relations have been fraught enough of late."

"I'm on it, Sir," replied Mereweather.

"And Caroline?" Ramsay asked.

"We'll leave a line of enquiry open. We can't make a move until we get a lead."

"But, surely we have to investigate every avenue to come up with a lead?" Ramsay stated. He looked at Mereweather, knew the man had a soft spot for Caroline. "Simon? We *are* searching for her, aren't we?"

The deputy director nodded. "We are. But we must bring King in first. Stop him rampaging over Europe, dancing to Helena's tune."

Ramsay nodded. "I'll get on with it then," he said and stood up. "Unless there's anything else?"

Amherst shook his head. "Thank you, Neil."

Mereweather walked out with Ramsay and into the outer office. Rashid was sitting in a comfortable leather chair. He was watching Amherst's secretary as she typed. She was smiling at him, a little coyly. Ramsay waited for the door to the director's office to close, then leaned into Mereweather. "We can't give up on her," he whispered.

"We're not," Mereweather said tersely. "But King needs bringing in."

Ramsay shook his head. "The two things should go hand in hand. But we've done so little to date, that she will probably never be found. King is our best shot. *Caroline's* best shot."

Mereweather shook his head. "Look, while I see our friend out, you get on with the task you've been set," he said sharply. "But come to my office and see me before you go. Understand?"

Ramsay nodded. He watched Simon Mereweather escort Rashid out of the office, then let out a sigh.

"Problems?" the secretary asked, her expression humorous and her eyes inviting comment.

"Always," Ramsay replied. "But I fear, there may soon be many more."

24

King wanted a target on the man's body to give him two things. Maximum noise and maximum incapacity. He wanted the man incapacitated, but he also wanted him to howl like a banshee and bring everybody running. This man had a better suited weapon than the guard with the Uzi, and King intended on using it and leaving the crossbow behind.

The crossbow sights appeared to be off centre judging from the miss on the first guard, either that, or the crossbow fired to the left because of human error. King put the vee and pin sights on the man's right buttock and eased them a little higher to compensate the distance. He knew that if the man gave up the fight, he may well survive long enough to receive and respond to medical attention. But he would never have known pain like it. He thought of Caroline, his motivation for such cruelty.

And then he squeezed the trigger.

The bolt hit the man between both buttcheeks. Penetration was deep, but the bolt stopped just short from going through and through as the solid plastic flights, like a set of mini aircraft wings, slowed the bolt to a stop. The man dropped the rifle and howled. King was up and moving towards the staggering man. He had managed to turn around and King saw the tip and shaft of the bolt sticking out from the man's blood-soaked genitals. The man looked on in horror at King as he barrelled towards him, but he was not able to put up a fight. King caught him by the throat to steady and incapacitate him further, then gave the bolt a twist with his right hand for good measure as he tripped his feet from under him and dropped him onto his back. The man hollered, then screamed when his buttocks hit the ground and the bolt took the impact.

He didn't stop screaming.

King stepped away, picked up the assault rifle and checked it. The man did not have a spare magazine on him, judging from his attire, but he did pick up the man's radio and tossed it over the fence. He looked back towards the property and could see two men on the lawn, two-hundred and fifty metres away, and one-hundred and fifty feet below. They were looking his way, but the sun was still in their eyes. King shouldered the rifle, took aim and fired three shots at each man, all aimed below the waist and above the knees. Both men dropped a moment later. He could hear their screams, even above the man squirming and hollering on the ground behind him.

King didn't look back. He started down the embankment, then crouched and took aim at the guard by the pool. He could see the woman on her feet, the children in the pool, their play having stopped as they stared up at him. King shouldered the weapon again. He fired two shots at the guard. Steadied his aim and fired another two rounds. The guard dropped to the ground, but he was alive and crawling desperately to safety. King sent half a dozen rounds into the pool and each impact threw a spray of water three-feet into the air. The bullets landed near the children, but he was never in doubt they would miss. The children screamed and scrambled to the side, their mother dashing towards them, desperately trying to pull them clear.

Luca Fortez appeared on the patio with a nickel-plated handgun and fired on King. The bullets went wide and low, sending up dust that showered his feet. King returned fire, making sure his bullets hit the glass doors behind. The glass showered the mafia boss and he ducked down, crouching low as he got to his wife's side and heaved his son out of the pool.

The radio in King's pocket chattered and he took it out, pressed down on the transmitter switch and tucked it into his belt making sure the switch remained activated. He had now jammed all communication between the security. The handset was ancient and only had the one channel. King stood up straight and fired two more rounds on Luca, aiming just a little to his left. He slung the weapon over his shoulder and calmly took the Uzi off his other shoulder. A guard ran onto the lawn and King mowed him down, taking the man's legs out from under him in a burst of 9mm copper-coated lead.

There were many screams now, calls for help and the sound of general panic and pandemonium. Gunfire erupted to King's left and he returned the rest of the magazine, hitting the gunman and the vehicle he had sheltered behind. The car's alarm added to the cacophony of noise. He changed magazines, then slung the Uzi over his shoulder and switched to the Heckler and Koch G36. He had barely noticed what make the weapon had been. All he knew was he was familiar with it and had it switched to selective fire mode as soon as he had picked it up. The 5.56mm rounds were more powerful than the 9mm pistol rounds in the Uzi, and the weapon was accurate to five-hundred metres.

King reached the lawn and the writhing men. He kicked the first man's weapon aside. Then covered the other two with the rifle. "Where… is… Luca… Fortez?" he asked harshly in carefully rehearsed, but poor Italian, with as much Russian accent as he could achieve speaking a language he would not even understand the answer to. He bent down and picked up one of the men's pistols and tucked it into his waistband. The man spat something in Italian at him, and King dropped the rifle butt down onto the man's ankle. He wailed, and King kicked the other man's rifle away.

Two guards ran out into the grounds from the buildings behind the mansion and fired on King with pistols. King turned and fired, but this time, the men were close, so he took no chances and gave each one two rounds, centre-mass. They went down hard and one rested still, the other squirmed, his legs kicking and striking the ground in an effort to push himself into cover. King turned towards the house and fired the rest of the magazine at the windows, then dropped the weapon and slipped the Uzi off his shoulder. He jogged down the side of the house towards the pool. Luca's wife was shepherding her children into the house, but the broken glass was making their escape on bare feet difficult. King was instantly regretful, not wanting the children to injure themselves, but he knew they would be ok. Nothing a few plasters wouldn't sort out. He had seen worse in Syria and Iraq; these two privileged children would cope with a few cuts and a day of discomfort. They may be traumatised, but then, maybe he had done them a favour. Maybe they would head clearly down a different path, a life without crime.

King looked at the woman. She was frozen to the spot, her feet bleeding on the broken glass. She didn't seem to notice the pain and was simply staring back at him, looking at the muzzle of the machine-pistol. King grabbed hold of her, twisted her around and held her in front of him for a human shield. Just as long as her husband did not fire upon them, she would be alright. Luca wouldn't be so lucky. He was going to feel some pain now. King saw him sheltering behind a large planter and opened fire. The terracotta pot smashed, and King aimed carefully at the man as he cowered.

Again, he used a carefully rehearsed line, strong on the Russian accent, "Nikolai has had a change of mind. He will be taking you over. He will own your empire, eat from your table and sleep with your woman…" King fired and hit him in the left shoulder with a single shot and the white shirt turned crimson around the hole. The woman screamed as Luca fell backwards, and King gave her a shove forward. And that was the last King saw of them as he turned and ran down the side of the house and across the lawns. He hoped the children were alright, but he hoped Luca Fortez was too. He was convinced it was a flesh wound and knew that the bullet had not hit organs or arteries. It may have broken bone, but he was convinced that if pressure was applied quickly and just so long as Luca did not go into shock, then he would survive.

25

Caroline was eagerly anticipating a visit from Michael. He was young, and seemed different, certainly more sensitive than the other men she had encountered so far. As if he were somebody caught up in something he had no control over. She had tried to create the human element, the personal factor. She had told him that he reminded her of her brother. She concentrated hard to create a person in her life to fit Michael's character. She was an only child. This was all a game, an avenue to explore and to exploit. She imagined things Michael might like, thought how to weave her fictional brother's life into her captor's mirroring image. She had no idea what her captors planned, but people were less willing to harm, or even kill a person they felt attachment to. If she could make Michael feel for her plight, she may even get the man to help her. But how far could she go? What would she be willing to do to buy her freedom?

She could hear a noise outside, footsteps on the landing. She unwrapped herself from the covers, slid off the bed and made her way around the bed to the desk. She figured she could get the leg off the desk in one swift movement. She held the wingnut in her palm, her fingers clenched around it, she quickly tucked it into her bra.

The bolt eased back. There were two sharp knocks, then the door eased open. Michael stood in the doorway with a flask. "Coffee," he said, and walked in. He looked at her, signalled for her to step backwards with a flick of his hand.

Caroline obliged, took a step backwards and smiled. "Thank you, Michael." She watched him pour the thick, black liquid into a dirty-looking cup on the desk. It was hardly appealing, but the thought of the warm drink made it more appetising than she ever thought it would have. She stepped over carefully, noticed that the man did not move. Was he letting his guard down? She picked up the cup, cradled it in her hands and took a sip. It was strong, tasted faintly of cigars, of burnt tobacco. She grimaced but found the warmth of the liquid and the caffeine hit most welcome and took another sip. It tasted better the second time. By the third mouthful, she was drinking as fast as the heat would allow. She held the cup, studied the man's face. "Where am I?" she asked.

He shook his head. "I not tell," he said. "I *cannot*."

"I was expecting Eastern Europe, but I think we travelled further. Perhaps into Russia? The scenery looks like I imagined Russia to look." She took another sip, thought more about the time they had travelled, the stops. "Those mountains are to the north. Ukraine perhaps?"

"Enough!" he snapped. He held out his hand for the cup. His sleeve rode up, exposing a tattooed forearm. Caroline recognised it. She was no football fan, but she knew Manchester United's insignia, briefly saw the name over and under the picture of the devil with the pitchfork.

"Okay," she said, acting more subdued than he could ever make her feel. She decided that it might be best to put the sight of his tattoo in the bank. She could work on a satisfactory backstory, weave her brother in somehow. Appeal more to the young man's conscience. "I just want to know where I am. I have family who will be worried. My brother…"

"I don't wish to know!"

"My brother looks just like you. I miss him. He's football crazy. You know, soccer? He supports Manchester United. Have you heard of them?"

"Of course!"

"He's a huge fan, took me to see them play."

"Where?" he asked curiously, his tone softening.

"Old Trafford," she said. This was unfamiliar territory for her. She decided not to try and be too detailed.

"Who did they play?"

She tried to think of another premiership team but was at a loss. She thought of the big cities. "Newcastle United, I think." She cursed inwardly. She couldn't remember if they had been relegated or not. She would have to be hazy on dates and players.

"You think?"

"It was a long time ago," she said flippantly. "I'm not a football fan, but it was fun to go. The atmosphere was incredible…"

"What colour shirts did they wear?"

"Red!" she said, smiling. She held out her cup. "Could I have some more, please Michael?"

He nodded, poured and filled the cup. "I mean, Newcastle."

"Oh," she said. She was concentrating hard. She knew their nickname was The Magpies. She went with it. "Black and white. It was a fun afternoon."

"What was the score?" he cocked his head. "You must remember the score?"

She shrugged. "I'm not sure, two-one, maybe? It was a long time ago, and as I said, I'm not a fan. But my brother is. You like Manchester United?"

He smiled. "Yes." He lifted his sleeve. "See?"

"Wow!" she exclaimed, hoping she wasn't overdoing it. "Have you seen them play, live, I mean?"

"I have," he said proudly. "But not at Old Trafford."

"My brother could set you up with a box. You and some friends. He does all sorts of corporate events with the club. PR work for his company. Other companies like the link, their managers enjoy a good box event with a free bar."

Michael nodded. "I would like that…" he trailed off. "I have to go now," he said.

"You said there were others here," Caroline ventured. "Other women like me?"

"No," he said, shaking his head. "Not like you." He backed away and caught hold of the door.

Caroline watched him leave. There was a moment when she thought she had blown it, but now she felt confident she had successfully formed a human link.

26

There was enough pandemonium to escape the property through the vineyard, but not without coming under fire from the guards. But as King had reckoned when he had first envisioned and formulated his plan, they were not of the standard of the Russians. Luca's men were comfortable. They were renowned through historical acts, a ruthless reputation. But there was a difference between tough and sadistic men outnumbering individuals and businesses, and highly trained ex-military recruited into the Russian brotherhoods. And this is what King had seen at their meeting in the mountain town. Not only a higher degree of professionalism, but the Russians were on foreign soil and would undoubtedly be ill at ease.

King hadn't underestimated the Italians, but he had used them. He had reached the edge of the vineyard and the plateau carved out of the mountainside. He was now into the trees and traversing the steep gradient. The ground was uneven, loose and dotted with giant boulders that he had to dodge around. He had thrown the radio handset behind him, and as he crouched low behind a thick pine tree to get his breath and bearings, he ejected the magazine of the Uzi and checked. He was down to two rounds. He thumbed them out and checked the breach of the Uzi. It was an original design Uzi, in that it fired off an open breach bolt. There was therefore no chambered round in the weapon. He dumped it down on the ground and pocketed the rounds. He took the pistol he had captured out of his waistband and checked it over. It was a Beretta APX in .40 calibre. He had never used one before but looked over the features and the trigger safety and decided it was similar in design and working function to a Glock. He checked the ten-round magazine and the weapon's chamber, then stood back up and checked the ground behind him. There was nobody on his tail yet, but he wasn't about to give them time to get organised and brave. He stripped off the suit jacket, and then tore off the ridiculous gold chains and tucked the bundle between a tree stump and a boulder which looked to have felled the tree in a landslide at some time. He wedged the Uzi and its magazine in there as well. Then, he started to take the slope, gaining in speed and agility as he grew used to the ground and momentum. He was carrying a lot of speed and ended up charging through one of the huge tarantula webs. He shook his head and brushed himself off the best he could as he ran, slid and leapt across the terrain. He tried not to think about the giant eight-legged creatures as he ran.

He was hot and soaked in sweat, but he reached the first mountain road, hopped the barrier and ran across the tarmac, clearing the second barrier and dropping six-feet to the slope below. He lost his footing and sprawled. He slid and rolled and came to a halt some thirty-feet later. He was cut and would certainly bruise, but he checked himself hastily and was lucky to have not broken anything. He had lost the pistol. He looked quickly, but the weapon had been electro-coated with olive-coloured paint and he did not hold out much hope finding it in a hurry in this environment. He still had the large sheath knife and the flick knife in his pocket, but he left them where they were, not wanting to chance another fall. The gun would not fire unless he pulled the trigger - and he wouldn't do that because his finger was nowhere near a trigger until he needed to fire – but he wouldn't want to fall with a sharp blade in his hand.

He knew he was clear, but he just hoped they would not gather, regroup and anticipate his escape. He needed to get to his car and get away as fast as he could. Right now, he imagined they were in a state of shock. But Luca Fortez was a man who had risen in his world by acting fast and striking hard. King knew that both his appearance and questions, the way he had asked them, would point them towards the Russians. But had he done enough? Would they fall for it? He thought they would. Was banking on it. But it was *how* they would react that would matter. He doubted the Italians would simply go round for a cappuccino and work things out. This was their turf and their boss had been hit. His family terrified. Their colleagues injured, some killed. They were red-blooded, hot-headed men and they would go after the Russians with everything they had.

King just hoped it would be enough.

27

London

"Is that halal beef, then?"

"Couldn't give a shit, mate," Rashid spoke as he chewed through a mouthful of his cheeseburger. "Why do you feel you can comment on my religious practices?"

Ramsay seemed taken aback. He hastily took a sip of his coffee. "I just…"

"You just what?" Rashid wiped a glob of secret sauce off his chin with the paper napkin and swallowed his mouthful.

"Well, your file states you're a Muslim."

"And I bet yours says simply, C of E. So, do you go to church every Sunday? Or just the Easter and Christmas stuff, when most white British get the *calling.*"

"No, I just thought your lot were strict on that sort of stuff."

"My *lot*? What, British citizens who were born here?"

"You know what I meant."

"Do I?"

"I wasn't being obtuse," Ramsay paused. "I thought it strange, that's all."

"I was born here. My parents were persecuted by Sikhs, who raided Pakistan from India, and they fled to England. My mother was pregnant. My father was so relieved that he and my mother made the journey over, were able to establish themselves and eventually granted citizenship, that he embraced his new country, and encouraged us all to as well. My sisters, my brothers; we were all westernised, I suppose you'd say. But we still practised Islam, in our own ways. We still went to the mosque, not because of God, the Divine, but because of the spiritual togetherness it brought us. I'm open-minded and intelligent enough to understand science, most people are. Religion is about more than that. I understand the big bang theory, the evidence of dinosaurs. But through Islam, we connected with people, our community. But we still took everything that western culture offered. My parents eat halal, but my dad likes sausages and kind of denies what may be inside them. My sisters do not wear the hajib, and they go to nightclubs to have a good time. One drinks, the other has chosen not to. But they both plan to marry Muslim men. Because they grew up with them and love them, not because it has been arranged. Both have had white boyfriends in the past. You see, we have embraced everything, and people like you see the colour of my skin, read a few statements on a file and have me down as a bad Muslim because I'm eating a burger. Some of my *kind* would call me *kafir* and would ridicule me for turning my back on my roots and my religion, and I can't help that. Those people in the extreme are the same people I fought in

Syria under the banner of ISIS," Rashid shook his head, put the burger down and sipped from his cup of tea. "People see practising Muslims, their heads covered, or dressed traditionally and they scoff at their prayers, their strict dietary requirements, and they hate that they have not immersed themselves into western society, given up on their heritage and culture and become more relaxed. Then I eat a couple of Big Macs and you come in here and have a pop at me that I'm not adhering to Islam. You see? We can't win. And it's *that* attitude which is creating a divide and making disenfranchised young men do terrible things in the name of Islam."

"Are you serious?" Ramsay stared at him incredulously.

"If you don't think any of that is true, then you aren't part of the solution," he paused. "And as we know, people who are not part of the solution are part of the problem." He shrugged. "Anyway, show me what you've got."

Ramsay moved Rashid's tray over and put down his briefcase. He opened it up and took out an array of papers. "I never thought about it like that," he admitted.

"Don't sweat it," Rashid replied. "I'm used to it. But tell me, MI5 has how many Muslim, Sikh, Jewish or Hindu personnel in the upper echelons? People who represent a cross section of Britain. Sure, a few of every colour and culture the recruiters or admin can think of; researchers, field agents and the like. But how many suited and booted senior-level staff that you and Mereweather, or Amherst meet daily? None, I bet."

Ramsay shrugged. "No. You're right." He passed Rashid the first paper and nodded. "It needs working on. Anyway, back to business…"

Rashid smiled. He doubted the issue would go any further than this table. He finished his last bite of the burger, which like all fast-food outlets, had now turned hard and tasteless as it had cooled. He chewed rapidly and picked up the sheet, leaving a thumbprint of secret sauce on the edge. He read quickly. It was a de-arrest form. He folded it and placed it in his pocket. The rest of the papers were recruitment contracts. In return, Rashid supplied his bank account and sort-code. Within ten minutes, he was an active and official member of the Security Service.

"What's the plan, then?" he asked, sipping the last of his tepid tea.

Ramsay looked at his watch. "We'll go back to Thames House and put in a few hours on the databases and see what we can get on the Russian's killed down in Biarritz. I have a techy working on gathering intel on Helena Milankovitch, formerly, or I guess, even currently Helena Snell. Either way, he's working the angles on that. We'll meet with him, see what he has found. You're booked into the Holiday Inn in Mayfair. Don't get excited, it's a standard double but breakfast is on us. I'll meet you there in the morning, work out the time later."

"Then?"

"Then, I think we had better get over to the continent and concentrate on finding King."

"Caroline is the one who needs finding," Rashid said. "King can handle himself."

"We're not worried about King handling himself. We don't want him becoming a problem that comes back onto the service. He took down a Russian mafia brotherhood. Those hoodlums are connected to all sorts of prominent Russian figures, all the way to the bloody top. King could soon have Britain involved in an international incident."

Rashid leaned forwards conspiratorially and said quietly, "Go after King before this is finished, and King will make you a target. Throw your resources and attention on getting Caroline back, and King will come in on his own."

"You can approach King," Ramsay commented. "You set up a meeting, I'll make sure we have enough personnel on hand to bring him back."

Rashid smiled. "And you'll be front and centre to make that happen?"

Ramsay nodded. "I like King. He'll see it for what it is. An intervention."

"Rather you than me."

"You and he are tight," Ramsay said, his fingers crossed, emphasising the fact. "You must know how to contact him?"

"Not a clue."

"So, how did you help him out in France?"

"He contacted me."

"Well, maybe he will again."

"Maybe."

"So, he used a phone to contact you, you must have his number stored on your phone," Ramsay ventured.

"Email."

"I'll need your device."

"It's a laptop in Hereford."

"I can arrange that."

Rashid shook his head. He took a pencil out of his pocket. It was small and had been sharpened using a knife, the edges around the nib were straight. He scribbled down his email address and handed it to Ramsay. "That's my personal email," he said. "You'll get my server and IP address with that. No need to go giving my landlady a fright."

"And that's it?" Ramsay asked. "No other way to contact King?"

"No. That's it."

"And what of your involvement with him in France?"

"We met for a drink."

"A drink."

"Pernod, I think."

Ramsay stared at him. "And you needed an assault rifle for that?"

"Boys will be boys," he smiled. "We let off some steam in the woods."

"Forensics will see if there is a bullet match to the Russian's that the French police recently found in the forest near Biarritz."

"Well, they would if they were investigating. But they're not going to be. You have me down as an official agent. You've informed Hereford that I was working with MI5. I have the paperwork in my pocket." Rashid stared, his dark eyes as black as jet and emotionless. He stood up. "It was a pleasure serving my country, as always. I'm sure the press will make quite a bit of clandestine wars fought in Europe. Brexit might make that even more tricky for you…"

"Okay, sit down," Ramsay said.

"No more bullshit tactics?"

"No."

Rashid sat back down, but his posture was defensive. He leaned back in his seat, his arms crossed. "Don't try and fuck me over again," he said. "I'll help you for one reason, and one reason alone. King. That's it, plain and simple. He's in a tight spot. He has some demented bitch using him in her vendetta, and she's holding all the aces. But what you and the suited and booted prats on the top floor don't seem to get is; King was on *your* payroll. King was serving his country and got shafted. His fiancé was abducted because he shut the terrorists down. MI5 should be moving heaven and earth to get her back. But not for King. She isn't his property. She is one of *your* agents and she got shafted, too. She was taken in the line of duty. Get that into your stupid heads. King is doing what he must, to keep her alive. The least you can do is get her back. Forget King. Your paths will cross again. Find Caroline."

Ramsay considered this for a moment. He nodded. "Okay."

"Just like that?" Rashid asked incredulously. "You'll get that past the top floor?"

"I agree. And that's enough. The top floor, as you call them, will get what reports I feed them."

"Good," said Rashid. "I just hope it's not too late."

28

King poured the water over his head and rubbed his fingers through his hair. It was greasy and thick, but the water had warmed in the inside of the car enough to take the worst of the butter out and leave it looking marginally cleaner.

He was sweating profusely, and he doused his armpits and chest, let the water run down his back. He had stripped off the black trousers and shirt and had crammed them into a bin sack, along with the shoes and the empty water bottle. He had drunk his fill of the tepid water when he reached the car, as thirsty as he had ever been. He knew he had been dehydrated, his vision and balance were off by the time he had reached the vehicle, but the water soon revived him.

He had driven away from the area, found a hunter's track and parked up, his heart pounding and his pulse thudding in his ears. He was wearing khaki cargoes, and once the water dripped from him enough, he slung on a loose-fitting blue cotton shirt and slipped on a pair of trainers that bordered on boat shoes. He put the flick-knife into one of the pockets on his right leg and tucked the sheath knife into the door pocket of the car. He still had the two 9mm bullets and was about to toss them away, when he thought of his old instructor, Peter Stewart and the man's insistence on utilising everything. *It isn't over until you check your bags at the airport*, the man would say. The bullets still had a use outside of ammunition. Melted lead could set a broken knife blade back into the hilt, the powder could start a fire, purify dirty water enough to drink, cauterise a wound, lower a heart arrhythmia – the brass could be flattened to form a makeshift blade. He tucked the two bullets back into his pocket and checked his reflection in the window. He looked like every other tourist, and nothing like the man he had been up at the vineyard and mansion. He donned a pair of black wraparound Oakley sunglasses, tossed the bag into the car and got back behind the wheel.

He did not see any of Luca Fortez's cars on the drive to Monteverdi Marittimo and when he reached the outskirts of the town, he pulled into a pine-clustered layby where there was a bank of general waste and recycling bins. He left the engine running while he got out and tossed the bag into the general waste bin and got back inside the vehicle. He paused on the side of the road, allowed the convoy of vehicles to drive past. He tensed, every fibre of his body on edge for no more than a second, as he realised the cars were Fortez's. Two red Alfa Romeos led the way, Luca's Maserati followed, with a new Lamborghini SUV and a Porsche Cayenne following closely, and another red Alfa Romeo bringing up the rear. All the cars had tinted windows, the darkest tint possible, verging on black. King had no way of knowing how many men there were, but he figured each car was rammed full of Italian muscle and a whole lot of guns.

He eased out behind them and followed. He was out-powered and had to work the gearbox and accelerator hard as the convoy snaked through the corners and into the town at over twice the speed limit. They veered off left on a mountain road King had not noticed during his time here, and the road was both narrow and twisted around a deep canyon descending rapidly. King realised he was down to just knives, and there would be enough firepower ahead of him to start and finish a small war. He kept his distance, tried to estimate from the satnav where the convoy was heading. He realised it was an alternative route that would snake around the mountain and come up onto the Russian's rented villa from what looked to be a series of tracks from the south.

King pulled to a halt. If the Italians were going to attack the Russians, then they would be doing so from the low ground. Tactically, a poor move. He scrolled on the screen and brought up the Russian's track that led off the road from Canneto to Monteverdi Marittimo. He had used the high ground to perform a reconnaissance on the Russian's villa. He needed to see what was happening and he needed to place himself somewhere with a tactical retreat. If the Italians were not heading for the Russians, then he would just have to take his chance. He wasn't about to blindly follow the Italians into a killing ground, and he wasn't going to chance detection as he followed them on their devious route.

He drove back to Monteverdi Marittimo and headed straight through, barely pausing for the pedestrians. He was tired, still hot and thirsty, as he threaded the car through the series of bends and steady incline. He got caught behind a slow-moving hatchback and cursed as he did not have enough power or road to overtake, but he wanted to get close to the villa and get himself into position before the Italians got there. Eventually, the car turned off sharply for Canneto, and King floored the accelerator and broached the hill affording a glorious view of the sea with the sun low on the horizon. It was almost dusk. The perfect time for Luca's men to attack.

King found the track he had used earlier and grounded the car over the rough lane, dropping harshly into the potholes and scraping the fronds of thorny bushes and the outspread branches of pine trees. He manoeuvred the vehicle around, so he was facing back out the way he had come, then switched off the engine. The silence was total, bar the ticking of the cooling engine. King got out and was instantly set upon by midges and the same type of horseflies that had terrorised him in the pool. He swiped them away, the best he could, but he was hot and perspiring and the insects had homed in on the only meal in the area. King rolled down his sleeves and reached back inside the car for the sheath knife. He slipped it onto his belt and checked he could draw it quietly. He then slipped the car keys under the driver's-side front wheel arch and stepped out into the thick brush, taking careful steps down the steep mountain slope.

It was five-hundred metres to the edge of the ledge, which dropped vertically three-hundred feet or so to the bottom, and the start of another steep slope. The villa was clearly visible to the right of the slope on a plateau below. King could see the rutted track running parallel. Uphill would eventually meet the road to Canneto, and King could only assume that the track ran downhill to the road that the Italians had taken, just outside the town of Monteverdi Marittimo. As if to confirm this, King saw the first man edging uphill. Another appeared behind him. Both carried what King could only identify as 'longs'. Too far away to see if they were assault rifles, hunting rifles or shotguns. A third, and then a fourth followed. They made their way up the track, edging closer but tentatively watching the ground either side of them.

King watched, voyeur to the assault from the sanctuary of the cliff edge. He felt strangely nervous. He had put a lot of stock into the personalities and traits of the two sides. He had the Russians down as professionals, and judging from their close protection performance, they had been far more switched on than the Italians. The Russians were ex-military, provided muscle and resources for enterprises like Luca Fortez had planned for the rival mafia families. And he had the Italians down as hot-headed, impetuous and able to muster resources at a moment's notice. He just hoped he'd not read too much into what he had seen in the town earlier that morning.

Any doubt King had over the Russian's professionalism was ruled out in a burst of automatic gunfire. He ducked down instinctively and watched as the first two men in the line dropped to the ground and lay still. The rear of the line was joined by more men, and they now dodged and darted their way across the lane and into the brush for cover. There were a few single shots, voices in Russian, returned shouts in Italian and then all hell broke loose. The two SUVs thundered up the track with men firing out of the windows towards the villa. More men came out of the trees. King could only assume that Luca Fortez's men had picked up friends or family, because there were now dozens of men breaking out from the trees. There was the sound of heavy-calibre hunting rifles, the sharp crack they made and the echo of sonic boom resonating off the cliffs. The pistols clattered away, short and sharp and far quieter but, what they lacked in noise they made up for in sheer quantity, as men paused beside trees and fired up to ten rounds at the house in one go, then dropped down to reload. King could hear shotguns as well, and then the crack of military-style assault rifles as they fired in bursts of three or four rounds, the men behind them more disciplined. King had these down as Luca's bodyguards. He tried to count the men, but he simply had to estimate as the men were moving fast and had amassed to thirty or more.

The Russians were fighting back hard. King could see them on all points of the house, on all levels. They had obviously managed to secure weapons for their excursion, most probably proving to Luca that they could put their hands on the hardware required to take out the other mafia families. King could hear the unmistakable clatter of the AK47 rifles, see the three-foot-long flashes from the muzzle in the dim light. He watched the men stay in formation, keeping cover using both the building and now upturned wooden dining furniture which featured on each of the patios and sundecks. King could not count them, which was a good thing for the Russians, as it showed they were disciplined and they were also using the windows of the villa to remain inside. They were defending a building, and they had the high ground. They could afford odds of 6 to 1.

There was a change in pace. In battle there usually is. But King couldn't work out what was happening in the sudden lull. The Italians had regrouped, mainly into groups of four and five, which gave King a chance to count them. He almost got it done but had reached forty when the men started to fire again upon the house. King could see it was going to go the Italian's way, when a vehicle bounced its way down the track, and five men spilled out. They took up position in the trees above the villa and started to fire on the house with hunting rifles. King had no idea what calibre the men were using, but they were powerful rifles, knocking great chunks of concrete out of the villa, which was no longer affording the Russian's protection. The new arrivals acted like a sniper unit, keeping the Russian's in place and unable to return fire as the main bulk of men approached the villa in a pincer movement on both sides. They were getting the hang of it too, if a little Napoleonic in their tactics, but they were getting the job done. Men would advance, drop to their knees and fire, more men would dash around them, drop and fire, and by the time they had rained shotgun lead or pistol bullets at the windows or the cowering men behind the solid oak furniture, the manoeuvre was repeated, and ground was constantly gained. All the time, Luca's security core was on the periphery laying down fire with automatic weapons and the snipers were either picking off Russians who attempted to return fire or keeping their enemy's heads down.

King was almost transfixed at the sight. He watched with a mixture of emotions. His plan was working. He had seen the Russian's as the more difficult target, been aware that he was operating without either the equipment of backup he would have needed for such a task. He had no friendlies to call on, no help on the ground to provide him with intelligence or weapons. The Italians seemed to him to be the easier target. And now, whatever the result of the pitched battle below, he could kill his quarry while they were battle weary, or Luca's men would have already done it for him. Like the wolf circling two fighting contenders to become the alpha male but striking the weary victor with a deadly attack when he had no fight left in him.

The sound of the battle changed. There were less gunshots, less automatic fire. King recognised this as reaching a conclusion. The Russian's were suffering from either personnel losses or were running low on ammunition. King had been both sides of that fence, and he knew the mental effect it could have. He knew the attackers would see the end in sight, but he also knew that the defenders could go two ways. Peter-out and think of surrender or go out with glory. Now was the time it could change and more often than not, for the unexpected.

The surge came from the house and three men exited, back to back. A Hail-Mary. They covered three points of a triangle and rained a hail of lead onto a three-hundred and sixty-degree field of fire. King saw many of the Italians drop, and the Russians kept up their shuffle towards the line of vehicles, which surprisingly, the Italians had failed to disable. Two more Russian guards followed giving one-hundred and eighty-degree arcs of fire, with Nicolai being firmly manhandled by a third guard. King saw the lights flash on the lead car, and one of the forward guards drop. They had a great deal of firepower and the advancing Italians were caught out, but not for long. The snipers were hunters and they were good. By the time Nicolai reached the car, only one guard remained, and he was struggling to get into the driver's seat. Another Russian bolted out of the villa and fired a pistol at the snipers' positions, but he was dead meat before his third shot and went down fast, bullets still hitting him and rocking his body after he was on the ground. The snipers then turned their attention to the car and shot out the tyres and front grille. King knew that enough lead and copper had hit the engine for it to be going nowhere. Luca's men made their way up on the Mercedes, and his personal security came out of the trees with their automatic weapons shouldered. There was a lot of shouting, but no more gunshots. At the villa there was movement at the doors and windows, and weapons were being tossed outside. Moments later, five Russians stepped hesitantly out of the building, their hands placed firmly on top of their heads. They were circled by three-times as many Italians. King knew what would happen next, and sure enough, the beating started.

Relentless, cruel and without mercy.

29

King had pulled back from the cliff edge, worked his way to the east two-hundred metres or so, pushing through thick scrub and dense pine. The slope was so steep, that it was almost sheer. He used the pine trees for footing, and slid down to the next tree, working his way down two-hundred feet or more to where the slope became less sheer. It was challenging work, and he was thirsty and hot, despite the noticeable drop in temperature as dusk gave way to night. A sanguine moon filled the sky, giving a dull, yellow hue by which, he could make his way through the trees.

He could hear voices, loud and commanding. They were Italian, and King had no ear for the language. But he got the gist of it. Pissed off was pissed off in any language.

He reached the wire boar fence, slid over carefully and made his way to the fringe of trees surrounding the property. When he found a suitable place to survey the scene, he almost wished he had stayed at the top of the cliff. But he needed to confirm, or at least control the outcome. He had come this far, it was imperative he see it through.

Nikolai was on his knees, a rope tied around his neck. A tough-looking man had a firm hold of each of his shoulders and a third held the rope as if the Russian were a stubborn mule. He was at the edge of the swimming pool. King judged it to be the deep end by the look of the metal ladder steps to the Russian's right and the scalloped Romanesque steps at the other end. King felt an ominous sinking in his gut. His plan had been to force the less professional side into overcoming the pros by numbers. He had forgotten, or rather neglected to think about what evil men can do when they were out for revenge. That, and had the elation inside that only the victorious in battle would experience.

King moved to his right, not for a better view, but to the body of an Italian heavy who had been killed during the last stages of the battle. The win was still fresh and the desire for vengeance was still coursing through their veins. They had yet to mop up their dead, dealing only fleetingly with the injured who could call out for help. Three men lay upon the steps of the villa's main entrance, but King could see that the two men tasked with attending to them were craning their necks towards the pool and intent on seeing what would happen next.

The man would have been around twenty-years-old and had died from a bullet to the chest. It was dead centre and had most probably hit the man's spine. His eyes were open, giving an indication of a swift demise. King bent down and picked up the man's pistol. It was a compact 9mm Beretta. He checked the magazine, but it was empty. The slide had not sprung back and held on the empty chamber, indicating that there was still a chambered round. He slid the slide open a touch and saw the flash of brass in the dull light. He smiled, thought of his old mentor, as he took out the two 9mm bullets and fed them into the magazine.

Old warriors got old for a reason.

King felt better for having the weapon, even if it only held three bullets. He edged his way through the treeline and looked back at the pool. Events had transpired, even in the brief time it had taken King to find the weapon, into a scene of torture. The Russians had been placed in a sitting position on the edge of the pool, their hands bound behind their backs, their legs facing away from the pool edge. One of the Italians had waded into the water, while two men pressed down on the prisoner's legs. King knew what would happen next, and he watched as the man in the water pulled backwards on the first Russian in the line and forced the man's head and shoulders under the water. The men on the legs had their work cut out as the Russian struggled and bucked under their weight but was at the mercy of the man in the water.

King's heart raced, knowing he was ultimately the instigator of this scene, but he soon checked his emotions, feeling a rage towards the Russian bitch who had set him on this course, held the woman he loved as his stake in her wicked game. He edged out of the treeline, kept within the shadows and moved behind the shot-up Mercedes. One of the Russians lay dead at his feet, and he tucked the pistol into his waistband and picked up the AK47. He crouched low, listened. The Italians and Russians only shared one common language, spoke English in thick accents, one slowly, commanding, the other desperate. King edged out, saw the mafia boss towering above the kneeling Russian. A coat draped over his shoulders, like a mafia Don from the fifties.

"Where is your man who attacked me? Where is the dog who did this?" Luca Fortez asked, his tone cold and impatient. He wore a sling on his arm, his shirt ripped open, a large dressing taped over the bullet wound and clearly visible underneath.

"Again, I know nothing of any attack!" Nikolai spat at him.

Fortez looked at the man who had been looking at him for confirmation. He shook his head at the man holding the prisoner's head under the water. He watched as the struggling Russian slowed his movements, then ceased altogether. The mafia boss walked to the prisoners. He nodded to the man in the water and he dutifully pulled the next terrified man under. Fortez looked down at the man beside him. "You will be next. After your friend has died, you will feel his pain, feel his loss. You will breathe the water through your lungs as if it were air, your life will play out before your eyes and you will wish you told me *everything*. Do you understand? Now, tell me," he paused. "Where is the man your pig of a boss sent to kill me?"

The man was panicked, could not get his words out quickly enough. "I… know… nothing… of… an… attack!" He looked at the struggling man beside him, then back at the man above him. "Please! Bring him up!"

"Then tell me about the attack!" Luca barked at him. "Tell me what you know!"

The man slowed, and like his colleague, stopped moving altogether. The man looked at Luca Fortez desperately.

"Please!"

"Tell me!"

"I don't know of any attack!" he screamed. "You had a deal with my boss! We were going to work for you on something! I don't know of any attack, it doesn't make sense!"

Luca nodded, and the man was pulled backwards. The men at his feet gripped tightly, making themselves ready.

"No! No…" the man's screams were cut off by a deep gargle and the thrashing of his limbs in the water.

Luca turned to Nikolai, unconcerned for the dying man and his struggle. "Tell me, tell me now."

"You stupid fucking wop! You have been told! There was no attack!" he screamed at him. "Not by us!"

Luca turned and watched the struggle until the man lay as still as the other two bodies. He stared at the scene for a moment, then looked at the man in the water. He said something in Italian and the man pulled both remaining guards into the water, catching the men holding their legs by surprise. They held on tightly as the men struggled and splashed and fought desperately, but futilely for their lives.

King looked on. He edged backwards, another body behind him, another AK lying on the ground. This time the weapon was an AK74. It fired a lighter 5.45x39mm round, technically less powerful than the AK47, but designed to be so, as the bullet was designed not to deform or fragment, but to yaw and create cavitation, or simply put: would tumble after penetration and cause more damage than a through and through shot from the 7.62x39mm round. He preferred the weapon, because it had less recoil and was easier to control. He looked back at the pool, the gathering of relaxed men watching the grisly scene, their leader undefeated, invulnerable in battle, merciless in his victory. The snipers, such as they were, rested on their rifles. King had felt anger at being pushed into this, rage at being used as a pawn in another person's game, but as he looked on, he felt contempt for the woman he now served. He had lost sight of what he was doing. He was so busy doing her bidding effectively, he had not stopped to ask himself why. Why? Why did she want these Russian mafia men dead? He thought back to the forest in France, the dead man's wife at the farmhouse. Helena Milankovitch wasn't just someone out for revenge for something in her past, she was working towards a future.

A future with these men removed from it.

King couldn't check the magazine of either weapon without making a noise. The AK rifle was a tool. A reliable tool you could count on, but it wasn't a supremely manufactured firearm intended for the range and competitions. For civilian shooters to coo over and upgrade with match-grade precision parts. It was hardy and rustic and worked. It was noisy and metallic in its operation, and that was without even firing it. King looked on. The men were drowning, and there wasn't anything he could do for them, and nor did he want to. They were men of the sword. They knew the score. But as he looked at the Russian brotherhood boss on his knees, he saw then a man who was merely a target.

He saw a link.

A link to the woman who had come crashing into his life and torn it apart.

King backed away, gave himself a better field of vision. He hoped the two weapons held enough rounds to do the job. He brought the AK47 up to his shoulder and tightened his finger on the trigger.

30

Georgia

She was exhausted. She had tried to keep her eyes open, but there was no fighting it. The coffee hadn't seemed to help. She knew she was tired and had had little more than naps for the past few days as she had travelled. The journey, adrenalin and fear had taken their toll. Her body needed rest. Her head lolled, her chin touching her chest, waking her with a start. Each time she raised her head, she almost dropped back to sleep.

Caroline slapped herself across the cheek. Hard. She felt the sting, but the sensation was nulled, quickly overcome. She could not succumb to this. It felt so unnatural, like no bout of tiredness she had ever experienced. She knew what had happened. Knew that the coffee had been spiked, contained a barbiturate of some description. Perhaps ground-down sleeping tablets, possibly something stronger. She slapped herself again, powered through her lethargy and rolled off the bed. She clawed at the floor, her fingernails digging into the gaps between the unfinished wooden floorboards, breaking and tearing away as they provided little purchase. She did not feel any pain, dug her toes in and pressed on, the bathroom offering sanctuary from the fate of what she believed would happen next.

She could hear the solid footsteps on the landing outside. She crawled onwards. Used the edge of the open door to pull herself inside the bathroom. Her eyelids were closing, and she bit down hard on the inside of her cheek, something to hurt her, to snap her consciousness back, put her equilibrium back under her control. She could hear the rattle of the lock outside. The key in the padlock, the rasp of the bolt. She rolled onto her back, heaved her leaden legs up and kicked the door closed. She could not rest there. She could feel the darkness washing over her, her eyelids heavy and unforgiving.

"Hey?" The voice whispered, muffled. She envisioned him peering through the darkness, his frame illuminated by the light behind him. "Hey, you?" Sharper now, louder.

Testing.

She knew what he wanted from her. She kept her feet pressed firmly against the door, arched her back, but had nothing to press against, provide purchase against the door. If he barged the door, she would simply slide backwards. She fought with all her might, battled the ebb in consciousness. Her eyelids heavy. She looked in the gloom, looked for something she could use, but he had taken all the wash things from her. If only she had something she could use... a wedge, something to jam the door with...

"Hey!" Loud, followed by a footstep as he entered the room. "What are you doing in there?"

She had it. The large wingnut she had removed from the leg of the dresser. She had anticipated its use as a knuckleduster. But now, it just might…

She slipped her hand under the linen dress, hooked it out from her bra. She could barely keep awake, let alone sit up straight, but she fought through it, bit at her cheek again and then at her lip to shock her system, to stem the drift downhill towards sleep. She half rolled, half sat up, pressed the wingnut under the gap, close to the door jamb. She pressed hard, part of the wingnut digging into a thin gap between two floorboards, the other half digging into the underside of the door. She fell back down, her head knocking on the floor. Her eyes, heavy now, no more resistance possible, caught sight of the handle moving, the door edging marginally inwards. It caught. She heard a curse; the sound of the door being kicked at. The door resisted, she prayed it would hold, but could do no more, as she entered a still, dreamless sleep.

31

King prioritised the targets. The hunters-come-snipers each leaned on their bolt-action hunting rifles. They would be slow to reload, their powerful scopes would be too close to fire accurately back at King, and in the low-light conditions afforded by the yellow moon, they may not make out King at all. The rest of the men had formed into two groups. The events in the pool were gruesome, and men thrown into this conclusion as voyeurs tended to watch shoulder to shoulder, rather than stand alone. Whether they took comfort or shared bravado watching such things in company, King did not know. But he had witnessed behaviour such as this in Iraq, Afghanistan and Syria. Even from the most battle-hardened ISIS fighters. Likewise, the perpetrators of these acts found both the will and the desire to continue the brutality, possibly feeding off the audience.

Men were always bigger men when weaker men looked on.

King glanced at the selector lever. It was all the way down to single-fire mode. That would do. The trigger was light, and he would fire once at each target. For they were targets now, not living, breathing men. He aimed, breathed steadily, then fired.

The first three men dropped without so much as a single man looking at the source of the noise.

King switched his aim and dropped two of the snipers for good measure, then turned back to the remainder of the group. He fired twice more, missing one man and hitting another. He moved to his right, just as someone managed to fire a pistol back at him. King fired at the muzzle flash, saw the man drop and then cursed himself as he remembered the three men tending to the casualties. He spun around and fired at the two figures on the edge of the patio. A double tap at one, a single shot at the other. The weapon dry-fired and King threw the AK47 down and reached for the AK74 on his back. He flicked the selector down and brought the weapon back on the main body of men. They had reached the point where they would either stand and fight, or scatter. King hoped they would stick around. He wouldn't have enough rounds for a pitched battle over various arcs of fire. He kept the weapon's sights low and fired at the men's stomachs. Gut wounds dropped men fast, they also gave room for an off-centre shot. King threw himself down across the bonnet of the Mercedes and rested the magazine. He aimed, fired, aimed, fired…

He was taking fire himself, but he maintained his onslaught, bringing down the last of the hunters, and turning his aim on the exposed men on the other side of the pool, illuminated in the pool lights in front of them and the moon behind. He reached Luca Fortez, who was frozen, transfixed at the muzzle flashes and commotion. He hesitated, thought of the woman he had used as a shield, the two children who had shredded their feet on the broken glass. King broke aim, sighted on the last of his guards and fired three shots. The next pull on the trigger yielded a click and King dropped the rifle and drew the pistol from his waistband. He broke cover, fired at a man in front of him, then a man to his left. He was being shot at from a gunman twenty-metres away. King fired, dropped the pistol and dived towards the man he had just killed in front of him. He snatched the dead man's pistol, brought it up on the last two guards standing and double tapped each of them in the chest.

Luca Fortez stared at King, now only ten-feet away from him. "It's you…" he said, bewildered and confused. "You're the man from town. The tourist…"

King levelled the pistol. He glanced around, aware there would be wounded men from the fight, and wounded men were extremely dangerous. "Live or die?" he said. "Your choice. I know where you live, where your family are. You walk away when I'm gone and it's over. I have no fight with you. No reason to return." He glanced down at Nikolai, then back at the Italian. "But he's coming with me."

Luca opened his mouth, but he struggled to process what was happening, and how quickly it had happened.

King crouched, picked up a dead guard's machine pistol. Another Uzi. He dipped the mag, knew by the weight it was more than half-full. He pressed it back in, saw the exposed round on the open chamber, the open bolt ready to fire. He switched weapons, tucking the pistol into his waistband, keeping the Uzi on Luca. "This is happening now," he said and stepped forwards, struck Luca in the throat with rigid fingertips. The Italian dropped to the ground, clutching his throat and fighting for breath. King grabbed Nikolai by his collar and heaved him up. He dragged him forward, man-handled him away. King glanced back, saw the mafia boss crawling towards a weapon on the ground.

"Leave it!" he shouted. "Lick your wounds and live for another day!" King reached the row of cars and saw two men advancing. He fired a short burst from the Uzi and both men fell. He turned toward Luca Fortez. The man had a pistol in his hand. King pushed the Russian to the ground and he fell onto his face, unable to break his fall with his hands still bound behind his back.

The mafia boss looked around him. The bodies were scattered, some having fallen onto their comrades and resting still. Others were wounded, but the 5.45x39mm was an evil little bullet, and they weren't getting up soon. Maybe never.

"I'll hunt you down, you bastard…" Luca shouted.

King fired a short burst and the man dropped, rolled forward and fell into the pool. The water started to turn crimson and Luca's body sunk to the bottom, his hands outstretched, gently clawing for the surface but going nowhere.

King watched, then said quietly, "No, you won't…" He had enough on his plate, couldn't afford a war on more than one front. He had taken enough risks and chances with his own life, knew he needed to remain alive to buy Caroline time. He'd given the man a chance to go and live a life with his family. King looked at the five drowned Russians as they drifted, neither floating nor entirely sunk, in the pool. King had felt for the man's family, given him a chance, but in truth, he hadn't deserved it. He'd got the end he deserved now, floating with the men he'd callously had tortured and killed. His wife and children would grieve, but they would eventually be better off without him.

King pulled the Russian to his feet and pushed him forwards without another thought of the scene of carnage behind him. He kept the Uzi aiming in front of him, the muzzle close to the Russian's head. He saw a man cowering in the bushes. His back was to King, his hands cradling his head. The three wounded men were nearby. It looked as though they had tried to crawl away at the sound of the gunshots but had frozen as King walked past.

"Stay down!" King said clearly and confidently. "Stay where you are. All the heroes are dead. Stay down and you will live to go back to your families…" He kept the weapon trained on them, right up until he reached the Lamborghini SUV. He opened the door, saw the control device on the centre console. King opened the rear door and pushed the

Russian inside. He fell, slipped down between the front seat and jammed in the footwell. He wasn't going anywhere. King slammed the door behind him and got into the driver's seat and started the engine. He dropped the Uzi on the seat beside him as he selected drive and floored the accelerator. He had never felt acceleration like it, as the twin-turbo diesel V8 dumped its six-hundred-plus horsepower onto the gravel track and shot forwards in a storm of thunderous engine and exhaust noise with a hail of gravel thrown onto everything behind it for twenty-metres. King almost lost control of the vehicle in a straight line, but he lifted his foot, brought the vehicle back towards the realms of sanity and aimed for the track ahead of him. He took the track fast, with little care for the potholes in the ruts or the boulders along the edges. The Lamborghini flew over the ruts, taking off occasionally and thudding down hard, Nikolai grunting as he was tossed and thrown in the rear. King roared up the incline and after a mile, which was taken in under a minute, King hit the tarmac and threaded the vehicle through a series of bends. He floored the accelerator on the straight and held on. The large vehicle was other-worldly fast. King daren't take his eyes off the road ahead to check his speed, but the bends ahead forced him to slow, even though the four-wheel-drive system seemed to grip as if the SUV was on rails. Once he had cleared the bends, King slammed on the brakes and hammered the vehicle down the lane where he had parked his hire car. The Lamborghini would only attract the wrong type of attention, so King would leave it behind. Cars like this were always fitted with a tracker. Usually a stipulation from the insurers or lease companies. But for mafia bosses, because they would want to find the person who stole their newest toy.

King killed the engine and got out of the vehicle. He opened the rear door and pulled Nikolai out. He pushed him ahead and into the rear of the car. He went back for the Uzi and slipped it under the driver's seat as he got in.

"Who are you?" Nikolai asked incredulously.

"I am life," King said. "Or I can be death." He started the car's tiny engine and by contrast to the premium SUV, their progress up the track was almost comically slow.

"And which will you be to me?"

"That depends on you," said King. He turned out onto the road, drove steadily and carefully. His lights were on, and he was just a tourist on an evening drive. No place to be, no agenda.

"Why? Why have you done this?"

"Helena Milankovitch," King said. "Do you know her?" He looked in the rear-view mirror, caught sight of the man's expression in the moonlight.

Nikolai nodded slowly. "I thought I'd never hear of her again," he said. He sat back in the seat, as much as his bound hands would allow. He looked up at the ceiling, his shoulders had sagged. "I thought it would never catch up with me…"

32

"I'm going to ask you some questions," said King. "You've seen what happens tonight when people don't get the answers they want."

"It was you," Nikolai sneered at him. "You did something to Luca Fortez. Something that drove him crazy. Crazy enough to wage war on us. Kill my men…"

King shrugged. "You ply your trade, make your living from bringing misery on others. You had it coming."

"Bullshit," the Russian paused. "You and I are one and the same. You are a man who has done many terrible things. I can see it. See it in your eyes. You are no different to me."

"I'm nothing like you."

Nikolai scoffed. "As I said, you are no different." He tried to sit up, but struggled in the deep sofa, his bindings restraining his hands and the use of his arms. He slumped back down. "Who do you work for? Helena Milankovitch?"

"Tell me more about her," said King. "It sounds like she has finally caught up with you. Why?"

"Why don't you ask her yourself?"

"I'm asking *you*."

"And I'm not telling."

"Want to bet?"

"I won't talk," Nikolai said defiantly. "Tougher men than you have tried before. They are all dead. You will be no different."

King took out the sheath knife. He unfastened his belt, removed the sheath and buckled back up again. The Russian watched. He stared at the blade, followed it as King placed it on the table.

"I don't really go in for torture," said King.

"Then what?"

"Maybe I'll appeal to your better nature?"

Nikolai smiled. "What is your name?"

"I'm asking the questions."

"What, I don't get to know who you are?"

"Always for the best."

"You're not hired help," he commented. "Who are you really working for?"

King walked out to the open-plan kitchen and picked up the kettle. He filled it with water, turned the dial and waited for the gas to ignite. He put the kettle on the gas jet and then turned around and stared at the Russian. "It won't take long."

"What? The hot water? What are you going to do with that?" he asked. His brow was perspiring, and his eyes were wide. He stared past King, his eyes transfixed on the kettle.

"I'm making a cup of tea," he said. "Or would you prefer coffee?"

Nikolai switched his eyes to King. He looked incredulously at him, his eyes flitting between him and the kettle, which was starting to steam from its spout. "Are you kidding?"

King took out two cups. He put a teabag in one and spooned some instant coffee into the other. He'd never met a Russian yet who drank tea, didn't assume for a moment that Nikolai would be any different. He poured on the water, replaced the kettle and switched off the gas ring. Again, he assumed black. Poured a little milk into his own. He had forgotten to buy sugar. But he had once been forced to make a brew with his own piss, so he'd cope.

He took the two cups into the lounge, placed them on the glass coffee table.

"How am I meant to drink that?"

King sipped his tea. He stared down at the Russian. "Helena Milankovitch."

Nikolai shrugged. "Trash. Married well."

"Didn't she just," King commented.

"Her husband died. She will be a wealthy woman."

"She had her husband killed," King paused. "She's on the run."

"And you're hunting her?"

"Sort of."

"What the hell does *sort of* mean?"

"I am hunting her, yes. And I'm going to kill her."

"Good. She'll be less trouble that way."

"To you, maybe."

"What has she done to you?" Nikolai stared at him, there was a knowing lilt to his chin. A cadence that did not need speaking. "She has done you wrong, hasn't she?"

King shook his head. "No. This is about you."

"May I have some coffee?"

King pulled over a chair, placed it around six-feet from the coffee table. The Uzi was resting on the chair. King had earlier checked it over, it held fourteen rounds. He picked up the sheath knife, walked around the table and pulled Nikolai forwards, sliced the man's bonds, then pushed him back into the chair. When he rounded the other side of the table, he pushed it firmly into the Russian's legs and sandwiched them to the chair. He pushed the coffee cup closer to the man, then sat back in his own chair. He placed the Uzi on the right arm of the chair and the knife on the other. He sipped his tea, watched the man in front of him drink the coffee. He noticed the man's hands shake. Nikolai placed the coffee cup back down on the table, rubbed his hands together, rubbed the circulation back into his wrists. He fiddled with his watch strap. King could see it had cut into his wrist. The Russian looked up at King, he was nervous. Understandable. He fiddled again with his watch.

"I will pay you," he said finally. "Pay for you to release me. Unharmed."

King sipped his tea, placed the cup back down. "What did you do to Helena?"

The Russian shrugged. "It doesn't matter."

"I think it does. You know Pyotr Sergeyev?"

Nikolai stared at King, the fear had left his eyes, replaced by annoyance. "I do."

"Elaborate."

"We worked together."

"And that's it?" asked King. "I asked you to elaborate."

Nikolai shrugged.

"That's not elaborating." King picked up the Uzi and selected single-fire. He aimed at the man's shoulder and squeezed the trigger.

The gunshot in the confines of the villa was deafening. Nikolai yelped, and his feet kicked out, pushing the coffee table away and splashing tea and coffee onto the glass. He had turned pale and the fleshy part on the tip of his shoulder was bright red, blood seeping through his shirt and running down his chest.

"What the...?" he grimaced, then cursed in Russian. He held his left hand on the wound, then looked around and picked up a cushion, pressed it hard against the bullet graze.

King understood the profanity, shrugged it off. He'd heard worse directed at him from his own mother. "Just a flesh wound," he said. "Bloody painful, though, I'd bet."

"Okay!" he snapped. "I worked with Pyotr Sergeyev. We were inducted into the same brotherhood as teenagers. We were gofers at first, then hard-men. Enforcers. We dealt out beatings, collected money." He was sweating, great beads running down his brow and into his eyes.

"But you went separate ways," King said. "Two rival mafia brotherhoods."

"Later, yes," Nikolai nodded. He winced, moved the cushion away and inspected the wound. The bleeding had slowed. It was a nick, a graze, nothing more. It might have needed a couple of stitches, but he wouldn't be getting them tonight. Too many people asked questions when they suspected a gunshot wound. "He's dead. I heard he'd been hit. Was that you?"

"Helena wanted Sergeyev killed."

"And?"

"So, he's dead."

"Shit, she must have something you *really* want back."

King ignored him. "And she wants you dead."

"I figured that."

"So, why?" King asked. "Why does she want the two of you dead?"

Nikolai smiled. "She's a vengeful bitch, that is why."

"No shit." King aimed the Uzi again.

"Wait!" The Russian held his hands up. The cushion dropped onto his lap. He was flinching, his hands in front of him like tiny shields. He winced at the pain. "I'll tell you!"

King lowered the machine pistol. "Go on then."

"Okay, jeez. I tell you, you ever need a job after this, you come to me, right? You get the Italians to take down my guys, then *you* take down the Italians? Shit, man, you got balls this big…" He raised his hands and made a gesture, his fingers and thumbs not touching. The motion hurt his shoulder and he winced again. "Look, we were hot shit. We knew we were untouchable. That bitch Helena worked the casinos and she danced in some places, too. Man, what a body! She would hang on a guy's arm, lucky charm sort of thing, whisper in his ear, ask for drinks. The guys lapped her up. She made the casino money getting guys to dump all their money on wild bets, and they made money on her drinks. Only French champagne, fifty US dollars a glass! Helena and girls like her, they were like gold mines. She was good too. She knew how to work a man for everything he had."

"And you had a cut of all this," King stated matter-of-factly.

"Of course," he said. "We supplied her, and other girls to the casinos."

"So, I'm guessing she tried to leave that life behind? Left you with a big hole in your income."

"Yes," Nikolai paused. "She did so a few times. Or at least, tried to. We took her back, encouraged her to stay."

"Encouraged?"

"Yes."

"You beat her?"

"No. Of course not," he said emphatically. "She was a pretty woman. No point damaging what makes you money, eh?"

"So, what happened?"

"I need a drink."

King raised the Uzi. "You'll get another bullet. Who knows, my aim might be a bit off next time. The bullet may go lower. Take a chunk of bone with it, nick an artery…"

"Okay!" Nikolai shifted in the chair. "Helena had done another one of her disappearing tricks. Her sister turned up in town…"

"She has a sister?"

"Yes. A fine-looking girl. She must have been about fifteen or sixteen. A good age. Ripe for the picking, but innocent enough to appeal to men with enough money. Helena went crazy when she turned up…"

"What was her name?"

"Catherine. Once seen, never forgotten. A real peach…"

"Get on with it!" King snapped.

"Helena got her out of town. Gave her a ton of money and sent her away," he paused, shaking his head. "A ton of the *brotherhood's* money. It didn't go down well. We decided to teach her a lesson. Bring her back to heel. Like a disloyal dog. We had some drinks, too much vodka, a little cocaine, then a lot of the stuff… It all got a bit out of hand."

King frowned.

"We had ourselves a little party. A sex party…"

"You raped her…"

"It wasn't like that! Just a gangbang. We all took a go, she didn't complain. But the drink, the drugs, it kind of went on all night. You know, for some people watching that keeps the mood up, a guy takes a turn, you drink, snort a line of coke, take your turn… The cocaine just keeps you going for hours."

"You fucking gang raped her!" King raised the machine pistol. "You raped her, and now she wants revenge! You and Sergeyev…"

"Hey, it wasn't *just* us! There were others…"

"Who?"

"Other enforcers."

"Their names!" King snapped.

"It can't have been so bad. There was another girl there. Sergeyev sort of kept her to himself. He ended up seeing her after that. They married a few years later."

"Anna?"

"Yes. Hey, what's it all to you anyway?"

"Because Helena Milankovitch is all out of options! She's on the run, waging a vendetta that started with you! I figured she wanted you out of the way, so she could make a claim on your business empire. Sergeyev, too. But this is revenge. If you hadn't done what you did, if you hadn't raped her, then my fiancé wouldn't be..."

King couldn't finish his sentence. The glass doors behind him smashed, sending thousands of shards of glass into the room along with a heavy oak sun-lounger that had been used as a battering ram. King dived to his left as his chair took the brunt of gunfire from something distinctly Kalashnikov. King swung the Uzi wide and fired, but the weapon had been set to single-fire and the effect was less dramatic than the attacker's. By the time he had realised and fired twice more, he was on the floor and Nikolai was on his feet and had kicked the glass coffee table into him, sending him sprawling into the kitchen. King rolled onto his back to see the muscle-bound bodyguard who had stopped him falling into his charge in the town earlier that day. The man was taking aim. King kicked his own chair into the man's legs and fired a short burst from the Uzi. The man wobbled as he returned fire, enough for King's bullets to miss him, but also enough for his own to pepper the floor to King's right. The AK was clicking as he dry-fired on an empty chamber. King took aim, was about to fire again, but the weapon was kicked out of his hand. He turned to see Nikolai lining up another kick and shunted himself backwards, the Russian's kick missing his face by inches. He looked back at the bodyguard, who had switched the assault rifle to hold it by the barrel. He raised it behind his head and threw it at him with considerable force. The rifle clattered into King's face and chest and he fell back down onto his back. He could feel wetness on his face, stinging in his right eye, and knew he was bleeding. He pushed himself up, but was kicked again by Nikolai, who had now given himself more room and was standing to his right. King was tightly confined by the coffee table, and now his own chair, which the bodyguard had kicked his way again. Nikolai went for another kick, but King punched out hard and struck the man's kneecap. He screamed as it dislodged, and he fell backwards onto the coffee table, falling through the broken glass and found himself caught up in the metal frame. The screaming did not stop, but the cuts and impalement of glass was nothing compared to the damaged joint.

The bodyguard was breathing hard, but he bent down and retrieved the knife which had fallen to the floor, and he smiled back at King. "Transmitter, asshole. In the watch. It's a Breitling and transmits to a dedicated receiver. That's how I found you. I guess you gave him the chance to activate it. Amateur."

"Didn't see you down at the villa," King said, as he got unsteadily to his feet. "You may have the knife, but you haven't got the fight. Run off into the woods, did you?"

"Fuck you!" He twisted the knife in his hand. "Looks sharp. And now I'm going to cut you up before you die."

King took a step forward. "Done talking?" He had dropped into a fighting stance, much like a boxer, but instead of waiting for the Russian, he lunged forward, like a sprinter off the blocks, and kicked the chair into the man's legs, but when it crashed into the man, he carried on, stepped onto the base of the chair with his right foot, and stepped up to the back of the chair with his left. At fourteen stone, even with a distinct size disadvantage against the muscle-bound bodyguard, King rode the chair right over the man. The bodyguard swiped with the knife but missed as he was driven downwards. King already had the flick-knife in his hand. He pressed the stud button and the four-inch blade whipped out. The bodyguard fell flat on his back, let out a gasp as he was winded, the chair on top of him, with King standing on the chair, legs apart and balancing like a surfer on a wave. King dropped down, drove the blade deep into the man's trachea. At the point where the breastbone met the throat. He dropped all his weight onto it, pressed so deeply the hilt went into the wound. The man gargled and gasped, but with each intake of breath, he took more blood into his lungs. King side-stepped the chair, keeping a grip on the knife. The man's eyes had glazed, his movements minimal. King gave the knife a twist as he pulled it clear and the blood flow more than doubled. The man was gone, his body just going through the motions. He wasn't breathing now, and as King wiped the blade on the man's jacket, he could tell that he was circling the drain. He stood up, turned and surveyed the scene. Nikolai was still caught up in the frame of the table, he was whimpering, had been watching intently, no doubt praying his man would win.

King bent down and checked the Uzi. The breach showed a round. He dropped the magazine and saw he only had the one bullet. He turned to Nikolai, kept the weapon trained on him.

"So much for appealing to your better nature," King said. "Where else gets the signal? The police? Rescue services? That's what those watches are for."

"Just my security."

King smiled. He glanced at his own vintage Rolex. He was merely estimating how long it would take to get clear of the villa. "Now I know you're lying," he said. "You're desperate enough to chance the local police. Well, I'll tell you now, they're being paid off by Luca Fortez."

"We'll see," said Nikolai. "Maybe their payments will stop now you've killed their meal ticket. Maybe they'll want to get even with you? Maybe they'll accept a deal from me?"

"Who else raped Helena Milankovitch?"

The Russian tried to move, but the glass was cutting into him badly, and his knee was beyond grinning and bearing it as he got out of the mess of twisted metal and broken glass. He looked back at King. He was beaten, and King knew it. What's more, he knew King knew it as well.

"Okay... Just help me out."

King put his foot against the frame, held out his hand and when the Russian took it, he heaved him out and spun him over into the deep chair. Nikolai cursed and yelled. He was as pale as a sheet, and he panted deep breaths to get through the pain, like a woman in labour.

"Who else is she wanting revenge on?"

"It's hazy, you know… There was a guy called Dimitri Romanovitch. He got out of the brotherhood. Started a series of businesses, legitimate ones. But once a Bratva, always a Bratva. He'll have done things to get where he is now."

"Who else?"

Nikolai glanced at his watch. King raised the machine pistol and the Russian looked back at him. He shrugged. "It won't do you any good." He smirked. "You may have killed Sergeyev, you may well kill me. You can kill Romanovitch if you like. But you won't get near the other man."

"Who is it?"

Nikolai smiled. "Oh, what a place the new Russia is. Like the Wild West, no? A man can do as he pleases. He can kill, have blood on his hands. He can take a man's property, business, empire even. And then what? When he has taken what he wants, what then? When is enough? Enough is a word some people have no understanding of. Enough is not even a word to a man like that."

King stared at the man. He was no longer the big, powerful mafia boss, leader of one of the most ruthless brotherhoods to emerge from behind the Iron Curtain. He looked broken, desperate. King knew he was biding his time. "I'm getting my fiancé back from Helena. I'll do it with or without your indulgence. So, another guy on her list is going to be difficult to get to. I get it. But I got to Sergeyev, and I got to you."

"You have no idea!" Nikolai spat at him. "You don't know what you're up against! You think you can fuck about in the shadows? Think again!"

"Who, then?" King snapped. "Who else raped her?"

"The fucking president, that's who!" Nikolai laughed and wiped a tear from his eye. He looked faint with the pain he was suffering, but the tear could well have been from the laugh. It seemed heart-felt and genuine. "Helena Milankovitch is just warming you up! Have you got a way to the president? Can you take on a million soldiers? Two million reserves?" Nikolai laughed again, he seemed delirious. He had either accepted his fate or was plaintively unaware that he was both crippled without medical attention, or at the very least, losing blood from the lacerations over his back, neck and legs. "Forget it! Forget your lover. Move on, it's done. You won't get to the new president of Russia! Just accept that you have lost, and Helena will kill your fiancé. Hopefully swiftly, but I doubt it…"

King squeezed the trigger and stopped the Russian mid-sentence. He sagged, his head lolling onto his chest like he'd fallen asleep. King glanced at his watch again. He estimated another five minutes before the police arrived in response to the GPS signal and recorded message they would have received from the tracker inside the Breitling watch. He was already packed, estimated he would be clear of the property inside three minutes.

33

London

Rashid had taken a run around the Thames, estimated it at five-miles and finished up sprinting at full pace back over Westminster Bridge. He had showered and changed and headed downstairs for breakfast, where the Holiday Inn had made it's first mistake. A breakfast-buffet. Rashid had filled a plate with toast and pastries, taken the entire jug of orange juice back to his table. He ordered coffee, then went back up to the buffet where he filled another plate with sausages, bacon, fried eggs, mushrooms and beans. The waitress raised an eyebrow when she brought his coffee, but he polished it off quickly and took advantage of the Holiday Inn's second mistake: there didn't seem to be a one-visit rule. Rashid filled his plate again, returned to his table and started all over, as Neil Ramsay walked in, caught the waitress to order a pot of tea, and headed over.

"Sleep well?" he asked, sitting down and watching him eat with amusement.

"Yes, before you ask; it's bacon and pork sausages."

"Wouldn't think of it," he smiled. "Looks like a heart attack on a plate to me. Didn't fancy muesli, then?"

"How far have you run this morning?"

Ramsay shrugged. "Fair point," he said. "Well, when you've finished stripping the Security Service's hospitality budget, we'll head back to Thames House and see what we have on Helena Snell."

"Milankovitch," Rashid said. "Snell will be a shadow. She married a billionaire, started a fashion concern, but she even kept her Russian lover the entire time. She then plotted with her lover, formed a terrorist organisation as a front to detract from the real motive of killing her husband. In doing this, she sacrificed people to act as a cover for her plan. She's a cold bitch. There will be nothing worth knowing from the time she was Helena Snell. But believe me, there will be something as Helena Milankovitch. That's the key. Her past."

34

Caroline came around slowly. The bright light shining through the bathroom window, shafts of golden light warming her face, forcing her to blink as she opened her eyes. She felt groggy, her mouth dry. Her head thudded like a hangover after a night of champagne. A sharp, incessant thud that she not only felt inside her head but heard incessantly in her ears.

She raised her head, had to fight through the light-headedness to refrain from falling back down. She could not place exactly where she was at first, but it flooded back to her and filled her with foreboding and fear. She sat up, blinked away her dry eyes. And then she felt herself all over. Her underwear was intact. The thought, as she checked, made her feel close to vomiting. She looked at the door. It was an inch ajar. She looked under the door, near the jamb. The wingnut had scarred the floorboard, dug in deeply. She got up slowly, knelt on the floor. Her head banging and pulsing. She pulled on the door, but it did not budge. She felt a wave of relief, a near-euphoria. But she was in no doubt that she had been drugged for sex.

She turned and ran the cold tap, splashed some water on her face and swilled her mouth out. Then she drank until she was full. The water would flush her system, take the toxin out of her, slowly bring her back. She rubbed some water around her neck, shuddered as it trickled down between her shoulder blades.

It was with a mixture of anger and a sense of hope that she kicked the door closed. The wingnut was pulled out of the floorboard, and she picked it up and tucked it back into her bra as she opened the door inwards and stepped back into the bedroom. She would not be a victim anymore. The coffee Michael had given her had been drugged. She would not let her guard down with him again. It was time to discover her fate. Or at least take a hand in controlling it.

35

King sipped his orange juice and picked at the pastries. They tasted like yesterday's. Maybe older. He'd always found breakfast in Italy to be a lacklustre affair, neither appealing to his appetite or constitution. Coffee, which he did not drink, a few biscuits, or perhaps bread and jam, or cheese and charcuterie. He wondered how the Italians got anything done before lunch. And he'd given up trying to order a pot of tea.

He had decided to put some distance between himself and the mountain. There was a lot happening up there, in all three locations, and he needed to be as far away as possible while the police scoured the mountain region for a person or people, undoubtedly armed, certainly dangerous.

As always, when making a getaway, King had driven right on the speed limit and made sure he observed traffic signs and signalled accordingly. He needed to be invisible, and he knew from his personal experience and cost that police could pull over a motorist and get lucky. It had happened to him a lifetime ago. Any lesson learned through pain and suffering did not need learning twice.

King had found the hotel in Siena using an app and Google Maps on his phone. Situated conveniently on the outskirts, overlooking the attractive, culture-rich city of spires and castles, fortified walls and towers. It had been on the list to visit with his wife Jane. Caroline had also put the city on her list, along with Florence, but King had merely agreed with her and not mentioned the fact he had dreamed of visiting with somebody in a previous life. Caroline had to have some things for the two of them, something she had not been beaten to, or be competing with a dead woman's dreams.

The hotel had a vacant double room, which out of habit, King took for two nights, although he did not plan on staying any longer than the time it took for him to eat his meagre breakfast on the balcony and plan his next move.

After he had arrived, he had tipped the barman for two buckets of ice and returned to his room where he ran a deep bath of cold water, tipped in the ice and set about soaking away his bruises, swelling, aches and pains. He had learned the practice as a boxer and it had stood him in good stead in later years. It was always agony at first, but if he remained until all the ice had melted, then he knew he would heal quickly. He had wrapped some of the ice in a towel and held it against his face. He was bruised and cut, but the swelling subsided soon after the ice worked its magic. The time was well-spent, but it had also given King time to think.

Counter surveillance measures like taking the room for an extra night, or moving the car, as he had and parking it in the street adjacent to the hotel's carpark, gave him the edge he needed. He had slipped comfortably back into the role he had been trained for. Another department, another life. That of an assassin. He had battled with the ethics, the ideals for so long. But he had always served his country, always been on the side of what seemed right. But as he contemplated over breakfast, the deaths of so many men on the mountain, he found there was no conflict battling within him. He had simply performed the tasks necessary to secure, or work towards the release of the woman he loved. For the first time in recent years, he had found the task of killing as simple and as functional as any other task within the parameters of his work.

He had decided to keep the mobile phone he had been given switched off. He had used his own to find the hotel, but this was not his MI5-issued phone. He had checked for messages but had none. He used it to check his various email accounts, and his data cloud. There was nothing there either. Apart from the one email from Mereweather asking him to return, a few days after he had left for Sweden. He checked the date again but knew the man would not email again. He had the man's email, unless there was a significant development regarding Caroline, King wouldn't bank on more contact from MI5. He was as out in the cold as he'd ever been.

King had been thrown by the Sweden thing. And he knew he had been played. It had made him doubt himself, because it made sense for Helena to return to her roots. A place where she would have familiarity, contacts and support. He would have bet everything that she was in Russia. But Sweden had brought nothing but the fog of indecision and doubt to him. What was the connection? Was it a random act? Something merely to throw him off the scent? While he kept the phone switched off, lengthened the tether Helena Milankovitch had on him, he was reminded of the feeling of empowerment. Caroline would be safe - no harm would come to her while he remained out of contact - she was still bait to him. It would strike back at Helena, too. She would not know if something had happened to King. She would hear about the Russians, she would be monitoring the correct channels for news. But she would not know about King; whether he lay wounded and dying, dead even, or whether he was homing in on her. It would unbalance her psyche, remove the illusion of control. He would have to act fast though. He would have to make some progress, too.

He had moved quickly. From Sweden to France to Italy. Barely had he had the chance to ponder events, calculate his options, the likelihood of finding Milankovitch or even where to start. But he was sure that if he found her, then he would find Caroline.

King finished his orange juice then picked up his mobile phone, thumbed the screen and checked his messages again. Nothing. He needed to get to an airport. He needed to get a flight and hand back the hire car. But first, he needed to make a call.

36

She watched the door handle turn. Slowly, ominously. The bolt had alerted her, raking backwards, scraping the metal as whoever was behind the door worked the locks. She had felt a pang of fear, of dread. She felt her legs stiffen, had to force herself to move, but she knew she wanted to be anywhere but on the bed. The thought of what could have happened to her last night, what she would have been unaware of under the control of the powerful drug that had been put in her coffee, chilled her to the bone.

The door eased inwards and Michael stood in the doorway, a paper bag in one hand, a pot of steaming coffee in the other. He nodded, stepped inside and poured some coffee into the stained mug. He said nothing as he threw the paper bag onto the bed. Caroline looked at the bag. It had been twisted closed but had started to unravel as it had hit the bed. She could see a bread roll of some description.

"Breakfast," he said. "Did you sleep well?"

"Where am I?" Caroline asked, ignoring his question. She looked at the steaming cup of coffee. She wanted the caffeine hit, felt she could never eat or drink while she was here again. She walked around the bed, looked at the man in front of her. "I know what you did," she said. "You drugged me. You came into this room, you were going to rape me."

"No!" he snapped.

"I was in the bathroom, you tried to open the door."

"I was concerned," he said. "I was trying to help you! I came to check on you, you had locked yourself in."

"You pushed the door, kicked at it. You were calling me."

"No, I…"

"Were trying to help me? Some help." She reached over the bed and picked up the bag. She looked at it, then tossed it at him and it bounced off his chest and onto the floor. "Take that back," she said. She picked up the coffee cup and looked at the murky liquid. Michael looked concerned. He stepped back, his eyes on the cup. "I thought you liked me, Michael. I thought we were getting along."

He shrugged. "I suppose," he said.

"It is not acceptable behaviour, Michael." She looked at him severely. "You have a mother, don't you?"

He nodded. "I…"

She shushed him, "I imagine you have a sister, or female cousins? Imagine if someone tried to do that to them?" She shook her head. "I thought I was going to try and get my brother to get you some tickets to see Manchester United. Had you forgotten that?" She stared at him. "You'd like that, wouldn't you? To see Old Trafford, see behind the scenes, meet some of the players?"

"Of course!"

"Good. Get me something to eat and drink. Sealed in packets. After that, you can get me some warmer clothes."

"You are cold?" he asked.

"No. I am not," she replied haughtily. "I am not comfortable in this flimsy dress. I want something more substantial."

"I…"

"Do it, Michael. Go and get me what I have asked for. You want to be my friend again, don't you?"

"Yes," he replied solemnly.

She turned her back on him. "Good. And Michael…"

"Yes?"

"I have a sweet tooth…"

37

Mr King,

You have cost me everything. You took away my security, my claim to a fortune rightfully mine. You cost me my freedom. And you ruined my future. You know what happened to my lover, while I lay awake, not knowing of his fate, and that I will likely never see him again. Never feel his touch on my skin, hear his voice.

But I have changed your life, too. What a month you must have had! You must ache for your lover. The uncertainty of what happened to her hurts you inside like an infected wound. You are viewed with suspicion by your employers. You have nowhere to go, no friends to turn to. I did this to you. I changed your future also.

I want you to know who did this to you. I want you to picture me in your sleep. In those darkest of hours, where demons goad you, rule over you, control you.

And now to Caroline. Your beautiful, feisty Caroline. I am enjoying her company. You will, by now, know of my past. Forced into becoming a whore. Passed around to filthy men, a prize, a sweetener for business deal after business deal. I escaped that life, but ended up in the same trap, before meeting my husband. Oh, and what a brute he was, too. Like the men on the Black Sea coast, those casino goers who would win at the roulette and buy me, my body – though my heart was never for sale. You see, he would beat me and bully me, and no amount of his money was worth that life. Viktor gave me the love and affection that my husband never would. And now, as I look at your beautiful Caroline, I see a woman who has seen none of this. A woman who gives herself to a man only when she is loved. A pristine example of a privileged life. She has loved few, and she has done so with all her heart. Shall I take this woman and make her a prize? Shall I see that she spends the rest of her days chained to a bed, screwing men for her own survival, or drugs, or perhaps just for food? Or shall I use her to gain more. Maybe if there were a man who would do absolutely anything to save her? Maybe if there was a man with skills I could use, manipulate for my own gains?

But there is such a man. And now I own him also. Because I know that you will do what is asked, because for you, Alex King, your payment is here, and I can control you in a way you have never known. I have your life in my hand. I can give it to you, I can take it from you, or I can destroy it in front of you.

There is a post office in the town of Sodertalje, near Stockholm, Sweden. It is on a crossroads with a coffee shop to its right and a sweet shop to its left. There is a safety deposit box number 427. The code to open it is 4478. You will go there on May 22nd and open the box at 0930.

Do not fail her.

Helena

Rashid dropped the letter back down on top of the pile of papers. He rubbed his face, with his palm, then fingered at the start of a goatee he had decided to leave in place when he had shaved earlier. "And King saw this letter?" he asked Ramsay but kept his gaze on the woman behind the computer terminal.

"Yes," he said. "Simon Mereweather took it to him. King left on a plane to Sweden that night."

"And how long did MI5 sit on it?"

Ramsay shrugged. "We had it a few days."

"And you didn't think to put an observation post on this post office?"

"In hindsight…"

"In hindsight, you fucked up," Rashid said coldly. "You could have had a lead on your missing agent. Instead, King went in cold and has been on the backfoot ever since." The woman behind the computer terminal looked Rashid up and down, then back to the screen. Rashid couldn't decide if she was attracted to him or hated his guts. He never really knew. All he knew was that they always hated his guts at the end of the fling. He wasn't boyfriend material. Couldn't give a damn either. "You alright, luv?" he asked her.

"Fine," she said, curtly.

"Caught you looking," he smiled.

"And?"

"Are you interested?"

"Of course not!"

"Good. So, get back to the computer and tell us what you've found."

Ramsay shifted awkwardly, but he didn't respond or interfere.

"Helena Milankovitch. Thirty-six. Born in Belarus, moved to Moscow when she was eight, later moved to the Ukraine. Left home at sixteen, wound up in Georgia around eighteen, worked in the Black Sea resorts of Batumi and Kobuleti. Dancer, exotic. Hostess, escort and then prostitute, by all accounts. She was involved in the Bratva, or the Russian brotherhood. The mafia. She was a hostess. The sort that hangs on your arm, encourages expensive drinks, big bets on the tables, sort of bleed the rich men dry."

"Met a few of them in my time," Rashid said. "Except I'm not rich, and drink shit lager, but you know…" He shrugged and gave the woman a wink. "I'd buy *you* a Cinzano and lemonade, though."

"You're all class."

"Class of one, luv." He smiled. "You'd get dinner as well. Well, some nuts to nibble on."

"What?"

"Nuts on the bar. Crikey, you're getting ahead of yourself."

Ramsay frowned. "You're breaking about four codes of conduct in the work place," he said.

"I haven't had the paperwork yet."

"It's about twenty pages long," the woman said, not taking her eyes off the screen. "So, I imagine you'd need to keep your entire weekend free to read it."

"Damn. I've got plans this weekend," he smiled. "I've got a hot date. A real looker."

"Really? What's her name?" the woman asked incredulously.

Rashid leaned forward, his chin almost touching her shoulder as he read from her ID and lanyard. "Marnie Adams…"

The woman smiled, but she also flushed red. She was an attractive brunette, her hair pulled back in a tight ponytail and the thin-rimmed glasses she wore had slid down her nose. She pushed them back up with her finger and smiled. "I think my boyfriend will have something to say about that," she said.

"Well, maybe you'd best not tell him you're spending the weekend with me just yet… You'll have to think of an excuse…"

"You can rest assured, I'll be spending the weekend with him."

"Meh…"

Ramsay coughed, but Rashid looked Marnie in the eyes, gave a little wink, then unhurriedly straightened up and turned his eyes back to the screen. "Yes, that's about half-a-dozen more codes of conduct right there."

"Best keep me in the field then," he replied.

"Well, I think we'd better work out a plan," Ramsay suggested. "And I'll tell you now; you're not going to be free this weekend." He took out his mobile phone as he heard the bleep, unlocked it and started to scroll the screen.

"You hear that, Marnie? We'll have to take a rain-check," Rashid said. He turned to Neil Ramsay. "Sweden," he said. "That should be our first port of call. We need to go to that post office and see what they can offer."

"Like what?" Ramsay asked, still distracted by his phone.

"CCTV for one. They'll have it for certain. We need to find footage of the safety deposit box. We need to see who put it inside, or even what they put inside."

Ramsay nodded. "Or… we could go via South Africa."

Rashid frowned. "Where exactly does South Africa figure?"

"This has just come through from Mereweather," he said, flicking the text down. "When Caroline was investigating a lead in South Africa, looking for the identity of the sniper Anarchy to Recreate Society used in their campaign, she was abducted and very nearly assassinated. Suffice to say she was okay, but she was assisted out of the country by an MI6 field officer, a man named Ryan Beard. He knew of King's reputation while he was with MI6. He has the name of the South African Secret Service agent who was corrupted by Helena Snell, as she was then, and who betrayed both Caroline and one of their own agents who was chaperoning her to her interview with a witness at Pollsmoor Prison."

"A link to Helena," Rashid said quietly. "Well, let's get going."

"I need to speak to Simon Mereweather first, get more on this Ryan Beard fellow.""Fine, you do that. I think Marnie better come," he said seriously. "She can work on finding out more, use this additional information in her searches, be on hand to keep us up to date."

"What?" Marnie exclaimed. She took off her glasses, stared at Rashid, but it had the opposite affect to what she imagined, making her features softer and altogether warmer. "Sir, I don't…"

"It's actually not a bad idea," Ramsay said. "You can work on Wi-Fi, and it will keep us in the loop with time zones."

"But South Africa is on the same time!"

"With Sweden then," he said. "We'll work on returning via Stockholm." He put his mobile phone into his pocket and picked up a file as he headed to the door. "Get ready, both of you. Meet back here with your passports and carry-on bags. No luggage." He checked his watch. "Say, in two hours? That should give you both enough time."

Rashid shrugged. "Suits me," he said. "Just got to go back to the Holiday Inn and grab my bag."

"But, Sir!" Marnie called after him, but it was too late. Ramsay had already closed the door and was hurrying down the corridor. She looked at Rashid, glared as she slipped on her glasses and took out her own mobile phone. "Happy?"

"Absolutely," Rashid smiled. "I told you I'd see you this weekend." He stood up and walked to the door. "Tell your boyfriend not to wait up…"

38

Caroline could see the mountains ahead of her, knew the distance would be deceptive. She had once driven towards the Rockies and they had appeared the same size after an hour on the road. She knew that these would not be in the same league as the Rockies, but she was aware they could be five miles away or thirty. There were scatterings of snow or ice at their peaks and given that it would be late May by now, that would indicate a great height and given their appearance, she estimated they were closer to thirty miles away than twenty. The thought of how long she had been captive made her eyes well-up. She missed Alex terribly, but more than that, to her sadness, she missed her freedom and detested the woman who had instigated this. What could she hope to achieve? She had only met her briefly, and that had been enough. She recognised madness, and clearly Helena Snell had been tipped over the edge. She had been seething with King, blamed him for the death of her lover. Blamed him for her being recognised as the instigator of a terrorist group, and their deadly manifesto. But it had been more than that, she had been in it for her own gain. To kill her husband and to gain financially from his death. And she had been both evil, or perhaps crazy enough to kill so many people as a cover for her agenda. With this knowledge, Caroline truly feared the woman. She knew she was a pawn, but she had no idea to what end.

Caroline considered the mountain region no more. With that direction ruled out, Caroline craned her neck to see what was to east and west. Naturally, if she were able to escape, she thought west would be her best option. Simply because it was in the direction of home. It would seem outlandish to head further away.

She heard footsteps, tensed at the sound. It took all her resolve to steel herself, assume the arrogant superior personality she had used with Michael earlier. She had trained in evasion and capture, knew all about Stockholm Syndrome, where captives can start to sympathise with their captors.

Well, that was not going to happen with her.

She would reverse it. She would have this cowardly little pervert eating out of her hand. She had taken a chance, and now she had to act on it. She would take each little victory she could.

The lock on the door raked back and she could hear keys rattling. The door eased inwards, and she stepped over to the dresser to be closer to her makeshift club. The wingnut was still tucked inside her bra. But she was trained in Krav Maga. She wouldn't be going quietly.

Michael skulked inside. He had a plastic grocery bag in one hand, some clothes tucked under his arm as he put the keys back into his pocket.

"Good," said Caroline. "Put the clothes on the bed." She waited while he placed a folded pair of jeans and thin sweater on the bed. "No shoes?"

Michael shrugged. "There are none."

Caroline considered this, glanced at the man's own. She estimated him to be a nine. She was a five and a half. She looked up at him. "What have you got me in there?" She nodded at the bag.

"Food, some drinks. All sealed, like you said." He looked behind him into the hallway, then stared back at her. "You will be moved soon," he said. "When I know, I will come and get the clothes from you. I will be in trouble otherwise…"

"Moved? Where?"

"I do not know."

"Find out for me," she said. "Please, Michael. We are friends, yes?"

"I…"

"Are you happy here, Michael?"

"I…"

She interrupted him again. "I could get you a place to stay in England. In Manchester, perhaps. A job, season tickets to watch Manchester United's home games. My brother could help me get those for you. You will be paid a great deal of money, by the people I work for, for helping me get home," she paused. She had hurried, but she was desperate. A new place could mean somebody less pliable. It could mean something altogether more terrible even. "What do you say?"

He glanced behind him, then said, "I have to go. I will think about what you have said."

"I mean it, Michael. I can help you have a better life."

He looked ashen, closed the door without saying anything else.

She cursed herself for rushing in. She tore off her dress and pulled on the jeans. They were a bit on the loose side, as was the sweater, but both made her feel less vulnerable than the white linen dress. She tore both straps off the dress, tied the ends in a reef-knot, then threaded it through the beltloops and pulled the jeans tighter around her waist. She sat down on the bed. She felt like crying, had to control herself. She knew the time to act was looming. She knew what it was to fight for her life. But she also knew the fear would subside quickly, as adrenalin and survival instincts took over. The first move was always the hardest. She breathed deeply, took her mind off it by checking inside the bag. There were two cans of full-sugar Coca Cola. She opened one, appreciated the caffeine and sugar hit as she drank half the can in one go. She placed the can on the floor and turned her attention to the crisps, biscuits and chocolate inside. They were all unfamiliar brands and it reminded her of holidays in Europe, or occasional visits to budget supermarkets. Apart from the cola, she did not recognise any of the brands. With all the fat and sugar content, it wasn't the healthiest meal, but it was the best she had eaten in a month.

39

Sodertalje, Sweden

Time had taken on another dimension. One that King felt it almost impossible to assimilate. He had barely paused for breath since Simon Mereweather had handed him the letter in Scotland. He could not tell, without concentrating hard, whether it had been weeks or days. But he had given his all, pushed through fatigue and his own fears to buy Caroline the time she needed. She was tough and resourceful, possibly one of the most intelligent people he had met, and he knew deep down, that the likelihood of a gallant rescue was slim. Caroline would have to use her military and intelligence training to get out of her situation. All he could hope for was to keep up what he had started. Keep Helena from seeing Caroline as a loose end of no future value, and now, unbalance the woman as he bought himself some precious time. He would have to act fast. It would be a fine line emotionally for Helena. She would undoubtedly be trying to find out what had happened to King, and while she was doing that she would be exposed. She would have to make enquiries, pay-off people in a position to extract information, and that would always create a trail.

King knew his time was limited. Stay under the radar too long and Helena may well abandon her plans and cut her losses, including her ties to Caroline. He would have to resurface soon.

He had already revisited the post office and been mildly rebuked at first, threatened with a call to the police when he had persisted. Data protection was a key right to living in Sweden, and the Swedish protected their freedom so fervently. King could tell that no amount of cajoling would work. He was unofficial, and a flash of his MI5 ID was about as useless as the mild flirting he had tried at first. He was ruggedly handsome, but certainly the wrong side of forty to have the desired effect on a twenty-year-old woman with looks worthy of *Vogue's* front cover. He had been told that all recordings were digital and held both on cloud and hard-drive, and only a court order would retrieve them. King had known that he had been close to the wire, knew he had to appear to give up and walk away. But appearances are deceptive, and King always played more than one card.

He watched the teenagers practice on the goals. There were a few girls, but mainly boys and the skill-level was high. It was called soccer in Sweden, but King would always call it football. Each player would dribble the ball a few metres, then power a kick towards the goal. It was quite an onslaught for the goalkeeper, but he was coping well, saving far more than he was conceding. After ten-minutes all the players were taking long passes and strikes towards the goal from just shy of the centre line. The goalkeeper coped admirably and saved all but a few. There was no element of surprise, and unsurprisingly he had more time to meet the ball. The coach seemed to recognise this quickly and he brought half the players in close, the other half split between the two corners. He shouted and made some gestures, and the players kicked in sequence to avoid a blast of multiple balls, and the goalkeeper let more than a few goals into the net. After five-minutes, the players ceased fire, gathered the balls and started to perform some warm-down exercises and stretches. The coach tossed a few spiky foam rollers into the mix and the players alternated working it along their hamstrings and quads. They all took on fluids, some drinking from bottles of water, others squeezing sachets into their water bottles. King guessed they were syrupy fruit cordials packed with electrolytes. It made him smile when he thought about playing football as a boy using jumpers as goal posts and downing a fizzy pop afterwards, or later training with the SAS on nothing more than tea, *Mars Bars* and bacon rolls. Perhaps a can of *Guinness* and paper-wrapped fish and chips smothered in salt and vinegar, his muscles aching and cramping after fifteen-mile runs with a fifty-pound Bergen on his back. But always up for a beer and some chips off base in the evening.

The coach was dismissing the players and packing the balls away in nets. He was forty-something, wore his thinning fair hair in a crew-cut. He had put on some weight in the years since King had seen him last. Par for the course. Not everyone lived such an active life as King did.

The coach dragged the nets of balls off the pitch, King guessed the Volvo estate backed up with its tailgate open belonged to him. It seemed the obvious choice, given that most of the parents waiting for their children had parked facing the pitch, most driving expensive SUVs and either talking on their phones, texting or surfing the internet on various devices. King got out of the Volkswagen hire car and made his way towards the coach. He walked unhurriedly, hands in his pockets. Just another parent waiting for their child to get changed.

The coach was pushing the nets in place, moving equipment to make room. He spoke before King could, didn't turn around.

"Time caught up with me?"

"It catches up with everyone."

The man wedged a cooler of bottled water between the nets of footballs, then turned around. He looked older than when King had last seen him. Of course he would, it had been over seventeen years, but even so, the crow's feet, wrinkles and extra weight in his face aged him considerably. "I thought the day would come," he said. "What can I do to change your mind?"

King looked him up and down. He was about to allay the man's fears, but saw the way he looked at him, noted the sense of foreboding in the man's voice. He needed some stick and carrot.

King simply shrugged. "I don't know, Simon…"

"Why so long?" he asked. "I mean, it's been, what? Seventeen… no, eighteen years?"

"Can't beat the Reaper," King said.

Simon Grant sat back down on the edge of the boot space. He sagged. He'd been with King on an operation, seen what the man could do. He wasn't a fighter, never had been. He knew if the man was there to kill him, then he was as good as dead. There was nothing he could do about it. Nothing more than delay the inevitable. "Can you give me some time?"

King had heard this before. In Switzerland, many years ago. A man who knew he had been beaten before the fight had begun. King had earned his moniker from that operation. *The Reaper.* The man had been a traitor and he had taken a softer ending with drink, a warm bath and a sharp knife.

"How's Lisa?" asked King.

Grant's expression hardened. "Fine," he said. "Please, leave her out of it."

"And David? He's what? Twenty-five?"

"Twenty-six," Grant said. King noticed his eyes brighten, could see the man's pride in his son. King felt a pang of indifference, jealousy even. Nobody had ever felt that way about him. "He's a teacher now. In Gothenburg. Married too. A little one on the way."

"About the same age I was when we met," King mused.

"Good times," Grant said sarcastically. "Seriously, why now?"

"I want you to do something for me," said King. "I want you to do one last job. Afterwards, you'll never see me again."

"What?" Grant asked incredulously.

"It's in Sodertalje, a quiet commuter town."

Grant nodded. "I know the place," he said.

"The target is a secure building. A post office. Time delays, motion sensors and a strong room," said King. "Inside the strong room is a computer server. I need to access it tonight."

"You can't seriously…" Grant shook his head. "I don't do that anymore," he said.

"You do tonight. I trust you. And I need your help."

"I coach football to rich kids after school. I drive a taxi at weekends. I haven't broken into anything since France, all those years ago."

"Simon, you were one of the best," said King. "And skills can go rusty, but not to someone like you. My hand is still in, and it's a two-man job. I need you."

"And afterwards?"

"I'm gone."

"Sure…"

"No, really. I don't ever intend to return to Sweden."

"And leave me dead? Or take me back with you."

"No."

"The money's gone."

"Life must be expensive in Sweden."

"I was on the run a while, still am I suppose," he said. "It costs money."

"I gather that."

"And Forsyth?"

King shook his head. "Dirty. And very dead."

"So, why are you here?"

"For your help."

"And not to arrest me?"

"No."

"So, you want me to break the law? Nothing more?"

King stared coldly at him. "I want you to help me. If you do, I'm gone. Nobody has to know where you are."

"Doesn't sound like anybody cares. Maybe I'll say no." Grant stood up, closed the boot lid. "I bet all those people in charge back then are retired by now. What are you, forty? Time you got out of this game."

"I watched you play with your son," King said quietly.

"What?"

"All those years ago. Lisa, your son and you. In the park. It started to snow. You kicked the ball with your son, left together. I walked away. I said I couldn't find you, told them the lead we had was a dead end. I was eventually reassigned. The case was closed."

"I…"

"I gave you those years," said King. "All of those birthdays and Christmases. All those school plays, sports days. Holidays the three of you took. You and Lisa had another child a few years later. I kept the odd tab on you, kept my ear to the ground to see if anybody fancied their chances tracing the money. All these years you had since Holman, O'Shea and Neeson had their claws into you. Everything you have done since is on me." King put a hand on the man's shoulder. "I'm not going to bully you, nor threaten what you have here. I need your help. Somebody has abducted my fiancé and is holding her. I think a lead may be in that post office. In fact, I'm certain of it. I love my fiancé. I need to get her back safely, and I need you to help me."

40

Cape Town, South Africa

"You're out on a limb here," Rashid said.

"I know."

"Is this official? MI6 are onto this person?" Ramsay asked.

"No."

"Then what gives?" Rashid asked dubiously. "You've dug into the South African Secret Service's affairs, come up with this guy?"

"No."

Rashid shook his head. "What then?"

"I liked Caroline."

"She's spoken for," said Ramsay.

"Not like that. Well, alright, but not for that reason."

Rashid glanced at Ramsay, then looked back and frowned. "Then what reason?"

Ryan Beard was tall and blonde, smartly dressed in a white linen suit. He looked like a model on assignment, the glistening sea behind him, Table Mountain to his right. He leaned against the white SUV and shrugged. "Various. Firstly, Caroline was a piece of work. She took out two would be rapists and assassins. She then carried on with her assignment, got ambushed by two guys. Between her and the South African Secret Service agent who died, she got out alive. The agent was sacrificed by a traitor in the SASS. We work closely with local intelligence. There's no room for traitors."

"And?" Ramsay asked incredulously.

"And, what?"

"You said, various reasons. Why else are you doing this?"

"I don't follow." Beard glanced back at the Mercedes hire car. Marnie was seated in the passenger seat and working on her laptop, apparently not having noticed the impressive sight of Table Mountain rising out of the rock before her, or the glistening ocean to her right.

"You don't want to catch this guy who was happy to have your agent killed?" Rashid studied him closely, looked the man directly in the eye. He wasn't trained in such techniques, but he knew a liar when he saw them. He would soon tell. "Were you expecting somebody else?"

Ryan Beard shrugged. "The Reaper, I suppose."

"Reaper?" Ramsay frowned.

"King."

"You know him?"

"Our paths crossed when I first took the job."

"And what job is that?"

"Embassy man. I help our *workers* with anything they may need."

"So, you get the kit, help with transport, that sort of thing?" Rashid clarified. He'd met a few in his time. One such man had helped him in Turkey getting through to Syria.

Beard nodded. "But not with The Reaper, no. I just greeted him. He did everything else."

"So, when was this?" Ramsay asked.

"Ten years ago, a couple of times since."

Ramsay frowned. "But King wasn't with MI6, he worked as an unofficial with MI5. He was our late Deputy Director, Charles Forester's man."

Ryan Beard looked adamant. "No, he was definitely an MI6 agent."

Ramsay considered this for a moment. Beard was silent. Rashid said nothing. He knew enough about King's nature not to have probed. The man was an enigma, and it was King's completion of the SAS selection course, not once but multiple times, that had cemented their friendship. Rashid had seen King once at Hereford. MI6 had a poor sense of humour, used the toughest selection process in the world to keep their agents both fit and on their toes.

"Okay," said Ramsay quietly. "So, what? Merely out of solidarity to the *Firm*?"

Beard shrugged. "Caroline and King are together. I figured he would show up sooner or later, I wanted to call the shots, offer the information before he chose to seek it for himself."

"And the *Reaper* tag?"

"Folklore," replied Beard. "Caroline rebuked some of it, but it was said that King was seated near an MI6 traitor in Switzerland. He was drinking coffee. When the guy looked over and spotted King, he went back to his hotel and killed himself," he paused. "Shit, it sounded better when I told it to Caroline…"

"Can't beat The Reaper…" Rashid mused quietly.

Ramsay nodded. "Okay, Mister Beard. Thank you for your cooperation. Where is this SASS traitor?"

"He has a place in vineyard country. Just outside Franschhoek."

"Is he under surveillance?" asked Rashid.

"Not yet. A contact inside the secret service has granted me forty-eight hours before he calls it."

"Meaning?" Ramsay prompted.

Beard shrugged. "Hey, I thought King would come."

"They want him dead?" Ramsay baulked. He glanced at Rashid, then looked back at the MI6 officer. "Really?"

"Look, this is bandit country," Beard paused. "They have the guy banged to rights. He has an account with a lot more money in it than he would ever be able to explain. He has taken payments, made the contacts and there is a trail to all four dead men left here in your agent's wake. My contact has granted me carte blanch. They want the information we glean from him, then they want him out of the picture. That's the price for a free lunch."

"Well, it's not exactly free, is it…" Ramsay said sardonically. He looked at Rashid. "Are you okay with that?"

"Am I fuck?"

"But…"

"I think I'm due a raise."

"You've worked for MI5 for two days."

"A big raise. I think I remember you mentioning it earlier."

Beard smiled. "Look, sort it out amongst yourselves. This is my little gift for you. MI6 will know nothing about it. MI5 get a link to that sniper and his paymasters who took out all the rich people last month."

"And in return?" Ramsay asked. It was *quid-pro-quo*. Nothing came for free.

"I have helped. King doesn't come around here cutting all the loose ends."

"Crikey," Ramsay paused while he considered it. "That man certainly *does* have a reputation." He looked at Rashid. "We can sort this out, yeah?"

Rashid shrugged. "I suppose."

Ramsay turned to Ryan Beard. "Okay. Lead the way. Rashid will travel with you, I'll follow in the Mercedes. Pull up a few miles short and we'll work out the order of things."

41

Caroline heard the footsteps, heavy and deliberate. She could tell they were not Michael's. They belonged to somebody heavier, and altogether more confident. She slid off the bed, waited near the dresser, close to her makeshift club with the big bolt protruding from the end.

The padlock clicked and grated, and the bolt slid cleanly through. Caroline watched the handle turn and the door open steadily. She could not see anyone until it was nudged wider, then she shivered when she stared into the face of the man who had touched her, felt her when she had been so vulnerable.

The Beast.

She was scared, and she knew the man could see it in her eyes. She shivered involuntarily.

The Beast reached behind his back and pulled out a small automatic. A 9mm Makarov. He smiled at her as he pulled out a pair of handcuffs from his pocket and threw them onto the bed. "Put these on," he drawled, his Russian accent thick and guttural. "No funny business, or you get a bullet. Okay?"

Caroline picked up the handcuffs and begrudgingly clipped them over each wrist. The Beast raised the pistol and walked over to her. He reached out and gripped her left wrist, squeezed the cuff and it ratcheted tightly. He smiled as she winced, repeated it again with her right wrist. He let go, reached for her hair and yanked hard, bringing the pistol up into her neck.

"No funny business," he said, then pushed her ahead of him, out of the bedroom and into the dark corridor.

Caroline's heart was pounding. She tried to assimilate what was happening, told herself there would be an opportunity at some point, but there was an over-powering sense of dread that she could not shift. Her legs became heavy and her breathing erratic.

Ahead of her, a narrow staircase was lit by a window high above. She could see clouds scudding across the blue sky. She looked at the stairs, a strip of well-worn carpet, almost threadbare and accented by grimy painted floorboards on both sides. She could tell the house had not received attention in many years. Perhaps even decades. But the wear indicated that it was in constant use.

"Downstairs, turn right, go into the room," The Beast ordered. "And no funny business…"

Caroline wondered if he had learned his English from forties American gangster movies. She did as she was ordered, slowly. She would not give the animal the satisfaction of obeying meekly. He moved closer to her and prodded her back with the muzzle of the pistol. She grimaced as she smelled stale cigarette smoke and body odour on him. She entered the room, a large innocuous area which had been set aside as a dining area. A large pine table some twenty-feet in length and half as wide and surrounded by at least twenty chairs. The table was grimy but had been wiped after use. The room was otherwise featureless and windowless.

"Sit," ordered The Beast.

Caroline pulled out a chair and sat down. The beast walked around the table and sat down as well, keeping the pistol in his hand and aiming towards her. He had relaxed his hand, placing the pistol on the table, his hand loosely holding the grips, but was far too distant for Caroline to attempt anything other than suicide.

"Now what?" she spat at him.

"You shut up and wait."

She did not have to wait long. Caroline looked up as a woman entered. She was strikingly beautiful, but predatory and severe. Her eyes were as dark as jet, her shiny black hair cut in a sharp bob. She looked different now though. Sad, where once she had exuded nothing but confidence. She had seen the woman once before. Until then, she had only seen her in magazines, barely-cohesive articles on the internet, or in a series of photographs from files within MI5. She had seen the woman in person in a derelict house. She had almost died, was still gasping for air and clearing her throat of muddy water when the woman had walked in. She had picked up the knife King had left for her, and for a moment, Caroline had thought she was going to help cut the bindings on her ankles. She had seen the look in the woman's eyes, knew she was in trouble, but had been left far too weak from her ordeal to fight her off.

"Caroline," she stated flatly, as she pulled out a chair and sat down next to The Beast.

"Helena Snell."

"It's Milankovitch now," she corrected her.

"Congratulations. I'm sorry I couldn't bring cake."

Helena looked her up and down. "I wonder if you will still be so feisty after you have been forced to sleep with a thousand men?"

Caroline looked at her warily. "What is your problem? You had your husband killed, got caught out and want revenge?"

"I want revenge for my soulmate! Not that piece of shit you call a husband!"

Caroline nodded. "Viktor Bukov?"

"Yes."

"So, where is he?"

"You killed him!" Helena snapped. "Or rather your precious organisation did."

Caroline shook her head. "I don't know anything about that."

"Liar!" She pushed her chair back and it scraped on the flagstone floor as she stood up. She paced around, her arms folded, accentuating her slim waist. "Viktor was slaughtered on a rooftop by a sniper…"

"And what was he doing on the roof? No doubt attempting to assassinate another person on your death list."

Helena glared. She had no answer. She had been waiting for him in the street below. It was to have been their last hit. They had almost been home and dry…

Helena smiled. "I think it's time I showed you around," she said. "Let you see what awaits you, if your boyfriend doesn't make contact with me soon."

"Why would he contact you?"

Helena smiled. "Do you know how the northern Sami and the Inuit use a wolf's character trait against it? No?"

"No," Caroline said quietly.

"Well, let me enlighten you. You see, the cold does many things to someone. Also, to the animals inhabiting the frozen wilderness. Feelings are one thing. The cold can numb the senses, dull the emotions. You are hungry, and there is food, but it takes so much effort. Nothing is easy. And therefore, nothing can be ignored. Every opportunity must be exploited. The wolf for instance, like your beloved Alex, well, it is in its nature to kill. It will use its skills to secure a kill, but it will also put itself at risk. This is in its nature. The opportunity cannot be passed up. And therefore, with a little ingenuity, the wolf easily becomes a target. Feared and revered, when it is known that a creature will exploit anything, it can be used against them. The wolf will be tricked, just by its very nature. And when you know that you are up against a wolf, well you have to use the wolf. You must use its tenacity, its persistence, its determination to trick it. You see, the hunters in the cold and unforgiving regions of the north use only two things to catch a wolf. An opportunity and a means of exploiting it. They take a knife and they sharpen it like a razor. Afterwards, they simply dip it in blood and allow the blood to freeze. They repeat this until the blade is heavy and thick with frozen blood. Then, they melt some ice, either with warm blood or their own piss, and then ram the handle of the knife into the melted ice. It freezes in no time at all. What then? They hide? They call the wolf? No. They simply leave the blade for the wolf to find. The wolf smells the blood, watches, but sees no sign of a trap, nothing but the blood. The wolf sniffs the blood, then starts to lick. It licks the blood, cold and hard. Its warm tongue melts the blood, and soon the wolf's tongue is slashed to pieces. Its mouth is cut and bleeding, but the blood adds to the taste, the frenzy it finds itself in. Blood, blood, more blood. Warm and delicious; its tongue numb from the lacerations. The wolf cannot believe how easy this meal has been to find, to exploit. But soon, the wolf is bleeding terribly, soon the wolf is weakening as it bleeds and bleeds and bleeds; yet continues to feed, to drink its own blood. The wolf is dying but does not realise. Not even at the end, when the wolf finally collapses and dies…" she paused. "You see, you are the bloodied knife. King is the wolf. He is doing my bidding, but he will die doing it…" She nodded to The Beast and he walked around the table and pulled Caroline roughly to her feet. "Because he's performing certain tasks for me. I suppose to buy you time while he mounts a grand rescue. It won't work out that way, but I guess he's desperate enough to believe he has a chance."

"What tasks?" asked Caroline, as she was propelled forwards and walked in front of them.

Helena said nothing as they reached a door and The Beast pushed Caroline up against the wall. Helena opened the door, then caught Caroline by the arm, linking her own inside. They stepped outside and to any casual observer, it could have looked like two old friends meeting for the first time in an age.

"Your man is a killer. I'm merely using him for business."

"He's killed, but he's done it for the right side," Caroline corrected her, but already she felt a sinking feeling.

"I was part of the Bratva, the brotherhood," she paused. "The Russian mafia. Well, I suppose I wasn't as much a part of it, as a sex slave for it. They used and abused me, degraded me. Sold me, bought me back, hired me out. But I learned many things. About myself, and about them…"

"I'm sorry," Caroline said. She meant it and sounded sincere. But she knew she wasn't going to win over this woman.

"I learned that vengeance is a dish best served cold, as they say. I also learned how powerplay works. That if someone in power dies, how you can exploit that position entirely."

Helena slowed her pace as they reached a stone-built barn. It had been refurbished, fitted with windows, but Caroline noticed that the windows were barred.

On the inside.

"What do you mean?" Caroline asked, to bide time as much as understand.

"King has killed two prominent brotherhood bosses for me. I had the resources and insight in place to take over. To appeal to those who were left, shown them that my way would be the best for all concerned."

"What? In the brief time since the rug was pulled from under you?" Caroline asked incredulously.

"I had no options open to me. I am a fugitive. I had some money in a few offshore accounts, got the funds out in time. Bought bitcoins, mined and sold them on. Digital currency quickly becomes untraceable. But what I had to give me my in, to get me ahead, was a great many contacts within the brotherhoods," Helena paused. She stood aside while The Beast stepped around Caroline and opened the door. It was padlocked and bolted from outside. "This has been up and running for years," she said, sweeping her hand across the façade of the building. "Come see inside…"

Caroline followed tentatively. She could hear voices, but they were hushed tones and the voices soon stopped altogether when the door closed again behind them. The light was dim. There was a dank smell, the odour of fear and of poor hygiene. Her legs felt so heavy, it was an effort to maintain forward motion. She knew she was being toyed with. She knew she was about to see something terrible, and as hard as it was to move, she felt compelled to discover what secrets lay within this prison. For any building locked from outside with people within, was exactly that.

Helena smiled, but it was a mirthless, crocodile smile. "This is what your boyfriend has killed for," she said. "To save you from this…"

Caroline rounded the end of the corridor and stopped when she saw the Perspex viewing panel. "What is this?" she asked, her eyes transfixed.

The room on the other side of the panel was approximately five-metres by twenty-five. At some time or other it had housed animals because the remains of the stalls were clearly visible where the blocks had been removed, and there were still metal cattle ties in place. Most were hanging uselessly, but a woman had been handcuffed to one of them and there were welts on her bare back. Another woman was giving her a drink from a dirty bottle. It was water, but it looked cloudy. The woman was drinking thirstily.

"Ignore her," Helena said. "She was naughty. Tried to escape. Jurgen here, gave her a lesson."

Caroline shuddered at the thought of The Beast whipping the poor woman. She shook her head. "Who are they?"

"Trash. Waifs and strays," Helena said lightly. "Girls wanting comfortable jobs in the west. A better life. Ironic really…"

"You're sick!" Caroline snapped.

"I'm a realist."

"You said you were in the sex industry, forced into it by the Russian mafia," Caroline paused, looked at her in bewilderment. "Have you no feeling for them? You've inflicted your own fate onto them. Worse, most probably."

Helena shook her head. "We control our own fate," she said. "Nobody was there to help me. Nobody came to my rescue…" She smiled cruelly. "… and nobody will come for you."

"I get it," Caroline said coolly. "But what happens to these girls?"

"Sex trade, mainly. Some will go back east, out to the Middle East. The blondes and the redheads. They'll be the lucky ones. They will have some sheik who will only get it up so much, and he will want them clean and well-tended to. Some of them will even enjoy the lifestyle. Others won't be so lucky and will go to super-brothels."

"Where?"

"On your own doorstep!" Helena laughed. "Right under the noses of the middle-classes. Many throughout Europe. And then there's pop-up brothels. The handlers bring the girls into a short-term house let, advertise locally and sit back and wait. A few weeks at a time, from town to town, always one step ahead of the police."

Caroline watched the women, who were looking back at her. The girls were aged from mid-teens to thirty. Some were prettier than others, but all were attractive, or would have been before their soul-sapping ordeal had started. "So, this is a holding area?"

"Of sorts."

"And you got into this line of work since…"

"It's been happening for years!" Helena interrupted. "I have taken over assets and ventures, have the men on my payroll. I offered better incentives, a clearer picture for them to work from."

"So, when do these girls get shipped out?"

"We're still testing and sorting them."

"Testing for what?" Caroline paused. "STDs?"

"Amongst other things," Helena smiled. "Keep walking."

Caroline glanced at the women again, as she walked onwards. There was a door ahead and another large room, which would have been a milking parlour once. It had been scrubbed clean and the stalls knocked down, but Caroline had spent summers on her uncle's farm as a child, and she recognised the building's former use. This next room had a hospital-style bed and medical equipment at the far end. Caroline watched as the door opened and a woman was walked in by two dirty-looking, wiry men. Another man followed, he wore a filthy white medical coat and carried a kidney dish with equipment in it. As Caroline neared, she saw it was a speculum. She stopped and stared at Helena, whose expression was impassive. "What the hell is this?"

The young woman was manhandled onto the bed and held down firmly while the man in the filthy, stained technician's coat pulled the woman's legs up and apart. Caroline took a step and went to rush forward but felt the impact of the tiny pistol on her ear. She fell forwards, sprawled on the hard, concrete floor, scraping her chin. She could hear the woman scream, heard the man grunting as he made his inspection. Caroline couldn't look, but she heard the woman scream again, then the sound of the speculum dropping into the dish. When she got back onto her feet, Caroline had tears on both her cheeks. She couldn't look at the woman, but she watched the man in the filthy medical coat labelling blood samples he had hastily extracted from the woman's arm. The woman was pulled off the bed and handled back out through the door. Caroline could see blood dripping from the woman's wrist, having travelled down her arm, the extraction points untended with cotton wool and tape, or even a sticking plaster.

"This is money," Helena said. "Keep walking."

Caroline's legs refused to move, and she felt as if she were set in cement. She could feel her heart hammering against her chest, her breathing was so rapid, she fought to catch her breath. She felt herself shoved in the back and she carried on the momentum with her first step. She was walking slowly, the door looming. "I…"

"Oh, bless you!" Helena smirked. "You're okay for a day or two," she said, then added, "As long as your boyfriend makes contact soon. He's been a naughty boy. He's killed the next man on my list, but he hasn't checked in. I do hope, for your sake, that he's not lying dead in a ditch somewhere…"

"He won't be!" Caroline snapped. "And he'll look you in the eye when he kills you, if I don't first!"

"Feisty!" Helena smiled, then looked at The Beast, her expression hardening. "Jurgen, punch her. Hard."

Caroline did not have time to dodge as The Beast punched her in the chest, hammering his meaty fist into her left breast. She yelped and fell backwards, then howled as the pain set in. She rolled on the floor, her teeth gritted and the agony for both to see on her face. Every fibre of her being wanted to stay down and recover from the pain, but she found herself dragging herself to her feet. She looked at The

Beast, sneered and said, "If that's the best you've got, then you'd better not be here when Alex turns up." She looked back at Helena. "But I don't need a man to do my dirty work. Mark my words, I'm going to kill you myself."

"Hah! Words are all you have, my dear." She pointed to the door. "Now, walk!"

Caroline did, and to her astonishment, she no longer felt the heavy legs, erratic breathing or the pounding of her heart. She held back while The Beast got the door and ahead of her she could see another Perspex panel. She was ready now. Or so she thought.

"The girls who are not good-looking enough to appeal to your average male punter are here. Well, most of them who make the grade."

"Grade?" Caroline asked curiously, but then she could see. She didn't need Helena to fill in the gaps for her.

"We have computer, or I should say web experts who can find the market. Buyers are easy to come by, transactions are made in cash or via automated bank transfers. We provide invoices for other goods, of course."

Caroline watched a heavily pregnant woman struggle into a chair. Another, seven months pregnant, or so Caroline estimated, was rubbing the lower back of a woman who looked about ready. In fact, as Caroline watched, she could see the woman panting short, sharp breaths. The woman was already in labour.

Caroline could not help the tears forming, she reached up with her handcuffed hands and rubbed them away from her eyes. "You're farming babies…"

Helena shrugged. "This has been in place for years. The dark web gives us the means and opportunity to plug a gap in the market," she paused. "I struggle to think what to do with you. You're a good-looking woman. You'll probably do well for a sheik, but you're pushing the age limit. Those horny bastards like women in their twenties, although we women knocking the door of forty know we'd certainly please them better than we would have fifteen years ago!" She laughed and shook her head. "But you don't have children, do you? I think it would be worth a try. At least one before we send you somewhere…"

Caroline lunged at her, dug her fingers into Helena's eyes and pushed her against the Perspex. The Beast was caught off-guard, but only for a moment. He smashed the butt of the pistol down onto the top of Caroline's head and she slumped to the floor. Helena was screaming, cupping her eyes tenderly, inspecting for damage amid blood and tears. She kicked out and caught Caroline in the face.

Caroline was out cold.

Helena screamed at The Beast, "Get her back into the house!" Then she gently touched the edges of her eyes, inspected the mess of crimson on her fingers. "You bitch!" she shouted, then turned and saw most of the women smiling behind the Perspex.

She turned and pushed past Jurgen, muttering in guttural Russian as she went.

42

Franschhoek, South Africa

The house was a ranch-style, or bungalow. It was constructed of wooden white-washed slats and red wooden shingle tiles on the roof. There was a modern stainless-steel chimney, the type so often paired with a wood-burning stove inside. The nights in South Africa could be cold, even in the summer. It was a tidy property, and not out of the realms of a senior intelligence service officer's finances. The house was sat square in half an acre of lawn with shrubs and trees and a gravelled driveway with a white BMW X5 taking up half of it. To the right, a larger property sat in an acre plot, the building being some seventy-metres distant. To the left; twenty metres of scrubland before a road that right-angled at a crossroads.

Rashid studied the property from across the road. The location of the house put the houses on this side of the road at sixty-metres distant. Considering what he had to do, it didn't get much better, other than a deserted farm. He was certain nobody would hear the man shout or scream, and he was confident he would be able to contain the situation. He had read the cobbled-together details on the journey over. An attachment on Ryan Beard's phone.

The man in question was an unmarried forty-year-old named Harvey Botha. He was an intelligence analyst and had been with the South African Secret Service for eleven years. His file hadn't been clean. There had been an allegation of sexual harassment, which had later been retracted. No further action had been taken. And then four years ago, there had been an embezzlement investigation. Botha had sought representation, fought the case and won his tribunal. It hadn't been cut and dried though, as the investigating team had taken shortcuts, not followed protocol and the case had been dropped. Botha had been side-lined for a promotion which should easily have been his, and his security clearance had been lowered. The man was on a short leash, and Ryan Beard's enquiry had flagged up a warning in certain circles. Funds had been traced to Botha via poorly set-up offshore accounts. Ryan Beard had not held out much hope for the SASS, but he knew that forensic accountants working for MI5 would be able to get details of the account that the money had been sent from. Neil Ramsay knew this as well, and had tasked Marnie with sending the details to the department that had worked on uncovering the terrorist organisation Anarchy to Recreate Society.

"What do you reckon?" Beard asked.

Rashid shrugged. "We need information, see if what the man knows can tell us more about Helena Snell, or Milankovitch, or whatever the hell she's calling herself."

"I'm sure your forensic accountants will get something from the account number."

"I hope so," Rashid paused. "For Caroline's sake."

"What do you mean?" Beard asked.

"You don't know?"

"Know what?"

"I thought that was why you contacted MI5?"

Beard shook his head. "What?"

"Caroline was abducted. Just over a month ago."

"Shit…"

"Exactly right. King is working for Helena Milankovitch, just to buy some time. She's using him, and she's using Caroline as collateral."

Ryan Beard seemed to ponder on this for a moment, looked at Rashid curiously. "You know her… boyfriend?"

"Yes."

Beard shrugged. "I thought he'd come out here, hell-bent on getting some payback for the attempts on her life. I kind of sold it to my contact in the SASS. I thought it would stand me in good stead. Caroline dropped his name, The Reaper's. I didn't want to be another loose end."

Rashid smiled. "Look, I don't think that would be the guy's style," he paused. "He's tough and resourceful, certainly isn't a guy to cross, but he's a decent bloke. Relax. He won't come gunning for you. So, you know his name. We all do. I gather there was some business or other in MI6 that he'd sooner forget, or have nobody know about, but he's one of the good guys."

Beard nodded. "So, you'll kill Botha?"

"I'll question him," Rashid said. "After that, we'll have to see how it pans out."

"But my contact was adamant," Beard protested. "That's the deal for giving him up. That's the deal for the account number I gave you!"

"Come on," Rashid said. He opened the door of the SUV and signalled across the street for Ramsay to follow. He turned back to the MI6 officer. "I never made a deal with the South African Secret Service."

"But I did!" Beard protested. "I agreed that in return for any information the British intelligence services get from Botha, and for the account number they have already given up, Botha would be eliminated!"

"Well, you best live up to your end of the bargain," Rashid said coldly.

43

Stockholm, Sweden

"So, no plans of the building?"

"No." King fished a piece of paper out of his pocket and handed it to Simon Grant. Grant unfolded it, frowned as he studied the drawing. "What?"

"You have kids?"

"No. Why?"

"I thought you were showing me something they'd scribbled out in nursery."

"Nice."

Grant handed it back. "I need better than that," he said.

"Good. Seeing you don't like my plan of the building, you can do a recce yourself."

"When?"

King looked at his watch. "About an hour. Leave your car here, I don't want you getting lost following me."

Grant shook his head. "No. You follow *me* home. We'll leave my car there to avoid suspicion. I can't leave it here on school grounds. While I'm there, I'll grab some tools."

"Thought you were out of that game."

"I am, but I have some tools that will get us in. We'll go to Sodertalje to scout out the post office, have some dinner, go back after dark and do the job.

After that, I'll go back home, and we'll never see each other again."

King studied the man for a moment. He seemed tougher than when he had last seen him. Fresh out of prison, railroaded into working for London criminals and the IRA. Then coerced to work for MI6. King couldn't blame him now. The man had long-thought he had been in the clear. Lived a good life in Sweden and had more to lose now than he ever had before. He had his freedom now, his wife, a grown-up son and another child. He had it all to lose, whereas before, he had lost everything and had it all to gain.

King already knew where Simon and Lisa Grant lived. He had checked before, knew more about the man than he would ever let on. There were many people King kept tabs on. Some were old friends he would consider being able to call upon in times of need. Others were people he had given the benefit of the doubt to. It never hurt to keep your friends close and your enemies closer. And then there were the people who were connected to fallen comrades. He never visited them, many would not even be aware he even existed. But he had bestowed acts of kindness upon them from time to time in one form or another. He had started this life almost twenty-years ago, drawn into a fight with a group of Royal Marines in a drinking den in Portsmouth. That night had changed his life. Two men had been killed in a savage brawl and King had fled, only to be captured and tried for murder. His recruiter and MI6 trainer, Peter Stewart, had arranged for his escape, provided the body of a homeless man, who had died of hypothermia on a London street, to be substituted for King in a bog on Dartmoor and Mark Jeffries had ceased to exist. And good riddance to him. A brawler, a chancer and a troublemaker. Alex King had been born, as he had been whisked away that night, and became a better man. He had learned much over the years, but he couldn't forget, and he had made regular payments to the families of those two dead soldiers ever since.

His penance.

Simon Grant had picked up his things and met King in his hire car around the street corner twenty-minutes later. King did not ask if he had spoken to his wife, although he suspected he had. That was Grant's business, and they were not exactly buddies. The drive southwest to Sodertalje was both quiet and taken up by early weekend traffic out of Stockholm. King checked his watch regularly, imperative they arrive at the post office with enough time for Grant to check out the inside of the building. When they arrived in Sodertalje they had forty-minutes to spare. King drove around the block twice, checking where he had thought he saw a curtain twitch all those weeks ago. The house had a for rent sign outside it. He guessed it had been rented solely to act as an observation position to watch King take delivery of the package which would change his life. And Caroline's too.

Simon Grant had walked into the post office ten-minutes before. He was enquiring on the premise of setting up a safe box before he set about travelling throughout Sweden. Somewhere to keep his tickets, credit cards he didn't plan on using, his passport even. With any luck he would get a quick tour of what facilities they had, terms and conditions, even what security they provided.

King could see the entrance to the post office, saw Grant come outside at closing time. He carried what looked like a folded brochure and an envelope. He walked unhurriedly, apparently without a care. King knew the man would have much on his mind, not least the situation he now found himself in, but he would be concentrating on the layout, committing it to memory.

Grant reached the car and got inside. He took a pen out of his pocket, and a notepad. He glanced at King, then started to sketch out the floor-plan. "Don't say anything," he said. "I need to concentrate."

King remained silent. He watched the post office, saw the woman pulling in a sign and closing the door behind her. It was the same woman that he had pathetically flirted with when he enquired earlier. He had been right not to go back in with Grant. A blind pulled down on the window. King figured there would be things to do, protocols to maintain. He imagined the woman cashing up the register, reconciliating the credit card terminal. He had no idea how to do all of that, but he'd seen it done and knew it was one of many behind-the-scenes tasks that businesses had to perform each day.

Grant had sketched out a detailed record of what he had seen inside the post office. King thought his own sketch had looked like a six-year-old's in comparison. He thought nothing more of it. Grant's was accurate and professional, and he would be working off his own plan.

"Standard PIR, or Passive Infrared," said Grant.

"I know what it stands for," King commented flatly.

"Well, I can re-route that, and I can get the alarm sorted, as long as the delay isn't stupidly quick."

"Good. But I'm sensing a but..."

"How are you going to get the computer logged onto the server and overcome any password protection?"

"You let me worry about that."

"Fine," said Grant curtly. "And you don't need to get into the saferoom?"

"Just the server."

"The server is in the office behind the counter. I saw it when she stepped out around the counter to show me the safe room," Grant nodded. "We should be okay then." He looked at his watch, glanced at the sky. There were still a couple hours of light left.

"*Should* be okay?"

Grant shrugged. "It will have a silent alarm for sure. I'm hoping it will be part of the master unit."

"Right…"

"I still don't see how you will get into that server."

King nodded. "I'll see to that," he said. "The silent alarm worries me. I should have thought about it. This is a bit rushed."

"You don't have much time, do you," Grant commented.

"I think I've already run out, pushed what little leeway I had."

"Nothing like having all you care about at stake, is there?"

King nodded. The man had been recruited the day he had left prison. His estranged wife had moved on but was in an abusive relationship and wanted out. His son had seen more than any child should have. Grant had been bullied and conned into one last job, his family dangled in front of him like a carrot. Before he could draw breath, he was working with an IRA splinter cell and then whisked up by MI6. If anybody knew what it was to be used and keep false hope, it was Simon Grant. And yet still, the man had made a break for it, managed to get word to his family and steal the money from both the criminal who had conned him and the IRA who had hunted him.

"How did it happen?"

King could feel his heart race. *Because I should have been there! Because I let emotion get in the way!* Instead, he said, "It was after a mission. Mopping up the details. Caroline, my fiancé, had been lucky to survive. I checked she was okay, but I went after one of the terrorists. When I got back, she was gone…"

"You haven't learned a thing," Grant said.

"What?"

"In France, all those years ago. If you hadn't blindly chased Forsyth out of the house and into the dunes, then you wouldn't have lost both me and the money…"

"Piss off!" King snapped. But he knew deep down it had been true. "I found you all those years ago, let you go free because you and your wife and child had such a shit time," he said coldly.

Grant held up his hand. "I know," he said. "And I thank you from the bottom of my heart. But you should know, a sense of justice or even revenge, only serves one purpose and it is *never* worthwhile. Tell me; did chasing this person, whatever they did, or whatever you did to them when you caught up with them, make losing Caroline an acceptable cost?"

"Of course not!"

"Then make sure you never find yourself in this situation again," Grant paused. "Don't be blinded. Look at the whole picture. Vengeance solves no purpose if it gets in the way of the ones you love. Look at what lengths you would go to for Caroline.

Look at what this person has made you do, how easy it was for them to own you. Love is the strongest emotion, but it can so easily be used against you by those who would do you harm."

King frowned. He said nothing as he started the engine and slammed the car into gear. He took off quickly and performed a U-turn in the road.

Grant fumbled with his seat belt. "Where are we going?"

King didn't answer. He was well and truly irked. But what hurt the most, was knowing that Simon Grant was right. He knew that he was running out of time, and he was not going to waste any more of it on fool's errands.

44

South Africa

Rashid wrapped his fingers around the chunky butt of the Sig Sauer P225 9mm pistol. He had already checked that the magazine was full, and the first round had been chambered. Safety off, finger resting on the frame, hammer cocked. He preferred to cock the hammer – the weapon's double-action trigger pull was off-putting and never made for the most accurate first shot.

The plan had been hastily cobbled together. Marnie was an analyst and computer technician. She would stay in the car and had no aspirations to do anything different. It had been over twenty-four hours and she was still seething towards Rashid for suggesting she come to South Africa with them, even more so each time he gave her a cheeky wink.

Not a trained or experienced field agent, but flexible and willing to give most things a go, Neil Ramsay had slipped around the house and positioned himself at the back door. He had simply shrugged when Rashid had told him what to do, replying that he had been a useful Rugby fly-half at school and university and could throw himself around the legs of any man who ran from him, and wasn't scared to either.

That left Beard and Rashid to go in the front. Rashid would hang back, let Beard do the talking. He was an experienced hand on the continent and had been in South Africa a few years. He looked at ease, and although the tan was not a factor with Rashid, he didn't have the most welcoming of appearances. Something that had helped him blend into his infiltration with ISIS, but not somebody you'd want to turn up on your doorstep. For that reason, he would hang back out of sight. They had decided against a hard entrance. If Botha was a man who had sold secrets and sacrificed one of his colleagues, then the chances are he would take his own well-being seriously enough to have security in place. That may simply be a heavy series of door locks, or a loaded shotgun in the hallway. Botha was unmarried and had no immediate family. A loaded gun close to hand was of no consequence to the safety of a child or family member. South Africa was a country dominated by violent crime, most houses would have a firearm of some description.

Ryan Beard hesitated at the front door, glanced at Rashid, who glared at him and signalled him with the muzzle of the pistol to get on with it. He knocked firmly and stood back a pace. There was no reply. He waited twenty-seconds, knocked again. A few seconds later there was a faint and muffled voice through the door.

"Who is it?"

"Police," Beard said. He glanced at Rashid, who was staring at him blankly. Beard shrugged. It had been agreed to simply ask for assistance using Botha's phone to call a tow-truck, in lieu of his dead mobile phone battery. He'd gone off-piste, had little choice but to go with it. "There was an accident on the road between here and Coopertown yesterday, I'm following up with witness statements," he paused. "I'd like to ask some questions, see if we can build a picture."

Rashid flexed his fingers around the butt of the pistol, tightened his grip. He was glaring at Beard.

"I didn't leave the house yesterday," came the muffled reply.

"If you could just open the door, please."

"Show me your ID."

And there it is, thought Rashid. *All gone to shit...*

He edged forwards, keeping his body against the wall. He then suddenly seemed to realise that the wall was constructed from timber, hesitated for a moment then crouched low.

Beard took out a wallet, thumbed through and held it up to the peephole quickly. All he had was his MI6 ID, but it did not say MI6 anywhere on it, and simply had a photo and small print. The MI6, or Secret Intelligence Service insignia was small. He hoped a quick flash would be ok. He glanced at Rashid, flustered and flushed red. He knew he'd messed up. He dropped the wallet on the decking and hurriedly bent down to retrieve it.

The door splintered at the same time as the almighty boom resonated and splinters of wood and lead shot that had slowed through the thick wooden door covered Beard's back. Beard stood back up, shocked at the noise, but realised his mistake. He tried to dodge both left and right but was frozen and hampered by indecision. There was a loud and metallic 'click-clack' from behind the door.

Rashid was moving. He barrelled into Beard and fell onto his right side as Beard was thrown clear of the doorway and landed in a heap out of range. The second shotgun blast opened-up another eight-inch diameter hole next to the first. Rashid was already firing, putting three shots through the holes and another just clipping the wood a few inches to the right. He knew he was firing from a low enough angle for the bullets to have sailed cleanly in front of a man standing three-feet back from the door. And Botha would have to be to accommodate the length of a shotgun, and the size of the spread pattern which had punched cleanly through as complete holes, rather than like Swiss cheese.

Another 'click-clack' of the pump-action and another blast powered through, connecting the two holes. Rashid felt the splinters hit his face, but he was already up and had jammed the pistol through the group of holes. He heard: 'click' as Botha worked the action back, ejecting the .12-gauge cartridge, and

Rashid fired four shots into the unknown. There was a yelp and a thud, and the sound of the shotgun hitting a hard, wooden floor. Rashid had already pulled back, putting himself behind the door-jamb. He swung around, aimed a kick at the door.

Nothing.

He kicked again, and again.

Nothing.

Ramsay appeared around the edge of the house. He caught sight of Beard on the ground, of Rashid kicking the door. He glanced at a heavy planter, caught hold of it and heaved it through the window. The glass gave, as did the clay planter and Ramsay punched out the remaining pieces of glass.

"Rashid!" he shouted.

Rashid was already moving and bounded across the decking, throwing himself cleanly through the window. He landed unceremoniously on the floor but got himself back up and out of the lounge towards the hall.

Botha was sliding himself backwards on the polished wood floor, pushing with his feet. He had the shotgun in his hands, pushed the pump-action forwards with a 'clack' and brought the weapon around on Rashid.

Rashid aimed, but did not have time to try and wound Botha, so double-tapped and stepped back into the lounge as the two 9mm bullets slammed through the man's midriff and into the floor behind him. He ducked his head back out and saw that Botha wasn't going anywhere. He stepped forwards, kicked the shotgun away and headed for the door. There were three serious-looking deadbolts and a five-lever lock. Rashid undid them, turned the key and pulled the door inwards.

Beard was dazed, but on his feet. Ramsay was breathless, his shirt-tails had come out and his white shirt was covered in red earth from the planter. Rashid looked past them, saw Marnie standing beside the Mercedes. She looked indecisive, had got out of the vehicle but was not sure if she should come and assist. Rashid beckoned her over. It would be better to keep together. He doubted whether the three shotgun blasts from inside the house would have been heard in the neighbourhood, but the volley of 9mm outside certainly would have. But this was South Africa, and people seemed to shoot regularly at the road signs. A semi-rural suburb like this may just absorb the sound. Or, the police could already be on the way.

"Containment," Ramsay said. He looked up at Beard and tossed him the keys to the Mercedes. "Bring both cars off the road and park them nose out." He turned to Marnie, who was staring at the blood on the floor, and Botha, who was not looking in the best of health. "Find the man's computer and get into it. We want to see banking history. And drain his files."

Marnie nodded and fished in her handbag for some USB sticks and an algorithm stick, which had been designed by GCHQ to find what she was interested in. A simple plug and play piece of hardware. She hesitated, then realised it was down to her to find Botha's computer. She walked across the hall, slipped in some blood and righted herself quickly. She grimaced, glared again at Rashid as she walked past. She was not enjoying her introduction to working in the field.

"Right, get him into the kitchen," said Ramsay.

Rashid was about to question him but shrugged and tucked the pistol into his waistband and bent down and caught hold of Botha by his shoulders. Ramsay took the legs and between them, they padded across the hall and by deduction, walked across the hall and into a large and well-appointed kitchen and diner.

"Pull out the chair," he said to Rashid.

Botha was in and out, groaning and on the cusp of unconsciousness. Ramsay dropped the man's legs when Rashid positioned him on the chair. Rashid stepped back, wiped his brow with his sleeve and watched as Ramsay took his mobile phone out and fiddled with the screen. He set the voice memo function and placed it down carefully on the kitchen table. Next, he removed a small graphite box from his pocket. Rashid could see that the box was marked: Insulin. Not that Ramsay was a diabetic – it was merely a ruse for airport authorities and customs officers. It was complete with a doctor's letter outlining Ramsay's medical needs.

Ramsay opened the box and picked up the first syringe. He twisted off the cap and revealed an enormously thick needle approximately four-inches long.

"We're way past a thorough interrogation," he explained. "A shot of adrenalin to stop him going down the drain, and then straight into sodium panthenol." He looked at Rashid, who looked puzzled. "Truth serum, I suppose. A large dose could cause brain damage, but I don't think that will be of any consequence, considering his condition and the brief." Rashid didn't speak. He'd killed many times, especially on the battlefield, but this all seemed quite clinical. He watched as Ramsay prepared the needle, wouldn't be so quick to discount the man's field abilities in future.

"Right, open up his shirt," Ramsay told him.

Rashid got back in the game, decisively catching hold of both sides of the shirt and ripping the buttons off. There were four bullet holes in his chest and stomach, one was bleeding badly, but the other three seemed to have sealed closed. He stepped back, wiped his hands on a tea towel and noticed the two exit wounds in the man's back. He could see Botha wasn't going anywhere. He doubted the man would live more than ten-minutes. There would be untold damage inside him.

Ramsay held the syringe like a knife, then pushed the man's chin back and stabbed him in the centre of his chest, straight through the wall of his chest cavity and into the heart. Botha wrenched himself upright and inhaled deeply. His legs kicked out wildly then went rigid, almost forcing himself backwards, had the chair not banged into the table and stopped him from going any further. Botha looked at them, grimaced then started to chatter.

"Who are you? What are you doing in my house?" He looked down at his stomach, then back at Ramsay. "Get me a doctor!"

"All in due course," Ramsay said, as he prepared the next vial. This time, the needle was far smaller. He looked at Rashid. "Get a vein up."

Rashid had done paramedicine training in the SAS. He snapped to, unfastened Botha's belt and pulled it clear of the loops. He wrapped it tightly around the man's bicep. Botha attempted to resist, but his new lease of life was in the mental, not the physical presence. His forearm started to change colour, and the veins in the crux of his elbow were more prominent. Ramsay bent down and carefully administered the dose of sodium panthenol. He stood back, looked up as Ryan Beard entered the room, clearly shocked by the sight of the man in the chair, the injuries he had sustained and the treatment he was receiving at the hands of the apparently bookish and rather forgettable looking man from MI5.

"Go and check on Marnie," Rashid said to Beard. "See if she needs help searching, then go and stand guard at the front door." He looked back at Ramsay. "How long does it take?"

Ramsay looked at his watch. "About five-minutes," he said. "We can start now though, see where it goes." He caught hold of Botha's chin, looked him in the eyes. He was in and out, like he'd seen off two bottles of wine and was trying to appear sober. Ramsay clicked his fingers in front of the man's face. Botha seemed oblivious. "I'm going to ask you about money in your offshore account," he said. "We have your account number, have seen the dates of the deposits and the amounts… I want to know where the money came from."

Botha's head lolled. "The Russian…" he said slowly. His mouth didn't seem to correspond with his words. The facial muscles were affected by the drug, the voice slurred. It looked like Botha was well into the third bottle now. "The woman…" he added. "Not the man…" he paused. "He was here last year… to shoot…"

"Viktor Bukov?"

"Victor…" Botha nodded.

"You met him?" Ramsay prompted.

Botha nodded.

"And the woman," Ramsay paused, watching the man's eyes. He caught hold of his wrist, checked for a pulse and glanced at his watch. The man's pulse was over one-fifty. His heart couldn't sustain the dose of sodium panthenol, nor the dramatic blood loss and whatever damage the 9mm bullets had done internally. "Who was the woman?"

"The... billionaire's wife," Botha said, but started to gasp for breath. "Snell..."

"Her name?"

"Helena..."

"What did she ask of you?"

He gasped again, his mouth opening and closing like a landed fish. "To... help the sniper in and out of the country," he paused, his head lolling listlessly from side to side. Another gasp. "And to block the British agent investigating..."

"What do you mean by block?" Ramsay asked.

"I... I don't feel well..."

"You'll be fine," Ramsay said curtly. "An ambulance has been called and is on its way. Now, what did Helena Snell mean by block?"

"Kill," Botha paused. He seemed to have trouble swallowing now. "I was asked to arrange for someone to kill her. To buy her and Bukov time..."

Ramsay turned to Rashid and said, "Get him some water."

Rashid did as he was asked and took a glass off the draining board, filled it and handed it to Ramsay, who was checking Botha's forehead with the back of his hand. He took the glass and offered the man a drink.

"He's burning up," Ramsay said. "He's about to go pop."

Rashid shrugged like it was nothing. "Well, hurry up, then," he urged. "We need a link to Helena. Not a back story…"

"I'm doing it!" Ramsay snapped. He tipped the remainder of the glass on the man's head and the water cascaded over his face and neck. Botha appeared not to notice. He pulled the man's eyelid up and could see they were dilated. They were also red, blood vessels had burst, most probably due to the man's high pulse. He checked Botha's wrist again, frowned. He monitored it for fifteen seconds, then looked up at Rashid. "Over two-hundred…"

"Can't sustain that with the gunshot wounds…"

"Nor the temperature," Ramsay paused. He snapped his fingers in front of Botha's face, then gave his cheek a gentle tap. The man was dazed and appeared intoxicated to the point of passing out. Ramsay stood up. "I could give another shot of adrenalin…"

Rashid shrugged. "Not my area of expertise."

Ramsay went back to the graphite box and drew a small amount into the syringe with the large needle. He checked for air, tapped the side and held it ready. "Hold him, would you?"

Rashid caught hold of the man's shoulders and braced. Ramsay brought the needle down through the chest wall and into the heart. Botha went rigid and kicked out, catching Ramsay in the shin. The man cursed and hobbled on the spot for a moment. He put the syringe back in the box and crouched down to look the man in the eyes.

"The ambulance is near," he lied. "You're going to be alright. I need you to tell us where Helena is. Where the Russian woman is," he said slowly. "I need to know how to contact her."

"She called me… the man, Bukov, gave me a cell phone…"

"What do you mean?"

Botha gasped, clutched his chest. He grimaced, spoke through gritted teeth. He couldn't resist the sodium panthenol, the urge to unburden and cooperate. "Bukov gave me a cell. It had her number on it…" He sucked air through his teeth. He was soaked in sweat, had started to shiver. "One number only… must keep it switched off… contact by text… turn it on at midnight, then every three hours for five minutes only… she will text back when she's ready…"

"Where is the phone?" Ramsay asked. He could see Botha shutting down, breathing less, his eyes fading. "Tell me!"

Rashid pushed his fingers deep into the carotid artery, on the left side of the man's throat. "Faint pulse," he said. "He's gone."

"Damn it!" Ramsay snapped the graphite box shut and put it back in his pocket. He picked up the glass and walked it to the sink where he washed it with detergent and left it in the sink. He rubbed the taps with the tea towel. "Let's try and find that phone," he said.

45

Caroline had regained consciousness before The Beast had returned her to her room. She had lolled over his shoulder, his body odour rancid and almost enough to make her gag. He had taken the stairs as if her weight had been unnoticeable. He was a huge man, his back as wide as a cart-horse. He smelled about as bad as one, too.

She knew he would try something when they reached the room. She managed to get the wingnut out of its hiding place, tucked into her bra, and got it between the knuckles of her right hand. The metal protruded over a quarter of an inch. Enough to make a mess of his eye if she could get a punch there quick enough. The shock and pain would disable him, perhaps only temporarily, but she would not stop there. Like she had been taught by her krav maga instructor, the service's close quarters combat instructors, and by Alex - who she sparred with as part of their fitness regime - she would just keep hitting, gouging and striking until The Beast stopped moving.

And she wouldn't stop there.

The Beast took the stairs easily. Her heart was pounding, not only because she knew that the man would be intent on violating her, but because she knew that the time had come.

She would fight or die.

It would be as simple as that, because if The Beast overpowered her, she knew he would not stop until he got what he wanted. And she would never allow that.

Not over her dead body.

The door had been left open. The Beast was tall enough to have to duck down under the doorframe. Caroline would put him at six-feet-six. His frame was large; muscular underneath an ample covering of fat. Caroline felt the weightlessness as she was tossed through the air and landed on the bed. The mattress was old and most probably a poor-quality item when it had been purchased, and she felt the slats of the bed against her spine as she landed heavily and bounced once. She gave up feigning unconsciousness, looked up at him with contempt.

"Convenient," he said, his accent thick and guttural. Barely pronouncing the vowels. "So good for you to be awake for this…"

Caroline tucked her legs up, turning herself into a ball. She was frightened, but it was also an integral part of her act. She would appear submissive, strike like lightening when he thought he had the upper hand.

"Jurgen!" Michael appeared in the doorway. He spoke Russian. A short sentence, but Caroline could make out Helena's name. It was spoken like an instruction.

The Beast looked at Michael sternly, then back at Caroline. He shrugged, then said, "Later sweet one. Later I will show you, *teach* you a lesson…"

Michael glanced at Caroline, held the door open for Jurgen, then closed the door behind them both. Caroline could hear the bolt slamming back in place, the sound of the padlock hasp locking tightly. She had been close, but was now a prisoner once again.

46

King was seated in the departure lounge at Stockholm Arlanda airport. He had eaten open snow-crab sandwiches with lemon and dill mayonnaise at a concession stall, dressed-up to look like a street food stall. It wasn't exactly convincing in its execution, but it offered him a chance to sit at the counter on a barstool and observe the rest of the lounge, and it was quiet which meant that nobody would be waiting for his seat or bother him with inane conversation. The server cleared away his plate and he turned his side to her while he washed the sandwiches down with a cold *Mariestads* beer.

He took out his mobile phone and scrolled through his address book. He thought about it for the third time in as many hours, decided against it again and slipped the phone back into his jacket pocket. He could not order things. It was like playing chess and thinking five moves ahead. He knew he was on the cusp of his mental capabilities. Helena Milankovitch was as devious and ruthless as anyone he'd ever been up against. But it was more than that. The tasks he had completed over the past couple of weeks and the threat of Caroline's life hanging over him had been both physically and emotionally draining. He was starting to over-think things, doubt his chances of success. Sweden had been a case in point. He had over-thought the importance of the post office. The effort and risk involved in gaining access to that computer server was a move too far. If he could find an image of the person planting the letter and the phone in the safety deposit box, but what then? Sweden was to be the turning point, because Simon Grant had unwittingly laid it out for him.

Love is the strongest emotion, but it can so easily be used against you by those who would do you harm…

And with that, King had the answer he needed, the key to winning this duel with Helena Milankovitch. He had missed it in Italy. But he knew that he could find out what he needed to in France.

King scrolled through his mobile phone again. He found the number for the fourth time and dialled. The ring tone reached a count for three before it was picked up.

"Took your time…"

"Had a few things to work out," replied King.

"Done now?"

"Pretty much."

"Where are you?"

"Sweden. Just checking out."

"Where next?"

"France. Unfinished business."

"Really?"

"I think I've found an in."

"Think?"

"It's not going to be easy."

"It never is."

"It's going to get dirty."

"It always does."

"I'm going to need your help."

"Figured as much."

"Can I count on you?"

"You have to ask?"

"Over and above."

"Always."

"I'll text the details."

"You'll owe me."

"Call it a pint?"

"Call it two."

"Shit, the rate doubled."

"You still owe me."

"Hang tight, I'll text you where and when." King ended the call and smiled. He looked up at the monitor with the flight details and boarding gate numbers. His flight was now boarding. He drained the remnants of his beer and smiled.

Home stretch.

47

Rashid slipped his phone back into his pocket and opened the balcony doors. Ramsay was seated on the king-sized bed, a brandy and soda in one hand, his mobile phone in the other, eyes transfixed on the screen. Marnie had taken up position at the dresser. She was seated in the room's only chair and was connected to the hotel's Wi-Fi, linked through the MI5 server at Thames House and was call-conferencing with a technician with GCHQ. She wore wireless headphones with a wraparound mouthpiece and her fingers danced across the keyboard with the ease and deftness of a concert pianist. Beside her, Botha's phone was open with a USB jack connecting it to the laptop. Botha's laptop was running a reverse malware that would open his files without security settings. The connection to the running software not only broke Botha's four-digit screen lock, but sent the details to GCHQ, where specialist equipment was running both a GPS history of Botha's phone and the phone he was connected to. A picture was being built, created through cell grids, satellite relays and network masts.

"Important call?" Ramsay asked without looking up.

"Just me Mam," Rashid replied. "She worries so…"

Ramsay shrugged. "Mothers…" he said somewhat cynically, his eyes not leaving the screen of his phone. He continued to scroll. "You'd tell us if your pal King ever got in touch, wouldn't you?"

"Absolutely."

"Good."

"He's *your* pal as well, right?"

"Of course."

Rashid picked up his bottle of Heineken and sipped. He had decided on just one beer tonight, they had all decided on a drink, but it was a de-stressing tool, nothing more. They weren't about to set Cape Town alight, but they needed something to calm them all down after the visit to Botha's house. Ramsay had been distant. He had administered the dose of sodium panthenol, and the two shots of adrenalin had made the man's heart beat like a drum. The MI5 field liaison officer did not seem comfortable with the way things had gone. Marnie had been quiet. Although she had not seen anything of the interrogation, she had seen more than her emit in the hallway. She had washed her shoes off in the sink in Ramsay's room, as if washing the memory away as much as the blood in her tread.

Rashid perched on the edge of the second bed. Ramsay had secured three rooms, but they were using Marnie's room as the hub. Marnie had been on her laptop for over an hour, ever since they had bid Ryan Beard goodbye and returned to the Victoria and Alfred Hotel.

"I put enough lead in Botha for him to die," Rashid said quietly. "He may have got to hospital, but he wouldn't have left. Besides, that was the deal for getting the information on him and access to him from the secret service."

Ramsay drained his glass and placed it on the bedside table. "Why are you telling me this?"

Rashid shrugged. "I've killed before," he said. "And I killed Botha. That's all you need to take away from this."

Ramsay nodded, smiled sagely. "Thanks."

"Got it!" Marnie said triumphantly. "The IP address used for the transfer. And in turn, an address to the registered user."

"Where?"

"Kensington," she said. "But no surprise there, it's Helena Snell's property. Or at least registered to Ian Snell's estate."

"Damn it!" Ramsay snapped.

"No," she said. "The IP address of the laptop has shown up at two separate locations."

"Where?"

"Georgia."

"America?" Rashid asked.

Marnie looked at him with enough contempt to show she was not over leaving her comfortable office in Thames House. And she blamed nobody else but Rashid. She wasn't getting over it anytime soon. "No. The one next to Russia. Former USSR satellite country. Skhimili, to be precise. A small village or town near K'ut'aisi. Sandwiched between the Caucasus Mountains and the Lesser Caucasus Mountains."

"Oh, yes. That one," Rashid smiled.

"Where else?" Ramsay asked.

"Stockholm." She looked at Rashid and sneered. "That's in Sweden."

"Nice…"

"You two!" Ramsay said tersely. He shook his head. "So, square one. The letter mentioned a safety deposit box in Sodertalje, a town outside of Stockholm. King went there and now two Russian mafia syndicates have been hit. Their leaders killed, at the very least. Helena Milankovitch had mafia links, in that she worked for them…"

"Was *forced* to work for them," Marnie interrupted. "There's a tremendous difference."

"Why?" Ramsay countered.

"Because one way indicates a desire to take over, to use what she knows to get the opposition out of the way and broach onto their territories," she paused, rubbed her tired eyes. "And the other means that this could be nothing to do with her wanting to branch out and everything to do with her wanting to pay them back. For the life she was forced to live, or for something else altogether."

Ramsay nodded. "Okay. Well, we've got nothing more to go on here," he said. "We need to get to where that laptop was previously used. Sweden is my bet, the logical place to go. It's where King was summoned. In the meantime, you can still work with Thames House and GCHQ to find that bank account. Internet access permitting, that is. Get on the phone for updates whenever you can."

Marnie glanced at Rashid. He could see she was not pleased to be going to Sweden. And nor was he, because it was a dead-end.

Marnie leaned back in the chair and sighed. "I'm fried. Are we eating anytime soon?"

Ramsay shrugged and looked at his watch. "It's getting late," he said quietly. "You two go and eat. You can leave all this running, can't you?"

Marnie nodded. "Sure. I'll grab a bite to eat and see what's happening when I get back."

Ramsay nodded. "Okay then. We're done for the day, unless of course, you can see any developments when you get back from dinner. I'm going back to my room, taking a shower and hitting the room service," he paused. "Marnie, you can book our flights to Stockholm."

"I think that's a waste of time," Rashid said quickly.

"Why?" Ramsay asked sharply.

"I think follow the trail to Russia. Or Georgia, at least. Helena Milankovitch is Russian, she worked with those dead mafia hoods around the Black Sea towns, we have GPS coordinates to a Georgian town…"

"But this started in Sweden," Ramsay corrected him.

"It started in Russia," Rashid argued.

"Georgia," Marnie corrected him.

"Whatever… But it started with Helena Milankovitch. And it started in Georgia many years before she became Helena Snell, a billionaire's wife and a long time before she left something in a safety deposit box in Sweden."

48

Georgia

She could not succumb to sleeping. She was nearing total exhaustion, but could not let down her guard enough, not even for the quick five minutes the weaker part of her brain bartered for in the darkness.

She had eaten some crisps and a sort of cheese turnover sealed in a plastic packet. She had squeezed the edge, watched the air build inside as she had tested for a pin-prick, the slightest puncture which could have administered another drug. Michael had quickly provided her with the food, as well as another can of cola. She was still undecided about him. Had he been the man in her room? The man pushing at the wedged door? When she had seen The Beast, she had started to believe Michael's protestations, but the way the man had carried her back to her room, like she was nothing more than a rolled-up blanket, made her doubt the ability of the tiny wingnut which had jammed the door shut. She imagined if The Beast had wanted to get in badly enough, then he could have reduced the door to mere splinters.

Caroline was an experienced agent with MI5. She had served in the army's 14 Intelligence Company, and she had been deployed to Afghanistan. She had seen many terrible things, witnessed the death of comrades, seen the destruction war had caused the beleaguered Afghan people. She had even been present when her former fiancé had been killed, along with many other security personnel, by a suicide bomber. But nothing had prepared her for the inhumanity, the sheer callousness of what she had seen today. Young women treated like farm animals. Herded, sorted and farmed out to where they were needed most. The sex-trade was abominable, but the baby farming was on another level. Life created as a commodity. The bodies of unwilling women used and abused as part of the process. And what of the women when they were of no further use? She thought of *The Town*, a thriller she had once read on holiday. A disused mine outside a remote, and controlled mountain town in Oregon, the sale of body parts from missing people. The waifs and strays, the lost and unmissed. She shuddered at the thought of the clinical barbarity. She imagined a process down the line. Maximum yield from a person, dehumanised and turned into nothing more than a product.

She rolled onto her side, and for the second time in as many minutes, started to cry again. Not entirely for what would become of her, but for those young women and the babies that were being created down in that building of depravity. She wiped her eyes with her sleeve, sniffed and curled into a ball. She felt like she had when she was a teenager and had unexpectantly lost her pony to colic. Vulnerable, as if there would never be any fun or love in the world again. Like she was not only mourning the loss of her beloved pet, her friend, but the loss of all the wonderful years she had had to date. It had severed a link to her childhood. And today, down in that place, a link had been severed between her and all the good in the world. She would never look at life the same way again. Like a dark, low cloud that enveloped everything around her, pushing heavily downwards until there was no place else to go and she was swallowed in despair.

A footstep on the landing made her freeze. She listened for another step, realised she had stopped breathing. She heard another step, then another. They were different to before, quieter, but in that certain way that told her the person was *trying* to be quiet. She wiped her eyes again, swung her legs over the side of the bed. She still had fight left in her. She thought of Alex, what he would be feeling after so long not knowing of her fate. She wanted to see him again, wanted to finish their plans of buying a new house together - a fresh start. Wanted to finally see the man wearing a suit for their wedding day. She fished out the wingnut from her bra, placed it between her knuckles, realising the dark cloud had gone. She had reached a point Alex had once described to her. Rock bottom. At rock bottom, live or die was not even a choice.

But fight was.

Fight decided over live or die. Doing nothing didn't give you that choice. There was no gain from doing nothing. And the wonderful thing, in that flecting moment, was that fear was nowhere in the equation.

Fight was all there was.

The deadbolt slid back, the key turned in the lock. Caroline reached the dressing table, pulled the leg she had undone away. The dresser simply rested back against the wall. Caroline felt the heft of it, positioned the bolt so she could swing it into whoever was going to come through the door. She let it rest on the floor, out of view behind her leg. Waited.

The door eased inwards. There was no light on the landing. She could see a figure, not The Beast, slightly built.

"It's me... Michael," he said. "Come with me, I am getting you out..."

Caroline gripped the table leg. She hesitated, her mind spinning, her adrenalin subsiding. "Really?" she asked.

Michael stepped inside, eased the door closed behind him. "We don't have long," he said, and threw a pair of shoes on the bed. Caroline could just about see enough through the gloom to make out a pair of ankle boots with a small heel. "They should fit," he added.

Caroline put down the table leg. She picked up the boots, slipped one on. A little on the big side, but they would do just fine. She slipped the other one on, pulled up the zip.

"Why?" she asked.

"It's wrong," he said, his accent thick and the whisper made it even more difficult to hear him clearly. "I needed job, money. The job was okay at first…" He shrugged. She couldn't see his face, but hoped he had shame written on it. "Just girls for sex," he said. "Not great, but not my problem. It goes on. But the babies…" he paused. "And they make us do things…" he hesitated. "To the women. You know, I am young man. Should be dream come true… but…"

"You raped them?" Caroline asked, trying her best to keep the shock out of her voice.

"Yes, I suppose. The other men here do, too. But it does not feel like rape… the women, they do not struggle any more… but it is wrong, and I want to leave this place now… there are more women coming next week. I do not want to do it all again…"

Caroline grimaced as she nodded. The man was her lifeline. She needed him, but she would not protect him if she got clear of this hell-on-earth. She looked at him closely, saw through the gloom that his eyes were dark and swollen.

"What happened to you?" she asked.

"It is nothing."

"Well, it certainly looks like something."

"Jurgen," he said quietly. "He found out that Helena was not looking for him. Taught me a lesson…" he trailed off.

"She wasn't looking for him?" Caroline could tell that the instruction mentioned Helena's name, but she figured he had been needed elsewhere. Jurgen clearly outranked Michael, and she thought it strange that the young man had called him so forcefully. "Why did you do that?"

"I saw him taking you back. You were unconscious, it was obvious what he was going to do…"

"But why?" she pressed.

"It's wrong. All of this is so very wrong."

"Well, thank you," she said sincerely. "So, what is your plan?"

Michael shrugged. "Everyone should be either asleep or relaxing. The girls have been fed," he paused, and Caroline grimaced at the thought. It made the women sound like animals. He continued, "A few men are drinking, they will pass-out later."

"How do we get clear of this place?"

"I have left a car at the village," he said. "It's a pile of junk, but it starts. Mostly."

"Mostly?" she queried, the worry clearly detectable in her tone.

He shrugged. "It will be okay. But we can't start car here, too much noise. Helena has fast car, a big Audi. Jurgen also has a fast car, an expensive SUV."

Caroline figured that he would. The man would barely fit inside anything else. She picked up the table leg. "Okay," she said decisively. "Let's go."

49

Cape Town, South Africa

"Admit it. You're warming to me."

"I can tolerate you."

"Brilliant," Rashid said. "From loathing to tolerating in three days."

"Don't get ahead of yourself," Marnie said, sipping from her chilled glass of Pinot Grigio. "It won't get any higher than tolerating."

Rashid smiled. "Shame. I was hoping for day six," he said. "Mind you, personally I wouldn't choose to have dinner with anybody I merely tolerated."

"I hate eating alone," she said. "In restaurants, at least."

"I don't eat out much."

"I can tell."

"Really?"

"For a moment, I was sure you would drink the finger bowl."

"Shit, was that what it was?" he chided. "I just didn't want to fill up before my steak."

She smiled. Moved over as the waiter swept in and cleared her plate. He stepped around the table, took Rashid's plate of empty prawn shells, reached for the finger bowl. Rashid looked up at the waiter.

"Send the chef out please."

"Sir?"

Rashid glanced at Marnie, who looked pensive. He looked back at the waiter. "That soup was bloody tasteless," he paused. "I couldn't eat any of it."

The waiter hesitated, then smiled. Rashid thought the man had heard it all before. He bustled away and Marnie visibly relaxed.

"Idiot," she said, but there was humour in her eyes.

"Undoubtedly."

"Well, that's agreed," she said. "We both think you're an idiot."

"See, you're lightening up," he said. "No need to thank me for getting you out of the office and away to South Africa. Sweden next."

"Thank you?"

"You're welcome."

"No, I'm questioning your logic, not thanking you."

"You don't like to travel?"

"It's nothing to do with traveling. It's my fiancé."

"He doesn't like you to travel?"

"Will you forget about the travel!" she snapped tersely. She looked up as the waiter appeared with her snapper. She remained silent, an awkwardness to it that was not helped by the waiter, who now seemed to take his time delivering Rashid's seared Springbok steak.

"Will there be anything else?" the waiter asked, apparently relishing the awkwardness, maybe because it redressed Rashid's joke earlier, but more likely it was because it was what waiters seemed to do.

"Ketchup, please," said Rashid.

"Sir?"

"Yes, you heard. Tomato ketchup. And don't stick it in a poncey dish you'd bring mustard out in. It's ketchup, you need about five times as much as mustard." He watched the waiter leave, then smiled at Marnie across the table. "That'll teach him."

"For a moment I thought you were really going to smother that seared steak and yam and spinach fondant with tomato sauce," she smiled. "Oh, wait. You're going to, aren't you?"

"Absolutely."

She smiled. "What on earth is a Springbok, anyway?"

"A gazelle," he said. "Like their national animal."

"Nice," she replied sardonically. "Oh look," she said. "Your tomato ketchup is here. And he doesn't look to be happy about it."

"He isn't paying the bill," Rashid said.

"Nor are you. It's on expenses."

"Will there be a hearing? Misuse of government funds? Moral turpitude regarding an inappropriate condiment?" he smiled, and she laughed; both ignoring the waiter as he placed the sizeable pot on the table and left.

"You sound like you know hearings. Been in trouble before, then?"

"Trouble could be my middle name," Rashid paused. "Except it's Mohammed."

She smiled. "So, you're not the first-born son, then?"

"No."

"And is he as big a pain in the arse as you?"

"Wouldn't know."

"Not close?"

"No. He died."

She looked shocked, held her fingers to her lips. "I'm sorry."

"Don't be," Rashid paused. "He died before I was born. An Indian raid in Pakistan. Sikhs verses Muslims, that sort of shit. They raided one day. Sliced and bludgeoned their way through our village. My parents fled, my mother got pregnant with me on the journey over. I was born here."

Marnie said nothing. There wasn't much she could say, and Rashid seemed to understand. She took a mouthful of her fish while Rashid smeared tomato ketchup onto a piece of his steak. They chewed in silence, Rashid sipped a mouthful of beer.

"So, what's with Neil?" she asked. "The whole Botha thing has sent him into himself."

"You noticed?"

"Difficult not to," she said, sipping some more wine. "You were the hero, by all accounts."

"I don't think so," he replied. "If it wasn't for Neil's quick thinking with that planter, I wouldn't have got into the house so quickly, Botha would have probably fired again. I doubt he would have missed Ryan a third time."

She nodded. She had been terrified, cowered in the car when she heard the gunshots. She had admitted it earlier, without shame. She was an analyst. She hadn't signed up for field work. The most strenuous thing she did was Zumba on a Tuesday and Thursday. She had settled into her duties within MI5, and that had been part of her problem with Rashid's suggestion she accompany them. She liked to be settled. Or at least, she thought she did. As she sipped her wine, ate her exotic fish and noodles and caught glimpses of Table Mountain in the setting sun from the restaurant window, she had her doubts. She watched Rashid across the table from her. He was ruggedly handsome. Medium height and physically fit. His eyes were almost black, his dark hair sat untended by recent cuts or product, sort of falling in an untidy mop that had once been shorn close at the sides and back. A military cut, long since grown out. His skin was a strong milk coffee colour but weathered from a life in the elements. She knew he was with the Army, guessed at the SAS because of his secondment with MI5. She knew those men were tough and silent types. She couldn't help but to contrast the man with her fiancé – a city trader who lived in either pin-stripe suits with his old school tie or five-hundred-pound pairs of jeans dubiously paired with rugby shirts and blazers. A man she would not have normally been attracted to, but for the ticking body clock and too much champagne at a mutual friend's wedding. Andrew was a generous man, but he should have been, he earned a fortune in the city. Enough to retire at the age of thirty-six if he wanted to. But to him, the status and rush that his work gave him meant that the money was less important than the thrill of earning it. She imagined the soldier opposite her would have little in either wealth or assets and could care less about the fact.

"How long have you been with the SAS?" she asked.

"Who said I was?"

"Obvious, really."

"I can't talk about that."

She smiled. "There's enough people who are. You know, SAS programmes on the television…"

"Ex-Royal Marine's turned tattoo models, putting civilian triathletes through five days of *hell*?" Rashid interrupted and laughed. "All tight-fitting shirts and Lycra? No, they're not what the SAS are about."

"So, you won't tell me?"

Rashid smiled, drank down the last of his beer and placed the glass carefully back down on the table. "Well, I could tell you, but…"

"You'd have to kill me?" she laughed. "That is a really old one. Tom Cruise said it in Top Gun, I believe."

"No," Rashid reached across the table and gently stroked the back of her hand. "No, I was going to say... I could tell you, but then I'd have to sleep with you..."

50

It was completely dark when Caroline tentatively followed Michael outside into the courtyard. There were a few noises, but those were behind them now, the sound of men drinking and playing cards. The night was clear, cloudless. The stars were out in all their heavenly glory, accentuated by the lack of light pollution. Caroline was reminded of how remote Eastern Europe could be.

"Where are we?" she asked, the thought coming to her now that Michael was on her side.

"Georgia," he said quietly.

She nodded. She had thought Eastern Europe or possibly the Ukraine. She hadn't been a million miles away. "So, what is that way?" she asked, pointing in the direction of the mountain range. There was nothing to see, simply the world disappearing into darkness.

"The Caucasus Mountains," Michael whispered. "Very big mountains. Only a few roads through and very dangerous."

"Dangerous?"

"Bad roads, bandits, bears, wolves," he paused. "You name it."

Caroline knew that the mountains lay to the north. Which meant the Black Sea was to the east. She visualised the location on a map. She had no idea of distances or scale, but she felt relieved to be able to put a marker on her location. It gave her a new-found confidence, put some reality into her world of disbelief, fear and uncertainty. Just the knowledge that she knew her location gave her a flush of confidence.

She followed Michael through the courtyard but hesitated as he bypassed the barn and made his way between two derelict-looking buildings. "Wait!" she whispered, but it wasn't loud enough to grab his attention. "Michael, wait!" she called, as quietly as she could, but as loud as she dared.

Michael stopped in his tracks, turned back and said, "What?"

"The women," Caroline said quietly. "What about all of the women?"

"We have to go!" he snapped.

"But we can't," she protested. "*I* can't…"

"There is no room!" He shook his head. "I have a small car… there are thirty women here… we can't!"

"No, he can't!" Jurgen said, a matter of feet away from Caroline. He flicked on a torch, catching their faces in surprise. "*Predatel'skiy ublyudok!*" he shouted, then as if for Caroline's benefit repeated it in English, "Treacherous bastard!" His voice filled the courtyard as he stepped forward, his massive frame bearing down on them.

Caroline lashed out with the table leg. She didn't have time to check if the bolt was going to hit first, but it didn't matter anyway because The Beast batted it away with his forearm, almost taking Caroline with it. She was quick to react, using her training, she went with the force, used it, spun around completely and kept the table leg moving around three-hundred and sixty degrees, striking him on the right hip. He let out a grunt, swung a punch which scythed through the air narrowly missing Caroline's jaw. She had been lucky. The blow could have killed her. She pulled the table leg clear, pushed it head on into the man's groin. He wheezed and fell backwards, sprawling into the wall of the building. She was readying another swing, when Michael caught hold of her and dragged her backwards.

"Come on!" he shouted.

Caroline had lost her momentum for attack, and saw The Beast already getting to his feet. He was reaching for his pocket and she decided not to be there when he got what he was after. She turned and ran, following Michael between the two buildings. Behind them, The Beast was screaming in Russian. Already, the courtyard was illuminated by the lights flicking on within the farmhouse. As Caroline caught up with Michael, their shadows were cast by a powerful outside light set high up on the lee of the farmhouse.

Michael was a fast runner and although Caroline ran regularly to maintain fitness, she could not match his pace. She dared a backwards glance and was horrified to see that The Beast, despite his bulk, had gained ground on her. She was sprinting hard, as best she could in the boots, but the heel put her at a disadvantage. She tried to increase her pace, but she realised that both fear and adrenalin had dealt her all the speed she was ever going to get. Michael dodged right, beside some bins and a pile of scrap metal. Caroline followed, the sharp turn in direction catching The Beast off guard. He missed the turning, cursed and doubled back. Ahead of them, Caroline saw the metal fence. She already knew she would not get clear before The Beast caught her. The track was narrow, and Michael would slow up to make the initial leap. He would reach half-way and climb, but Caroline did not have enough distance between herself and The Beast to make it. She had another twenty-metres to go, saw her opportunity and went for it. The barn to her right was constructed of wood, but a sizable section had rotted away. Caroline leaped to her right, partially clipping the wood, which splintered as she crashed through into the darkness. She tripped and fell, but rolled loosely, and got back onto her feet in time to see The Beast run past. Two gunshots shattered the night air and she heard The Beast before she saw him, he was breathing hard, rasping and grunting. He seemed to have spent every ounce of resolve in the long sprint, even swallowing sounded an effort. He bent his massive frame to get into the hole in the wall, his broad shoulders wedging briefly as he pushed himself through. Caroline had broken the rotten wood away when she had flung herself through at speed. Maybe she had more momentum, or maybe the rotten wood had been trimmed away, but The Beast struggled to push himself through.

And that was all Caroline needed.

She stepped out of the darkness. Shafts of light penetrated the gloom and she stepped closer. The Beast had both hands on the floor, his backside high in the air, like a great ape about to spring up and pound his chest, except he wasn't going to spring anywhere. Not with his shoulders and neck touching the wood, and nor with the table leg crashing down onto his skull.

The Beast grunted, dropped onto the ground. Until then he had the tiny automatic pistol in his right hand but sandwiched between his palm and the ground as his arms took his weight. Now his hands were free. He waved the pistol towards her, but she was already taking another swing. The table leg cracked his skull again and the tiny pistol scattered out of his hand and across the ground.

"You will have to do better," he grunted.

He was still moving, crawling closer to her, his body now completely through the hole and inside the building. He pushed himself up onto all fours, his legs scrabbling on pieces of broken wood and discarded waste from years of neglect.

Caroline struck again, this time on his shoulder, shattering his clavicle. He screamed, grit his teeth and continued to push himself up. Caroline adjusted her grip on the table leg, positioned the two-inches or so of protruding bolt and swung as hard as she could. The table leg travelled in a wide arc, but The Beast raised his arm and met the attack. The impact shook Caroline to the core and the table leg rebounded off his arm. Enough force to break most men's arms, but his arms were like most people's legs. He didn't make a sound, stared into her eyes through the gloom and stood up to his full height, towering above her. Caroline took a step backwards, trod on the pistol and skidded, losing balance. She fell backwards but was already scrabbling for the pistol as The Beast stepped forwards. She slapped the floor repeatedly with her palms, desperately searching for the pistol in the darkness. She glanced upwards, saw how close he was, and dropped onto her belly as she searched.

"Just where I want you, bitch!"

Caroline's fingers groped the pistol. She got her hand around the butt, brought the weapon up to The Beast's groin and fired. The pistol jumped in her hand and the noise inside the confines of the building was deafening. The Beast screamed, cupped his crotch and dropped down onto his knees, his sheer weight enough to shake the ground she laid on.

Caroline pushed herself up and pushed the hot muzzle into the man's right eye and fired. She said nothing, didn't so much as give a backward glance as she walked on past the man as he dropped to the ground and lay still.

51

The shouts and commotion pierced the cool night air. Vehicles started their engines, headlights cut swathes of light through the darkness. Caroline had dropped heavily over the fence, curled up in the undergrowth to wait. She needed to get a handle on what was happening. She did not want to stumble blindly into her captors. A few minutes to assess, and she'd move on.

She had given up on Michael. The man had not waited for her, nor had he come back to help. She could not entirely blame him. He had played his hand with these people and he would have been called out by now. It would only be a matter of time before they caught up with him, she was sure about that. She needed to accept that she was on her own and plan accordingly. She had The Beast's pistol, which made her feel more secure. The weapon only had three bullets remaining, but it was still an advantage. She knew that to head north was not an option. The mountains were indeed a solid range of towering peaks, interjected by few passes, and like Michael had said, a dangerous place. To the south, the mountains were less dramatic, but she doubted the problems would be different. To the east? The opposite direction from home, towards Azerbaijan or Chechnya and the Caspian Sea? Not an option. Not for an attractive western woman with blonde hair travelling alone. She may as well hand herself back in and resume her role as prisoner. Which left west. A limited alley through which to travel, hemmed in by mountains, funnelling out to the Black Sea and the same towns where Helena Milankovitch once spent her time along the coast of Russia, Georgia and the Ukraine, imprisoned by the Russian mafia in the sex trade. For Caroline, the choices were coming down to just one. But what she feared more than her imminent situation, was that Helena would work out her choices as well. Which meant she had to get moving.

Caroline got slowly and carefully to her feet, making sure she did not disrupt the bushes as she pushed her way through the undergrowth. She needed to remain out of sight, and that meant everything around her should stay still, too. The way ahead was no longer illuminated by the lights around the farmhouse and courtyard, but the ambient glow seemed to create a halo around the area, making the night sky difficult to see in detail. She could no longer ascertain the direction of the mountains, which she knew to be due north. Without knowing the direction of north, and without being able to pick out the stars for reference, she would not be able to work out which way was west. She walked onward, keeping the farmyard behind her, which at least meant she was not heading east or south. She would have to best-guess until she could find a marker.

Keeping low, Caroline negotiated the brush. She knew that from what she had seen from the bedroom window, that it would thin-out soon and open out to farmland before long. From there, it was almost uninterrupted meadowland thirty or so miles to the foothills of the Caucasus Mountains. She kept the automatic in her right hand, her finger off the trigger with well-instilled discipline. The Makarov was chambered for a unique 9.2mm cartridge that made for a hard-hitting round in such a small pistol. The fact that she had killed The Beast and had his weapon to offer herself protection did much to bolster her resolve and confidence. She had been captured when she had been in a vulnerable state and she had not had an opportunity to escape until now. She was an ex-soldier, a trained agent with MI5 and she would be a tougher opponent than they could ever imagine.

Armed and dangerous.

She almost stood on Michael. Stopped herself in time. She crouched down and prodded him. He groaned. Her eyes were well-adjusted by now and she could see he was bleeding from his chest and stomach.

"My back," he said weakly. "My back hurts…"

Caroline tried to roll him and examine the wound, but he was a dead weight and he wheezed, a trickle of blood reaching the corner of his mouth. She looked at the two holes, both were ragged and large enough for a golf ball to pass through. She could picture it happening, The Beast shooting him as he climbed the fence. He would have dropped over heavily, crawled desperately to this place.

"Michael," she said, prompting him to answer. He didn't, but he was still breathing. "Michael, tell me about the car. Where is it?"

"The Village," he grunted. "Skhimili."

"Where is the village?"

"I need a doctor," he said.

"I need the car," she paused. "We can't go anywhere without the car. Where are the keys?" He tapped his hip pocket, but his hand was almost moving in slow motion. Caroline snatched them out and stuffed the bunch into her pocket.

"Green Opel Corsa," he said. "It is parked beside a general store," he paused. "Where I got you the foods in sealed bags… the cola…" He was trailing off, his eyes opening and closing in time with his shallow breathing.

"The village, Michael," she urged. "Where is the village?"

"Keep going," he said. "Keep heading the way you were. It is two-kilometres. You will come back for me?"

"Of course," she lied.

She wasn't being malicious. The man had helped her, but he would be dead within ten to twenty-minutes. There was no point in telling him so. She was about to leave when the thought of him being discovered occurred to her. If they found him, pressed him for information, he could tell them where she was heading. She bent down and spoke slowly and clearly into his ear.

"Michael. I must end this. Helena will not stop looking for us. I am going to double back around the farmhouse and kill her. I have Jurgen's gun, she won't expect me to go back." She tucked the pistol into her back pocket and took the keys out. She looked at the keys, quickly worked out which one was for the car and which looked like house keys and she slipped the car key off the bunch. "Take these Michael. Keep them safe. I will be back for you soon. You are going to be okay." She pressed the bunch of keys into his hand and stood up. She took a pace, then stopped and turned around. "Thank you, Michael," she said with genuine emotion in her voice. "Thank you for getting me out…"

52

Neil Ramsay gratefully accepted the coffee and paced over to the window. His own window afforded glimpses of Table Mountain, while Marnie's looked over the choppy blue-green waters of the Atlantic Ocean. He couldn't decide which view was better, but as he sipped the milky coffee and mulled it over, he decided he could watch the Atlantic from his usual holiday retreat in Cornwall but would probably never see the beauty of a sunrise over the prodigious landmark again.

Rashid perched on the edge of Marnie's hastily made king-sized bed and sipped his breakfast tea. "Nice view, isn't it?" he said to Ramsay's back.

"Not bad," he said. "I'm surprised you noticed it."

Marnie had powered up her laptop, purchased their tickets and had already been briefed by the technician at GCHQ. She glanced up at Ramsay, then shared a glance at Rashid.

"Anything I should know?" Ramsay asked, his back still turned on them, the rising sun casting a golden hue across the surface of the water in front of him.

"The account used to pay Botha was set up in the Channel Islands, but the money made its way to it via Luxemburg and Switzerland," said Marnie.

"Not that," Ramsay said curtly. He sipped some more coffee and turned around. "I'm referring to the poorly-made bed, Rashid still wearing the same clothes he wore last night."

"I was sleeping, then threw the bed together when Rashid knocked!"

"Yeah, and I couldn't sleep, thought I'd come around and see what was happening."

"And the clothes?"

"I'm a grubby sod." Rashid shrugged. "Hey, I'm travelling light."

"And I'm engaged!" Marnie protested indignantly.

Ramsay held up his hands in mock surrender. "Okay," he conceded. "I was mistaken. Just doesn't help things, people getting together in the service. There's too much at stake. Pillow talk for one thing, conflicts of interest for another," he paused. "Just look at King. He's storming around Europe taking out mafia brotherhoods. He wouldn't be doing that if he was not emotionally involved with Caroline."

"*Brotherhoods*?" Rashid asked.

Ramsay took out his phone and thumbed to a text. "This was sent in the night, from Mereweather," he paused, before reading out the name in his best Italian accent. "Monteverdi Marittimo," he said. "Some mountain town in Tuscany, Italy. An Italian mafioso called Luca Fortez was hit at his home, his family threatened. He was a real piece of work. Took down other mafia families, moved in on their assets. A cold, vicious bastard, by all accounts."

Rashid shrugged. "Good. The world is a safer place. Or at least Italy will be."

Ramsay nodded. "No doubt. But it doesn't end there. A deal was being struck between Luca Fortez and a group of Russian gangsters, or *Bratva*. The Russian boss was a man called Nikolai. Not sure it it's a Christian name or his surname, but he was an even bigger piece of work. He wound up dead as well. The police suspected the deal went wrong, but I have it on good authority that it was merely made to look that way."

"Whose authority?" Rashid asked.

"We have an open line of communication with Interpol. They are working with Italian intelligence, their internal intelligence and security agency."

"And?" Rashid prompted.

"This Nikolai character was in deep with Sergeyev once. They were enforcers for the Bratva. They worked along the Black Sea resorts at the same time Helena Milankovitch was there."

"Coincidence," Rashid countered. "All these Russian shits know each other. And they move on each other's territory all the time. They're backstabbers. Just because they are both dead, it doesn't mean King had anything to do with it. It's a dangerous lifestyle."

"CCTV showed King was there."
"Where?"
"This Monteverdi place."
"So?"

"So, the man was *there*."

Rashid shrugged. "He was there, big deal! A lot of people would have been there. It's Tuscany. It's a popular tourist spot. Half the middle-classes go there to drink prosecco and become cultured twats for a weekend. See some shitty leaning tower and reflect how good it is that the all the chavs still go to the Costas."

"You're a loyal friend."

"Only type of friend in my book," Rashid said, glaring at him. "Unless they have footage of King popping some guy in the head, deny it and move on."

"Now, look here…"

"Deny it!" Rashid shouted, interrupting him. "And move on… Caroline is in trouble and King is working the angles, the only way he knows how. He's buying her time."

"And we're looking for Helena. To find Caroline," Ramsay protested. "Find Helena, find Caroline. That was *your* input, I'll remind you!"

"Stop!" Marnie shouted. She stood up and walked over, hovering between them. "Let's take a moment. We have her secret bank account. We have traceability, a link that she paid a South African government agent to set up his colleague and organise a hit. In doing so, he endangered a British government agent. But what use is all that? Botha is dead. There's no material witnesses and nobody to prosecute. The South African's aren't going to come forward because they passed up one of their own. Had us do the dirty work in return for questioning him and gaining access to his computer. This investigation has dried up. We need to concentrate on location. And we have that with this place in Georgia. A location where Helena's laptop has been recently."

Ramsay considered this for a moment. He placed his coffee cup down on the table and looked at Rashid. "Have you heard from King?"

"No," he lied.

"And do you think Georgia is the next logical step?"

Rashid nodded. "I do. We know Helena was in Sweden, and we know that King went there, as instructed in the letter. But we don't know what happened in Georgia, or how important it is, but if the laptop was there, the IP address used, then we need to check it out."

Ramsay turned to Marnie. "All right then, cancel the tickets to Stockholm. Get us on the next flight you can find to Tbilisi. Unless there's somewhere closer?" he paused thoughtfully, looking at his watch. "Okay. Let's meet downstairs for breakfast in half an hour. That will give you enough time to get some tickets booked. I'll check in with Thames House, let Simon Mereweather know what our next line in investigation is." He walked to the door, let himself out as Rashid finished his cup of tea.

Rashid drained the remnants, placed his cup down on the table and smiled. "Close?"

"Close."

"Well, I'm glad he went for Georgia," he said.

"It would have been awkward telling him I'd already bought them," she smiled. "God, I was worried, began to wish I hadn't listened to you."

"I'm glad you did."

She walked over to him, stood barely half a pace away. "Well, you were extremely persuasive…"

Rashid moved in close, bent down and kissed her. She responded, her tongue slipping inside his mouth, both searching. She pulled away first. "Oh god," she said. "You've made me cheat on my fiancé!"

"I haven't *made* you do anything. You wanted to. You just didn't know it until last night."

Marnie sighed and nodded. "Neil said half an hour," she said. "And I've already bought three tickets to Tbilisi."

Rashid wrapped his hands around her and guided her to the bed. He gave her a firm shove and she fell backwards and giggled. "More than enough time," he smiled. "For me, that is."

"Great, just what every girl wants to hear…"

53

With no time difference between Sweden and France King arrived in Bordeaux International airport at a little after midnight. He cleared passport control quickly, and with just a carry-on leather overnight bag, he was through the airport and at the Hertz car hire desk within twenty-minutes of touching down.

He hadn't slept on the flight, couldn't remember the last time he had. He was tired but was comfortable driving the two-and-a-half-hour drive, stopping at a service station and truck stop for a pot of tea and some pastries just outside of Bayonne. Fuelled and quenched, he drove the Renault hire car to the furthest and quietest part of the car park, switched off, reclined the seat and fell asleep almost instantly.

He hadn't slept well, waking each time a large articulated lorry activated its airbrakes manoeuvring at slow speeds at the fuel stop. But he had been tired, dropping back off to sleep almost as quickly as he had awoken. At seven he drove back to the service station and washed quickly in the filthy toilets, grabbing a cup of tea to go on his way out. He stopped at the tobacco kiosk and bought a gas lighter and a medium-sized flick-knife. He pocketed both. They were useful tools to have, although he hoped he wouldn't need them. He only had around five miles to travel and figured that he would be early enough to catch her, but not too early as to descend upon her at an unsociable hour and risk finding her uncooperative at the intrusion. That was if she was still around, hadn't been found or disappeared.

King parked the car just down from the chalet. He watched, waited for a sign she was there. The BMW was parked on the driveway, but it was in a different position to when he had left it. Anna Sergeyev had used the vehicle, even if she had moved elsewhere. She had said she had funds, enough to live on, and King had told her the chalet was hers for up to two-weeks. That seemed so long ago now, but it had only been just over a week. He glanced at himself in the rear-view mirror. He was gaunt and drawn, his eye sockets dark. He had not taken care of himself after Caroline had been taken. He imagined he'd lost a stone or more from not eating properly. He was a big man, but still hadn't carried enough flesh to take such dramatic weight loss. It was more than that though, weeks of poor sleep had taken its toll too. He looked hollowed out, and his dark close-cropped hair now carried more salt than pepper at the sides.

King stepped out of the car. He checked the flick-knife in his pocket, relaxed a little. A good blade was as good as a small pistol up close. In many cases, he thought he could do more damage with a knife than a small calibre pistol ever would. He hoped he wouldn't need to put the theory to the test.

The house stood in its own grounds of about half an acre. There was a pool to the rear and the grounds were largely turned to lawn with shrubs and rockeries and a bank of four-foot-high bushes along the rear of the property separating it from farmland in the form of meadows. To the front of the property, a narrow road cut through the fields and a low wire fence with rustic wooden posts served as a barrier but had seen better days. From what King could make out, the grass was now far too long for grazing and would most likely be turned to hay or silage before long. Which meant that this area would not have been looked in on by the landowners for weeks. The house was about as private as it could get.

King hovered around the entrance and checked over the gardens. There were no signs of anyone. As he looked at the house, scanned over the windows, he saw nothing. He slipped over the stone garden wall and walked along the side of the house. He saw the pool, noticed swimwear hanging on the line. He thought about testing them to see if they were wet or dry, but it was early and there was dew on the grass and it would tell him nothing. If they had been used this morning, then they would be wet. If they had been left out all night, he imagined they would be in the same state. He continued but paused after a few steps as his senses caught both smell and sound at once. He could smell the aroma of coffee, hear the faintest clink of china. He knew that there was an alcove with a firepit-come-barbeque in the lee of the building, the perfect place to catch the morning sun. As he rounded the corner, he saw Anna Sergeyev sipping coffee, clad only in the skimpiest of beach wraps. He could see her body, the outline of her nipples against the damp cotton. He averted his eyes as he glimpsed lower, catching everything she had to bare. Anna looked up, stunned for a moment, but visibly relaxed. She did nothing to cover herself, adjust the position she was seated in. King was sure she made a point of it.

"I didn't think I would see you again," she said. "My husband's murderer, my saviour…"

"I needed to talk."

"Talk, talk, talk," she said. "And there was I thinking you were a man of action."

King pulled out a chair and sat down. It changed his view, as well as the dynamic. "I need to ask you some questions about…"

"Helena!" she interrupted. "Always about Helena."

"Why do you say it like that?"

"It was always about her," she said. "The most popular, the most sought after. I was a whore. I am not ashamed, because I was both popular and good at it, and in turn, that kept me alive. It kept me in better places, with less grimy men. Men who tipped and treated me and after they did what they did, cared enough to call again. If I was not so good at it, then I would have spent my life in a hovel chained to a bed and thrown scraps. Worse than a dog."

"I'm sorry," King said awkwardly.

"Don't be. I met my husband doing such work. He gave me a wonderful daughter, and he was kind to me. He was an evil man, a beast and a killer. He could be cruel. But not with me, nor our daughter. He kept me a prisoner, this is true, but it was an incarceration of luxury and privilege." Anna sipped some coffee, placed the cup down thoughtfully and looked at King. "Helena was the one every man wanted, my husband included. But she was too spirited to control. She brought many problems to my husband, to the men he worked with."

"Nikolai? Romanovitch?"

"Oh, you've done your homework," she said sardonically. "And don't forget Russia's esteemed leader! Do you know about him?"

King nodded. "I do. Or at least, I have been told."

"But do you believe it?"

"I'm not sure."

"Well, be damned sure. Only in Russia can a murderer and rapist, a former Bratva piece of scum become president. He is seen as a man of the people because he came from a poor background, served in the military for three years, just a foot soldier but he did his service. And then he held roles in construction, was instrumental in large developments and connecting Russia through its road networks. He was behind the trans-continental road development, theoretically connecting Europe to America via

Siberia and an ice road across the Bering Sea in winter."

King had heard of the project, even thought it would be a fantastic thing to do when he finally left playing cowboys and Indians behind. "And nothing ever comes up of his past, working in the Bratva?"

"He has paid off, bribed or killed all those who would do him harm."

"Except Helena."

"I think he thought she was a woman who would never tell of her past. Married to one of the wealthiest men in the world, making Britain her home, a changed woman. A professional business woman with her own clothing line, a woman who courted the press and frequently went to openings and official engagements. She was hardly going to start talking about working as a whore in her homeland."

King nodded. In a way, it made sense. Secrets relied upon staying that way only by two people's silence. The Russian president obviously felt that there was a status quo between them, but what he wouldn't have counted on was Helena's fall from grace. She had resumed her affair with her former lover, used his exceptionally specialised military skills as a way of getting out of her relationship with her billionaire husband, and keep what assets she would have been entitled to. She had deceived, connived and conspired with others to make her husband's death look like a murder, but as part of a terrorist organization's bigger plan. But she had been caught, by chance, as King had investigated the Home Secretary, a silent partner in her husband's company. Misappropriation of government funds, an undeclared conflict of interest had sparked King's investigation, but had crossed paths along the way. Helena had been found out by dumb luck. Now, she was discredited, a wanted criminal and her assets had been seized. She would have known this at once, severed all links with her current life and looked at how to come out on top. She knew all about the Bratva, knew the world they lived in. And at the same time as she built an empire, she sought revenge for what they had done.

"Please, if it's not too painful for you?" King ventured. "Tell me about that night."

Anna scoffed. "It was nothing," she said. "Or it was everything."

"I don't understand."

"You are a man," she sneered. She felt her breasts, squeezed them and lifted them upwards. "You see these?" She slid her hand lower, pulled the swim robe apart revealing herself fully. "That?" She stared at King as he did his best not to look either interested or too uncomfortable. "That is for me to give someone or to deny them. There is no in between. Some people don't think it is possible to rape a whore. But let me tell you; it is. I could sleep with a dozen men in a day. But if someone did not stop when I wanted them to, then it is rape. As much as it would be if I were a nun."

King nodded. "I get that."

"Do you? Because few men do," she sneered. "Those Bratva bastards, my husband included, they took what they wanted. That night was wild and crazy and changed my life. Pyotr decided he wanted me for himself, swore off the others. It was madness. Too much champagne and vodka, too many drugs. Line upon line of coke. They were snorting it out of the girl's parts, off their boobs… madness. There was Viagra too. As if they needed it with all the cocaine and ecstasy. Helena had cost them a lot of time and money. She had whisked her sister out of there, took some money to do so. They were mad. Pretty soon I was just laying down on a sofa and they were just concentrating on Helena. There was nothing they didn't put that woman through. Nothing." She drank the remnants of coffee and looked thoughtfully past King and out across the meadowland. "I hooked up with Pyotr after that night. I did it for survival. I figured if I had to fuck, I would rather it was just one man. Whether I liked him or not. He was on the cusp of making it big, so I took my chance."

King said nothing. He had shot the man in the head, a simple sorry wasn't going to sit well with her. It was another world. He had seen most of the evil in it, but it never ceased to amaze him how life could be.

Anna looked back at King and smiled. "I suppose I should thank you," she said. "It's weird, you know? I feel numb to it. I will not see him again, but I don't feel happy about that. I have money, plenty stashed away here and there. I need to be able to get to it. I went down to Bayonne and bought clothes yesterday. A prepaid phone. And you said I could keep the car, right?"

"Sure," he said. "I mean, put some false plates on it when you can, but yeah, keep it."

She nodded. "I can't thank you enough for letting us use this place," she said. She smiled, smoothed her hands over her breasts and stomach. "Or I could thank you in another way?"

"You don't owe me anything."

"Perhaps I want to?"

King smiled. "Those days are behind you."

"I still have needs," she said sharply.

"Then find someone who loves you, love them back and forget the past."

She laughed. "You are a kind man," she said. She stood up, showing King everything he had passed up on. "I will get us some coffee," she said.

King didn't stop her. He didn't drink coffee as a rule, but he doubted she had tea. He hadn't come for breakfast anyway. He leaned back in the chair, watched the glow of the sunrise across the hills of grass and orchards. It was a beautiful place, and he wished he could have been there with Caroline. The thought made him anxious again, and he fought hard to control his emotions. He looked up as Anna returned with a pot of coffee and another cup. She poured him a cup with no offer of sugar or cream, then topped up her own cup.

"Tell me about Catherine."

Anna nodded. "Helena's little sister. I suppose by now she'd be twenty-four or twenty-five, so not *that* little," she paused. "She looked a lot like Helena, so beautiful, beguiling even. Helena knew that she would end up in the same situation, knew she would be sought after. That is why she got her out. The money she stole from the Bratva was given to her to give her a start someplace."

"Do you know where she is?"

Anna hesitated, then said, "No."

King stared at her but said nothing. He tapped his fingers on the table, watched her grow uncomfortable and look away from him. "I think you do," he said.

She sighed, and King noticed her hand was shaking. She caught him looking, moved it to her thigh and rested it there. "And what will you do?"

King shrugged. "My fiancé is being held. I don't know where, I don't even know if she's still alive," he said, his voice wobbling a little. He took a breath, steadied himself. "I want a bargaining chip. I want like for like. I want to find Catherine Milankovitch and trade her for the woman I love."

Anna smirked. "And for this woman, you have killed my husband, and who else?"

"The man called Sergeyev. He is dead too."

"And Romanovitch?"

"No. Not yet."

Anna looked at him. "I know where he is," she said.

King nodded. "And you'll tell me?"

"Perhaps," she said. "But I know more than this. I know where Catherine Milankovitch is."

"But you have a price," King stated flatly.

"There is a price for everything," she said.

"I thought you had money."

"I do."

"So how about giving me the information for free?"

She laughed. "Oh, my dear, nothing is free."

"I doubt I can afford it then."

"You are a government man," she said. "I know the type."

"Okay…"

"Anonymity. That is my price. For my daughter and myself," she paused. "A new name, social security details, British identity… that is all. I do not need money, I just want to disappear."

King had tried to disappear once, and it hadn't worked. A man had found him, brought him back into the fold. A new role, but life felt very much the same right now.

He nodded. "Go on," he said.

"You can do this for me? For my daughter?"

"Yes." He knew that Amherst would be able to swing it. What was a name, a national insurance number and a passport? What price was that for getting their MI5 agent back? "But time is sensitive," he said. "I don't break my word, but I need you to tell me. I need you to trust me, and I will make arrangements for both you and your daughter."

She considered this for a moment, then stood up and nodded. "Okay. We will go inside, and I will write it down."

King followed her, the swim robe covering little of her backside as she took the three stone steps up into the house. The room was a large, open-plan living area where a lounge, dining room and kitchen merged into one. Anna found a pad and started to write down an address. King could see she was drawing a map as well. "My husband spoke with Romanovitch the day before you killed him," she said neutrally. "He always goaded Pyotr, delighted in emasculating him whenever he could. Dick measuring, I suppose. Romanovitch had wised up to Helena being on the scene. She had made some moves, paying mercenary types to build a platform from which to operate. He suspected what she was going to do, or at least that she could be after revenge. He took out certain insurances and goaded my husband. Pyotr said he would never hide or cower from her like some damned dog. I suppose that was Pyotr trying to out-dick Romanovitch."

"What insurances?" King asked, taking the note off her and studying it before folding it and placing it in his pocket.

"Romanovitch found Catherine and took her."

"Took her?"

"Yes," she paused. "I don't know where he took her, or even if she is still alive. But all I know is that Romanovitch is a merciless bastard and he will use her in any way he can to protect himself."

"And this address, it is his main home?"

"Yes."

"Why help me?"

The question seemed to stun her for a moment, she shrugged and said, "Maybe Helena needs to end this, maybe things will be better for me if she does. She will not like the fact that I got together with Pyotr. She will have seen that as me siding with him, gaining from that night."

"And if Romanovitch dies, well that's one less person to come after you for the secrets you know about your husband's business affairs."

Again, she shrugged like it meant nothing. "Win, win."

King nodded, was about to thank her for her cooperation, but something outside caught his eye. He moved to the edge of the window, keeping far enough back to remain unseen. A large black Mercedes and a black Range Rover Sport had pulled up and parked on the road opposite the house. "Your husband's men… would you recognise them all?"

"Most of them," she said. She walked up to King and stood at his shoulder. "Those cars are his, I'm certain of it."

King stepped back and looked at her. "You said you bought things yesterday," he paused. "How did you purchase them?"

"On my credit card…" she trailed off, realising her mistake.

"And the phone?"

"Card," she said. "I bought two of them. My daughter was missing her friends. The phones should be fine, they're pay as you go."

King frowned. "But if your daughter called somebody and they got hold of that person's phone, they could use the find my phone feature."

Anna covered her mouth with her hand. "Oh god! They've probably gone to Anushka's house, Dina's best friend from the international school. Another Russian family living in Biarritz."

"Go upstairs and get your daughter," he paused. "And get some clothes on. Don't pack, just be ready to move. And leave both of those phones upstairs."

He returned to the window, saw the passenger door of the Range Rover open and the man get out. He had to be six-feet-six and two-hundred and fifty pounds, and he looked like he lived in the gym. Another man got out of the rear door and stood beside him as they both surveyed the house. He was five-six and wiry. A stark contrast to the giant, but by the look of him, no less dangerous. King could see that both men were armed – the contours of their leather jackets indicated sizeable firearms of some description.

King checked the lock on the door, then hurried over to the door the two of them had come in through and locked that also. He could see that the windows were closed as he crossed the kitchen and went into a utility room that branched off it. There were shelves with washing powder and liquids, ant-killer, slug-pellets and drain-cleaner. Below were stacks of newspaper and magazines, and alongside the shelving were recycling bins filled with glass bottles, and another two with tins and plastic. At the far end of the twelve-by-fifteen utility were domestic appliances and a small generator. Next to the generator was a five-litre can of petrol.

King went back to the kitchen, saw the large man in the middle of the road, his eyes on the upstairs of the house. The smaller man was opening the gate, about to step into the garden. He didn't have much time, but he already had a plan. Of sorts.

Petrol is an evaporate. Once spilt it will not last long in a flammable state. It has a low flash-point, high burn-rate and because of this, it expels its energy quickly. King took three glass bottles out of the recycling bin. One had previously contained wine, another vodka and the third still had remnants of orange juice at the bottom. King placed them on the ironing board and picked up the tub of slug pellets. He glanced at the back of the box, then opened it and scooped out handfuls, dropping them into the bottles until they were around one-third full. King then picked up the stack of newspapers and tore the sheets off, rolling stacks of ten or twelve sheets into tight tubes. He put them to one side, picked up the petrol can and poured the petrol into each bottle, leaving a gap of about three inches from the top. He had spilt some petrol, but it would soon evaporate. He then pushed the paper tubes into the bottles, where they soaked up the fuel almost instantly. The pellets were soluble and had already started to turn into a purply mush at the bottom of the bottles. King peered around the doorway, before he eased out, carrying the three bottles carefully. He could no longer see the men, but he knew they would be checking the back of the house.

Anna appeared at the top of the steps, her face ashen and her eyes wide. She had changed into jeans and a shirt and wore a pair of pumps with sequins all over them. "They are here," she said. "They are trying to get in one of the windows!"

"Where?"

"Come with me," she said. "You will see them." She looked at him, precariously carrying the three bottles. "What are those?"

"Something your motherland came up with," he said. "Molotov Cocktails…" He placed two of them on the kitchen counter, carried the larger of the three – the vodka bottle – with him as he bounded up the stairs. "Show me," he said to her.

There were four large bedrooms upstairs and a mezzanine area set aside as a cosy-corner with a selection of paperbacks on the windowsill acting as a mini library. Anna veered to the right, stepped past one of two double beds and stopped just short of the window. "Down there," she said.

King peered down, saw the larger man prising the shutter with a large screwdriver, the smaller man standing back a few paces with a mini-Uzi machine pistol held at the ready. He placed the bottle on the floor, then reached for the locks.

"What are you doing?"

"Getting us out of here."

"But you'll kill them both!"

"They have guns," King said. "Machine guns. They'll cut us to shreds."

"But while they're round the back, we could get out the front way!"

King looked at her. "Yes. You're right," he said. "Get your daughter and wait for me downstairs."

He watched her go, then turned back to the window and eased the catch. It was stiff, and he applied enough dynamic tension to avoid it giving suddenly and making a noise. He got it undone and started to ease the window outwards when the smaller man looked up, his eyes on the window to the room next door. He then looked directly at King, brought the mini-Uzi up to aim.

King ducked backwards, the window shattering and a trail of bullets slamming into the ceiling. Plaster dust fell and debris from the ceiling and shards of glass scattered across the wooden floor. King reached for the lighter in his pocket, got it lit and dabbed the flame on the petrol-soaked paper wad. It flamed instantly, and he grabbed the bottle and threw it down hard in their general direction. He did not know if the men had moved, but he guessed they hadn't when he heard the screams above the woof of the petrol igniting. He got to his feet, chanced a look and saw the smaller man on his back, his feet on fire as he scrabbled backwards on his backside. He had dropped the machine pistol and was looking horrified as the giant clawed the air, staggering onto the lawn, leaving a sticky trail of burning fuel that singed the grass in his wake. The addition of the slug-pellets, largely consisting of Methiocarb - a substance which liquifies at 114°c and turns to syrup - meant that the fuel stuck in place and allowed the petrol vapour to burn for longer and more intensely than it normally would have, like an improvised napalm.

The giant's blood-curdling screams started to die down but were replaced by those of the smaller man. King peeked out, saw he was patting his feet with his hands, but the sticky fuel merely stuck and burned. The man leapt up, staggered the twenty-metres or so to the pool and threw himself in.

King bolted down the stairs, barging Anna out of the way as he reached the bottom. She was in shock, her expression one of terror as she shielded her daughter.

"I'm sorry..."

King silenced her with a right jab to her jaw and she fell to the floor, already unconscious. Dina screamed, and King glared at her. "Stay there!" he shouted.

He dashed over to the window, saw two men at the Range Rover. They were taking cover behind, aiming pistols at the house, unsure what to do next. They had heard the gunfire, the screams, but it took a lot to run towards that, and these men were not that type.

King unlocked the door, lit one of the tapers of newspaper, and picked up the bottle. He took a deep breath to ready himself, then opened the door and darted outside.

The men froze for a second, enough time to get the bottle airborne and travelling in a gentle arc across the road. He ducked down, as they opened fire. One man had a fully-automatic Glock and wasted his twenty-rounds on the house, the garden wall and the open doorway. King hoped that the girl had stayed put. He heard the vehicle engulf with flames, the woof that petrol makes in large quantities when it ignites. He ducked back into the house, used the doorframe for cover as he peered back outside. The bottle had landed just short of the Range Rover, but the liquid had spilt underneath and engulfed the vehicle in flames. The men were on fire, stumbling into the fence and unable to escape the horror of the flames. Everywhere they trod started to burn, the syrupy fuel sticking to and burning whatever it encountered. The Mercedes had started up and was reversing erratically away. It had caught some of the burning fuel, its front wheels burning fiercely.

King turned and walked along the side of the house. He could see the man in the pool. He was clinging to the side, breathing erratically, fighting the pain. He looked up at King as he walked past. The giant was dead, but still burning. King never ate roast pork, something he had learned many years before whilst operating in areas where war had been fought from the air, or rebels had ethnically cleansed entire villages. The smell would always stay with him – the smell of fuel, of rendered fat, of burned meat. It clung inside the nostrils, the sweet and sickly essence of death. There was a distinct likeness to over-done pork that always took King back to those hellish scenes.

King picked up the smaller man's machine pistol. It was an older version, where the action fired from an open bolt. The bullet visible in the neck of the magazine. A squeeze of the trigger and the bolt would slam forward, the firing pin fixed and take the bullet to the breach where it would fire instantly and cycle until the trigger was released. Not an ideal design for grime and debris, but it was instantly recognisable as empty or loaded. He walked over to the pool, aimed at the man clinging to the side.

"What were your orders?"

"Fuck you…" the man winced, the side of his face was burned too.

"She warned you, didn't she?" King asked. "At the window."

The man smirked. "What the hell did you expect? You killed her husband."

"And you came here to kill me?" The man shrugged like it was nothing. "And her?" King asked.

"What?"

"Did you come here to kill her too? Her daughter as well?"

"Why the hell would I kill *them*?" the man asked incredulously.

King shot the man in the forehead, turned and walked back to the house without seeing him sink to the bottom of the pool, a trail of blood discolouring the water like a pale, crimson mist. He checked the weapon's magazine as he walked, best guessed there were ten rounds left. He could see the Mercedes on fire a hundred metres up the road. The burning wheels had set something alight in the engine bay, or perhaps the fuel lines underneath, and the flames had taken hold. King had no way of telling if the driver or whoever else had been inside had gotten clear. He couldn't see anybody, so entered the house vigilantly, the weapon aimed in front of him.

Anna was on the floor, her back perched against the sofa, her daughter cradling her as she rubbed her jaw. She looked groggy, possibly only coming round in that moment. She looked up at King, her eyes wild and her expression full of hate.

"Bastard!" she shouted at him.

"You called them, didn't you?" he said quietly. "When you got the coffee."

"Of course," she said. "I said what I said to you, because it suited me. I survive. That's what I do. I survived back in those days with the Bratva, and I continued to survive by marrying one of them. I knew they would be looking for me, and I knew they would leave me alone if I helped them. And I rated their chances more than yours."

"Let me know how that's worked out for you?"

"Bastard!" she shouted again. The girl flinched, and Anna held her arm, squeezing tightly. "This is the man who killed your father, my dear."

The girl looked puzzled for a moment, then sad. She said nothing, but tears were welling in her eyes.

King ignored Anna, looked at the girl and crouched down. "I'm sorry for you, Dina. Truly I am," he paused. "I understand your pain. But I gave your father a chance to live. More of a chance than he gave me."

"Bastard!" Anna shouted.

King raised the machine pistol at Anna. "Shut up!" he snapped at her, his eyes as cold and blue as glacier water. He turned back to the girl. "You look like a smart girl," he said. "You can choose to hate me for what happened, perhaps even wish me dead. Or you can let it go and get on with the rest of your life. The first option will bring you nothing but misery. The second option will define you, bring you happiness. The ability to love the people you get close to and enjoy life to the fullest." He stood back up and walked to the door, pausing briefly to turn back and look at her. "My name is Alex King," he said. "Remember it. If you want to get even one day, well I'll most likely deserve it. But believe me, I'll be ready, and I don't die easily. And I won't think twice about killing you."

54

"About time. You're playing fast and loose with the woman you love."

"I was injured after taking down Nikolai. I needed a few days to get sorted," King lied seamlessly, then paused. "And the area got pretty hot with the police. I had to lie low for a while."

"But you're ready for your next task now?"

"Yes."

"Good. I will text it to you now. And no contact with me until it's done."

"Whatever."

"No, Mister King. You will receive the target and the address. You will do the job and you will keep all communication switched off until it is done. Do I make myself clear?"

"Crystal."

"And no collateral damage."

"Sometimes it's inevitable."

"Not in this case!" Helena snapped.

"I'll see how it goes."

"The guards are one thing, but no civilians. No non-combatants. Understand?"

"Like I said, I'll see how it goes."

"There will be no collateral damage, or you will never see your woman again…"

"Is there something you're not telling me?"

"Plenty. But make sure you understand. No collateral."

"Send me the details."

"Nearly there," she paused. *"And then you will see your beautiful, feisty Caroline again. Unless of course, you fail…"*

King heard the line go dead. He smiled, feeling that she had been suitably rattled. He held the phone in front of him, willing the text to come through. He took out the piece of paper that Anna Sergeyev had written Romanovitch's details on. She could have been lying, but he doubted it. She seemed to want Helena Milankovitch derailed as much as he did. She ran with the fox and hunted with the hounds. He suspected he couldn't trust a word she said.

The text came through, a silent vibrate that King had set the phone to. He unlocked it and read the text. Goran Romanovitch was the target. King held up the paper alongside the phone. Helena had included GPS coordinates with her text, but the two addresses were identical.

King had his next target.

He was another step closer.

But there was no mention of Catherine Milankovitch. Only Helena's insistence upon zero collateral damage.

Not only was King a step closer, he was now decidedly out in front.

55

Tbilisi International Airport (TBS), Georgia

"I'll get the car," Ramsay said. "You two stay here and keep an eye on the bags."

"Yes, Dad," Rashid quipped as Ramsay walked away from them.

"You like winding him up, don't you," Marnie stated flatly. "He's not so bad."

"No, he's okay," Rashid agreed. "But he's done a lot of desk work, pressed the flesh and signed a lot of documents off. Not to mention had a few lunches on expenses."

"He was pretty handy at Botha's place," she countered. "Got you inside quickly when everyone was being shot at."

"True," he conceded. His phone vibrated in his pocket and he looked at the screen as he took it out. He turned away from Marnie and spoke quietly. Marnie watched him, as he nodded, concentrating on the voice on the other end. She caught his eye and smiled, but he turned away without returning her gesture. Rashid slipped the phone back into his pocket and walked back over to her.

"Everything okay?" she asked.

Rashid watched Ramsay signing documents at the Hertz desk, showing his licence and talking animatedly with the hire company agent. He turned back to Marnie and bent down, kissed her firmly on the lips. She went to pull away, but he tucked his hand behind her head, felt her submit and kiss him passionately back. When he pulled away, he smiled. "Sorry, luv," he said. "Got to go. Don't try and find me, I have something to do."

"What?" she asked, shocked and confused. She looked over at Ramsay, who caught her eye, but looked back to the hire car rep. "What do you mean; go?"

"Got to see a man about a dog," he said. He slung his travel bag over his shoulder and headed for the exit without another glance.

56

London

Another day of drizzle, the humidity of summer exacerbated by the heat and fumes of the heavy traffic. Simon Mereweather had left the COBRA meeting and was on his way back to Thames House. It was only a short drive, but as expected, the traffic was gridlocked. MI5 were using motorcades less frequently in recent months, preferring to blend in with the rest of the London traffic. Mereweather travelled in the rear passenger seat of a pool car, the anonymous Ford Mondeo crawling with the flow of commuters, sight-seers and taxis. Upfront, his regular driver was accompanied by Mereweather's bodyguard.

His phone was hot, messages, texts and calls coming in from MI6, GCHQ, the MOD and various departments within MI5. The impending visit from the Russian president was first and foremost on the security and intelligence community's agenda, given the dire lack of relations between the two countries after the Russian's had been accused of biological attacks on former KGB double-agents on British soil. Russia's relationship with many countries who had supported Britain, expelling Russian diplomats, was at an all-time low. Now, with a new Russian president and a new British Prime Minister in place, the visit was viewed as critically important on the world stage. However, with Russia's involvement in supporting the Syrian regime, and an accusation of covert biological attacks in predominantly Muslim Chechnya, many Islamic extremist suspects had been heard on what GCHQ called network chatter. Their Echelon listening system had picked up talk of assassinating the Russian president.

Mereweather looked at his phone for the tenth time in as many minutes. He was about to ignore it for a moment, collecting his thoughts for the imminent COBRA debriefing he would have with Director Amherst back at Thames House. There was barely a number he didn't have stored, but the number was an international one, and he felt compelled to take it. He answered and was greeted by a woman's voice, heavy in accent with a little background white noise.

"Operator services, I have a reverse-charge call from Georgia, will you accept the charge?"

"Yes." A series of clicks followed, more white noise, then Mereweather said, "Hello?"

"Simon! It's Caroline..."

"Caroline! Oh my god! Are you alright?"

"I am," she hesitated. *"But I'm not safe."*

"Are you free?"

"I am."

"Where? Tell me and I'll get an asset to you."

"Seems to be becoming a habit..."

"Where are you?"

"*Batumi,*" she said. "*On the Georgian Black Sea coast.*"

"Where?"

"*Hard to say. I have a vehicle, but no money and no phone. The British embassy is in Tbilisi, but it wasn't practical to head that way. I don't have enough fuel to reach Tbilisi.*"

"Neil Ramsay is in Georgia. He traced Helena's IP address to a deserted farmhouse on the outskirts of Skhimili."

"*That's where I was being held!*" she gushed, the relief and knowledge that they had been looking for her was almost too much, the emotion heavy in her voice.

"He's up there now. The police are all over it. But it's deserted."

"*They haven't found anything?*"

"They are taking swabs and prints as we speak."

"*People. What about people? Women?*"

"Women? No. The place was empty."

"*Simon, it was hell. It was a staging post for sex trafficking, baby farms… There were many women there…*"

"Well, they've cleared out now," Mereweather paused. "I'll call Neil right back, get him to come and get you. Where can you meet?"

Caroline hesitated, then said, "*There is a lighthouse and Ferris wheel on the seafront. I'll meet him there.*"

"Hang tight," Mereweather said. "He'll come straight over."

"Simon," Caroline said quietly. *"Is Alex okay?"*

"Why do you ask?" he paused. "Apart from the obvious?"

"Helena said she had him working for her. To keep me from harm. Is that true?"

"I'm afraid so."

"Is he okay?" she asked again.

"We don't know," Mereweather paused. "He's taken down half the Russian mafia and an Italian mafia syndicate for good measure. In short, we don't know where he is."

"Helena needs to be caught."

"Well, we're working on it. Look, stay put, I have to go so I can get you picked up," he paused. "It's brilliant to hear your voice again. Stay safe…" Mereweather ended the call, scrolled and dialled Neil Ramsay's number.

57

The Georgian police seemed to have a unique approach to securing a crime scene. Once every officer had trod their way through with muddy boots, they gathered and smoked a cigarette each. Talked in low voices and agreed it would be a good idea to walk the mud through again, this time picking up everything within reach without gloves, regroup and smoke again, each man flicking their cigarette stubs in different directions. Some long and low conversations later, and relatives of the police were now on scene to assist, smoke, traipse mud of their own through the crime scene, then confer over more cigarettes. Somebody had found a bottle of alcohol and a few of the lower-ranked officers gathered behind one of the barns to share it. After a few more smokes, a vehicle arrived and then a man got out wearing a suit and carrying a medical case. He conferred with the group of officers, accepted a cigarette and smoked it on his way in.

Ramsay looked up, glanced at Marnie, then looked back at the man in the suit.

"I am officer Danko, I am the forensic scientist."

"I'm with the British Home Office," Ramsay said without offering his name or department. "There looks to be evidence of people being held here. One of our people may have been held prisoner here," he paused. "We are sending over a DNA sample, fingerprints, blood type and photograph to your headquarters." He looked dejectedly at the mud on the floor, the officers walking through. "In the event of a miracle and you actually finding any forensic evidence that hasn't been corrupted by your colleagues, the British Government would appreciate you correlating this data and sharing it immediately."

The forensic scientist shrugged and walked over to two police officers, who pointed towards the stairs. He left the room without a glance.

"Fat lot of good this will do," Marnie said. "I only know about these things from watching *Silent Witness* and *CSI*, but I'm guessing they don't excel in the world of forensic science out here. I doubt they even watch those shows."

"I doubt they even get *Quincy*," Ramsay commented flatly. He felt his mobile phone vibrate in his pocket and took it out. He saw Simon Mereweather's number on the display. "Hello?"

"Drop whatever you're doing and get down to Batumi on the coast. There is a lighthouse and a Ferris wheel on the seafront. Caroline will be there."

"What?" Ramsay asked incredulously. "A trade?"

"No. She escaped, and she'll be waiting for you."

Ramsay was already walking, Marnie snapped to and followed, her expression one of concern. He strode out across the farmyard, talking as he went. "Is she okay?"

"She sounds shaken, and she has no money or phone, so hurry and pick her up. Call me as soon as you have her."

Ramsay put the phone back in his pocket and reached for the keys to the hire car.

"Problem?" Marnie asked.

"No. Caroline is safe. But she has no funds, no way of contacting us and we have to drive to a town called Batumi and pick her up. She escaped…"

"Escaped?" Marnie interrupted.

"Yes," Ramsay replied tersely. "I don't have the details yet, because I'm sure Simon hasn't either."

"What about Rashid?"

"Screw him."

"No, seriously."

"Seriously, screw him. He isn't going to be with MI5 after that little stunt he pulled."

"Well, it must have been important," Marnie protested. "Rashid is a good man."

"Tell that to your boyfriend," Ramsay paused, shaking his head. "I saw you and him kissing at the airport."

Marnie stopped walking. "Firstly, that is between me, and my soon to be ex-fiancé. Rashid actually made me realise I was making a mistake, whatever happens or doesn't happen between Rashid and myself when we get home."

Ramsay stopped and turned around. "And secondly?"

"Secondly, don't take a cheap shot at *me* because you're pissed off with *him*."

He turned back and carried on walking. "All right," he said. "I'm sorry, it was uncalled for."

"Forget it," she said. She took out her mobile and started searching for the name of the town. "Okay, I've got it. I'll start satnav guidance now."

"How far is it?"

"One-hundred and thirty-eight kilometres."

"About two-hours then."

"Try four and a half."

"What?"

"That's what it says here. It's not the M1, that's for sure."

Ramsay got into the Skoda Superb, had the engine started before Marnie got in. As her backside hit the seat he took off at speed, the front wheels throwing up gravel that scattered down the side of the vehicle. Her door closed when enough wind force pushed it shut. She was struggling with the seatbelt, which had locked up when the wheels lost traction.

"Holy crap!" she shouted.

"Four and a half hours, my arse," he said, and took the car up to eighty miles per hour down the narrow country lane. The car scudded over potholes large enough for a corpse to be buried in, the car bouncing and weaving its way down the track. "I said two-hours, and by Christ we'll do it in two."

58

Batumi, Georgia

King could see the lighthouse in the distance. It had been recently painted and he imagined that the up and coming town had seen some investment with the intention of seeing Batumi elevate to a holiday resort that appealed to couples and families, as well as casino goers and clubbers. The Ferris wheel would indicate that the town's council envisaged more for the resort than blackjack and slot machines. Further up the seafront, King could see towers and other fairground attractions, that looked set in place for the summer. Perhaps the town council would follow the Spanish and import better sand, rather than the dark quarry dust and chippings the beach was made up of.

King knew the difference a few streets could make. The tourists wouldn't see this aspect of Batumi though. Tenement housing, run down businesses and vacant properties. Some properties looked to have been broken into, squatters taking up residence. A few hundred metres off the strip, set back from the three parallel streets running along the seafront. There were a couple of bars, but they were dark and foreboding-looking places only the hardened traveller or misguided fool would wander into in a state of inebriation.

There were three of them. King had watched for an hour and was certain of the system they were using. He watched as a white Mercedes with large after-market exhausts and spinning wheel hubs pulled in, its windows as dark as coal. The driver's window lowered, and a man casually walked over, his gait more swagger than purpose. He bent down, said very little as King watched the driver hand over a fold of banknotes. The man turned and walked back to the bar, where a youth of around fourteen took the money and darted down the alleyway. King had a good enough view to see the boy hover at the entrance to a tenement block. A scruffy-looking man appeared, took the money and stepped back inside. King watched for a few minutes, and then saw the man appear in the entrance and hand the youth a package. The boy ran back along the alley and stopped at the edge of the bar, handed the package to the frontman, who sauntered back over to the Mercedes. The window lowered again, and King could hear rap music fill the air. The man stepped back, and the Mercedes powered away, its rear wheels lighting up on the rough tarmac. The man sat back down at a table outside the bar and the youth had faded away into the alleyway. It was like a smooth-running restaurant – front of house, dining staff and chef. A drug chain that could easily be broken if the police happened by. Each heading their separate ways.

King started the car and drove past the bar, then turned first right, and then again. He parked the car near some dumpster bins and looked around. The car was a new model Dacia. A nothing car, but everything to somebody living here. He doubted it would be long before somebody tried to steal it, but he had taken out the insurance and he had noticed an *Avis* and *Eurocar* in the business centre of Batumi. It was only a short walk to the seafront and its lighthouse and Ferris wheel, he would head that way and work his way in on better streets.

He got out and opened the boot. He rummaged underneath the carpet and retrieved a single head tyre iron. He slipped it up his sleeve and closed the boot lid. The alley was open-ended, and King figured he'd found it as he crossed the road and glanced around, keeping alert, but making himself seem alert too. Trouble rarely looked for trouble, and with his broad shoulders and chest, athletic waist, close-cropped hair and pugilist's brow, he looked like a serious opponent. The cat-like grace with which he crossed the road, hopped the pavement, his fists ready and his motions fluid, he could well have been heading through the crowd to a boxing ring.

King best-guessed the building – now on his left – and stepped into the doorway on his right. He had a good eyes-on for both the entrance of the tenement block and the youth who would come with the money and take back the drugs. It was now only a matter of time.

The alley smelled of urine and damp over domestic waste. It was closely hemmed in by buildings built in the Soviet era, where thought was only towards housing the masses and ensuring workers of certain demographics had accommodation and were close to work. In this case, most probably the port for which Batumi had once been a crucial link for the Soviet empire. King guessed the place had seen better days. Most of it appeared empty now. Since it broke away from the Soviet Union, Georgia had become a hub for travellers, people looking for the next best thing. The beach resorts of the Black Sea were never going to compete against the Costas or the south of France, but they were no worse than much of Italy's or Cyprus', and holidays on the Black Sea could cost half the price as those destinations. The money put into Batumi's seafront and new town showed that commerce was set to grow. Places like this, the rotten, degraded pockets of poverty would be gone before long. And the drug dealers would have to ply their trade elsewhere.

King could see a garish yellow Range Rover slow and pull up outside the bar. It was an old model vogue lowered and kitted out to loosely represent a Range Rover Sport. The windows were blacked out, and already King could hear some R&B coming out hard. A moment later, the boy ran down the alleyway towards him. The boy shouted when he reached the entrance and thirty seconds later the man appeared. King could see him clearly now. Shaved head, bearded, tattooed and muscular. He snapped at the boy as he took the money. King could see he had a pistol tucked into the back of his waistband. He disappeared, came back moments later with the package. The boy ran back towards the bar and King stepped out of the doorway and crossed the alleyway.

The entrance was dark, and a cage door was propped open, the man almost through when King stepped inside. He let the tyre iron drop down his sleeve. He was only two paces behind the man when he turned around. King swung the iron, but the man was quick. He dodged left, drew backwards and went for the pistol. King swung again, the iron swiping an inch in front of the man's face. He kicked out, caught the man in the groin. The man dropped, but caught hold of King's shirt as he fell, and he pulled King downward. King smashed the iron down on the man's back and he cried out as he let go and fell. He had fight training, and as he curled into a ball, his hands held in a tight boxer's guard, he kicked wildly and repeatedly, stopping King from attacking further. King kicked downwards, keeping his eyes on the man's hands. There was still a firearm in the mix, but it was ok until the man reached for it, which he would do if King did not keep up the momentum of the assault. He struck the man's shin with the tyre iron, then went to take a better swing when he felt himself pulled from behind. Both the frontman and the boy were grabbing at him, and it was enough time for the man on the ground to get into a better position. The frontman was reaching for a blade. King had left the flick-knife in France, without hold luggage, he couldn't risk it in his carry-on. King kicked backwards, keeping the man on the ground busy. He caught him in the face, heard the crunch of bone, keeping his eyes on the knife. The frontman swung, as King caught hold of the boy by his shirt collar and met the attack head on, using him as a shield. The boy was slightly built, and after his back took the swipe of the blade – a grimace on his face – King smashed the youth back into the frontman, putting distance between himself and the blade. The back of the boy's head was in front of the frontman's face, and King cupped his face with the palm of his hand and smashed his head backwards into the frontman's jaw. Once, twice, three times… By the fourth time, the man had slumped enough for the boy's head to smash his nose flat. He slid down the wall and King let the youth go, where he fell and joined him. As he turned, the man on the floor was reaching for the pistol. King darted forward and punched the man with a right-cross to his jaw. He was out cold before he fell backwards onto the urine-soaked concrete.

King was heaving for breath. It hadn't gone like he had wanted it to. But things seldom ever did. He took the pistol out of the man's jeans. And tucked it into his own. He turned to the boy, who although wasn't out cold, was lying down, clearly shocked. He was holding the back of his head, tears in his eyes and panting for breath. King caught hold of him and pulled him forwards to check the wound. His head was swelling, but not bleeding. His back had taken a slash, but it wasn't deep. The knife had been blunt and had pulled across the boy's shirt, cutting in places, scratching for the most-part. The blade was most likely dirty, and the boy would need medical attention. But it was the swelling to his head that King was most concerned about. He had taken quite a battering. He cursed quietly to himself. But he pushed the boy back down onto the unconscious body of the frontman and went about checking the other man's pockets. There was a spare magazine for the 9mm Makarov pistol which King took, along with the roll of banknotes from the drugs transaction.

He looked back at the boy. "You speak English?"

The boy nodded.

"How old are you?"

"Fifteen."

King could see a wispy moustache beginning to poke through, but he was a long way off shaving. He looked the boy up and down. He didn't feel guilty, worse things had happened to him by that age. But he felt compassion, because he knew when these men woke up, the boy would be ferrying drugs and money and would not be going anywhere near a hospital.

"I'm sorry you got hurt," he said. "Come with me, and I'll drop you outside the medical centre. I've seen one in the new town."

The boy looked hesitant, but he removed his hand from the back of his head, checked his fingers for blood and shrugged.

"Your head needs a cold pack," King explained. "And you may need a stitch or two in your back, but you definitely need it cleaned and perhaps some antibiotics in case it gets infected." King looked at the state of the floor, was certain it was most likely infected already.

"Okay," the boy shrugged, like it was an everyday occurrence.

King led the way and the boy followed. He had no idea why the boy did not run, but as he stepped out into the light upon leaving the alleyway, he wondered if the boy had any choice in the work he did.

Thankfully the car had been left alone, and King opened the door, let the boy slide gingerly into the front seat.

"Who are those men?" King asked.

The boy shrugged again. "Just men," he said. "My mother died, my father went to work in the Ukraine last year, picking flowers. He hasn't been in touch since…"

King nodded. He should have been back between the growing season. He knew that tulips, poppies, orchids and roses were grown in the Ukraine. It was seasonal work relying on migrant workers. He doubted the boy would see him again.

"Those men, they pay you?"

"Some."

King drove quickly, threaded his way through the streets until he found himself on the seafront. He passed the lighthouse, then followed the road around to the left, away from the seafront and towards the new town. He fished out the wad of banknotes, around a thousand Lari worth approximately three-hundred pounds. He tossed it into the boy's lap. "Take this," he said. "Maybe it will be enough to get away from here. You have relatives?"

"An aunt and cousins in Tbilisi."

"Go there. Don't go back to those men. They're using you and no good will come from it. I know. I started dealing drugs for people like that, pretty soon I was handing out beatings and in and out of prison." He pulled up in front of the medical centre and took out his wallet, retrieved a stack of Lari, around fifty-pounds Stirling. "Get yourself patched up. Get the wound cleaned, stitched and ask for antibiotics. And get a cold pack on that head bump."

The boy opened the door, went to thank him, but King pulled away and the door shut of its own accord once he got up to about thirty-miles-per-hour. He checked his watch. He had made good time. He had a gun and ammunition, and he had an hour's drive ahead of him before he had to use it.

59

King had stopped at a builder's merchants, having been unable to find an extensive DIY store. He had found most of the things he needed, paying in cash, but had also stopped at a pharmacy, a supermarket and a service station for the rest of the things he would need. A military surplus store located on the side of the road which had been advertised by a Soviet T-62 tank, provided him with the last of his purchases. Although the store did not sell firearms, it still provided King with a sturdy combat knife, a gas stove, some mess-tins and a dozen aluminium water bottles in canvas sleeves. He picked out some olive cargo trousers to go with his grey T-shirt and tan leather jacket, and a pair of surplus boots to help him blend into the landscape and provide solid foot-ware for the rocky terrain. He wore a balanced combination that would afford him cover, but not have him dressed like a soldier if he found himself in a different situation that required him to blend into a crowd.

The mountain road took him higher, winding through woodland and pastures, affording glimpses of the Black Sea. King could see how the sea got its name. Not land-locked, but separated by the narrow Bosporus straight, the Sea of Marmara and the Aegean Sea from the sparkling blue waters of the Mediterranean. The Black Sea was dark and slick, with choppy waves rather than small rollers, and the waters looked deep and black on all but the brightest and clearest of skies, or calmest of seas.

King found a track and pulled off the road, checking his mobile phone signal and sending a short text, before making his way cautiously down the track, the Dacia coping with the ruts and potholes without grounding. The track led to nothing more than a turning point, where King switched off the engine and typed a text, he checked for mistakes forced by the auto-correct before sending.

The silence as King got out of the car was blissful. The air was warm, but clean. He felt the sun on his face and was buoyed by the promise of getting ahead of Helena. He would soon be in control, and he relished turning the tables on his enemy. He received a message back, checked it and smiled. He had felt so alone until now. He had spent his entire career working alone and even when he had assistance or joined forces with another intelligence service, or agency from another country, he knew he would ultimately be alone. He had been a deniable asset. Nobody would trade for him, negotiate his release. He should have been used to it, but in his short-time working with MI5 and partnering Caroline on various cases, he had grown used to being a part of a team. But it wasn't only that. King had felt from the outset, that the price of Caroline being held for ransom was too high, as was the risk of failure on his part. The pressure was insurmountable.

King opened the hatch of the car and started to take out the equipment and items he had bought. He set up the gas stove and arranged the mess-tins around it. Next, he took out the aluminium water bottles and set about puncturing the lids with his knife. He then arranged them in the boot of the car where it was a decidedly smoother surface than the ground. He opened a bottle of thick bleach and poured it into a mess-tin. Then he scooped out petroleum jelly from a large tub and placed it in the bleach, along with just the right amount of borax and potassium nitrate, also known as salt-peter. King placed the mess-tin on the gas stove and watched it melt the petroleum jelly. He sprinkled in the iron filings - to aid as an electrical conductor rather than shrapnel - and stirred the mix together with a stick. As the mix boiled and licked the edges of the mess-tin, King took it off the heat and stirred gently, the mix thinning further and gradually darkening in colour. He placed the tin in the boot of the car, then opened the bag of two-inch screws into his hand and fed them into two of the bottles, each about half-full. He then poured the mix into the bottles right up to the top and threw the mess-tin onto the ground. He took out a length of electrical wire, East-European spec, with just a negative and a positive. He used a pair of snips to cut the length, then fed the wires through the lid until approximately four-inches of wire protruded. Next, he coiled the wires separately around his finger so that both lengths of negative and positive resembled a spring. King eased the lengths into the warm liquid and fastened the lids in place. He then took two battery power units and a pin-timer delay out of the boot and wired the connections, leaving the batteries out until he was ready. He set the timers for five-minutes and taped the consumer units to the side of the bottles with duct-tape. King repeated the process twice more, imperative he use clean mess-tins and did not change the order in which he made the mixes, and finally stood back to admire his handiwork. Six time-delay Improvised Explosive Devices – or IED's - each one capable of blowing a car into the air into pieces, or he estimated enough to take down two average-sized houses if set correctly.

King then set about cutting lengths of string and soaking them in sugar and liquid paraffin. He left them for twenty-minutes while he made four more bottles of the mix. He checked that the holes in the lids were made larger, to allow for air, then took the string out of the paraffin and allowed them to dry in the warm air. Once they were dry enough to the touch, he folded them in half, and pushed both ends through the lid and deep into the liquid compound, which was already starting to thicken. He tightened up the lids, leaving a ten-inch loop protruding. He tested a spare length of the string with his lighter, watched as it burned fiercely, counting the whole time. The length of string burned away, and King dropped the ember to the ground. He then adjusted the lengths of string in the bottles and taped them in place. He figured they would burn for ten-seconds before heating the mix enough to initiate and cause detonation. The initiation would use a third of the mix, making detonation around two-thirds as powerful as the electrically-detonated devices. Enough to disable a car, breach a door or take down a group of men effectively.

King took out a bottle of water, drank down half a litre or so and washed his hands thoroughly. He dried them on his shirt then took out the 9mm Makarov pistol and checked it over. He unloaded the magazine, inspected the bullets. They looked like factory loads as far as he could tell, and the shell cases were in good condition. He never fired anything he hadn't re-loaded himself, or that wasn't factory-loaded if he could help it. But beggars couldn't be choosers. He unloaded the second magazine, checked the bullets, then stripped the pistol down. An easy weapon to take apart – he simply pulled down the trigger guard, slipped it sideways onto its internal holding lug, then pulled back the slide all the way, lifted and dropped it forward and off the barrel. He sprayed the weapon well with what he guessed was Georgia or Russia's equivalent of WD40 and rubbed it all over with a dry cloth. He oiled the spring, inspected the barrel, squirted a little oil down it and allowed it to drain. Drug dealers tended to pose and threaten with their firearms, but there was no telling whether this weapon had been fired in forty-years. King suspected it had started off life as a well-used military piece but would have been stolen and sold on many times over since then. It looked in ok condition. He oiled and checked the magazines, reloaded them checking the spring tension. He put them down, put the pistol back together, checked the action, then loaded one of the magazines, chambered a round and applied the safety, which dropped the hammer onto the safe bar. He tucked the pistol into his right trouser pocket and put the spare magazine into the other.

"Well, you managed to get a piece, more than I could do."

King spun around, but he had already figured out who it was and refrained from grabbing the pistol. "You made decent time," he said lightly, but he was mad with himself for being crept up on. Fatigue and circumstance was putting him at a disadvantage.

Rashid walked up, held out his hand. King took it, shook it warmly. It was relief to have help, to see a friendly face.

"How is it on the outside?"

"Flying blind," King replied. He told him about Sweden, what he had been about to do, and the idea that Simon Grant had unwittingly given him about using leverage. He told him about Anna and the way she had played both sides. The two men that he had killed, the unknown number of men in the burned-out Mercedes. He hadn't seen the need to check.

"You've been busy," Rashid commented as he looked inside the boot of the car. He saw the IEDs. "Blast radius?"

"A hundred feet for the electrical charges, fifty-feet for the taper fuse ones," King said with a shrug. "Or thereabouts."

"Shrapnel?"

"About two-hundred grams of screws in each. The taper fuse ones will be less powerful, but still enough to wreck a vehicle."

"I'll be sure to duck, then," Rashid said. He updated King on what he, Ramsay and Marnie had found. He told them about South Africa, working with Ryan Beard from MI6 and what had happened at Botha's property. And then he told him about the IP address and that Marnie and Ramsay were heading there to investigate.

King listened intently. This last piece could lead them directly to Caroline. He wondered whether he should pack up and go, but he was so close, and they could find themselves at another dead end. He needed to hold his nerve.

"I'll stick to what I'm doing here. I just want a hand with a diversion," King said. "As far as I'm concerned, I'm getting Catherine Milankovitch out. Romanovitch is Helena's problem. With Catherine, I have a bargaining chip, a fair trade for Caroline. Anna Sergeyev told me that Romanovitch snatched Catherine and has kept her ever since Helena funded some mercenaries to move in on the Bratva's assets.

He covered his arse, even taunted Pyotr Sergeyev about it, telling him to hide."

Rashid nodded. "So, what do we know about Romanovitch's place?"

"I've found it with Google Earth, worked out the borders, which way is north, seen the gates. Nothing more."

"So, flying blind," Rashid said flatly. "I haven't got a weapon," he said.

"If all goes well, I just want some big bangs. There are outbuildings, cars, and of course, a huge gate. If some of those things go skywards, I plan on slipping in through the back and finding Catherine."

"And if she's being held in one of those outbuildings and gets blown to kingdom-come?" Rashid shook his head decisively. "No, we need to do a thorough recce. You've come so far, buying time, getting Helena to trust you, discovering both the existence and whereabouts of Catherine. Now you have an edge. We can't risk harming the one person who can get Caroline back unharmed."

King nodded. He was not only fatigued, he wasn't thinking straight. "Agreed," he paused. "I bought some binoculars. There is plenty of high ground above his property. If we can work our way up there, it will be worth it."

"What about a recce, then hitting him in the middle of the night? We can be stealthy, use the demolition stuff to aid our escape instead of storming the castle, so to speak. Could keep the body count down too."

"We'll see," King said. The end was in sight. He was so close to transferring the power between Helena and himself, so eager with anticipation, that he felt like a child at the end of term. He was glad that Rashid was here to play devil's advocate, lend a sense of perspective. He looked at Rashid and nodded. "I guess you're right," he admitted.

Rashid patted him on the shoulder. "We'll get her back," he said. "It isn't over till it's over."

60

She had waited two-hours and twenty minutes and it had felt like a day. Parked on the road overlooking the seafront, the doors to the car locked, the windows wound up and the keys in the ignition. She had positioned the mirrors to watch the road behind her, affording little in the way of blind-spots and had spent the entire time studying all who came near. She kept the tiny pistol with its three rounds under her thigh. An easy reach.

Her nerve was gone. She was frightened, now that she was away from that place of hell, terrified she would be caught and bound and returned. Or taken someplace new and equally as hideous. She was hungry and thirsty, tired and desperately in need of a shower. The clothes Michael had given her were muddy, torn and blood-splattered. Her hair was tangled and lank, and as she caught sight of herself in the mirror, she would acknowledge that she looked hollow and worn. She was a beautiful woman, although she would never allude to thinking that, but she could see some light had left her eyes, some sparkle was gone, and she doubted it would ever return. She had been through much in her life – the killing of colleagues in both the army and MI5, as well as the death her fiancé in a terrorist attack – but she knew that these past weeks had extracted more from her than bereavement ever would. She thought of those poor women, their bastard children – innocent and compromised by fate, and whether they would ever know freedom again. She vowed, as she sat and stared at the stranger in the mirror, that she would help them. She would make it her life's work if she had to.

Caroline watched Ramsay's Skoda saloon pull up and park. He got out and looked around, then walk towards the lighthouse. There was a woman in the passenger seat. Her hair was dark and shoulder-length, her shoulders slender. Caroline felt a pang of familiarity. The same profile and build as Helena. Caroline continued to watch, noticed the woman looking around uneasily. She could see it was not Helena. While attractive, she wasn't in the same league of beauty, and she wore a pair of small, rectangular glasses set in trendy designer frames.

She realised that she was being paranoid, but her ordeal had infected her, changed her. She doubted she'd ever feel truly free again.

Trust nobody, rely on nobody.

She unlocked the car, took the keys out of the ignition and slipped them into her pocket. She did not lock the car door behind her, preferring to know she could save an extra second getting back in if she had to. Why was she dubious? She should have trusted Ramsay, thrown herself at him as he arrived. But she didn't feel she could let down her guard, put her safety into someone else's hands. No rescue had come for her. She worried about Alex. Had he come to harm going through who knew what for Helena's agenda? She had faith in him, but she couldn't worry unduly. She needed to think about herself. But she knew that safety was an illusion. She wanted to flee back to London, but London was where she was abducted from. She knew she wouldn't be any safer there than right here, right now. Leaving Georgia was putting the place behind her, but not the threat. The threat lay with Helena. And until she was dead or imprisoned for her crimes, then Caroline knew she would never truly be safe.

She glanced at the woman inside the car. She did not recognise her, but much of MI5's work was compartmentalised and many people from various departments never met until they were pulled in to work on something specific. Support staff, analysts and technical departments would work together regularly, but field agents like Caroline and King rarely rubbed shoulders with them. In fact, since the attack on Thames House by Russian terrorists last year, most of her briefings had taken place in temporary offices in Whitehall or the MOD.

The woman was working on a laptop, balancing it on her lap and checking a smartphone at the same time. Caroline walked onwards, watched all around Ramsay and behind her, feigning interest in the giant Ferris wheel. Nobody seemed to be watching him, which was Caroline's fear. She had come too far to be led unwittingly into an ambush. There were only a small number of places where it would have made sense for Caroline to go, it wouldn't be too difficult for Helena with her resources to have people looking out for her. After all, Caroline could link her with a number of major crimes and would be a witness to her sex trafficking and baby farming schemes. Both of which would be crimes where sentences would be handed out in decades rather than years.

Ramsay turned and saw her. He strode over, stopped short of hugging her and hesitated. Caroline hugged him, relief catching up with her. She pulled away, looked at him. There were tears in her eyes.

"God, I'm glad to see you," he said.

"Ditto," she replied, a little croak in her voice. She coughed, took a breath and said, "Where's Alex?"

Ramsay sighed. He glanced around and said, "Let's talk in the car. We'll get a hotel room, you can have a shower."

Caroline stopped in her tracks. "I asked you where Alex was."

Ramsay shook his head. "I don't know," he paused. "I haven't had contact with him since this started."

"So, you don't know if he's okay?" she asked. "Helena said that he was working for her, doing tasks to keep me safe."

Ramsay nodded. "He has been," he paused. "I don't want to go into it here, but he's a skilful chap. A certain *set* of skills, few possess. He has used them to good effect."

"So where would be your best guess?"

"I imagine getting closer to Helena," he said nonchalantly. "There's nothing high-profile on the grapevine since his visits to France and Italy. Those weren't exactly subtle affairs."

"So, you've no clue?"

"No. But an SAS officer on secondment to five, a man King knows well, by all accounts, was working with us to help find Helena," Ramsay paused. "Find Helena, find King. That was his angle. But I fear he has played us; been in contact with King throughout."

"Rashid?"

"Yes."

"Alex has no other friends in Hereford. He hates the place. I have met Rashid. He's a solid character. Where is he?"

Ramsay hesitated. "Well, that's just it," he said. "We arrived in Tbilisi and while I was hiring the car, he upped and went."

"Just like that?"

"The technician I have working with me, well, they both got fairly well acquainted…"

"And that's why he left?"

"No. Marnie was with him when he got a call. He listened, didn't speak much and left her standing there."

"You think it was Alex?"

"I do," he said.

"And he left through the airport, out onto the concourse?"

"Yes."

"Then if it was Alex, that would mean he was in Georgia," she said hopefully. "Which means Helena is still in Georgia and Alex is closing in on her."

"Precisely."

Caroline nodded. "We need to contact Rashid, see if he is with Alex. He'll need to know I'm safe and well."

"And are you?"

Caroline shrugged. "I've been through a lot, but I've seen a lot worse. Others did not have it as easy as I did," she paused. "I was eventually held at a farm…"

"We've been there," Ramsay said. "Near Skhimili. It was evident it had been in recent use, but it was deserted."

"Oh, no…" Caroline said quietly. She looked at Ramsay, her expression sorrowful. "There were girls there, young women… they were being held, ready to go out to the sex trade. Pop-up brothels, the internet, sex-slaves to the wealthy and immoral. They also had women set aside for a baby farming venture."

"Jesus…" Ramsay trailed off.

Caroline sighed. "The dark web, or deep web, or whatever the hell it's called. A place where babies can be bought and sold. To the highest bidder, naturally."

Ramsay shook his head and said, "I don't get it. I just don't understand how a British billionaire's wife can get so low, so quickly."

"She always was," Caroline said. "She worked in the sex trade herself, was part of the Russian mafia. She married well, that's all. She was the same person all the time. She cheated, keeping her long-time lover, Viktor Bukov, planned and schemed her husband's death all along. Together, they came up with Anarchy to Recreate Society. A terrorist organisation praying on the rich and powerful. Modern-day Robin Hoods. But that was all a cover, a way of making Sir Ian Snell's death look like part of a bigger picture. In doing so, she gladly sacrificed three other men, and people like the Jameson family, who simply died because they owned and lived at a house that was perfect for Bukov to take his shot from to kill Snell while he was down in Cornwall."

"And both King and yourself thwarted their plans, uncovered them."

"She's a spiteful and vengeful bitch," Caroline said bitterly.

"And clever too. Or at least smart."

"But not as smart as Alex. He was onto them from the moment he investigated the murder scene. He knew that they had taken more than one shot from such a great distance. He knew that from the position Snell had been sitting in, and the granite wall behind him, meant he would have been drugged. Snell simply would have known he was being shot at. He would have moved at least."

"Well, if Alex is onto her, we need to find out where he is so that we can be of assistance," Ramsay said thoughtfully. "It just doesn't feel right. The woman managed to be involved with the Russian mafia all this time, overthrew them using you as bait and a British agent to do her dirty work, and cleaned away her operation and evaded capture in a matter of hours, but she allows King to get near her? I don't see it. With the best will in the world, the woman is out for vengeance, and I just can't see her letting King get near her after all that has happened."

"You think Alex is walking into a trap?"

Ramsay nodded. "I'm convinced of it."

61

The mountain road led to a former communications outpost, chosen for the uninterrupted signal it would both receive or generate, high atop the tallest mountain in the range. It would have dated back to the original cold war, and King imagined bored and weary, undisciplined Soviet troops milling around, Kalashnikovs slung over their shoulders, waiting for word from Moscow, or counting down until their tour led them to something a little more favourable than a deserted mountain ridge. The posting would have been a punishment, or perhaps a last-chance shot across the bow for junior soldiers. A trained radio operator, and a handful of conscripts to cook, clean, guard and maintain the series of huts and bunks. Inspections would depend on the senior ranking soldier, and their own balance between social acceptance and fear of a snap inspection. The person in charge of this place would either be ostracised by his men or hauled over the coals when an officer turned up with high-ranking KGB officials for a report.

The buildings were now largely torn down. Graffiti and what King recognised as Russian profanity was tagged in garish colours on the remaining walls, and the roofing, windows and doors had all been stripped and stolen, most likely making up somebody's house soon after the fall of the Iron Curtain.

Rashid had left his car further down the mountain, parked off the road in a mountain track and tucked the keys under the front wheel arch. He had then ridden the rest of the way up with King, who had turned around and parked nose facing outwards, ready to escape if they needed to. Rashid's car would serve as a back-up plan if they were compromised by Romanovitch's men and could not make it back to King's car. Leaving the keys was merely soldier thinking – Rashid may not make it back, but it didn't mean that King would be out of escape options. King did the same with his hire car, returning the favour for Rashid. The two men now made their way down the mountain slope, where they could see the Russian mafia boss' property spread out below.

"I'm going to have to up my rate," Rashid said, following King's route through some loose boulders. "I keep getting into shit with you, and you never pay your bar tab."

"Pretty sure I saved your arse in that mosque."

"Wasn't it the other way around?" Rashid laughed.

"It's all a bit hazy now," King said and ducked down behind a large boulder.

"Well, I saved your backside in France, that's for sure."

"Quit your bitching," King replied. "At least I get you out from behind a desk."

"It's not exactly slow in the regiment."

"It is if you ravage the daughters of senior officers who can block your career path."

Rashid shrugged. "He should watch out. He's got a fit wife too…"

King smiled, checked the position of the sun before he raised the binoculars and studied the property below. He could see that Romanovitch had undertaken work since Google Earth had been overhead. The main building was a *McMansion*. Two-tone colours, pillars and tall windows. He estimated twenty rooms or more and could see that not only did the property boast an Olympic-sized swimming pool, but a sizable pool ran along the south side of the building, entirely enclosed in glass. The gardens reminded King of French palace lawns, with striped mowing patterns, water features and statues of women in vulnerable poses.

"The guy's got it going on," Rashid commented.

"And then some."

"Let's have a peek."

King handed him the binoculars, turned his attention to the boundaries where the well-cultivated lawns and shrub borders met the Georgian mountain scrub.

"No fences," Rashid said. "Other than the front gate and wall across the front of the property. Have to watch for motion sensors, but I doubt it. This is wild land. I imagine there are mountain goats, deer and wolves up here. Small vermin too. The sensors would be going off constantly."

King could see that the property was set back from the entrance road like a horseshoe. A wall ran along the road, with large iron gates to the driveway, but the sides of the mountain rose up on three sides like a quarry.

"Got a few toys." Rashid handed him back the binoculars. "Ferrari, I think. And a Rolls Royce."

"Standard," King replied. "Most probably got a few more in one of those barns."

"We're in the wrong business," Rashid paused. "Or at least, on the wrong side."

"Never."

"Ever thought about selling those skills?"

"Nope."

"Liar."

King stared at him. "Not once."

"Me neither. Just shitting with you."

King raised the binoculars again and skirted the perimeter. He watched a man walking across one of the lawns. He stooped and picked something up. King could see it was a hoe. The man reached an area of concrete, in the centre of which was a water feature. The man started to scrape something off the hard ground. King watched for a moment, then moved on. He could see that the Ferrari was a new model. He didn't covet such cars, but he had flicked through enough magazines and satellite channels to recognise it. Car models changed so quickly these days that he could barely keep up, but he knew this one had electric capabilities that was more of a nod for pairing it to its petrol engine for almighty starship performance, rather than to save the planet. It cost north of a million and that's when King started to lose interest. He liked the idea of a car a tenth of the price, providing he won the lottery, but he had seen too much of the worst in the world to know what a million pounds would do in some places, and the lives it would change. He saw such spending as a finger up to the rest of the world. Especially when it was criminals like Romanovitch who held the finger. He thought about the misery the man would have caused. He thought about the IEDs he had made, and how they would send the cars up into the air with the Russian mafia boss inside. An easy way to get the job done. But the job had now turned into a snatch and escape. And he could care less what happened to Romanovitch.

"There's a guard coming out of what looks like a bunkhouse."

"How can you tell?"

"That he's a guard or that it's a bunkhouse?"

"Both," said Rashid.

"He has a sidearm. Can't leave it alone. And the unit looks both drab and strategically placed," King said, handing him the binoculars. "There's a blue hue in the window. I reckon it's coming from a bank of CCTV monitors."

"Or a laptop."

"Possible."

"And the strategic element?"

"Close to the gate, enough distance from the house to be discreet and there are no cameras on the building. Every other building has a CCTV camera fixed to it, providing eyes-on across all points on the compass. The building is in the line of sight for at least three of those cameras, which provides the security personnel with a reference-point. If the worst-case scenario happened for them, then they can monitor an enemy's progress in relation to their position."

"Fair one." Rashid slid down behind a large boulder and wiped his brow with his sleeve. He said, "I think the cars would make a great diversion. One of your fireworks up the exhaust and it will be a bunch of headless chickens down there."

"If that is a bunkhouse, an IED in there would see our job easier."

"That's a lot of collateral, my friend."

"There's also a wireless receiver unit, solar panels and switch-feed generator on the roof. That place is the hub. If it goes up, the CCTV cameras on the house and other buildings mean nothing." King shook his head. "As for collateral? It raises the odds a little more in our favour. I've got a Makarov and fourteen rounds. A few homemade bombs and an unarmed lothario who looks like he came dressed for the roulette tables in Monaco…" He looked at Rashid and shrugged. "Just saying…"

Rashid smiled. "But you've still got your sense of humour, so it will be okay."

King ignored him, turned his attention to the house and its many windows. Romanovitch had invested in security measures there too. In the shape of net curtains bought for a few lari per pane in the local market. Or perhaps several thousand euros in Milan. Either way, King could not see in, but whoever was inside would undoubtedly be able to see out. They would be going in blind. It could only be done at night. As if to confirm this, four men stepped out of the hub. They loosened up, seemed to stretch as they talked. One man broke away and walked to the house, the other two waited for another man to step outside and they walked to one of the large outbuildings. He could not see if the men were armed, but he expected them to be.

"I'm thinking I get close, or at least, as close as I can," King said. "There's little moon tonight, I'll use as much cover as I can and be ready to use an IED to breach the door to the main house."

"While I create a diversion?"

"Exactly."

"And you want that diversion to include putting an IED through the door to that security hub?"

"Best option."

"Not for them."

"There's a lot of men down there. A lot of muscle, undoubtedly armed." King looked at him earnestly. "I have everything riding on this. I really do appreciate your help so far," he paused. "And I guarantee I will be there for you if you ever need me in the future, but I think it may be best if we part company."

"You do?"

King shrugged. "I don't think I can ask you to drop an IED through that door, not knowing how many are inside. And I don't think it's fair to. You have reservations. That much is clear. I'll take it from here." He raised the binoculars and looked back at the property below.

"Just like that?"

"Better all round."

"I just think there's a better way."

"If I don't get this done, I won't see Caroline again. I know that."

"Then kill Romanovitch and exfiltrate. Don't complicate things taking a hostage of your own. For all you know, Catherine Milankovitch might not even be here."

King rubbed a hand through his short hair. The thick strands sprung back as his hand moved further towards the back of his head. He sighed, shook his head.

"Your vision has become clouded."

"You're surprised?"

"No," replied Rashid. "But this is a big deal. The man has security personnel and adequate measures. You have a short-ranged pistol and nowhere near enough rounds for a pitched battle with multiple targets. And *I'm* not armed at all."

"I'll manage," he paused. "I always have."

"Like in France?"

"I knew you'd show up."

"And in that bloody mosque?"

"You had a gun, and your bindings were almost cut through."

"You must have a death wish."

"I'm still here," King replied tersely.

"And so am I. But if we get down there and into a battle with hardened Russian mafia, most of whom are probably ex-Spetsnaz, we'll get in trouble. We don't have enough firepower. Or men."

King shrugged. "No hard feelings," he said. "Get out of here. Go back and help Ramsay, to find Caroline through Helena. Keep it a two-pronged attack."

Rashid stood up, took another look down at the distant property. He glanced at King, but he was studying something in the binoculars. He didn't say anything more. It was a suicide mission with ten men, let alone one.

King watched Romanovitch step out onto the patio and make his way towards the Olympic-sized pool. He had studied the photographs that Helena had attached to her text message. The man looked a little older and greyer. A little fleshier. But there was no mistaking him. He rested the binoculars down beside him and turned around.

Rashid had gone.

62

Caroline had showered twice and stared into the mirror for a good while before showering again. She hadn't seen her own reflection for a month and it seemed a novelty. In the car, she had looked haggard and worn. Now she looked cleaner, but still unfamiliar. There was something different about the way she looked, the way she looked back at herself. She knew part of her had died, lamented the feeling of loss. She hoped one day the sparkle in her eyes would return.

She couldn't seem to rid herself of her ordeal, cleanse herself of the degradation of her capture and trafficking to the east. No amount of showering left her feeling clean. The way The Beast had touched her in the first house she had been taken to, the threat of what he was going to try back at the farmhouse and what he was going to do to her in that derelict, pitch-dark barn during her escape. And the blood that had splattered over her when she had killed him, and that too of Michael's. It seemed as if it would never wash out. She stared at herself, deep into her eyes. She had taken a life. She had killed The Beast and she was not sorry.

She would do it again.

Ramsay had ordered her room service, told her he would meet later to discuss their next move. It was a decent hotel, and she had relaxed on the king-sized bed and eaten the club sandwich and fries, drank the gin and tonic and ordered more of the same. She hadn't realised how famished she had been, nor how the comforts of a decent hotel and a nerve-steadying drink could relax her so.

She had met Marnie briefly, and decided she liked her. The woman had no agenda. She had bought Caroline a selection of clothes and underwear, and she had bought well. No under sizing, nor over sizing – simply the right size and suitable for the occasion. It could have been so easy to buy too small and feign surprise that they would not fit or buy too large and look as if she had sized-her up wrong. Caroline had experience of such women all her life, and it was a refreshing change, especially as Marnie was at least a size larger than Caroline. Her taste in clothes suited Caroline, and she imagined that given the opportunity, or completely different circumstances, they could become firm friends.

Caroline looked up as she heard the knock on the door. Sharp and business-like. For a fleeting moment, she had jumped at the shock, unnerved. She imagined she would react that way for some time. She walked over, stood to one side.

"Yes?"

"It's Neil, let me in."

Caroline could hear a tone in his voice but was unsure how to read it through the door. She flicked off the security chain and opened the door.

His face showed concern, but she imagined he would think he hid it well.

She walked back a few steps. Ramsay looked at her, nodded approvingly.

"You look better."

"Thanks," Caroline replied indignantly.

"Oh, I didn't mean anything," he said.

"Forget it," she said coolly. "What's up?"

"There was a triangulation on Rashid's phone," he paused. "Further down the coast. It's a monied place, not so much a poor man's Monaco, as a place where the rich and criminally wanted choose to hang out. Much like the Costa Del Sol in the eighties and nineties. Only Russia's rich and criminally wanted. Georgia affords them both a police force and regional governments who are susceptible to bribes and turn a blind eye to criminal activity."

"And you think Rashid is there with Alex?" She sat down on the bed and crossed her legs. Marnie had picked out a tastefully cut silk blouse and Caroline had paired it with dark, tight jeans and a cream lamb's wool cardigan. The jeans were tucked into tan leather knee-length boots.

Ramsay glanced at the boots as Caroline crossed her legs. "Crikey, that's the budget gone this month!"

"I do hope so," she replied sardonically. "Marnie did well."

"I'll have to have a word."

"You'll do no such thing," she said. "And I think I'm due a pay rise."

Ramsay nodded. "I suspect it will be on the cards."

Caroline nodded. She knew they'd reassess her status – just as long as she promised not to talk to legal or sell her story someday. Standard. They had made her sign all sorts of papers when her fiancé Peter Redwood had died in a terrorist explosion. She hadn't been thinking straight, both relieved she had lived, and crippled with grief at the same time. The legal department at MI5 knew how to pick their moments.

"Marnie is running software on Rashid's phone," Ramsay paused. "The moment the man switches it on, we'll know where he is to within two square metres."

"You've tried messaging him, or ringing?"

"Of course. But you know how it is. If you leave a couple of messages, then leaving more won't make them ring you sooner."

"Enough of your love life," she grinned.

Ramsay smiled. He could see that she was slowly returning to her normal self. He guessed it would take time, but she would get there.

"What did you find at the farm?" she asked.

Ramsay shook his head. "It was cleaned out. The place was a shell."

"I killed a man," she said. "He died in a derelict barn."

"I'm sorry," he said.

"I'm not."

"Okay."

"You found nothing else?"

"Nothing."

"What about the police? Forensics?"

"Rank amateurs. They will have corrupted more than they'll ever find."

"So that's it? Nothing else to go on?"

Ramsay shrugged. "I think it may come down to King. He must have had a breakthrough, for the way Rashid ditched us and disappeared. He must be close."

Caroline said, "I certainly hope so."

63

Rashid pulled his car over in a layby behind a selection of parked heavy plant vehicles and took out his phone. He switched it on and waited for it to run through its start-up sequence. He could see that he had two text messages and two missed calls. He didn't need to look at the call list to know who it would be. He put the phone on the passenger seat, leaned back in his seat and stared at the headlining as he sighed. He was nowhere. He hadn't helped King – certain the man was on a suicide mission, that he wanted no part of – and he was no longer aiding in the search for Caroline or Helena Milankovitch.

He had helped King twice in the past, hadn't really been able to reason why, other than he knew King was a man who bent the rules, acted spontaneously and had completed the gruelling SAS selection course many times. For Rashid, the selection process had been the toughest experience he had ever known, but for King, it had been MI6's idea of maintaining fitness. King had not only completed the course, but he had been dropped into it many times for three or four weeks at a time, at every stage over a dozen years. If he was honest with his reasoning, Rashid probably couldn't think of any other reason than that. It said more about King than anything else ever would. He supposed he respected him more than anyone he had met.

And now the man was going up against impossible odds.

Rashid punched the steering wheel and screamed, cursing a half-a-dozen times. He gripped the wheel and went to put the car in gear but stopped himself and picked up the phone. He read the curt messages. Neil Ramsay asking him where he was and to call him back immediately. Rashid looked at the time the message had been sent. Immediately had long-gone. He tossed the phone back down and drove the car out around the enormous digger and pulled back out into the road. He didn't see the car, rather than misjudged and was almost rear-ended amid a blast of horn. He stuck up a finger and cursed again, accelerating hard down the mountain road. The driver behind pulled out around him, his modified twenty-year-old Audi blasting past with gunfire erupting from his exhausts. The driver held up his fingers like a child mimed a pistol and was gone with the exhaust popping and banging. Rashid cursed again. Cursing his own stupidity, his own carelessness. He heard his phone ringing, saw the false name he'd used for Ramsay, and cursed again. He ignored it. He was heading for civilisation and a decent road. Then he would call and speak to the MI5 man. He'd use the time to concoct a story as he drove. He had a feeling he'd be back on a desk assignment in Hereford before long, his brief career with MI5 nothing more than a fleeting memory.

64

"Damn it! No answer!"

"I've got a cell triangulation." Marnie played her fingertips across the keypad and brought up the software map. It was a detailed survey map complete with topographical height increments. "Near the border with Abkhazia."

"Bugger. That border is hot, isn't it?"

"Yes. Abkhazia broke away from Georgia and became an independent state."

"I remember. A horrible little war not many heard about in the west. Plenty of ethnic cleansing on both sides, but the Abkhazians had support from Armenia and Russia, who had scores to settle with Georgia for breaking away from the USSR. How close is he to the border?"

Marnie worked the keys and adjusted the map. "Close. Practically straddling the two countries." She pushed the tiny glasses back up onto the bridge of her nose as she read. "You can't get in without a letter of authority, which converts to a visa. It's a relatively straightforward process but takes around five days. And you can't fly in because the Georgians have vowed to shoot down anything flying in or out across its airspace."

"Nice."

"Needless to say; Georgia doesn't recognise their independence."

"Nor does anyone apart from Russia and about four pacific islands they paid off."

"And the Armenians, but they stand with Russia because of the war crimes. They need their protection from the UN."

"I *love* these fleapit countries," Ramsay said sardonically.

Marnie leaned back in her chair and sipped some tepid coffee. She looked at Caroline, who was standing in the window looking out at the Black Sea. She had been uncharacteristically silent until now.

"If Rashid is that close to an ambiguous area, do you think Helena is holing up in Abkhazia?" she asked, not taking her eyes off the view.

"It might make sense," Ramsay replied. "It's a tricky place to police. Bribes are commonplace, the law more easily corrupted than even this place."

"Call him again," Caroline said. The sun was golden above the sea, working its way west, leaving everything in its wake vulnerable to darkness. Caroline shivered. She did not like the thought of darkness and night. "Tell him you've found me. Tell him we need to find Alex for his own safety. There's no pressure on him anymore. He can pull back, regroup with us and we can start anew. The hunt for Helena can now be methodical and well-planned."

Ramsay hesitated. He looked at his phone. He had no missed calls.

Marnie looked up at him from the desk. "It makes sense, Sir," she said. "I know I'm not a field agent, but the pressure is off. If King is doing what he is solely to find Caroline, then he no longer needs to. If Rashid is close to him, then he can be the messenger."

Ramsay looked agitated. MI5 protocols dictated that communications were concise. Text messages were no more than a recall system. Nothing was ever discussed. It made for clear deniability. But Rashid was not answering his phone.

"We don't know where Helena is, and we have no idea as to the locations of Alex or Rashid. But Alex has clearly been in contact with her, and Rashid has been in contact with Alex. If Rashid disappeared so suddenly like he did, it was because he knew Alex was close. This is it, Neil," Caroline said looking at him earnestly. "It's all going down soon. And right here in Georgia. And that is too bloody close to that border."

"She's right, Sir," Marnie said. "And Caroline is safe, after all. We need to pull back. Abkhazia is a militarised zone. If anything happens on that border, then the world will soon know. And Russia will be playing the propaganda card, just like those bio-weapon attacks on the former KGB agents back home, and just like in Syria."

"Shit!" Ramsay looked at his phone hopefully, willing it to ring.

He unlocked it, selected his messages and started to type.

65

King was used to operating alone. He'd spent a lifetime that way. From fending for himself as a child, to working menial tasks or even stealing to feed his younger siblings, he had always done what was necessary to survive. His mother had been a crack whore, his father unknown. When his mother had arranged for a *client* to be alone with his ten-year-old sister, a neighbour had thankfully intervened in time. The family had been put into care. King, being older and unruly, had gone through a succession of foster families, and when they eventually proved unable to tame him, children's homes had been his shelter. Open to bullying, abuse and neglect, King had fled and grown up on the streets. His mother had died of an overdose and his brothers and sister had been successfully adopted. But King was too old, too ruined by fate and circumstance. Nobody wanted a fifteen-year-old who had already reached a shade under six-foot and looked like a twenty-five-year-old man. Prison followed, as did release and more trouble, and prison again. Nobody had ever been there for him, and he had grown to accept it. Eventually, thrive from it. Although he never saw his siblings again.

When his wife had died from ovarian cancer, King had vowed to return to his lone wolf existence. To count on and care for nobody. He did not need baggage or responsibilities. He had spent five years alone, but Caroline had changed that, had shown him there was more to life than merely surviving, and in turn, working with a team in MI5, he had grown used to the support. But he knew he had softened because of it. He had found himself giving the enemy options, relying on back-up, as he had done in the forest in France, waiting for Rashid to make his move. But no more. King was in control now. Win or lose, live or die. He was alone, and he knew the consequence. He could accept it.

No quarter given; none asked.

It was time to do what he did best.

He had parked the car, much like in Tuscany, lower down the mountain slope. Hidden from the road in a narrow track, he had cut branches and layered them over the roof and bonnet to hide it from view from oncoming headlights. He had then broken a branch on the edge of the road and folded it over so that it hung at a right-angle. It would act as a marker for him in the darkness but would hopefully be ignored by anyone else. With the car secured and more easily accessible in the event of a hasty retreat, King swung the rucksack he had bought over his shoulder, leaving the car unlocked and the keys under the driver's wheel arch.

The hike up the mountainside was difficult; the rocky terrain was loose and jagged. He found smoother progress made following the deeper culverts which had been carved out by torrents of running rainwater. The light had faded and there was no moon at present. King estimated it would poke above the horizon ahead of him in another two hours, but he knew it would be no more than a slither, added to which, there was noctilucent cloud cover, which acted like a lace blanket, shutting out most of the stars and only letting the merest of opaque light through.

The temperature had dropped, but his exertion up the steep gradient stopped him from becoming chilled, and by the time he had worked his way over a mile, and at least two-thousand feet in elevation, he was perspiring and wishing he'd packed more water.

At approximately four-thousand-feet above sea level and at least two miles from where he had parked the car, King removed the rucksack and dropped it onto the dry earth. He finished his litre bottle of water and wedged it between two rocks rather than risk it making a noise in his rucksack. He then removed another plastic bottle, but this one had been wrapped in tape. He had earlier drilled two-dozen equally-spaced holes into some plastic tubing he had bought from the builder's merchants. He had then marked a hole of the same diameter into the bottom of a one-litre plastic water bottle, cut it out carefully and wedged the tube in place so that it ran all the way through the bottle and out of the neck. He wedged cotton wool inside the neck and poked it towards the bottom until it was heavily packed, and the tube was even. He had then cut the length of tube and tested it against the muzzle of the Makarov pistol.

Now that King had reached his insertion point, he carefully taped the bottle in place. He tested it for straightness, then applied more plumbing tape as he made fine corrections by eye. The moving action of the pistol would make this silencer a one-shot deal, but in King's experience it would be utterly soundless. The bullet would travel out of the muzzle of the pistol and through the tube without touching the sides and the gasses that carried the sound would vent through the holes and become absorbed by the cotton wool. He had used one before to significant effect on a Ruger .22 rifle, and although the 9x18mm Makarov round was louder, it carried less velocity than a .22 round from a longer barrel. King estimated the result would be about the same. A short-range, silent first kill.

King put the rucksack back on and stood up slowly, mindful to keep his movements slow and his profile low. There were five things to remember when moving in on an enemy's position. They were known as the *Five S's*. Shine, shape, sound, silhouette and shadow. King had one thing that could shine in the moonlight, and that was his vintage Rolex Submariner watch and he made sure his sleeve was pulled down covering the stainless-steel bracelet. He kept his shape profile low and fluid, using cover when available. He would stand next to a tree, rather than away from it, or squat down and use a rock to break up his shape. Sound was a no-brainer and he watched his footsteps, choosing to backtrack a pace rather than step on dry twigs or loose gravel, and he had emptied his pockets of coins and checked the rattle of the rucksack before setting off. Silhouette was most prominent on top of gradients, and he always avoided the skyline, choosing to traverse slopes and keep the high ground above him. The shadow element shouldn't be a problem tonight, but a bright moon or backlight could cast shadows every bit as noticeable as on the brightest of days.

Below him he knew that Romanovitch's property would be quiet and inactive. It was one AM and as he reached the edge of the slope he could see that there was only one light on within the house, and a faint blue hue emitted from the security hub. He watched, using the binoculars, which were assisted for low-light conditions by a lithium battery and passive infrared beam. They struggled at this distance for night capability, but he could pick out the buildings and the two cars still parked on the driveway. King checked the perimeter, tracking the fence and using his own mantra of the five S's to see if he could spot anybody in the darkness. To look past the form of a person and turn his attention to the visible tell-tale signs they could emit. His eyes slowly tuned in. Before long, he was seeing what he had clearly not been meant to. Throughout the grounds, there were dozens of men. He could make out the DPM, or disruptive pattern material of the camouflage clothing by looking for just the lighter patterns at first, and he could see the dead-straight lines - the shapes and angles at odds with nature - of long guns. Shotguns and rifles. Under the magnification of the binoculars some rifles even looked modified and customised with scopes, lights, laser dot pointers and underslung shotguns.

They knew he was coming.

66

A diversion wasn't going to cut it. It would bring the men running. And they would be shooting. King had seen the focus of men were placed on both sides of the eastern gable of the house. This made the driveway a column with the attack at both sides at the end. As if he were going to come up the driveway as bold as brass. Highly unlikely. The pincer movement was a fine idea, but the men had deployed parallel to the drive, directly opposite each other and not at acute angles. This would mean that in a firefight, they would inflict casualties on each other, rather than merely obliterate their intended target. It was an idea from somebody without combat experience. Which was encouraging. King had assumed most of Romanovitch's men would be ex-military. Maybe they were, but unlike the US, UK and NATO troops, there was a generation of Russian soldiers who had served their country with no combat deployment.

King had worked his way down the mountainside and made out more men flanking the house. Each man was placed at intervals of fifty-feet. If King couldn't make his way between two men at fifty-feet, he wouldn't be doing this. He had trained as a sniper and could use his surroundings to remain invisible. He had lain in wait for a target for four days, not thirty-feet from a manned Taliban observation post in Afghanistan. When the target had finally presented himself, King had taken the shot, waited another day and exfiltrated without being seen. But that was then, and this was now. He had had time on his side back then. With these men of Romanovitch's waiting for him, King knew it was now or never. He either got Catherine Milankovitch out as a bargaining chip, or he killed Romanovitch to appease Helena.

There was no turning back.

King could see that the men had assumed that any attack would be coming from the front, with the men at the sides of the house being a backup to any attack, or perhaps a security cordon for Romanovitch inside. King neared the perimeter where the scrub met shrubs. In this case, a belt of privet. He shuffled forward on his belly, raised the binoculars and breathed steadily as he scanned the ground ahead of him. The binoculars gave him the low-light illumination, so he wound down the magnification to increase his field of view. The men were closer now, and he could see the slight movements which had alerted him further up the mountainside. The men were fidgeting. Weapons were moving. Eyes were on the driveway. King was sure that with this amount of men within the grounds, there couldn't have been any motion sensors, and nor would the cameras be much use, unless they were all focused on the perimeter. He felt in the bag for the first IED and planted one of the electrical timer charges on the ground behind the belt of privet. He set the timer for fifteen-minutes and crawled steadily down the line of the perimeter, towing the bag behind him on a length of paracord. When he was opposite the largest group of men, he took out another electrical charge, checked the luminous dials of his watch, then set the second IED for ten-minutes. Against his normal SOP, or standard operating procedure, he made his way back along the line and crossed past the first IED with eight-minutes showing on his watch. He used his elbows and toes, keeping lizard-low as he reached the end of the garden and where the mountain slope extended upwards at ninety-degrees. The ground was difficult to cross quietly here, gravel had washed down, and the area was patchy grass and scrub, along with planted shrubs that hadn't quite had the tending they needed. A buffer between the manicured ground and the wild mountainside. King took advantage of the cover and untied the rucksack, slipping it quietly over his shoulders. He tucked up into a crouch, his eyes on the last man in the line, who was watching the garden ahead. King tucked the pistol and its bulky silencer under his left armpit, then slipped the knife out of its sheath and held it down by his side as he made his way silently across the edge of exposed ground. He got within two paces of the first guard, checked his breathing to steady himself, then hesitated as a second guard stepped away from the edge of the house and came into view three-paces in front of the first guard. King slipped the knife silently back into its sheaf. The second guard turned to say something to his colleague, but King already had the Makarov in his hand and took the shot before the man could mutter a warning. The man took the shot in the forehead and dropped in a heap. King ripped the modified silencer off the pistol and stepped in close, the hot muzzle burning the man's throat, his left hand clutching his mouth and nose closed. He whispered in Russian, "Don't move. Don't resist..." He removed his left hand and took the machine carbine out of the man's hands, then walked the man backwards and around the side of the house and pushed him face-first against the wall. He said, "Show me the staff entrance." He slung the weapon over his left shoulder and let it hang loosely from its strap.

"He knows you're coming," the man drawled quietly in English. "You don't have a chance..."

King pressed the pistol in hard, stifling the man's artery. It was enough to get his attention, the blood pounding up his neck, but going no further. He released it and the man sagged. "Do you have a key to the staff entrance?"

"There *is* no staff entrance," he croaked.

"The kitchen then. Romanovitch doesn't cook his own meals. He has people to do that. Show me."

"The key is in my pocket," he said.

He slipped his hand inside and before King could say anything, he snapped his head backwards, catching King on the bridge of the nose. King recoiled, dropping the pistol, his eyes watering, not yet feeling the pain that went along with the light-headedness. The man spun around, a spring-loaded knife in his hand. He shouted a warning to his comrades but was drowned out by the first of the IEDs.

The night sky lit up and the noise was deafening. King darted forwards and jabbed his knife at the man's throat, but he blocked the attack, taking the length of King's blade across his wrist. Blood spurted a long way and the man stared at the wound, grimacing as King's second strike plunged deep into his liver. King switched his left hand, cupping the blunt top edge of the knife's blade, and in a powerful downward motion, he yanked both hands and engaged his core for extra strength, driving his legs down into a squat. The man dropped onto his knees, his torso opened-up and spilling his steaming bowels onto the ground. King stood back up and turned away, taking the man's machine carbine off his back. He could hear the screaming of the group of men caught in the IED's blast. He knew how it would have gone down – the heat of the blast, the thud in their chests from the shockwave, the ringing in their ears as they tried to make sense of what had just happened, the pain from the shrapnel – the fear and indignity at having been felled by an unseen enemy. There were shouts of instruction and King envisioned braver men going to their comrade's aid. He was in too deep. Too personal. More committed than he had ever been in what felt like a lifetime in these situations. Which was why he didn't feel the same level of guilt when the second IED lit up the sky and it happened all over again for the men in front of the house.

67

There were shouts and commotion and King knew what would be happening. Most of the men would have hunkered down, not chancing being caught in a third explosion. Weapons would be trained impotently on unseen threats, shadows playing eerily across the scorched earth as stubborn flames licked the grass. Ringing ears and shouts of both fear and concern was enough opportunity for King to place a single 5.45x39mm round through the door lock. He shoulder-barged the door open, then closed it behind him and took off the rucksack. He could hear multiple gunshots outside, the men taking no chances and firing into the treeline at would-be attackers. He used two wooden wedges tapering from two inches to a thin tip, both carved from a piece of wood bought from the builder's merchants. He dropped them down on the floor, positioned them away from the hinges and kicked them in place with his size-twelve boot. He kicked again for good measure, then slung the rucksack back over his shoulders and picked up the AKU machine carbine – essentially a smaller version of the infamous AK47 but chambered for a lighter, faster bullet. The result was a weapon which effectively took down the enemy, its bullets creating a more devastating wound than the old AK47's 7.62x39mm rounds, but not over-penetrating walls and chancing collateral damage. The short design was both light to handle and easy to use in close quarter combat scenarios.

The kitchen was dark, but light emitted from the next room, which King could already see was a large hall. He shouldered the rifle and stepped cautiously out. Lights were flicking on upstairs. King saw the first guard, a tall man carrying a semi-automatic pistol. King dispatched him with a double tap, moved onwards and up the stairs. He assumed Romanovitch would be inside and leave the dirty work to his men. King was going in blind and had no plans of the building, nor information regarding its occupants. He knew that Romanovitch was married, but he did not know if there were children in the house. He hoped not, but he wouldn't let that affect him now. Caroline was his priority. Romanovitch was a ruthless mafia boss who had lived his life, built his riches on other people's defeat and misery. He didn't care if the man was a father or not. He had already decided that Catherine was his best chance of seeing Caroline again, but it would cover all his bases if Romanovitch was taken out of the picture.

King reached the landing and could see the chaos below him through the window. He could hear gunfire, and now he could see men firing their weapons at the mountainside and the treeline beyond the perimeter. They were convinced that the IEDs had been grenades, fired or thrown from the top of the first slope. King checked behind him, then slipped off the rucksack and took out two of the taper-fuse IEDs.

He used a cheap disposable lighter he had bought in a service station and lit both fuses. They burned fiercely, and King worked the catch to open the window, but it was stuck firm. He cursed his stupidity, should have opened the window first. He used the butt of the rifle to smash out the glass, but the glass was toughened. Cursing again, he fired two shots through the glass and used the butt of the rifle again. The glass gave way, but a few of the men had turned and were looking up at the window. King was cursing a little more fluidly as he lobbed both IEDs out of the window amongst the men. They looked at the burning water bottles, but the first exploded before anybody worked out what was going on. Mud, shrapnel and debris blew high in the air and two of the men were thrown backwards, the third man was obliterated by the blast. The explosion had sent the second IED high into the air, and when it detonated, it showered molten-hot screws across the garden, felling men and sending shrapnel into the side of the house. King ducked and felt the wave of heat, glass blowing over his back. When he looked back up the man was standing firm, the pistol aimed at his head. King dodged left and the gun fired. He dropped low, clawed for the AKU and got a couple of rounds off, both hitting the top tread of the stairs. The man fired twice more as he ducked back around the landing. King fired three more shots, smashing the banister spindles and taking chunks of plaster out of the wall. He had a better hold on the rifle, a better aim and he shouldered it and took the stairs two at a time. The man ducked out, the pistol held in a two-handed grip, he fired at the same time as King and went down squirming. King took another step, aimed and fired. The man's head rocked backwards, and he didn't have to stick around to know he was dead. He took a step forwards, turned the weapon sideways and reached to detach the magazine to check how many rounds he had left. His left arm wouldn't move as fast as it should, and he felt a stab of pain. He looked down, saw the blood on his sleeve. He'd killed the man at the top of the stairs, but he'd gone down fighting. King had been hit by one of the 9mm bullets. He checked the magazine, wincing at the pain and pushing through the barrier to get the task done. He pivoted the awkward backward alignment of the Kalashnikov's magazine and clicked it back in place. He estimated twenty-rounds remaining. He moved on, but as he passed the largest of the windows, a bay window with an area that had been turned into a reading corner with leather sofas and books piled high on antique wooden sideboards, he caught sight of lights and gunfire at the main gate. He watched as a digger, a JCB, he thought, crashed through the gates and drove up the driveway, part on the grass and part on the road, tearing up a line of privet hedge on its front grille. It lowered its front bucket and rammed hard into the Ferrari, smashing it into the Rolls Royce. As it met resistance, the Ferrari went further into the bucket, which was already rising. The digger swung out and then braked suddenly, and the Ferrari carried on, landing in front of the men who were lining up and firing at the digger. The wrecked Ferrari smashed onto the ground and rolled into some of them as they dodged in all directions trying to avoid it. The digger swung around, the bucket lowering and drove into the security hub, taking out a complete wall and making the roof collapse.

King shot out the glass and crouched down. He took out the last two electrical-timer IEDs and set them for one-minute a piece. He counted down in his head, then threw them both out, one left and one right, when he estimated fifteen seconds remaining. He did not wait to see what effect they had on the men down below as he headed for the first of many doors along the south wing of the building.

68

Rashid hadn't driven a digger before, but the three-mile drive to Romanovitch's property had given him plenty of scope. He wasn't about to consider a second career, but he could make it move – much like any heavy vehicle – with gears and brakes and throttle, although the throttle was steering wheel mounted and he discovered the brakes could be split to turn on a coin. The front bucket went down and up and tilted accordingly by use of another lever. He hadn't had the time to study the back-hoe, which required revolving the seat, but he didn't think he'd be digging a trench anytime soon. In his opinion, he'd done a pretty good job, raising the bucket as a bullet trap, and destroying the security hub as well as the two cars, but he was starting to take fire and the glass all around him had either completely shattered, or was strewn with individual bullet holes.

After leaving King, Rashid had deliberated for some time and had eventually responded to Neil Ramsay's text message, when he had seen the subject matter. King no longer had to either kill the Russian, or snatch Catherine Milankovitch. Caroline was safe and well. Ramsay was demanding a regroup and debrief. As far as Rashid was concerned, his friend had crossed the line. He wanted to help, but he could only see the odds as a suicide mission. If King had reached the point where he couldn't see reason, then

Rashid had wanted no further part of it. He had driven near, hoping to catch King before his assault. He had texted him, and then, when he received no response, he had called. Straight to voicemail. He knew King would have switched off his phone. It was then that he had heard a thud and echo across the mountainside. The first of King's IEDs.

Rashid had acted quickly, remembering the road building equipment parked up in the layby. He had no weapon, and his hire car would be torn to shreds if he tried to drive in. He had driven at breakneck speed and decided to steal the massive digger. Hereford had taught him many things, not least how to hotwire enemy vehicles. A skill he had already deployed in Syria many times. The drive back to Romanovitch's property was a fraught one - the digger could only reach forty-miles-per-hour and Rashid imagined King cornered and taking fire, or worse.

Now he was taking fire of his own. He had heard ricochets in the cab, had pressed his chin to his chest as a fragment zinged past his ear. He had just tossed the mangled Ferrari at the group of men and taken a few out with the wreckage. He slipped his foot on the right brake pedal and spun the wheel clockwise as he pulled hard back on the throttle. The digger span quickly and Rashid lowered the front loader bucket, scything through the air and catching two men who were thrown twenty-metres into the wall of the house. They wouldn't be getting up.

To counter the nauseous feeling from the inertia of the spinning cab, Rashid swung the wheel the other way and depressed the other brake pedal. The digger practically rotated on the spot, its bucket midway and spinning quickly. The men were starting to gather on the lawn. They were reloading or swapping magazines with each other or picking up scattered weapons from the men killed or injured in the IED blasts. Rashid didn't give them time. He straightened up and the giant machine lurched forwards towards them. His main concern was a man getting level or behind him and leaping either onto the side ladders or the rear-mounted back-hoe. From there, they would be able to take a shot at their leisure. He countered this by swinging the machine in a zig-zag. The men scattered, some firing, others fleeing. But all the time, Rashid drove like he was demented. The digger turned so severely that it looked as if it may well keel over. Rashid stopped suddenly and reversed. He soon had fifty-metres between himself and the remaining men. He swung the vehicle around and faced off the men he had first engaged at the entrance to the drive. They had regrouped and were advancing. Rashid lowered the bucket and repeated his zig-zag as he neared them. Again, the men reacted in the same way, dodging but failing to anticipate how erratic ten-tonnes of metal could be. Rashid heard the thuds as bodies hit the metal but felt nothing as he kept the digger moving at maximum speed through the grounds. He drove a wide circle, the headlights lighting up the vast area of lawn. As he came around towards the house, he could see that he had allowed too much time for the men to regroup and he saw the muzzle flashes a split second before he heard the bullets hitting the body of the digger. He turned and raised the bucket so that it completely blocked his view, and the bullet strikes as they impacted on the toughened steel of the bucket changed two octaves higher.

Wishing he had gone along with King's plan of a diversion, Rashid steeled himself momentarily, then yanked back the throttle for a final charge. He bounced out of his seat as he drove over a line of flower beds, then crashed through a water feature and was left with fifty-metres of sparking, pinging bullet strikes over the front loader arms and the bucket. He was closing fast, but the bucket suddenly dropped without warning and hit the ground. The hydraulic cylinder had been hit and hydraulic fluid sprayed over what was left of the windscreen and into Rashid's face. A mound of neatly manicured lawn was pushing up over the already full bucket and he felt the vehicle halve in speed. Rashid hit the brakes and slammed the machine into reverse. He moved backwards at full speed, the bullets pinging off the grille and bonnet. The range was increasing with every second, and Rashid kept the machine reversing hard all the way towards the front wall. He could already see men at the gates. Some were injured and crawling, others were kneeling and getting ready to fire. Rashid nailed the brake and swung the wheel hard. The digger spun, throwing up huge clods of earth. He was twenty-five metres from the wall when he changed gear and pulled back the throttle. The digger lurched forwards and he had just enough time to change into second and brace himself for impact. The bucket smashed through the wall and the digger hit the rubble and became airborne, crashing down onto the road. Rashid was thrown out of his seat and through the shattered windscreen. He slid onto the hot bonnet, scrambled off the side and limped off the road and into the brush. Gunshots echoed, and bullets sparked and pinged off the digger, but already Rashid was well out of their line of fire, picking his way through the treeline and making his way back towards the entrance, parallel to the road.

69

There were many rooms upstairs, but King already knew which one he wanted. But as he made his way down the corridor he kept the weapon trained on every doorway he passed nonetheless. The door he was heading for was a double oak door, approximately eight-feet high. It had to indicate a master bedroom. It seemed the most fitting. And the facing end of the building featured a large balcony, which spanned the entire façade. King imagined the southwest-facing balcony soaked up the sun for much of the day. It seemed the obvious choice for the master suite to benefit from such a feature.

King edged to the side as he drew near. He unslung the rucksack and dropped it on the floor before reaching across and testing the handle. Splinters of wood burst out, the bullets punching ragged holes through and spitting out across the landing. He snatched his arm back and the door continued to take a pummelling, the sharp report of a pistol filling his already ringing ears, the lead hammering the solid oak door and careening at all angles down the corridor as it penetrated the thick wood. He raised the rifle, but the thought of Catherine being caught in a crossfire at this stage, made him lower it. He had come too far to lose his bargaining chip now. And he had no idea who else could be inside the room, and although he knew Romanovitch was married, he still didn't know if the man had any children.

The gunfire ceased, and King raised the rifle, the butt held out from his shoulder and high in the air, the barrel aimed mere inches from the door handles. He was at such an acute angle as to do nothing more than put his rounds through the floor a foot or so inside the room. He took the chance and fired six rapid rounds across the door locks. The powerful 5.45x39mm bullets smashed the locks out and took one of the round gold-plated doorknobs clean off, leaving a six-inch hole, the doors opening a few inches.

The wood splintered, three gunshots filling the air. King reversed a hook kick, keeping his body away from the door, but sending his heel powering into both doors. They sprung back, and as King pulled back his foot, he swung the rifle out one-handed, like a pistol and lined the sights up on the man standing between two facing leather chairs.

Only it wasn't just a man standing there.

And he no longer aimed the pistol at the door.

Romanovitch was tall and thin, but broad. Like a coat hanger. He reminded King of a scarecrow. The dossier that King had read on him mentioned a period of five-years spent in a Russian gulag. Five years in the baking, mosquito-ridden swamps of a Siberian summer, and one of the coldest, most unforgiving places on the planet in winter. King could see that the man had done hard time. It showed in his eyes. They were dead. His features were chiselled and gaunt. He looked like a man who had starved to the bone. There was never a full recovery from that sort of existence. No matter what luxury he had in his life now, the damage had been done. Like holocaust victims. There was no leaving the camps behind.

The woman was tall, her long hair dark and glossy. Standard Russian or east European trash. She had the looks and the figure to have model pretensions, but there was no warmth in her eyes. No sparkle. She was a predator. She had hooked up. Paid a price she thought worth paying. She was another Anna.

Another Helena.

Romanovitch held a pistol to her head. He was a whole foot taller, but he hid well behind her not inconsiderable height. King had the short rifle held loosely in his hands, the sights hovering somewhere between Romanovitch's face and the woman's shoulder. He couldn't get a clear shot at the man, and through his mind was running with the notion of clipping her shoulder to reach his face. But the round from the AKU wasn't like the 9mm Romanovitch was holding. It could slice straight through, or it could clip bone, tumble and take her entire arm off. The 5.45x39mm had been solely designed to take personnel off the battlefield. It was a savage round and King would rather go for a clean shot.

King could see the woman shared features with Helena Milankovitch. He saw Helena a thousand times a day. He pictured her staring at him as he investigated her husband's murder. Her long-time lover standing at her side, seething at his interference. But it was the way she had looked at him that haunted him at night. She had been staring at him impassively, but King knew now that she had been planning how best to hurt him. How to destroy him. Now King saw that same look in this woman's eyes.

She wasn't scared.

She was planning.

Catherine moved her arm a touch and King saw the pistol too late. She fired, and King ducked to his right, but this took Romanovitch out of his line of fire. He squeezed off two rounds in front of them, the noise and muzzle flash shocking them and ruining their follow-up measure. King swung the rifle and the barrel hit Catherine in the jaw. She yelped and fell, between the two armchairs. Romanovitch was bringing the pistol around on King, but the swing of the rifle now meant he was way off target, so he swung back and caught the pistol with the muzzle of the AKU as it went off.

Romanovitch kicked out and King felt the rifle wrench out of his hands. He ducked his head and powered into the Russian, headbutting the man in his diaphragm. King could feel the bone and as he got his arms up and gripped the man's shirt with both hands, he could feel the sinewy muscle and thin wrap of skin around his ribs.

Romanovitch was no stranger to fighting and used his elbows to strike down on King's broad back. It was a large target and the Russian was using it well. Not blindly beating him but aiming his blows into the vertebrae. He was working his way up between King's shoulder blades, trying to get them down onto the base of his neck. He had invested in the strategy, knew that a well-placed blow would take King out of the fight, so he gripped King around his chest with his left arm, wrapping him in a bear-hug, as he used more force and precision to deliver his blows. King was taken by surprise at the man's strength. He pulled backwards but met resistance. King always countered resistance and used it to his benefit. He pushed instead, but Romanovitch had been waiting for this and ran backwards with him, keeping up his savage attack on King's spine.

King was breathless now, and knew he needed to get out of the man's grasp. He dropped lower but caught a well-placed knee in his eye as Romanovitch countered. He now took successive blows from above and below, but he blocked the knee as best he could with his forearms, feeling the rawness of the bullet wound more now that it was taking a pummelling from Romanovitch's knee. The man's knee was undoubtedly stronger and harder than King's arms, but the power of the blows was being drained enough to have minimal effect on his face. King drew a deep breath, then dropped lower and powered up through his legs like a weightlifter. He drove both fists up into

Romanovitch's stomach in a double blow but carried on through as he straightened his legs. The Russian's eleven-stone or so was taken clear from the ground and King kept on lifting until Romanovitch teetered and was thrown clear over King's back and onto the parquet wooden floor. King heaved for breath but was quick turning around to meet his opponent. Romanovitch was stunned, but he knew - or rather had a well-tuned animalistic instinct – the importance of getting off the ground. He rolled onto his side, and when he glanced back up at King, he rolled twice more and put a favourable distance between them. King took a step forwards, but was wrenched backwards, the wind sucking from his lungs as a hard, slim forearm wrapped around his throat and Catherine pulled backwards with all her might.

The parameters of King's mind were being warped. He had entered the room and found a clear hostage situation but was now being attacked by two people. Both equally hell-bent on killing him. He couldn't process it, couldn't compute what was happening. But he had two enemies in this fight and that was all he could focus on right now. He countered Catherine the same as he would anyone else attacking in such a manner, and snapped his head backwards, his cranium impacting on the woman's nose. Her clasp released, and King felt welcome air rush into his lungs. He saw Romanovitch watching the scene, temporarily transfixed on the woman. Rage filled his eyes as she fell backwards, and he pushed himself up and charged at him, screaming in Russian and lowering his head. King dropped into a wide fighting stance, and when the man closed the gap enough, he swept his left hand onto the back of Romanovitch's neck and drew him further downwards until the man's head was far lower than he was meaning it to be and he lost balance. King caught hold of the Russian's collar and dragged him closer, then guided him through and sandwiched his head between his legs, gripping as if he were a rodeo rider out of the gate. He wrapped both hands around the man's waist, bear hugged and heaved until Romanovitch's legs were clear of the ground and he was upside down. King gripped the man's head like a vice. And then he kicked out both legs and dropped onto his backside. The man's head met the parquet flooring first, King's entire weight driving the blow to an impact with no give or mercy.

One hundred percent compression.

King released his grip and glanced over at Catherine's unconscious body as he got back to his feet. He picked up Romanovitch's pistol and checked it over. It was a 9mm CZ85. A reliable and handy tool. It had five rounds remaining and King tucked it into his pocket as he stepped over the contents of Romanovitch's shattered skull and over to Catherine. He could hear gunfire, but it was distant and sporadic. He realised he had outstayed his luck.

It was time to get moving.

70

Darkness was his friend, his ally. He could use darkness, turn it against his enemy. He had done so many times before.

Rashid kept to the mantra of the five S's. He was wearing dark navy trousers and jacket, with a light blue open collared shirt. The navy wasn't a problem, but he turned up his collar and buttoned up the jacket to eliminate the lighter shade underneath. He shadowed the trees until he reached the gate. The road was single lane, and he could already tell from the ruts and potholes, that it wasn't a main route to anywhere. He eased out slowly from the trees, crouching in the dried-up drainage ditch. He could see two guards milling around in the smashed-open gateway. By the looks of them, both had been injured when Rashid had rampaged through the gates. One was limping, favouring a leg, the other was rubbing his shoulder and nursing a cigarette. He carried an assault rifle and was holding its muzzle towards the ground. Both men were watching as several men approached the stationary digger. They had offloaded enough ammunition for a small war and were tactically advancing as if the person inside might still pose a threat.

Rashid turned his attention further up the driveway. He could see clusters of men regrouping. His thoughts were of King and whether he had reached his objective. He had undoubtedly created a diversion, but now he needed to buy King some time.

Rashid stood up and crept across the road. He had twenty-metres to go when one of the men started to turn. Rashid sprinted, suddenly realising he was favouring an injury of his own. His knee was stiffening with swelling; he must have clouted it on the dash as he was thrown through the windscreen. He powered onwards, the man completing his turn when he was five paces away. The barrel of the AK74 started to rise, and Rashid could see the fear in the man's eyes as he closed the gap and barrelled into him at alarming rate. Both men hit the ground and sprawled at the other man's feet. Rashid knew the man he had taken down was less of a threat than the other, and he kicked him in the knee. It wasn't enough to take him down, but it was the injured leg and it bought him enough time to scramble for the rifle. He caught hold of the barrel and swung it like a baseball bat, the man taking the wooden stock to the side of his head. He was out cold and falling before Rashid finished the swing. He elbowed the other man in the face, then got up onto his knees and straddled him as he hammered down a flurry of fists into the man's face. They weren't killer blows, but they were fast and there were so many of them that the man was soon unconscious.

Rashid got up and limped over to the rifle. He checked it over, then took three spare magazines from one of the inert men. He noticed the other rifle on the ground. A Russian AK15. This was a modern version of the famous AK47. Designed to take on the west's silky-smooth assault rifles, it was a short-ranged sniper weapon for the urban environment. Good for six-hundred metres, chambered for the 7.62x39mm cartridge and equipped with a chunky suppressor for quiet operation, and a handy x6 magnification wide-angle scope. It covered a multitude of bases and was possibly a more complete package than what many NATO countries were using. Rashid had never been so close to one, and he checked the magazine and slung the weapon over his shoulder. If he could get it to the British embassy, he knew the boys at Hereford would want to take a look at it.

Rashid turned his attention back to the forty-year-old design of the AK74. He tucked the spare magazines into his waistband and took cover against the wall. He started to take single shots at the men at the house, then turned to the men advancing on the digger and fired several rounds at them, before turning his aim back on the men who were scattering at the house. He repeated the process until there was all-out gun battles ensuing. He changed magazines and switched to rapid fire sending volleys the three-hundred metres or so to the house, then short burst to the men in the open and those who were now using the digger as cover. He was soon out of ammunition and he dropped the rifle onto the ground. He unslung the AK15 and held it ready but did not fire. He could see the pandemonium at the house, and the men at the digger were firing off rounds ineffectively at the wall that Rashid hid behind.

He backed out of the gateway, his eyes on the house. "Well, my friend, I've got to get going now," he said. "I hope that bought you enough time…"

71

"Are you going to kill me?"

King couldn't answer that. He looked down at the blood on his stomach. He felt weak. He had made the call: *I have what you want,* he had said. He gave the location and told her not to be late. *Get here if you want to see her alive...*

He looked down at the Black Sea. It wasn't living up to its name today. It was glistening like the med, the sun turning it a hue of gold in places. The pine trees across the mountainside were rich in scent and shimmied in the gentle breeze. He ran a hand down to his stomach and looked at the blood on his fingers. He tore a strip off the lining of his jacket and felt under his shirt, tucking the strip inside the wound like packing wad. He grimaced, his face bruised and swelling from the fight.

The fight of all fights.

"I'm sorry," Catherine said, looking at his stomach.

"You loved him?"

She shrugged. "He treated me well," she said solemnly.

"He was married."

She nodded. "To me."

"But Anna Sergeyev said you had been recently abducted."

"And you trusted her?" Catherine smirked. "More fool you…"

King stared at her coldly. "Then why does Helena want you? Surely she would know you and Romanovitch were together?"

Catherine looked back at him. From inside the boot of the car. It was the coldest expression he could recall. "Because she hates him. Hates him more than she loves me…" she paused. "Perhaps she genuinely thought I needed help," she said, but she did not sound all that convincing. "But she will have seen me as a way to get to him. Helena is always five moves ahead of everyone else."

"We'll see," said King. But he had already called her and set her on her way. He was wounded and needed medical attention. He took out his phone and made two calls. When he had finished, he closed the boot-lid, hearing Catherine's screaming become quieter as he walked away.

72

Helena Milankovitch was seething. She had been attempting to contact King, but he had not replied to either texts or calls. She had put her plans into escape and evasion. She had lost. She knew it. She had shut down the farm, paid off her workers and hastily sent the girls destined for the sex industry to her contacts, accepting a reduced rate for the inconvenience of the short notice. The baby-farming enterprise had been moved to another location, with several of her workforce assuming the role in her absence. Helena, meanwhile would be relocating and organising by phone until she was satisfied the heat had died down, and that she could regroup with her contacts and organise a base from which to work. She was planning a period of laying low in Chechnya. Nobody bothered with Chechnya.

But King's call had halted that. With Romanovitch dead and his organisation in chaos, she had what she wanted. She could assume her role as head of the Bratva and had paid off – with money or promises of power and influence – enough people who could otherwise have stood in her way.

And now she had the key.

Catherine.

The bitch sister who had ignored her efforts to keep her away from that life and married her tormentor and rapist and pimp instead. But also, the same sister who knew Romanovitch's most intimate secrets. His accounts, his holdings, his inner workings. Catherine would come around. And if she didn't, then she would tell Helena anyway. Helena knew the sort of people who could get anybody talking.

She had ordered King to bring Catherine to her, but King had said no and told her to listen. He had told her where and when and he had hung up on her when she had refused. He had not answered her call when she returned it. Twice more she had rung the number before he eventually picked up. He had told her how it would work and reiterated both where and when. And then he had hung up again.

But he had told her to bring Caroline.

She was still in with a chance.

King had not been aware of Caroline's escape. She still had a card to play, and she would bluff her hand until she won.

Because she always won.

73

"I can't let him go through with this," Caroline said emphatically. "*We* can't let him go through with this."

Ramsay glanced at his watch. He took the next winding section of mountain road, slowed for the hairpin bend, and accelerated the modest Skoda as he exited the corner, and the section of road unfolded to another long straight. "Try him again," he said, concentrating on the road ahead.

Caroline knew that King would hear her first voice message and return her call. There was no question about that. But she no longer had a mobile phone of her own and was calling from Ramsay's number. Better to text, hope he saw the opening message on the locked screen. The annoyance of iPhone's lack of privacy feature - often a curse for leaving the phone in front of her at meetings to have King text an intimate or downright rude message - may actually play into her hands. She couldn't think what else to text, having sent a handful of messages already, but decided on:

Caroline is with us! – call ASAP – danger ahead!

She pressed the send icon then cursed loudly.

"What?" Ramsay snapped.

"No signal."

"Wait one," Marnie said, holding onto the hand-loop in the rear seat, bracing herself for another hairpin. She rummaged through her bag, retrieved a satellite phone with an antenna that looked like a child had fashioned it out of thirty Lego bricks. She twisted the antenna and handed it to her. "You'll have to program in his number."

"Bugger!" Caroline snapped. She looked back at her phone and saw that the message had not been sent. She re-sent it, watched the blue line trundle slowly across the screen, the signal indicator hover around one to two bars. She watched the blue line get close to the end and the signal bar dropped to no service. She cursed again, snatched the large phone off Marnie and set about typing in the number.

Ramsay wound the car around the bend, then slammed on the brakes, a lorry in their path and nowhere to go. The car skidded, then gripped as the traction control cut in and the ABS did its thing, but too late. He swung the car into the mountain face, sparks raining on the windows as the car scraped down the rock. Caroline screamed and Marnie, who had been leaning forwards, ended up thrown between the seats and head first into Caroline's footwell. The lorry impacted on the front quarter with a glancing blow, but enough to fire off the airbags, throwing Marnie back the way she had come, where she slumped onto the rear seat. The lorry scraped down the side and the glass shattered. Caroline dropped the phones and rested back in her seat, shocked and confused. Her ears were ringing from the explosion of the airbags and the car had stalled, its hot and overworked engine ticking in the silence.

The lorry had carried on around the bend as if nothing had happened and was out of sight.

74

King watched the Audi approaching. He had chosen the stretch of road for its long approach in both directions. He hadn't known which direction Helena would come from, but he knew the car. He had been adamant she tell him that. And so far, she was obeying his instructions. The Audi stopped. The lights flashed twice, and then it moved on slowly and steadily. No sudden movements or change in speed or direction. It entered the dusty and rocky layby and stopped. The road wound entirely around the top third of the mountain affording an uninterrupted view of the Black Sea. The layby would have made a wonderful vista stop. But not at this time of the morning. The rising sun was reaching the lower peaks, casting its golden hue on the sea and the town below. It was Sunday. And apart from two dedicated cyclists, intent on testing themselves against the challenges of the mountain pass, King had yet to see anyone else.

Helena got out of the car and as instructed, placed the keys on the ground. She took a step forward.

"That's far enough!" King shouted. He held Romanovitch's pistol by his side.

Helena kept on walking.

King raised the pistol.

"I said; that's far enough!"

"Show me my sister."

"Let me see Caroline."

Helena swept a hand towards the car. It's windows heavily tinted, and the windscreen taking the full glare of the rising sun. "See her for yourself…"

"That's not how this works."

"Don't tell me how this works! *I* tell you how this works!"

"Go back to the car and bring her to me."

"The same," Helena replied. "I want to see my sister before this goes any further."

Helena was fifty-metres from King and ten-metres from her car. King kept the pistol on her, but she was entirely unfazed.

King had never felt fear, nor anticipation like this. He was so close to getting Caroline back safely. He just had to remember he was dealing with Helena. It was like petting a cobra.

"Don't move," said King.

He edged backwards to the car and opened the boot-lid. Catherine was still bound at the wrists and cramped from the confined space. King could care less. She had tricked him, shot him and tried to strangle him.

He was past compassion.

Catherine limped with stiff legs in front of King, with him guiding her by the shoulder. She was wincing at the daylight, blinking and straining to see her sister. She said nothing. It wasn't much of a reunion.

"Now get Caroline."

Helena looked at her sister and smiled. It was a sly and impassive expression, like a weary and tormented older sibling gave when their tormentor was getting the punishment for something they hadn't done.

"She's not here…"

King pushed Catherine to the ground and raised the pistol. He could see there was no love lost between the two women. She wasn't going to make a human shield, she was more likely to get in his way.

"You think I would come up here, with the directions and instructions you gave me and not take a counter measure?"

King said nothing, but he saw a flicker in her eye. Her expression changed slowly, recognition dawning. She looked past King, but he wasn't new to this. He wasn't going to turn around. And open himself up to a *look behind you* pantomime trick.

Helena was ashen. She took a step backwards. She was a hell of an actress. But King knew even she wasn't a good enough actress to drain the colour in her face.

"Alex!"

King couldn't help himself, spun around to see Caroline running down the edge of the road. She looked exhausted and was favouring a leg. She was soaked in sweat and encrusted with dust. There was blood smeared across her face where she had wiped it away from her nose. She was holding a small pistol in her right hand.

He turned back to Helena, but she already had a gun in her hand. A stainless steel snub-nosed revolver, glistening in the morning sun.

King had his pistol half-raised. Or fully raised, if he were to shoot her knee. But she was close, and the revolver looked steady.

"Counter measure…" King said quietly.

"Not even close," she said.

She looked up at the mountainside and held up her hand. She made a chopping motion and pointed to Caroline, who had almost reached King. Helena scowled, looked at the mountainside again and repeated the chopping motion. She turned back to King, uncertainty in her eyes. He could tell it was an emotion she wasn't used to.

"Counter measure," King said. "My guy beat your guy," he paused, stared at her intently and smiled. A cruel, mirthless smile. He added, "Again."

"No!" Helena fired the revolver.

She was incandescent with rage, and it affected her aim. The bullet sliced through the air an inch from King's ear and he was already dodging to his right to put himself between the gunfire and Caroline. He heard another gunshot and returned one of his own, but it went wide, and Helena was still standing. The reports of the revolver were loud and crisp and as King caught sight again of Caroline, he could see Helena in his periphery adjusting her aim. Caroline fell forwards and hit the dirt hard. King threw himself down, slid close to Caroline on his belly and spun around, holding the pistol in a two-handed grip. He took aim and fired.

Miss.

He aimed lower, central body mass.

A larger target.

Concentrate.

Only three rounds left.

Catherine had got to her feet and was running for cover. She crossed in front of King and he lost sight of Helena in his sights, couldn't shoot without hitting Catherine in the back. Helena tracked her aim across to Caroline, no longer fearing King, only intent on killing the person he loved. She wanted to hurt him more than killing him. She fired three shots. Catherine took two of them in the chest and fell.

Helena froze for a moment, realization kicking in. She looked at King fleetingly as he adjusted his aim, and then she dropped to the ground, a red hole appearing on her chest and a crimson splash leaving her back.

King got up and dashed to Caroline. He hugged her close.

"Help me up," she said.

"No, stay there, I'll get help…"

"Help me up. I'm not hit," she said. "I fell…"

King hugged her like she would float away from him if he let her go. He felt her arms squeeze him tightly, her tears soaking his cheek.

"I thought I'd lost you," he said quietly. He pulled away and looked at her inquisitively. "Where the hell did you come from?"

Caroline shifted in the dirt and sat up. "Ramsay had a text from Rashid. We high-tailed it up here, but a lorry hit us about six miles back," she paused, wiped dust and tears and blood from her face. "Marnie was knocked out cold, Ramsay said you're a big boy and his priority was to get her to hospital."

King nodded, although he had no idea who Marnie was. "Why didn't Ramsay tell Rashid that you were safe?"

"He did."

They both looked up and saw Rashid looking down at Helena. He had a grey blanket over his shoulders, a load of foliage poking out of the weave, the AK15 rifle in his hand. He kicked the revolver away from Helena's body and strode over. "For a start, you don't return my calls," he paused. "And that bitch needed to go down. End it for you both. You were too close, needed to keep your head in the game. She's still alive by the way."

King got up, limped over to Helena. He ached and bled and felt weak. The wound to his stomach had stopped bleeding. It was packed with dirty cloth, and he needed to get medical attention imminently. He had seen enough gunshot wounds to know he had been lucky. On closer inspection he had seen that the bullet had slowed through his leather belt and was stuck in the muscle wall. His arm ached though, and he put his missed shots down to the lack of movement. It was still bleeding, despite his makeshift dressing.

Helena looked up at him. Her breathing was shallow and there was blood at her lips. Her eyes, for the first time, did not show indignity, cruelty or spite. They were the eyes of someone close to the destination of their journey. The only destination we all ultimately reach yet are completely unprepared for. She looked a different person.

"Counter measures," King said. "My guy was better than your guy."

She tried to speak, but the rattle left her lips and she closed her eyes, her face frozen, her body relaxing and resting still.

King turned around and walked back to Caroline. He put his arm around her and looked at Rashid. "I guess I owe you a pint?"

Rashid smiled, looked at the two of them and shook his head. "Nah, I'll buy you both a drink when we get home."

75

London

"I've spoken with Bérénice Duvall my contact with Interpol in the Anarchy to Recreate Society case," Caroline said, hesitantly enough for King to sit up and look at her. "She is arranging a tour for me. I've spoken to Director Amherst, Simon Mereweather too. They have agreed for me to take a sabbatical from MI5. Six months."

King sat up in the sofa, he struggled with his bandaged arm, pinned to his chest in a sling. He had stitches in his side and had only just found a comfortable position. Somehow, slouching didn't seem appropriate with Caroline's revelation hanging in the air. "To go and work with Interpol?" he asked.

"Yes."

"I see," King paused. It was a rare thing for him to appear shocked, but he could not play it down. Didn't want to. "Is this goodbye?"

Caroline cocked her head to one side, reached out and stroked his leg. "No," she said quietly. "But this is something I *have* to do."

"Georgia?"

"It's a start," she said confidently. "I can't let it go. I've tried. Believe me, I've tried. But those girls… the things I saw…"

"It eats you up."

"Exactly."

"Caroline, I'll never ask what happened, other than what you've already told me," King said. "I've seen enough crap, gone through enough to understand what needs to be known, and what is better left buried. But will this help you?"

Caroline's eyes flashed momentarily. "It's past the point of whether it helps *me* or not. I need to do it for *them*."

"The Georgian police are investigating."

"You really think they'll close the loop? Ramsay said that Cub Scouts could have done a better investigation. Interpol will lend their expertise. It's a wild west country. The police and government officials are all on the take. Sure, it's closed-down now, but another venture will start up again. If not there, then in the Ukraine, Belarus, another anonymous spec on the map."

King nodded. "I can imagine that," he agreed. He could see how important it was to her, but he didn't want to lose her. He wanted to fight for her, but he could see that if he stopped her from doing what both her heart and mind was set upon, then he would ultimately lose her anyway.

"Bérénice is excited. She has contacts who want to do more to shut-down these ventures. She has a couple of people in mind who will jump at the chance and together, we may make a difference."

King nodded. He sipped some of his tea, but it was tepid. He recognised Caroline's drive, her desire to do something as survivor's guilt. She had fled that night. There was no way she could have fought for those girls and women. To have done so would have been futile. But Caroline had gotten away. She had done what nobody else had. She had escaped. Now, she was not only driven by justice, but by her own guilt at having walked away. The Georgian police had moved in, women had been rescued, but he knew that the investigation would have stalled at their end. Caroline's connection with Interpol, having been seconded to them earlier in the year had given her an insight into what the international facilitator could do. She saw that she had a chance to make a difference, and King knew the cost of not trying. He had walked away from death and despair. He had performed his tasks for Queen and country, but he had lived with the fallout ever since. He carried guilt, carried the memories of the things he had seen along the way. Could he have done more?

Undoubtedly.

"I think it's a good idea," he said. He touched her hand. "I know you need to do this."

She wrapped her arms around him and hugged him closely. Her breath was warm in his ear and her perfume, the way it clung subtly to her body, stirred him. He pulled back and kissed her, but he could already tell she was in Georgia. She was with Interpol, planning her first move.

"What will you do?" she asked. Her eyes were moist, and they glistened like diamonds, but it was more than that, there was renewed vigour, more life behind them. As if his consent, or at least acceptance of it had lifted her.

"Well, if MI5 are handing out sabbaticals, I think I'll take one of my own," he said. He watched the television screen for a moment. The Russian president was waving at the top of the steps about to board his plane back to Russia. He had conceded nothing. The recent biological attacks killing former KGB agents turned British informants had been vehemently denied. Deals had been restructured to secure pricing and supply of natural gas. It had been an awkward accord, but all the King could see was that Russia had taken a big slice of cake and eaten it in front of the rest of the world.

"Sabbatical? You?" Caroline said, almost laughing. "Where would you go? What would you do?"

King watched the man who had raped Helena Milankovitch turn and step from view into the airplane. Maybe fate always played a part in life. Maybe action and consequence were inextricably linked to fate. He watched the door to the plane close, the ticker-tape on the bottom of the screen round-up a summary of the Russian president's visit. Could this one man have led to Helena having people killed, of taking Caroline prisoner? Of taking over the concessions of the other men who had been a part of it? Of the girls trafficked, heinously abused and dehumanised? And now, Caroline was a part of it.

She had lived a nightmare, was going off to live many more in her quest to redress the balance and look for justice, a stop to this outrage. One man's actions a dozen years ago, destroying and claiming so many lives all these years later.

King watched the plane taxi onto the runway. The ticker-tape highlighted the success of the president's visit. King just saw a series of scraps the Russians had tossed a country who had to be seen to keep face but was desperate for what they could get in a post-Brexit world. A world where the alliance between the countries it once surrounded itself with were uneasy towards its new-found independence. Russia increasingly took no notice of NATO, America or indeed, the rest of the world. It was a country with no allies, no friends, and nor did it care. It was a country that bullied the world but heeded nothing. A country whose president merely shrugged at the footage of ballot-box discrepancies and of blatant vote rigging. A president who intimidated the opposition. Who failed to sanction investigations into the disappearance of his political opponents. A leader who merely did as he chose, dared countries to respond and taunted governments at their lack of resolve. A man who considered himself untouchable.

"Do you believe in fate?" he asked.

"Sort of," she replied. "I suppose there's a case for it."

King nodded. "Do you believe it catches up with you?"

"What, like cheating death?"

"I suppose," he said. "The cards get dealt. I've known some of the best operators in the field catch an unlucky bullet. I've seen rebels with no training, discipline or skill fight and live through hell on the battlefield. Sometimes it just boils down to fate."

"You're sounding distinctly profound tonight," she said, digging him the ribs with her elbow. "Are you worried I cheated fate? Worried that my true destiny lies in Georgia?"

King smiled. "No. I think you'll take care of yourself."

She edged a little closer, rested her head on her shoulder and watched the television. The Russian president's plane was nearing the end of its taxi to the runway. A picture of him appeared in the top righthand corner, the ticker-tape relaying his position on the discovery of biological nerve agents that killed the two Russian KGB defectors.

"So, tell me more of this sabbatical idea," she said softly.

"I thought I'd go to Russia," he said.

"Russia?"

King nodded. "I hear it's a beautiful country," he said. "Might be worth it."

"I guess so," Caroline paused. "But don't go worrying about fate. I don't think you can change it anyway. When your time is up, your time is up."

King knew that was all too true. But he had commanded a degree of fate. He had served it up to many people over the years. Some deserving; others less so. Maybe you couldn't beat fate, but you could guide it towards others.

"I agree." King stared at the picture of the Russian president on the screen, before picking up the remote and switching off the television.

"You can't beat The Reaper," said Caroline.

"No," King agreed. "You most certainly can't."

Author's Note

Hi – thanks for reading, and I hope you enjoyed the story!

It goes without saying, if you didn't buy and read my stories, I wouldn't be doing this. I appreciate my readers, look forward to meeting you all at signings and events, and I always respond to messages if you want to get in touch.

Once again, if you have time I'd appreciate a review – just a rating and a few lines – this keeps my work visible in today's algorithm-led searches. Plus, it puts a huge grin on my face and often lifts me through tediously difficult plot lines in whatever I'm writing next!

If you need links for this, or would like to join my mailing list and stay ahead of the pack for updates, new releases and competitions, or simply want to say hi, you can find all this and more on -
www.apbateman.com

Thank you

A P Bateman

Printed in Great Britain
by Amazon